LONGING FOR Home

A PROPER ROMANCE

SARAH M. EDEN

SHADOW
MOUNTAIN

Visit us at ShadowMountain.com

This is a work of fiction. Characters and events in this book are products of the author's imagination or are represented fictitiously.

Library of Congress Cataloging-in-Publication Data
Eden, Sarah M., author.
  Longing for home / Sarah M. Eden.
    pages cm
  ISBN 978-1-60907-461-6 (paperbound)
1. Irish American women—Fiction. 2. Nativism—Fiction. 3. Wyoming—Fiction. I. Title.
PS3605.D45365L66 2013
  813'.6—dc23   2013014178

Printed in the United States of America
Edwards Brothers Malloy, Ann Arbor, MI

10 9 8 7 6 5 4 3 2 1

To Anne,
who left her beloved Ireland in search of a better life
and, in doing so, blessed generations

Chapter One

WYOMING TERRITORY, 1870

Eighteen years had passed since Katie Macauley killed her sister. Time hadn't erased the memory of poor Eimear lying pale and still in the biting cold of an Irish winter. Even some two decades later, sitting in the back of a stranger's wagon, surrounded by the vast desert of the American West, Katie knew if she closed her eyes for more than a moment, she would see her sister's face.

The five children climbing around the covered wagon bed bumped and jostled each other and Katie with them. She'd taken to sitting on the very back, facing the direction they'd come, with her legs hanging free. The Garrison family was kind but a bit much to take in. She'd not been truly at ease with children since Eimear's death, and the Garrisons had children in abundance.

"Take care," Mrs. Garrison called out from the front. "You'll knock Miss Macauley clear out of the wagon."

'Twasn't an exaggeration in the least. She'd nearly toppled out a few times over the past two days. The tiniest Garrison offered her a gap-toothed grin before returning immediately to his mischief.

She clasped her hands in front of her. She'd helped prepare meals and see the wagon ready for each day's journey since they'd left the train station. Keeping busy meant never being asked to tend the children. Otherwise she'd have spent every moment reliving her sister's death. Children did that to her every time.

"Hello, there!" Mr. Garrison, driving the wagon, called out to someone Katie couldn't see from her place in the back.

Every face turned at the sound, necks craning as the wagon slowed to a stop. The children rushed to the front for a peek. They'd not come upon another soul in two full days. Katie found a welcome comfort in the loneliness of the place, despite the constant ebb and flow of the Garrisons' ocean of offspring.

"Are you men headed home by chance?" Mr. Garrison asked. "We have someone here bound for Hope Springs."

Mr. Garrison had addressed them as "you men." Katie didn't care for the idea of traveling with a group of men she'd never met. She carefully lowered herself off the back of the wagon and leaned around, keeping herself half-hidden behind it.

Another wagon stood near the Garrisons', pointed in nearly the same direction. Neatly stacked crates filled the back. Two men sat up front.

The driver was a fine-featured man, his ginger coloring familiar to one who'd grown up in Ireland. His was a pleasant face, ordinary enough to not be worrisome. The man sitting next to him was far too handsome for anyone's good.

He had hair the color of a lake in the darkest hours of night, and a teasing hint of a smile played on his lips. He sat with one arm bent over the bench back, his sleeves rolled up, collar hanging limply open. Something his companion said brought out his smile. Where he'd been handsome before, the change rendered him rather breathtaking.

"If that just doesn't beat all," she whispered to herself. The handsome men always were the most trouble. She'd do well to keep her distance from that one.

Katie realized with no small degree of alarm that she'd caught the dark-haired man's attention. He'd turned about on his seat just enough for his eyes to settle on her. He gave her a questioning look before moving to slide off the bench he sat on.

She stepped quickly back, fully behind the wagon once more. Eighteen years of living on her own had taught her to hit and kick and use her knee to great effect. She could do so again if need be. Still, there was some comfort in knowing that the Garrisons and their children were near at hand. Surely even the worst of rogues would cause no trouble with a wagon full of freckle-faced imps grinning out the back at him.

The handsome stranger stepped around the wagon, stopping within reach of her. Katie held herself still and alert, careful not to show even a hint of wariness. She'd appear confident, whether she felt it or not, and she'd keep a close watch on him.

"I hear tell you're on the road to Hope Springs." He spoke with the flavor of Ireland.

"Aye," she said. "That I am."

Surprise turned his expression. "Ah, you're an Irish lass."

"As are you."

His smile tipped and laughter twinkled in his eyes. "Not a lass, exactly, but Irish-born, for sure."

Wasn't that just like a man. Knew exactly what she meant and yet turned her words about. "You know full well I didn't mean you were a lass."

"Didn't you now?" He leaned against the back of the wagon, arms folded across his chest, and kept grinning as though he'd never enjoyed himself so much in all his life. Katie didn't relax her guard in the least— even a snake in the grass knew how to smile.

The children had made their way to the back of the wagon, watching Katie and this stranger with curious eyes.

"My name's Tavish O'Connor," he said. "And it's very pleased I am to meet you."

Katie held her ground and kept her peace. There was nothing that irritated an arrogant man more than a woman who showed no interest in him.

Tavish's smile remained in place. "Might you see your way to telling me what it is I'm to call you?"

Katie didn't trust this mysterious Tavish O'Connor and his twinkling blue eyes, not for one moment. Handsome he was. Talkative to be sure. But she'd not give him credit for more than that.

"Come now," he said. "It seems we're to take you on to Hope Springs. Wouldn't do to be calling you Miss for the next two hours."

"You're taking me to Hope Springs?" When had that been decided? "I don't even know you."

His smile flashed once more. "Aye, but you needn't be overly worried. I'm not." The twinkle in his eyes reached ridiculous levels. "You don't seem the type to kill a person when he's not looking."

She looked away, her tiny sister's pale, still face filling her thoughts for one searing moment. *Not the type to kill a person,* he said. He'd be surprised.

Katie squinted against the bright sunlight, bracing herself against the constant wind, and kept silent.

"I don't suppose it would set your mind at ease if I told you I'm quite trustworthy." Tavish gave her a smile that sat with such ease on his face, she didn't doubt for a moment he knew just how effective it could be.

"Not in the least." Katie shrugged a casual shoulder. Let the man make of her lack of interest what he would. "If you *are* untrustworthy, you'd have no qualms saying you were honest and all, though it were a bold-faced lie."

"You don't mean to trust me even an inch?"

Katie looked him dead in the eye. "Not even half an inch."

She couldn't say if he looked more intrigued or entertained. Either way, he didn't seem the least discouraged. Katie had dealt with gnats who were less persistent.

"It seems I'm to have plenty of time to convince you. You're headed to my town in my company."

He knew she'd be going along despite her uncertainty—she could see the triumph plain in his eyes. She wasn't ready to label him a saint by any means, but giving him her name seemed reasonable.

"I am Katie Macauley." She added, with emphasis, "And I don't particularly like you."

"A great pleasure to be making your acquaintance, Miss Macauley." He tipped his hat. "And I'll wager you'll most particularly like me before too long."

Katie kept her expression unimpressed and painfully neutral.

The infuriating man laughed. Their young audience laughed as well, pulling Tavish's eyes in that direction.

"A fine day to you, Josephine and Henry," he said.

"Hello, Mr. Tavish," Josephine, the Garrisons' ten-year-old daughter answered, a bit of a blush heating her freckled face. Handsome men did that to females of all ages.

"You know the Garrisons?" Katie couldn't say if the revelation was comforting or shocking.

"Aye," he answered. "I've passed through their town a time or two. You didn't think they meant to send you off with two strange men, now did you?"

Katie'd had no reason not to think that. The Garrisons hadn't known her three days earlier. They'd taken her up in their wagon as an act of charity, but that didn't mean they wouldn't wash their hands of her at the first opportunity.

"Now," he said, "might you tell me just what it is that has you headed for Hope Springs? 'Tis not a place most people have even heard of, let alone seek out."

Before she could reply, a voice interrupted. "Tavish O'Connor, you right lazy bum, quit your jawin' and let's get on the road."

The Garrison children laughed at that. Katie leaned around the wagon once more. 'Twas Tavish's riding companion who had called out.

"Your boss?" she asked.

"My older brother," Tavish answered, "which amounts to the same thing, really."

"Your brother's fair glaring you into an early grave." Katie liked his brother. "Maybe you'd best return."

Tavish didn't so much as glance in his brother's direction. "I still haven't learned what it is that's bringing you to Hope Springs. I hadn't heard any of our Irish families had sent for anyone."

"I've not been sent for." She tipped her chin up a notch. "I'm to work as a housekeeper."

"Ah." Understanding dawned on his face, mixed with a bit of shock. "For Joseph Archer, no doubt."

How had he pieced that together so quickly? She held her hand up once more to shade her eyes from the sun. "Do you know Mr. Archer?"

His smile grew ironic. "Everyone knows Joseph Archer. What's more, they all know he's missing a housekeeper this week or more." Tavish motioned her in the direction of his waiting wagon. She followed, though more than a touch warily. "Ian! See who I've found."

"She'd best be Queen Victoria herself for all the time you've spent bending her ear."

"Better even than that," Tavish said. "This here is Joseph Archer's missing housekeeper."

The oldest O'Connor's mouth dropped open. "Oh aye, she isn't."

"As I live and breathe."

The brothers spoke to each other but looked directly at Katie. With both turned fully facing her, she could see them quite well. The family resemblance was well nigh ridiculous. Little except their coloring differed between them. That didn't bode well for her liking this Ian O'Connor. She didn't like his brother at all.

"Now won't that cause an uproar when we ride into town with her sitting up beside us," Ian said, his expression growing more amused.

"Better than that, even. She's an Irish lass, her brogue so wide and deep that I'm certain she's only just been tossed off the boat. She likely tripped on a shamrock and landed on American soil."

Ian finally looked at his younger brother. In perfect unison their musical laughter rang out. Laughing at her, were they? The Garrisons had been overwhelming, with children climbing about constantly, but at least they didn't mock her.

The oldest Garrison girl took Katie's fiddle case to the O'Connor wagon, her father close behind with Katie's carpetbag. Tavish took both and set them in the wagon bed. Her acceptance of their hospitality was a foregone conclusion.

Mrs. Garrison had alighted as well. She squeezed Katie's hands in a reassuring way. "We've known the O'Connor brothers for five years now. We would not have even suggested you ride with them if we didn't completely trust them both."

Her sincerity could not have been more apparent. Katie's worries eased a small bit. A very small bit. "Thank you for bringing me this far. I know it was out of your way."

Mrs. Garrison smiled in return. A moment later the family was all back in the wagon and, another moment after that, on their way once more.

"We'd best be off," Tavish said.

She'd first begun wearing a long, thick, sinister hatpin while a scullery maid in the town of Derry. That pin resided in her bonnet even then. A fine weapon in a pinch.

"Give your seat over to the lass, will you?" Ian said.

"And just where do you mean to put me?" Tavish eyed his brother. "In the back with the crates?"

Ian looked entirely unrepentant. "Seems a good solution to me."

Katie agreed. Tavish made her far more uncomfortable than did his kind-eyed brother. If Ian would stow Tavish as near to the back as could be arranged, she would be quite satisfied.

"Not a chance of it," Tavish said. "I'll drive, and you can stand up for the next two hours."

Ian shook his head. "I'll be driving, and don't you doubt it."

"What'll your Biddy say, brother, if you come driving into town with a beautiful young lass up next to you? I think you'd best let me drive."

Ian didn't budge. "Tell me, Tavish, which is most likely to set gums flapping? A beautiful young lass arriving alongside the town's most sought-after bachelor or sitting up next to a man everyone knows to be quite happily married?"

So Ian was a husband, was he? That improved Katie's opinion of him. Tavish, however, was not, which didn't help his cause in the least.

The brothers' argument ended there. Tavish handed her up into the wagon. Katie snatched her hand back in the first possible moment.

He did not climb in with the crates and burlap sacks in the back. Instead, he sat directly beside her on the narrow bench.

She slipped her trusted hatpin from her bonnet as discreetly as she could manage and held it hidden within her clenched hands. She'd learned a thing or two about preparing for the worst in the eighteen years she'd had no one but herself to care what happened to her.

The wagon lumbered northward. Katie kept quiet and pulled herself in as small as she could. The bench wasn't large, but so help her, she'd do her utmost to avoid actually touching either of her traveling companions.

Tavish waited only a minute or two before speaking again. "Would you care to make a wager, brother?"

Ian shot him a questioning look. "About what?"

"On just how long it'll take after arriving in Hope Springs for Miss Katie Macauley here to start a war."

Chapter Two

This Katie Macauley clearly thought he was exaggerating, but he knew full well her arrival would stir up trouble in town. Not only were single women thin on the ground in Wyoming but another Irish settler in Hope Springs would be greatly frowned on by those who didn't hail from the Emerald Isle.

"Don't take it to heart, Miss Macauley," Ian said. "He's stretching the truth a bit, as usual."

Tavish shot his brother a look of pained betrayal he knew didn't look at all sincere.

Katie set her gaze forward once more, pointedly not looking at either of them. A stubborn lass, he'd quickly discovered.

"I've not taken to heart a thing your brother's said, I assure you," she said firmly.

Ian chuckled, the traitor. "Took your measure right quick, she did."

Tavish leaned a touch closer to her and nearly laughed out loud to see her clutching that nasty-looking hatpin tighter in her fist. Did the woman think he meant to toss her in the back of the wagon and ravish her right there and then?

"I'll thank you to keep a proper distance, Mr. Tavish O'Connor."

He managed to keep his grin tucked firmly away as he moved back a bit. "My apologies, Miss Katie." The woman clearly had no idea how amusing her show of defiance was. She made quite a show of appearing as though he didn't worry the very life out of her. "Seeing as I have but an inch to spare on this bench here, do you consider this a proper enough distance, or shall I get out and run alongside the wagon?"

She didn't so much as glance at him. Did she mean to ignore him through the entire two-hour drive to Hope Springs? They'd just have to see about that.

"Do the world a favor, would you, Miss Macauley," Ian said. "Belt him hard in the gob and see if you can't shut his mouth for a while."

Tavish's attempts to keep his laughter in check proved entirely insufficient after that comment. He had a feeling Miss Katie Macauley could belt him a good one and would, too, if the need arose. He'd lived his entire life with a large family of feisty women; he wasn't easily intimidated.

"You wouldn't really knock my teeth out, now would you, Sweet Katie?"

"Sweet Katie?" She repeated the name he'd thought up for her as though it were a rotten potato.

He shrugged. "I think it suits you, despite the fine show you're making of being all prickles and thorns." Truth be told, he wasn't sure if she was anything but prickles and thorns, but he was intrigued enough to find out.

"My prickles and thorns are no concern of yours. And I'll thank you to call me Katie, plain Katie, as that be my name."

He shook his head slowly. "I don't think I could do that. The Katie part suits you, but you're not the least bit plain."

That was the truth, with no twists or turns to it. Her clothes were worn with heavy use and hardly of the latest fashion. Her overly serious expression might have discouraged some. But her eyes had pulled at him from that first moment behind the Garrisons' wagon. A deeper, richer brown he'd never seen in any woman's eyes. He had his suspicions that if she would only smile, the stubborn colleen would be stunning.

She adjusted herself to sit full forward once more. Here was a woman who could make a statement without a single word. She didn't like him. Not in the least.

"He's only teasing you," Ian said.

"I don't care for your brother's teasing."

"Then you're the first." Ian's tone held not a note of brotherly loyalty.

"But likely not the last," Katie muttered.

Ian laughed. "I like you, Katie Macauley. Maybe with you around, Tavish's head'll shrink back down to normal size."

Leave it to a brother to take a woman's side against his own kin.

"Don't you listen to a single word falling out of his mouth, Sweet Katie. Ian isn't the brightest of us all. 'Tis not his fault, I suppose. He was such an ugly baby, Ma was startled every time she picked him up, and she dropped him on his head a great deal."

Ian grinned, just as Tavish knew he would. With five years between them, they'd grown up with just enough of an age difference not to be rivals but with few enough years between them to get on rather well.

Tavish kept an eye on their quiet passenger as the wagon rolled on. He felt certain she was listening, though she pretended to pay them no mind whatsoever. He turned the conversation to the townsfolk and saw with satisfaction that she glanced from one to the other of them covertly. She was curious about her destination, then. Not so indifferent as she pretended to be.

This Katie Macauley was a full mystery to him and an intriguing one at that. He'd never known any woman who so quickly and readily pushed him away. She wasn't quite as cold to Ian. So was she wary of strangers in general, or was there something about him in particular that she didn't like? These were questions a man needed answers to.

"You're keeping right quiet, Miss Macauley," Ian said after they'd talked for nearly the entire two hours. "Tell us of yourself. Have you any brothers and sisters?"

"I've three brothers," she said in the tone of one who'd said all she meant to say.

Clearly Katie didn't wish to discuss her family in greater detail. Bless him, Ian didn't allow her to leave it at that curt response.

"And are they still in Ireland?"

She gave a quick shake of her head. "In Manchester."

"And why is it you're not in England, as well?"

Katie's hands clenched so tight Tavish wondered if she'd managed to bend that vicious hatpin.

"Ours were different paths, I suppose." She cast her eyes directly in front of them. "How close to those mountains is Hope Springs?"

Tavish shot his brother a surprised look. Katie had just executed an enormous and graceless change of topic. Apparently discussing her family was even more unwelcome than his earlier teasing. He easily interpreted the question in Ian's eyes: should he move on and follow her lead?

Tavish shrugged.

"Hope Springs sits a good distance from them," Ian said. "They're just tall."

"Very tall, I'd say." Katie's tone of curiosity rang a bit false.

She grew more intriguing all the time. He didn't doubt she was as strong and independent as she'd let on, but there was something in her tense and uneasy demeanor that struck him as terribly vulnerable. A contradiction she was.

"I've seen nothing in Wyoming but distant mountains and a vast brown emptiness," she said. "How does one farm in a place as dry as this?" Her thoughtful frown was surprisingly endearing. She was too serious by half.

A bit of teasing seemed more than called for. "Dry? Why, it looks like rain even now, and we had rain only last week."

"Aye." Ian nodded. Tavish knew that look of feigned seriousness. "A mere ten days ago."

"I heard a rumor that an ark's being built back behind the mercantile," Tavish said. "Should it rain again in ten days, we'll have farmers lined up by the twos, we will. Three downpours in a month's time. 'Twill be the end days, it will."

Katie's posture grew stiffer at his teasing. "I don't like you, Tavish O'Connor."

How could a man not grin at such a declaration made with such an overdone look of displeasure? "I know."

Katie clutched her hatpin tighter and kept her gaze on the road ahead. If ever a woman were determined to dislike a man, she was. It was that stubborn effort at disapproval that piqued his interest.

Over the next quarter-hour, he watched Katie's expression flit between confusion and irritation, worry and no interest all. She likely had no idea how much of her thoughts showed in her face. She was nervous but didn't want them to know. More likely than not, she didn't want *him* to know.

Did he truly frighten her as much as he seemed to, or was she simply set on keeping everyone at a distance?

"You're determined to make everyone your friend, Tavish," Da had often said over his growing-up years. "Not everyone's goin' to like you."

To which he'd always replied, "But more of them will than if I ignored them all."

And most people did decide in the end he was worth being called friend. Katie Macauley, though, didn't seem like most people.

"Keep your eyes fixed on that bonnie wee mountain just ahead." Tavish pointed directly in front of them at the hill that hid the town. They didn't get many visitors; a person had to know where Hope Springs was to find it, so well was it hidden from view. "Just on the other side runs a river. Over that river stands a bridge. Beyond that bridge you'll find Hope Springs."

For the first time since they'd taken her up in the wagon, stubborn Katie Macauley didn't make a show of ignoring him. Her gaze took in the very sights he pointed out. She didn't argue, didn't turn her back. She was curious enough to drop her defenses for a moment.

The wagon went around the low point between two hills and into a vast valley.

"Here we come, Sweet Katie. Just ahead."

"You've told her that once already, you looby." Ian shook his head. "Shut your gob and let her enjoy a moment's peace."

Leave it to Ian to ruin the one moment of attention their companion had paid him in the entire two hours they'd been together.

Into view came the very outskirts of the tiny town the O'Connors had called home for ten years. Would Katie think it quaint and picturesque, or insignificantly small? He tried to see it through a stranger's eyes. The river ran slow and lazy as it often did in the heat of summer. The wooden bridge was made of rough-hewn wood, perhaps less than pleasing to the eye. The town itself could boast nothing beyond a single street with a building on either side.

He tried to gauge Katie's reaction to it. But she'd closed her expression up tight. The window to her feelings was shuttered and locked.

The wagon rolled over the bridge.

"Sit up nice and tall, Sweet Katie. We're about to parade you through the center of town."

Her mouth tightened in an annoyed line. "I've asked you not to call me that."

"Too late, I'm afraid," he answered. "The name fits, and I suspect it'll stick."

Indeed, he meant to call her that for as long as he knew her, if only because it pulled her from her determination to be standoffish and unapproachable. He was generally good at reading people, and he firmly suspected Katie Macauley was not the cold, unapproachable woman she worked hard to appear.

Ian led his team directly down the street through the center of their town. Katie grew noticeably uncomfortable.

Ah. There is a bit of her puzzle, then. She doesn't care for scrutiny.

"You couldn't see fit to go a back way, I suppose," she murmured.

"And miss the chance to be seen riding about with a lovely young lady?" Tavish said. "Not on your life."

He expected her to blush. She only looked further put out with him. Stubborn lass.

"Actually, there is no way to reach any of the farms in this valley except right through the center of town. So nothing happens here that doesn't spread as gossip faster than a wildfire in the dry season."

They rolled slowly down the street. The few people in town would take note of them immediately. By nightfall every farm nearby, the far-off ranches even, would know the O'Connor brothers had arrived with a young lady alongside them.

Katie'll hate that. Perfect.

"The first building way up ahead is the mercantile." He gestured toward the very thing he spoke of. "Across the way from that is the blacksmith. The white building farther down a piece is the schoolhouse and church on Sundays."

"And this stretch of dirt we're riding on is the road." Ian gave him a quick look of annoyance. "The woman's got eyes, Tavish. No need pointing out every little thing."

He shot him a pleading look he knew his brother wouldn't believe for a moment. "Don't take away my chance to brag a bit. She'll think me whip smart for knowin' so much."

"More likely she'll think you talk too much about nothing. I'm saving you from your own self, if only you'd listen."

Katie glanced between the two, brow knit and mouth twisted a bit. "Do you always bicker this way?"

"Not bicker, Sweet Katie. 'Tis banter, this is. *Banter.*"

Ian came terribly close to rolling his eyes. "When we were growing up, Da would take a switch to us for bickering. But banter was permitted."

"Put on your airs if you got them," Tavish said under his breath as they reached the edge of town. "We're about to be the very center of attention."

As predicted, all eyes turned in their direction as the wagon slowly rolled down the town's one and only road. Those walking about stopped and turned to watch, studying the wagon's occupants. Seamus Kelly stepped out of the blacksmith shop and leaned against a post holding up the overhang. A gaggle of women stood outside the mercantile to watch them pass.

Katie kept her eyes forward, her back straight and chin up. She clearly meant to tell the entire town that their opinion of her mattered very little. But if she truly didn't care what they thought, why make such a show of it?

She glanced behind her at the town as they left it behind. For someone so indifferent, she certainly kept her eye on things.

"'Tis a bonnie wee place, is it not?" Tavish said.

"'Bonnie wee?' I lived in Ireland all my life and never once heard anyone actually say that." She shook her head. "I'm beginning to suspect you're only pretending to hail from Erin's Isle."

He grinned mischievously. "Around here we like to make quite a deal out of being Irish. Perhaps we've come to overdo it a bit."

"Aye. A bonnie wee bit," she said under her breath.

"Well turned, Katie," Ian said. "Well turned."

Well turned, indeed. There was intelligence under that stubborn mask. She would be a joy to know, if only she'd give him the opportunity.

"There's Archer's place." Tavish motioned with his head directly in front of them.

Katie turned forward again, eyeing the white, two-story home with dark blue trim and a gabled roof, sitting in the midst of a neat and orderly yard. The Archer home was by far the nicest in the area. No rough plank walls and river-rock chimneys for the wealthy Joseph Archer. He owned the largest home, the most fertile fields. He alone had the means of hiring servants to see to the keeping of his house. Tavish tried very hard not to envy the man but didn't always succeed.

Ian pulled the wagon up in front of the barn. Almost the next moment their youngest brother, Finbarr, stepped out and glanced up at them.

The lad had worked for Archer these past three years. During that time, he'd grown from a scrawny, timid boy to a quietly confident young lad of sixteen. If for no other reason than that, Tavish had long since decided not to hate Joseph Archer.

"Is Joseph about?" Ian asked.

Finbarr nodded and motioned to the barn behind him.

"Tell him we've come with something he's been looking for."

The boy's eyes shifted immediately to Katie, curiosity clear on his face. She fidgeted under the scrutiny. She'd best grow accustomed to that. The entire town would be wondering about her.

"He is an O'Connor, I daresay." She sounded more irritated by the realization than anything else.

"The youngest of us," Tavish said.

"Aye, but that one knows how to hold his tongue, something I hadn't thought was an O'Connor trait."

Ian, who'd begun climbing down from his perch on the wagon, stopped midway and smiled across at her. "I've a feeling you're going to get on quite well with my wife, Biddy."

Tavish hoped that proved true. A friendship between the two meant he'd see more of this intriguing Katie Macauley.

Joseph Archer emerged from his barn, walking with determined step toward the wagon. Ian greeted him a few paces away. "Good day to you, Joseph."

"That's Joseph Archer?" Katie asked Tavish in a low whisper. She sounded both surprised and unhappy with the thought.

"Aye. Joseph Archer he is."

Her expression pulled tight with surprise. "He's younger than I expected."

"How old did you think he'd be?"

"Nearly ancient."

Just what in his letters had made her think that? Tavish wondered.

Ian and Joseph approached the wagon. Katie kept herself quite still, studying her employer, a look of dissatisfaction written all over her face.

Joseph looked up at her. "I'm told you are my missing housekeeper. I expected you over a week ago."

Tavish bristled a bit on her behalf at the scolding tone Joseph had used.

"I know I'm late, sir, but it's not my fault. I missed a train back a piece, and that threw off the whole schedule. Before I knew what I was about, I found myself later and later and standing quite alone in a station a full week after I might have expected to be retrieved." She took a quick breath and finished her explanation. "I have managed to get myself here, though, and I hope you'll not be holding it against me that I did so a week after my time."

Joseph's face shifted from neutrality to surprise to near annoyance as she spoke. He looked over at Ian. "She's Irish."

Ah. There was the reason for Joseph's obvious disapproval.

"As a shamrock," Ian replied.

Joseph shook his head adamantly. "She can't stay. You'll have to take her back."

"What?" Katie's eyes pulled open wide. Even her mouth went slack.

"I'm sorry." He didn't look particularly sorry. "But you cannot stay here." He turned away.

"He is serious?" Katie asked Tavish.

"I'd imagine so." While he knew Joseph wouldn't like the idea of another Irish employee, he'd not have thought the man would turn her away out of hand. "We told you your arrival was likely to cause a stir. Looks like it's starting here."

A look of alarm flitted through her eyes. This seemingly unflappable woman had been dealt a hard blow. She sat mute, staring at Joseph Archer's retreating back.

A woman alone with no employment and no family and no place to go would be well within her rights to panic. He'd been amused by her stubbornness, intrigued by the contradictions he saw in her. But watching her defensive wall crumble, even for the briefest moment, and seeing the frightened person she hid there, tugged at his heart almost alarmingly.

"Do you want me to talk to him?" He couldn't guarantee he'd succeed, but the woman ought to at least know she had an ally in this unfamiliar town.

Katie shook her head, and the blanket of fierce determination she'd wrapped herself in throughout their journey made a tenacious reappearance. "I learned long ago how to fight my own battles, Tavish O'Connor. That man promised me a job, and I mean to see that he gives it to me."

Chapter Three

Katie climbed down from the wagon with absolutely no grace to speak of. Speed was more essential than elegance. She pushed her hatpin back through her bonnet, needing both her hands free.

"Hand down my things, please."

Tavish eyed her with curiosity even as he complied with her request. "You mean to confront him, do you?"

"I mean to keep my job," she said crisply.

She hadn't the slightest idea how to accomplish that. This was hardly the fiercest storm she'd weathered. Knocking on door after door in Derry looking for a job at eight years of age came to mind. She'd not once been without work since that time. Today would not be the day she failed in that.

She squared her shoulders, set her eyes firmly on Mr. Archer's retreating back, and marched in his direction. She'd think of something, so help her.

Mr. Archer had just reached the barn doors when she caught up with him. He glanced at her only briefly.

"If you'll be telling me where my room is, sir, I'll put down my things and set straight to my work." Her first approach would be to call his bluff. If he weren't firmly set on sending her off, he just might back down.

Mr. Archer stopped and turned to face her. His was a stern and un-yielding expression. This was a man accustomed to getting his way. "I told you that you would have to go."

"No. What you told me was that I had a job keeping house for you here. What you told me was I'd get room and board and pay." She empha-sized each declaration with a pointing of her finger. "What you can tell me next is where to set my things as I'm a week behind on my duties." She hoped her frustration made her seem more confident than she felt. In truth, her knees were knocking beneath her skirts.

Mr. Archer only shook his head. "I am not hiring Irish."

He most certainly was, whether the man had admitted it to himself or not. She needed a job. "That's your policy, is it? You'd have done well to have said something before you offered me the position, before I dragged myself across this continent on the strength of your word of honor."

"I didn't realize you were Irish."

"Macauley is not exactly an Italian name."

"It sounds far more Irish when you say it than it did in my mind when I read it."

Ian stepped up near them, his posture reluctant but his expression thoroughly amused. "Can Finbarr come along home now?"

Mr. Archer nodded. "He's done for the day." He called into the dim depths of the barn. "Finbarr. Your brothers are going to take you home now."

The lad emerged a brief moment later. He nodded to Mr. Archer, gave Katie a curious look, and moved to join the others by the wagon.

"I'll see you in the morning," Mr. Archer said.

The O'Connors piled into their wagon. Ian set the team in motion.

"We're down the road just a piece," Tavish called out to her. "If you need anything, you come find us, Sweet Katie."

She was in no mood for Tavish O'Connor's teasing. No matter that he was fine looking and smiled more handsomely than any man had a right to. She'd had quite enough of him. "I told you not to call me that," she called back after him.

Tavish only grinned. Impossible man!

He could simply take his cheekiness and his offer of hospitality and hie himself on home. She meant to stay and keep her job.

She set her things on the ground, then planted her fists firmly on her hips. "Finbarr O'Connor? You cannot tell me you didn't realize that name belonged to an Irish lad." She glared him down in much the way the first housekeeper she'd worked under used to do to her. She'd found it most effective. A person couldn't help feeling at least a bit abashed having their judgment shot through so neatly by someone eyeing them in just that way.

Mr. Archer didn't so much as flinch. "I don't have general objections to hiring Irish. I don't have objections to Irish at all."

"But that's the reason you're intending to turn me off." He'd give over even if she had to talk him around for hours. "Sounds like an objection to me."

"My personal feelings have nothing to do with not keeping you here." His tone had grown more tense. Even his posture spoke of irritation. Clearly Mr. Archer was not accustomed to being argued with.

"Then what is your reason, sir?" She held herself still, unwilling to appear intimidated. Her livelihood stood on the line and with it every dream she'd clung to since childhood. "I crossed this country on the promise of a job, and now you're meaning to take it away from me. I believe you owe me an explanation at the very least, sir."

He raised a single questioning eyebrow at that. For a fraction of a moment they stood, each watching the other, neither giving an inch. She hoped her gaze looked half as sure and challenging as his did.

"An *explanation*, Miss Macauley?"

She winced at his horrid pronunciation of her name. 'Twas no wonder he hadn't realized her name was Irish. His version of it might have hailed from anywhere at all.

"Very well," he said. "Come." Without waiting to see if she followed, he strode to the front of his house.

Katie followed close on his heels, moving swiftly to keep up with his much longer strides. Joseph Archer was a tall man, one who moved with more confidence than any man ought. He stopped but a few paces from the road that ran past his property. Katie could see he was annoyed. How could he possibly think she'd simply hang her head and walk away after his dismissal?

She ignored his angry posture, refusing to be cowed by it. He would be made to give over, one way or another.

"Tell me what you see," he said.

"I see a great many things, sir. You'll have to give me some indication of just what it is you're wanting me to see."

He motioned to the very road they stood beside.

"A road, sir?"

"More specifically," he said, "a fork in the road. Half the town lives down that branch." He pointed to their right, where the road continued far off into the distance. "Everyone in that direction despises the Irish." He shifted and pointed to the left, the other side of the road running up to and past a bridge. "Over the river is the other half of the town. Everyone who lives down that road *is* Irish." His piercing gaze settled once more on her. "Now, where does that put me?"

She glanced down each road in turn and back to where the two met directly in front of them. His property sat on neither branch but exactly at the meeting of the two. "That rather puts you in the middle, I'd say."

"Which is exactly where I do not wish to be. The people of each side of the town have been ready to strangle each other for years, and all they need is an excuse to do it." He gave her a pointed look that clearly meant he saw her as that excuse. "They argued enough about my loyalties when I hired Finbarr. If I take on another Irish employee, they'll all come down on me. The Irish will want me joining their side of the argument. The others will insist I publicly declare my agreement with them." He stepped back and shook his head. "I have no intention of becoming part of their feud."

His words sobered her a great deal. She'd encountered Irish hatred in Baltimore. Heavens, she'd encountered it in Ireland—the English hated the Irish and the Irish hated the English, the wealthy hated the poor and the poor hated the wealthy—but never had she lived in a town as sharply divided as this seemed to be.

"And that, Miss Macauley, is the reason you cannot stay." Mr. Archer spoke with finality. He left her standing there and made his way back to the barn.

She sympathized with him, could fully understand his wish to be left alone. Heavens, she herself craved peace and quiet and knew well the frustration of not finding it. But she couldn't allow him to send her off. Years of saving every penny possible had left her but one hundred dollars from her goal. After earning enough for train fare back, she'd have that last one hundred in only a half-year at this job. Then she could go home, back to Ireland, back to her tiny home in Cornagillah. She could be with her family again.

"You promised me a job, Mr. Archer," she called after him. "I have your written word on that." She hoped he wouldn't demand she produce the telegram in which he'd made the offer. She had all three of the wires he sent but, not knowing how to read, could not have pinpointed the right one. "I may be small and poor and Irish and female and a thousand other things that count against me in this world, but those aren't reason enough for you to lie to me."

Mr. Archer stopped, though he didn't turn back. The sound of the wind rustling the leaves on the nearby tree filled the silence between them. He didn't move and neither did she.

Katie hardly dared breathe. Suppose she couldn't talk him around? Without a job and the salary he'd promised her, she was in deep water indeed.

She stepped closer to him so she could lower her voice. She took a moment to calm her nerves.

"You're needing a housekeeper, sir, and I'm needing a job. Makes no sense for us both not to get what we need."

He yet stood with his back to her, his hat in his hand. If his rigid shoulders were any indication, he hadn't softened.

"What I need more than anything," he finally said, "is to be left in peace."

"Believe me, Mr. Archer, I appreciate that, likely more than you realize. I'm not the sort to pry into others' concerns. You've assumed since I'm Irish-born that I must be inclined to fight on the Irish side of this town's disagreement. I assure you that isn't the case."

He looked at her, though he barely turned in her direction. "You plan to side against your own people?" Clearly he didn't believe her.

"You say their feud isn't yours—it's even less mine. I know not a single person here. I've no family, no friends, no associates. Indeed, I consider myself only passing through. I've come for no other reason than to work. Once I've enough to return to Ireland, I mean to go back. I'm no threat to anyone."

Mr. Archer shook his head. "They won't accept that."

"They will soon enough. I keep to myself as a rule, one I've not broken from the time I was a little thing. You'll find me quiet and more likely to blend in with the walls than to stir up a hornet's nest." She'd found that approach by far the best. Leave people alone, and they'll do the same.

"I won't have my land or home become a battlefield." 'Twas as much a warning as a statement.

Katie nodded. "I understand, sir. I'd not like living in such a place myself, no matter how short or long the stay."

Perhaps it was her own wishful thinking, but Katie thought she saw him waver. The tiniest hint of uncertainty lurked deep in his eyes.

"Give me a chance, sir."

He watched her but didn't give any indication that he agreed or disagreed.

"Let me do the work, and you can see if I make trouble for you."

"And if you do?"

"Then I'd say you have every right to send me off. I'd be going back on my sworn word to you, and that's always reason to dismiss an employee." It wouldn't come to that, though, she vowed. Katie had not given anyone a hint of trouble since that horrible day eighteen years earlier. She'd caused enough people pain and heartache and loss in that single night to fill a lifetime and more.

"I suppose that's only fair," he said. "But if you start a war, you'll have to go."

"Yes, Mr. Archer, sir."

He slammed his hat on his head, likely hoping to wedge it on tightly enough to keep it there despite the wind that was picking up quick and fierce. He pushed the barn door open with a heave. She could see he was not entirely happy with the decision he'd made.

Katie wasn't convinced herself. 'Twas hardly the quiet situation she'd prefer.

"You need only stay a year," she told herself. "In a year you'll have enough saved to go home, and all will be well again."

Chapter Four

"An Irishwoman," Joseph muttered to himself.

How had he managed to hire an Irishwoman? Any other nationality, *any* other, would have been fine. She could have spoken not a word of English and known only how to cook dishes that were hardly recognizable, and he would have simply shrugged and accepted it. But having a second Irish employee would cause him no end of trouble.

I should have sent her away. The O'Connors would have taken her in. He still didn't understand what had made him change his mind.

"Yes, you do," he said to himself as he stepped inside the barn. "She accused you of lying to her."

He couldn't entirely refute her accusation. He'd promised her a job without asking her nationality. Firing her for her Irish roots when he hadn't stated that as a requirement was not honest. He had failings like any other man, but he was not a liar.

Joseph looked back, watching her step onto the back porch and go inside the house. He should have asked far more questions in those telegrams than he had. Besides her nationality, he should have made entirely certain she was the grandmotherly type he wanted.

When he'd read in her first response that she'd worked nearly twenty years as a servant in various households, he had assumed she was older than he was by quite a few years. That thick brown hair of hers showed not a single strand of gray. Her face was not lined with age, her posture not stooped and weary with time. She was likely not much more than twenty-five years old.

A young, attractive, unmarried woman living under the same roof as a young, widowed man. That would likely cause as many whispers as her nationality.

He muttered a few choice words under his breath. She was going to be trouble, he could sense it. But Miss Macauley had his back against the wall, and she knew it. He had to have a housekeeper. Six months of attempting to do the cooking and cleaning, along with all the work required to maintain a farm, had all but knocked his feet out from under him.

He took up his pitchfork again and set himself to the task of mucking out the stall he'd been working on when Miss Macauley arrived. He'd gone to the station a week earlier to fetch her, but she hadn't been on any train in the twenty-four hours he'd waited. Five days he'd spent in getting there, waiting, and getting back. He believed the story she'd told about missing one train and its ruining her schedule. The fair part of his brain knew he couldn't hold that against her, but he still felt frustration bubbling deep inside. Nothing about hiring this new housekeeper had gone as it should.

As he flung dirty straw into the waiting wheelbarrow, his mind churned over the aggravation of it all. His late wife would have known all the questions to ask. She would have found the perfect housekeeper. He had managed to hire himself a sharp-tongued, demanding, stern-faced bundle of difficulty. The passage of nearly four years had lessened a great deal of his pain over Vivian's death, but in moments like this, he missed her acutely. Their marriage had not been perfect but neither had life without her.

He led his black gelding back into its newly cleaned stall, speaking to it reassuringly. A little attention and some affectionate rubbing of its nose and the animal seemed to forgive him for the disruption to its otherwise peaceful afternoon.

"I have made a mess of things, Copperfield." He hung a bucket of oats on its peg inside the stall. "There's a woman in my kitchen. A young Irish woman, with a tongue capable of filleting a man with little effort. But one I cannot, in good conscience, send off." He pushed out a weary breath. "I have a feeling I should prepare for a disaster."

Copperfield whinnied appreciatively as he swallowed a mouthful of oats.

Joseph smiled a bit at that. "I know. She'll feed us edible food for the first time in half a year. That is definitely worth something."

Especially when he reminded himself how hard his daughters worked to eat the food he cooked for them. Further, they'd taken to sleeping in the tiny corners of their beds that weren't piled high with toys and clothes awaiting washing. The house was a mess. Their meals were a disaster.

Miss Macauley would have to stay. The girls needed her. He would put up with a great many things for his girls' sake.

He pushed the wheelbarrow from the barn and out to the dump pile. A storm was brewing overhead. He watched the dark, churning clouds. They would be pounded with rain, he was absolutely certain.

What was taking Ian so long?

Joseph wanted his girls home before the storm broke. Little Ivy's health wasn't always good, and a thorough wetting might lead to lung inflammation.

A gust of wind snapped the open barn door back and forth, pulling his eyes in that direction. Miss Macauley had left her battered traveling bag and violin case there.

Joseph grabbed her belongings and made his way to the house. It seemed as good an excuse as any to check on his new housekeeper. He hesitated a moment on the porch before shaking his head at himself. This was *his* house. Why should he second-guess his decision to go inside? He'd never done so with the last housekeeper.

He turned the knob and gave the door a push, his hands full. The wind did the rest of the work for him, flinging the door completely open. Miss Macauley stood near the stove, a startled expression on her face as she looked at him. Leaves and dust blew in as the wind rustled loose tendrils of hair in her face. In that unguarded moment, she looked almost approachable, not at all like the shrew she'd seemed out in the yard.

"You left these by the barn." He held up the carpetbag and fiddle case.

"Thank you, sir."

He inwardly cringed at hearing himself addressed that way. The servants who had worked in his home during the years he was growing up had scraped and bowed and sirred his father through nearly every waking moment. Father required their subservience as his due. Mother kept them in line with threats of dismissal and looks of haughty superiority. His distaste for such palpable class distinctions was one of the things that had driven him west.

Still, he'd argued with his new housekeeper enough that day. He could let a sir or two pass without comment.

He closed the door and crossed the kitchen, setting her things beside the door in the wall opposite the stove, the door to her bedroom. He looked back at Miss Macauley. She stood in front of the stove, watching it with her hands on her hips. The stove sat cold, nothing being prepared there as far as he could see.

"Are you having difficulties with the stove?" He moved toward her.

She shook her head. "I hadn't lit it yet is all."

"But you do know how?" It would be just his luck to have hired a woman who couldn't even light the stove.

"Of course." Miss Macauley pulled her dignity around her and looked down her nose at him. "I've worked as a servant nearly all my life. I believe you'll find me quite competent in all areas of household management, sir."

There was that sir again. "Let's begin there, shall we?" He heard the annoyance in his voice. It likely showed in his eyes as well.

She looked instantly wary. They were not making a very good beginning.

"I would rather not be called sir," he said. "Especially not at the end of every single sentence. Mr. Archer or Joseph will be fine." He gave her a final nod for emphasis, then made his way to the kitchen window. The girls weren't home yet.

"I will remember that, Mr. Archer." Miss Macauley spoke from her position near the stove. "And I would ask you to call me Katie, as I far prefer that to Miss Macauley."

"If that is what you want." His gaze remained on the window. He hoped she would set herself to cleaning it soon. The grime had doubled many times over since he'd last had a moment to scrub the glass.

Miss Macauley didn't sound as though she were seeing to the meal. A glance in her direction confirmed that. The stove still wasn't lit.

"Were you planning to cook dinner?" Surely she understood that was a basic requirement of her employment.

"You were expecting to eat, then?"

He gave her an uncertain look. "Yes." The word emerged like a question.

"And this is something you'll be wanting on a regular basis, is it?"

Her sarcastic tone spoke volumes. He had offended her. "I did not intend to question your competency."

Miss Macauley—no, Katie; she preferred Katie—gave a brief nod, as if acknowledging he had ceded an argument to her. Yes, this new housekeeper of his was going to be difficult.

"I'll see to your meal, Mr. Archer, just as soon as I've found enough clean dishes."

He looked briefly toward the window, not liking the increase he heard in the wind. Where was Ian? Of course, at the rate Katie was going, the stove would still be cold and the girls would go hungry.

"Would it speed things along if I lit the stove?"

She held her chin at that defiant angle she continually assumed.

Perhaps he should have made "an accommodating disposition" one of his requirements for the job.

"I will light the stove," she said crisply. "I am certain you have plenty of your own chores to see to."

Her professional pride might take a bit of a beating, but he fully intended to see that his daughters were fed. Despite her look of surprised displeasure, he took the box of matches from the shelf.

"Sir."

He looked back at her even as he hunched down beside the stove. "I do not answer to sir."

She watched him closely as he lit the match, brow creased deeply, mouth set in a tight line. Did she think he wasn't capable of lighting a stove? He couldn't cook worth anything, but he could certainly manage a fire.

"I thank you for seeing to that, Mr. Archer." Her tight tone told him clearly that his efforts grated on her and she thanked him only because she felt she must.

He stood and faced her. "I know how irritating it can be to have someone looking over your shoulder while you work. I'll leave you alone while you see to your tasks."

A bit of the defensiveness left her posture and snapping eyes. She even managed the tiniest, fleeting hint of a smile. Maybe that would be the key to a peaceful coexistence. He would simply avoid her whenever possible.

"Thank you, Mr. Archer. I'm a little nervous about my first day, I suppose. Things didn't begin well."

"I know." He could give her that much. "I'll just be out on the back porch if you can't find something or need anything."

She nodded and turned back to the pile of potatoes and carrots and such she'd set on a hastily cleared corner of the table.

Joseph walked to the back door. He opened it, letting the storm in once more. Heavy drops of rain joined the burst of wind. The temperature had dropped. They'd be under a deluge soon.

"Come on, Ian," he muttered as he closed the door behind him. "Get my girls home while you still can."

Time crawled as he stood waiting. He never could be easy while Emma and Ivy were away. He liked having them nearby where he could see they were healthy and happy. He needed them there.

How would Katie treat the girls? He had envisioned their new house-keeper as something of a grandmother or at the very least a matronly aunt, someone who would adore them and give them the tender affection they both needed so much. Katie didn't seem the type.

He couldn't very well fire her for being less cheerful than he'd expected. They'd have to make the best of things. So long as she didn't mistreat the girls, they could get along.

From out of sight came the sound of hooves and wheels splashing through the gathering puddles. Joseph leaned out into the rain. The silhouette of an approaching wagon. That would be the girls. At last.

The wagon pulled into the yard directly in front of the barn. He stepped out into the rain to meet it. Ian tipped his hat. Joseph returned the silent greeting with a quick nod of his head.

"Quickly, girls," he called up to the wagon bed. "You're soaked through."

Emma reached down for him first. He lowered her to the ground. Tiny Ivy came next. Even for five years old, she was very small. Joseph hugged her to him and rushed toward the porch, quickly catching up to Emma.

The sounds of Ian's wagon pulling back out could barely be heard over the increasingly heavy rain. Thank the heavens the girls had reached home before the full downpour.

He opened the kitchen door and pushed the girls inside, thankful for the warmth radiating from the stove. Katie stood at the stove, stirring something in the steaming pot and watching their entrance.

Joseph watched her as well. How would she treat Emma and Ivy?

What if she was as stern and snappish with them as she'd been with him? He wouldn't put up with it, she would quickly discover.

He set Ivy on her feet beside Emma, who clung close to his side. They were both dripping from their ride in the rain.

"There's a fire in the stove, girls. Stand near it and warm up."

Neither girl moved at all. They watched Katie with obvious uncertainty. Katie didn't look any more at ease than they did.

"This is Miss Katie Macauley. She will be looking after the house and the meals."

"And looking after us, Papa?" Emma asked.

Surprise touched Katie's expression, though Joseph wasn't sure just what struck her as odd. Why could he not have found a housekeeper who was as uncomplicated and contented as Mrs. Jones had been?

Joseph pulled his thoughts back enough to answer Emma's question. "Yes. She'll be looking after the two of you."

At that, Katie turned back to her pot, a look of unhappy contemplation on her face. He braced himself, knowing almost instinctively that the situation was about to go from bad to worse.

Chapter Five

Katie's lungs froze in shock. These were his very own children. None of Mr. Archer's telegrams had mentioned that. Not a one. Katie would have remembered. Indeed, she had been struck by the fact that he didn't have children. She'd considered herself fortunate for finding a position that didn't involve children. An absolute miracle, she'd told herself. His lack of children was the primary reason she'd expected him to be stooped and elderly.

Had she known children were part of the bargain, she would never have applied for the position. She would have told the housekeeper in Baltimore to stop reading immediately and tear the telegram into tiny pieces. Had children been even hinted at, Katie would never have come.

She could clean a house, milk a cow, throw together a meal in a trice, even cross an unfamiliar continent on her own. But tending children was another matter entirely. The last time she'd been placed in charge of a child, that child hadn't lived to see morning.

Katie looked from one girl to the other, her mind frantically trying to determine what to do. The littler one held her attention longest. She couldn't have been more than five years old, the age her sister, Eimear, had been when she died. This girl even had brown eyes and a sprinkle of freckles across her nose. 'Twas like looking into her own past directly at a face she'd spent eighteen years trying to forget.

Something had to be done.

"'Twill be a moment before your dinner is ready, Mr. Archer. Might I jaw a piece with you while you're waiting?"

"She doesn't even speak English, Papa," the older girl said.

Why was it Americans had such trouble understanding her? She'd had to repeat herself to more people than she could count since coming across the ocean. "I'm wanting to talk with you just a bit before your meal, sir."

Her words surprised him. "Is that really what you just said?"

"Aye, it is."

"Hmm."

She hadn't the slightest idea what to make of that.

"Would you grant me a moment of your time?" Katie asked once more. "Alone, if you please."

He motioned in the direction of the back door. Katie hadn't expected a conversation out in the weather, but she'd not argue. The difficulty had to be seen to. She simply couldn't be left in charge of children.

They stopped beneath the roof of the back porch. Mr. Archer pulled the door shut behind them. Katie studied his face a moment, wishing to know his state of mind. The man's feelings, however, were impossible to decipher. He'd been that way from the first moment she'd met him. His mouth pulled in a stern line, his eyes watching her closely. His posture was rigid and unbending.

She'd best hit at the heart of the matter and resolve things quickly. "I was only wanting to know why it is you didn't think to mention your daughters in the wires you sent."

That brought confusion to his expression. "I did most certainly mention them. I was quite thorough, in fact, including in my description their names, ages, temperaments."

He spoke very formally, his accent as refined as any of the fine ladies and gentlemen she'd served in the hotel in Baltimore. Her confidence flagged a moment. Clearly this man was no simple farmer.

Rally yourself, Katie. This difficulty must be seen to.

"No." Katie shook her head. She'd listened quite closely as Mrs. Hendricks, the housekeeper at the hotel where she'd worked, read the telegram explaining the job opportunity. "I remember clearly what you wrote of this position. Cooking, mending, laundering, cleaning. You said it was a small town in the middle of nothing. You gave instructions on trains and stations. But there was no mention of children nor needing to look after them."

"Does it seem likely to you that I would hire someone to tend my children without mentioning them at the very least?" His tone rang with impatience.

It didn't seem at all likely, and yet Katie knew she'd been told nothing of children.

"Perhaps you should reread my wires, in case there's anything else you missed."

He was talking slowly, as though he doubted her intelligence. Her throat tightened as embarrassment tiptoed over her. She was not stupid, no matter her lack of education.

"Have you any other children, sir?"

A tight sigh escaped him. "Mr. Archer or Joseph but not sir."

Katie nodded. "I'll try to remember, Mr. Archer."

"The two girls are my only children."

Now they were getting somewhere. "Have they names?"

"No, I opted not to name them." His voice was dry as a hot summer day. "It simplifies things."

He meant to become sarcastic, did he? "No need to sharpen your tongue on my back, Mr. Archer. I'm only trying to sort this all out."

He offered no apology and didn't look repentant. Behind him rain fell hard and steady in the yard, the view appropriately bleak.

"The older one is Emma and the younger one is Ivy," he said. "They are nine and five, respectively. Shall I itemize their personalities next?"

He obviously was reciting the very information he'd written to her. Confessing she hadn't read the telegrams, couldn't read them, would only further convince him she was not very bright.

"I've no experience with children, Mr. Archer. I wouldn't have the first idea how to see to them or meet their needs. I'd be as turned about as a ship in a gale."

That admission hung heavy in the air between them. Katie's hair and skirts whipped around her, more than a few drops of rain wetting the side of her face.

"Didn't you grow up with any siblings to look after?" he asked, his gaze still boring into her.

Katie shook her head. "Only older brothers, sir." The familiarity of the lie didn't make it easier to hear. A lie was a lie, no matter how necessary. Telling the truth meant confessing her only sister had died and that she bore the guilt of that. She'd never once admitted to anything related to her sister in the years since she'd died, not even her very existence.

"And you don't think yourself capable of keeping an eye on two relatively quiet, sweet-tempered girls?"

Quiet and sweet-tempered. Would the similarities never cease? Katie couldn't bear it. Though she felt she'd changed in the years since Eimear's death, Katie nearly panicked at the idea of the girls left solely in her charge.

"I don't know that it would be the best arrangement."

"Very well." Had he no intention of trying to talk her round? "I said earlier you couldn't stay. It seems that is more true than ever."

The man meant to let her go. Katie hadn't expected that. A change of duties, perhaps, but not dismissal.

"Mr. Archer?"

"I have offered a large salary because I expect a great deal of work.

That includes looking after the girls. If you feel yourself unequal to that task or unwilling to take it on, then I will simply have to keep looking."

He actually looked relieved. Suspicious, that. Had he been hoping for a reason to fire her again?

What a day she was having. A rather horrid and awful day.

If Mr. Archer truly let her go, she'd be without a job, without a roof over her head, without a means of earning her way back home. Katie grasped the sides of her skirts in her fists, a heavy weight settling in her chest.

Mr. Archer left her on the porch. She stood, attempting to choose a path. After twenty years of working, she'd have the money she needed in a year at the salary he'd offered her. She'd have what she needed to go home at last. How could she turn away from that opportunity?

"One question remains, Katie," she whispered to herself. "Can you be trusted?"

Trouble was, she didn't know the answer. Surely she could see to it that the girls didn't come to any harm. Katie closed her eyes and breathed slowly, forcing back the memory of her sister's lifeless body. The situation was different, she told herself. She was only a child herself the day she killed her sister. With age had come some bit of wisdom. Further, Mr. Archer would be nearby. And the girls would look out for each other.

She needed the job. But to accept a position she felt herself unequal to, one that involved the welfare of innocents . . .

"A selfish person you are, Katie Macauley," she scolded herself. "You know full well you're about to march into that kitchen and insist on keeping the job."

Katie gave a firm nod and turned back toward the house. She needed the job and the money and a roof over her head. She vowed to be very careful in her interactions with the Archer girls. They'd not come to harm at her hands. If time showed she was as incapable as she'd been with Eimear, Katie would resign her post. She'd return to Baltimore and look for something that suited her limitations, though the cut in pay would set her back by several years.

'Twas an acceptable arrangement, she told herself. Trouble was, she didn't entirely believe it.

She pulled open the door. Mr. Archer stood glancing doubtfully at the pot of boiling potatoes. The girls were nowhere to be seen. Katie hated feeling that their absence was a relief. If ever anyone was unsuited to the task of tending children, she was.

"Dinner will be ready in a trice, Mr. Archer." She'd do well to keep to areas she knew.

He poked at her boiling potatoes with the wooden spoon, not even glancing in her direction. "You seem to have forgotten you were just let go."

"About that, Mr. Archer. I know I had some misgivings, but—"

"Misgivings?" His was not an empathetic expression in the least. "You told me that putting you in charge of my daughters was not a good idea."

She hadn't said that exactly. "I said it wasn't the *best* idea. Only because I haven't any experience, not because I can't be trusted to look after them." The lie sat thick in her throat. She didn't entirely trust herself, so why on earth should he?

"Katie." He held himself with a confident air Katie could not help finding intimidating. "You have been quite clear in admitting you are not qualified. That, to any father who cares at all for his children—and I assure you I care a great deal for mine—is completely unacceptable. I will find someone else who is capable of looking after this house and my girls."

Though her first thought was to insist she could do both, the words died on Katie's tongue unspoken. Her history wouldn't support her claim. And she'd done far more lying already that day than she could be comfortable with.

What could she say in her own defense that wouldn't be completely untrue? Perhaps she could call upon his sympathies. "I've nowhere to go, no family hereabout."

"I made my requirements very clear in my telegrams. That you have arrived unsuited for this position is not my fault."

"Aye, that's a truth, sir." Neither was it her fault she hadn't been read his messages in their entirety. But arguing the fact seemed pointless.

"Then you will understand why there is nothing more to discuss. The O'Connors said you could seek them out if this didn't work." He nodded his head in the direction of the back door. "Theirs is the fifth house down the left side of the Irish Road, over the bridge. It is about three miles."

Could circumstances possibly grow worse? "You're in earnest, sir?"

"I am always in earnest."

She could see by the determined set of his chin that he'd hear no more appeals from her. She'd lost enough battles to know how to accept defeat with dignity.

"The soda bread will be ready to come out of the oven in another minute or so." She didn't allow her shoulders to stoop or her voice to shake in the least. "The praties should be boiled nicely not long after that. 'Tis a humble meal, but it'll fill you."

She moved swiftly to the far side of the room where Mr. Archer had set her bag and fiddle. She picked up the bag and held it firm in her grip. The fiddle case was old and worn clear through in places. She'd no desire to see the fiddle ruined by the rain. She would simply have to come back in the morning.

The wafting smell of bread filled the kitchen as Mr. Archer pulled the soda bread from the oven. Katie told her stomach to hush its begging. She wasn't sure when or from where her next meal would come. She'd do well to push ahead and not think on it.

The sound of something heavy toppling over in another room pulled Mr. Archer's attention away from the oven. He set the pan, steam rising from the bread, atop a dish towel on the table and left to investigate.

Katie stepped to the back door. A person couldn't leave behind the smell of warm bread without some regret. How often her stomach had sat empty during The Hunger. She'd come out of that terrible time strong and determined to survive, but she'd also emerged scarred. She knew too well the gnawing pain of hunger. The mere thought of facing it again frightened her, tensed her from head to toe.

She took her heavy wool shawl from her carpetbag and pulled it over her head, the only protection she had against the rain that continued to fall. How she hoped the O'Connors really would take her in, at least for the night.

"The fifth house down the left of side of the Irish Road," she repeated aloud. That was the road that ran over the bridge.

She left behind the porch and the respite it offered from the elements. Before she'd even walked around the side of the house, rain had left her skirts heavy and wet. She pushed against the continual gusts back toward the road. Did the wind always blow so fierce in Wyoming?

By the time she reached the bridge, Katie was shivering. Damp hair was plastered to her face. The smell of wet wool filled the air around her. Everything she owned must have been soaked through in her secondhand carpetbag.

She'd considered Mr. Archer's telegram a miracle when it arrived. The salary was more than she'd ever hoped to make, and, at least as she'd understood it, he was looking for someone with her particular qualifications. She'd even rejoiced at the rarity of finding such a position in a home without children. Her fortunes had changed, she'd confidently declared. What an utter fool she'd been.

For two months she'd sought this job. Two months of dictating her qualifications and sending them off, hoping to be chosen, then planning the journey and undertaking it. She would have had enough money to go home, not just to Ireland but to the very place she'd grown up, where life had, at one time, been good and hopeful. She could have put so many things right with the money she would have earned at the Archer home. Her family might even have welcomed her back after seeing what she'd made of herself.

She'd been let go after less than an hour on the job. Two months for one single hour.

Katie stood on the bridge, too overwhelmed to take another step. She turned her face toward the heavens, rain pelting her mercilessly.

"Another failure?" she called out. "I have been trying to make this right since I was eight years old. Why can nothing I do ever be enough? Why must every day be a punishment?"

Even as her bold words faded to silence, Katie knew the answer. She'd always known. Her sister was dead, and it was her fault. Forgiveness for such a thing did not come without suffering.

Chapter Six

Walking through the deepening mud and unending downpour, Katie couldn't keep thoughts of the past at bay. Too often she'd been out in the elements with no place to turn for relief. The skies had been steely gray the day Father walked her from back door to back door down the finer streets of Derry begging the housekeepers to give her a job.

Katie had cried the whole day long but hadn't spoken a word against his efforts. What parent would wish to keep a child who'd killed another? When at last someone agreed to take her, Father left her there without a backward glance, shoulders hung in wearied defeat. Pain had broken him. Pain she'd caused.

He'd mourned the loss of his land, wept at not having the means of giving his dead daughter a proper headstone, railed against The Famine for taking so much from him and his family. For two decades Katie had worked, trying to save enough to get back all he'd lost. Nothing she did could bring her sister back, but if she could only return her father's land and the pride he'd once taken in working it, surely he'd forgive her all she'd done. Surely he'd love her again.

Thunder rumbled around her. Katie eyed the sky with misgivings. The last thing she needed was lightning joining the fall of rain.

She blew away the water dripping off her nose and running down her lips. Water had long since seeped into her badly worn shoes. She could endure a cold face, aching hands, wind piercing through her clothes. Hair heavy with rain could be borne. But when the cold reached her feet, Katie fought not to panic. She'd spent too many days and nights as a little girl crying from the pain of feet unprotected against the elements.

"My feet are beginning to ache, Eimear," she whispered into the punishing wind. Talking to her sister had become an oddly soothing habit over the years, one that gave her a sense of being less alone. "They're growing cold."

But at least they are cold. Katie well remembered what it meant when one's limbs stopped feeling frozen.

A flash of lightning lit the sky, followed quickly by an ear-splitting crash of thunder. She'd best find shelter quickly. Katie had passed only two houses. The O'Connor home was the fifth down that road, a long distance to cover with a storm breaking overhead.

She could see lights in a house not far distant but none beyond. Either the rain made seeing further impossible, or the next farm was quite far off. She'd not be making it to the O'Connors' house in this storm.

"Now what am I to do, Eimear? Continue on in the lightning, or turn in at a stranger's farm?"

Just beyond the small farmhouse sat a barn, silhouetted against the darkened night sky. No lights burned inside the barn, a sign the family who owned it had finished their work for the night. She could likely slip in without being seen.

Another thunderous crash overhead made up her mind for her. Shelter was necessary sooner rather than later.

For more than six weeks she'd followed her parents into barns or abandoned homes under the cover of night. Taking refuge in either place was against the law. They'd risked imprisonment every time, but winter weather was unforgiving in the vast openness of the Irish countryside. There'd been no money, no food, no home to return to.

The storm brewed ever louder as she turned toward the barn, careful not to make more noise than necessary. She glanced now and then in the direction of the home as she passed. Quick flashes of light lit the sky, followed quickly by the deep roll of thunder.

Her hand shook as she slowly pushed open the barn door. Blessed warmth sat inside. The rain no longer pelted her. The wind did not come inside, save the tiniest bit of a draft under the door. She could hear the sounds of animals moving about and talking in their own way to one another. They'd likely pay her little heed if she stayed near the door and kept quiet. Katie pressed her palm to the wall, following it almost blindly. A few paces inside, she set her carpetbag down before sliding to the ground herself.

Katie pulled the wet woolen shawl off her head, laying it out across her bag. Perhaps it would dry out a bit before she need brave the storm once more. Water dripped down her face, off her nose and chin. She pulled her arms around herself, grateful for the respite despite the chill seeping through her wet clothes. A miserable, miserable night.

She wiggled her toes, finding a deep sense of relief in knowing she still could. 'Twas a childish and silly fear of hers, but she worried that every moment of cold and wet would prove disastrous. Yet the worry never fully left her.

She allowed her head to fall back against the barn wall, tired to her core. A barn was not the place she'd expected to spend the night. The smell of animals would almost certainly linger with her in the morning. The darker corners and piles of hay likely hid rats and mice. She'd spent most of the two weeks' journey across the Atlantic worrying over the vermin that made their homes alongside the poorest passengers, like herself, who endured that voyage in steerage class.

"Meaning," she told herself firmly, "you're perfectly capable of enduring this. 'Tis nothing you haven't borne before."

Endure it she could. But how long could she hide out there? She'd need to eat eventually. She'd need a job. 'Twas always the same. Work and money. She seemed to forever be chasing down both.

"It's not a selfish thing I'm wanting. I'm not looking to challenge the queen herself for riches. I only want to go home."

Home. Speaking that word hadn't broken her voice in years, yet, sitting there in the dark of a stranger's barn, she couldn't push the word out whole. She shook her head at herself, shook it again and again. There would be no tears, she silently insisted. None.

"Enough now," she whispered. "You made this bed eighteen years ago, and you'll lie in it until you've earned the right to get out."

Katie rubbed her chilled arms. What was she to do now? If she couldn't find work elsewhere in town, she was in a pinch, to be sure. 'Twas more than two days' wagon ride back to the train station, and she hadn't so much as a pony or a mule to her name.

"A fine fix, this," she muttered. "A fine, fine fix."

A burst of fierce wind sounded through the cracks and gaps of the barn. The door flew open, slamming against the wall not far from where Katie sat. She leaped to her feet and pushed hard against the door, grateful when the wind died down enough to allow her to close it again.

Her pulse continued racing some moments after calm returned to the barn. The door had come too close to pinning her against the barn wall. The animals were noisy after the disruption to their peace. Katie moved slowly back to where she'd been. 'Twas a very good thing she'd been inside during that gust. It would've knocked her off her feet.

Just as she made to sit once more, Katie heard a sound that unnerved her more than the continued wind: approaching footsteps.

She froze, listening and frantically thinking. Katie knew herself in the wrong, trespassing on another's land. She might try hiding but hadn't the slightest idea where nor the time to look about. Huddling further in the corner wouldn't help much, for there was nothing to slip behind. She'd be seen for certain.

She heard the door creak open.

Oh, help.

Katie stepped back, away from the doorway, as far into the corner as she could quickly and quietly get. She couldn't hide, precisely, but perhaps whoever stepped through wouldn't look in her direction. She lowered herself to the ground, tucked into the corner, just as the door opened fully.

'Twas a man, largely built. Katie froze, her heart pounding through every inch of her. He held a lantern up, moving it from one side to the other as he stepped further inside. If only he would turn back and go. The man was searching and no doubt about it. He must have seen the wind blow the door open, then watched as it closed seemingly on its own. He'd have known someone was inside. He'd know it as surely as a cloud knows the sky.

Help me!

He had already passed her when he turned toward the side of the barn where she hid. Even through the slats of the stall near her, she could see he'd come with more than his lantern. The man held a shotgun, held it like he knew just how to use it.

Katie pressed a hand over her mouth to muffle the sound of her breathing. Saints, if the man found her there she was good as dead. Cold and fear set her shaking. Katie only hoped she didn't make enough noise to draw his attention.

Please walk on past. Walk past.

He stopped a bit beyond halfway and held the lantern high, glancing in all directions. If only he'd decide there was no one to be found and go about his way. He glanced toward the front once, then twice, the second time keeping his gaze there. By the tilt of his broad-brimmed hat, he wasn't looking at the door but something on the ground.

She'd left her shawl and bag near the door. Saints above! There they sat, in full view of this stranger and his gun, testament to her presence. She couldn't slip out. He'd look until he found her.

Panic seized her. There'd be no sneaking away, no hiding. He hung the lantern on a peg beside the door and hunched down, taking the wet shawl in his hand. He turned his head in her direction. The man must have been looking directly at her from under his hat. She knew he saw her there.

Saints o' mercy. Just don't kill me.

Katie opened her mouth to explain, but no sound would emerge. He yet held his gun and was well within his rights to use it. She couldn't breathe.

His head tipped a bit to the side. "Katie?"

What, begorra, was Katie doing hiding in the corner of Ian's barn? Tavish leaned his shotgun against the wall.

"Have you gone and lost your mind, woman?" he asked. "I might've shot you if I'd not recognized you first."

"Tavish?" Had she only just realized who he was?

He took off his hat. "Now how about you answer my question? What are you doing hiding in my brother's barn?"

The stubborn woman with sharp eyes and a sharper tongue fell to pieces right there in front of him. Her face crumbled. She dropped her head into her hands, her breath coming broken and unsteady.

Tavish strongly suspected he'd scared her out of her wits by coming into the barn with a gun. If he'd had any idea she was the one who'd closed the door, he wouldn't have arrived armed.

He squatted down in front of her, thrown by the fact that she still hadn't spoken. She must have really been upset. "Come now, Katie. No harm done. Don't cry."

She pressed her fingers against the bridge of her nose but still didn't look at him. Several deep breaths seemed to calm her a bit. She even hazarded a terribly uncertain glance at him.

He gave her his most winning smile. "Are you fond of barns, then, that you sit about in them in all kinds of weather?"

Katie shook her head. "I was so very wet, and the lightning seemed terrible close, and . . ." She let out another long breath. "I'm sorry."

She chose the barn to escape the elements?

Tavish shook his head at that bit of female logic. "But why didn't you knock at the house?"

"I didn't know who lived here." She pulled her arms around herself and dropped her gaze again.

Her hair sat wet and heavy against her face. He had the strongest urge to brush it back out of her way but felt certain she'd not appreciate his doing so. The Katie Macauley he'd shared a wagon bench with only that afternoon would likely have broken his fingers for touching her. Where had that banshee of a woman gone?

"Mr. Archer said the O'Connors were the fifth house down, and I hadn't gone that far."

"My parents' house is the fifth one. My sister's is fourth. This is Ian's. Mine's the second. Another sister sits first after the bridge."

"There are a lot of O'Connors," Katie said.

He had to smile at that. "Some might say too many." His eyes didn't leave her face. She was such an unexpected combination of independence and need. She looked away from his scrutiny, noticeably pulling into herself.

"Joseph Archer let you go, did he?" Tavish honestly hadn't expected that of him.

Katie nodded.

Odd. "He and I don't always agree, but I'd at least have thought him above throwing a woman out in a storm."

"I've endured worse, I assure you."

Her declaration, devoid as it was of self-pity, struck right at his heart. He didn't like the idea of anyone, let alone a woman he suspected was very much alone in the world, being treated so poorly. "Why don't you come up to the house? We're about to sit down to eat."

She didn't take even a moment to consider his offer. "I won't take food off your brother's table. I owe him yet for driving me into town."

"We don't keep tallies of such things in this family, Katie."

"I do," she answered. "I don't care to be beholden to anyone."

That determined chin of hers rose once more. The feisty colleen was back again.

"Why do I suspect I ought to have named you Stubborn Katie rather than Sweet Katie?"

"You needn't mock me." There was the slow-burning dislike he'd heard in the wagon. Katie was returning to herself in spades now.

Did she have any idea how intrigued he was by her?

"I wasn't mocking in the least. Some of my favorite people are terribly stubborn. Ian's wife, for example. If she hears you hid out here in the barn rather than accept her hospitality, she'll skin you and me both alive for it."

"*She* didn't offer hospitality. *You* did."

Stubborn woman. "It amounts to the same thing."

"No, it doesn't." Her words shook a bit, but so did her very frame.

"You're fair freezing." He moved to take off his coat.

"You needn't do that, Tavish."

He nodded even as he pulled it off the rest of the way. "But I intend to just the same." Tavish eyed her doubtfully. "The question remaining is whether or not you're going to refuse it and sit there cold and wet and miserable or accept the offer graciously."

"Stubborn I may be," Katie said, "but I'd like to think I'm not stupid."

He took that as encouragement and put his coat about her shoulders. He fully expected her to glare at him or act as though she despised him. What he hadn't anticipated was the rush of tenderness he felt. He hardly knew her. Why would he feel anything beyond curiosity and, perhaps, a tug of compassion?

"Thank you for the coat." She pulled it more firmly about her. "I haven't a proper one of my own, and this is something of a merciless rain you're having tonight."

"Aye, that's Wyoming for you. Weeks of dry nothingness followed by a downpour you can hardly abide."

"That's *Wyoming*?" Katie shook her head. "You've just described life itself, is what you've done."

He knew that for a fact. "Ah, but that's far too often true."

Katie looked away from him. Uncomfortable with being in agreement with him, was she? Tavish wasn't sure how to get around that, nor why he wanted to so much. Perhaps it was the challenge of a woman who'd decided so quickly to hate him.

"What do you say we make our way up to the house, Katie? I've a feeling you're as hungry as I."

"I don't like being an imposition."

What she didn't like, he felt certain, was being noticed. "Then I suggest you come directly. The entire family'll march out here to talk you into coming in if you insist on staying behind."

She looked up at last. He made certain his face showed that he was fully serious about the family running her to ground. He'd rally them himself if need be.

"You don't have to tell them I'm here," she said with an uncertain hopefulness.

"Ah, but I do. I most certainly do."

Surely she would see there was nothing for it but to give over. There was no way on God's green earth he would leave her to spend the night in a barn. He'd not do that to any woman.

Some of her stubbornness slipped from her expression but not all. "Do you think they could find a few chores for me to do, in exchange for their kindness?"

She wished to work for her keep? An admirable trait, that. "If you'd like. There's always plenty of work to go around."

Katie nodded, apparently satisfied. "Then I suppose we'd best be on our way up to the house."

He'd fully expected a long, drawn-out battle of wills. "That was easier than I thought it would be."

"Maybe I'm not as stubborn as you've accused me of being." If not for the way her chin jutted out and her mouth pressed into a tight line, he might just have believed her.

"I'm certain you're every bit as stubborn as I suspect you are." He rose to his feet. "I'd offer you my hand, but I've a feeling you'd refuse."

He nearly laughed out loud at the look of fierce independence that immediately entered her eyes.

"And now I'm being glared at." Saints, but he would love to spend time with such a maddening woman as she seemed to be. Kept a man on his feet, she did. Gave him a challenge.

She stood, though not without effort. The cold, it seemed, had left her stiff. She took up her bag and shawl.

He grabbed his lantern and shotgun. "Shall we?"

Katie nodded. "But this doesn't mean I like you."

"Yet," he added as he opened the barn door.

She stopped in the doorway. "I didn't say *yet*."

"Ah, but you meant it." He motioned her the rest of the way through. "Out into the rain with you, you troublesome woman. We've a hot meal waiting for us."

"You're going to get wet without your coat," Katie warned him.

"And well worth it, I assure you."

Getting to know her better would be more than adequate compensation for a wee soaking. Indeed, he'd discovered one thing about her already: she responded better to a challenge than she did to a show of sympathy.

He stepped past her, calling back through the downpour. "Run like the banshee's hot on your heels!"

Chapter Seven

Katie ran through the rain but not because Tavish said she ought to. She ran because it was the sensible thing to do.

He didn't pause to so much as knock on his brother's front door.

She hesitated. "You're certain they'll not mind?"

He stood, holding the door open, smiling as he ever did. "They'll not mind."

Katie took a long, deep breath, gathering her courage. For one who preferred keeping quietly to herself, she'd spent far too much of the day convincing strangers to keep her around. She'd be hard pressed to feel less welcome were she a three-legged horse in a speed race.

Just as ridiculous, she'd let this man with his teasing smiles and twinkling eyes see her on the verge of tears, hurting and frightened. Showing such weakness scared her more than she cared to admit. She vowed to herself as she stood on the porch that Tavish O'Connor wouldn't see another crack in her walls again.

"You're letting in the rain, Sweet Katie."

She was indeed. Katie slipped in, taking up a position directly beside the door. She'd stay out of the way until she could figure out what to do with herself. A quick and careful study of the small room revealed two children, a boy and a girl, and a woman stirring the contents of an iron pot in the fireplace. Ian and Finbarr O'Connor stood over an upturned chair they appeared to be mending, not paying the least heed to their brother's return.

"You should have been back quite some time ago," the woman said. "What kept you so—"

The words stopped abruptly as her eyes settled on Katie. Surprise and curiosity filled their depths. The woman, either Ian's wife or the family's hired help, was likely not much older than Katie was, perhaps nearing thirty, with hair a vibrant nut-brown.

The woman's gaze shifted to Tavish. She indicated Katie with a nod of her head. "Something you found blowing about in the storm?"

"Aye. The heavens blew her right to me, they did."

"Sounds like a sign from above to me." The woman tapped her wooden spoon on the edge of the iron pot she tended before replacing the lid. "I'll send Ian out for the preacher. We'll have the two of you married before the stew's done cooking."

Married? Katie eyed the woman, relieved to see a glint of teasing in her eyes.

"I'd be much obliged to you, Biddy." Tavish's tone of gratitude was far too overdone. "Though Miss Macauley, here, might object."

Biddy. She felt certain that was the name of Ian's wife.

Katie brushed at a drip of water hovering on the tip of her nose. She didn't care to be stared at when in fine form, let alone standing drenched to her very skin, in boots and a dress covered in mud.

"Miss Macauley, is it?"

Mrs. O'Connor seemed happy at the thought. An uninvited stranger stood dripping water and mud on her floors, and she found this a pleasing turn of events? What was the matter with these O'Connors? Were they all daft?

"I've heard more than a little about you since the men returned from their trip," Mrs. O'Connor said. "I'm pleased to have you drop in on us."

Ian spoke up, his tone not so light as his wife's. "What brings you out in this weather? Is something wrong up at Archers'?"

Katie shook her head. Shivers and nerves and exhaustion all joined forces to keep her mum. No words would come.

Ian abandoned his project and moved with determination toward the door. "Joseph wouldn't send a person out in a storm for any small thing."

A bubble of dismay surfaced in her. She'd caused trouble again. But how to stop Ian from rushing into the rain himself and bothering the Archers?

Tavish managed the thing with only two words. "Joseph's fine."

Ian halted on the spot. "You know it for a fact?"

"Like a priest knows his prayers."

The children were still watching Katie. She tried to smile at them but knew the effort fell flat. Finbarr's eyes were on her as well. And Ian's. And Tavish's. She clasped her hands in front of her, the only thing that ever truly stopped her from fussing with them. She dropped her gaze to the muddied toes of her battered shoes. If she couldn't see them studying her, she might manage to convince herself they weren't.

Ian at last broke the silence. "Then why is Miss—"

"Your questions can wait, dear," Mrs. O'Connor interrupted. "The poor woman's teeth are chattering louder than a town full of gossips. Let her dry off and warm up, will you?"

Though she didn't look up properly, Katie saw Mrs. O'Connor cross to where she stood. Why hadn't Tavish let her remain in the barn? 'Twas quiet in there, and no one need be bothered by her. Bothersome man. How had he talked her into this?

"Won't you come sit near the fire?" Mrs. O'Connor asked. "Fetch her a quilt from the chest, will you, Tavish?" She laid a hand on her husband's arm, addressing her next request to him. "You and Finbarr set back to your repairing. I can see to Miss Macauley."

The room was quite suddenly in motion once more. The children returned to their book and toys. Tavish crossed to a cedar chest on the far side of the fireplace. Ian and Finbarr took up their tools.

"'Twasn't my intention to disrupt your evening, Mrs. O'Connor. I only wished a moment free from the rain and lightning. If you've a back porch or a corner that'd be out of your way, I'd be quite content standing there until the storm passes."

Mrs. O'Connor's eyes widened. Though Katie couldn't be certain, she thought a hint of tears shone in the woman's eyes. What had she done to cause such distress? She inched further in the direction of the door, trying to think of an excuse to slip out.

"Saints, but you sound like home," Mrs. O'Connor whispered.

"I told you my very self she was only just tossed off the boat." Tavish turned back toward them, a quilt in shades of brown and green folded over his arm. "Why is it you never believe a word coming out of my mouth?"

Mrs. O'Connor tipped him a look of exasperation. "It's not as though you're regularly giving me reason to believe the words coming out of your mouth, now is it? One never knows with you if you're joking or being serious." She shifted her gaze from Tavish to Katie and smiled kindly at her, though doing so didn't set Katie's mind at ease. "Come the rest of the way in, now. The air's far warmer near the fire."

Katie kept right where she was. "If not for Tavish being so infernally bossy, I'd have stayed out of your way entirely."

"'Infernally bossy.'" Mrs. O'Connor smiled broadly. "I don't think I've ever heard him described so perfectly."

Tavish shook his head but didn't seem offended.

"Come on now." Mrs. O'Connor motioned her over again.

"I'm not meaning to put you out at all, only to wait for the rain to pass."

"Oh, and I suppose the storm'll pass faster if you martyr yourself in the coldest corner of the house?" She clicked her tongue and shook her head.

Tavish crossed back to them. "You'd best give over, Sweet Katie. The only woman I've ever known who could beat Biddy for stubbornness was my own mother, and that is saying something."

From across the room, Ian tossed out a remark of his own. "Keep on standing there insulting both my mother and my sweetheart, and I'll see to it you don't eat tonight, brother."

The jab didn't seem to affect Tavish in the least. He held the blanket out to Katie. She slipped off his coat and traded him for it. Their hands brushed. The tiny moment of contact sent a shiver through her that had nothing to do with how cold she was.

Oh no you don't, Katie Macauley. There'll be none of that.

She snatched her hands back quickly. "I thank you for the blanket." She spoke in her most freezing tones.

Tavish raised an eyebrow but didn't comment.

Mrs. O'Connor eyed her with concern. "I've a feeling that quilt won't be enough, even with the fire. What you need is a fresh change of clothes."

Her other two dresses were in her carpetbag, likely near as soaked as the one she had on.

"I can lend her my clothes," Tavish said, his tone thoughtful to the point of drama. "Of course, I'd have nothing to wear then, myself."

Katie refused to blush at that comment. Indeed, she set herself quite firmly on ignoring it.

Mrs. O'Connor rolled her eyes, something Katie had rarely seen a grown person do. The childlike gesture made Katie smile inside despite the awful day she was having.

"Miss Macauley's been through enough tonight without being subjected to that," Mrs. O'Connor said. "You leave your clothes on and quit trying to embarrass the poor thing."

"Trying to make her smile was all I was hoping for."

"And you setting the table was all *I* was hoping for," Mrs. O'Connor replied. "Set yourself to it while I find Miss Macauley a dress of mine."

"I couldn't take one of your dresses, Mrs. O'Connor." Katie's wish to keep in the corner was evaporating like water on a summer's day.

"I'm not making you a present of it. I'll be wanting it back just as soon as your own clothes are fit for wearing again." She stepped nearer a curtain hanging in a doorway. "Come on, then. Let's find you something dry."

Katie might have objected again but remembered Tavish's warning in the barn. The O'Connors would insist on helping her, would work at getting her to accept their help. She'd be less of a burden if she accepted gracefully. Katie resigned herself to it.

They stepped past the curtain into a small bedroom. The bed took up nearly the entire space, save a trunk at the foot and a small table. Mrs. O'Connor opened the trunk and pulled out a neatly folded dress in a shade of very light blue and a pair of homespun woolen stockings.

"You're not quite my height," she said, "but I think this'll fit well enough."

Katie accepted the bundle. "It's thankful I am for your kindness, Mrs. O'Connor. I fear I've nothing to offer in return beyond an eagerness to do whatever work you might have for me."

Mrs. O'Connor's eyes brightened as she smiled. "Promise to call me Biddy, and I'll consider us quite even."

'Twasn't remotely a fair trade, but Katie nodded her agreement.

"Bring your clothes with you when you've changed, and we'll lay it all out by the fire to dry."

"Thank you, Biddy."

A moment later, she was alone. What a day. Handed off to strangers, let go from a job twice, drenched, cold, and embarrassed into a blush by a man she felt certain she'd do best to dislike. She'd expected Wyoming to hold the answer to all her difficulties, not simply create an entirely new set of worries.

Katie changed quickly. She shivered more with every layer that came off. How she wished she yet had the quilt. She made quite an effort at rubbing the water from her skin, though doing so only added to the puddle she left on the floor. She hoped Biddy O'Connor didn't prove too stubborn to allow her to clean the mess.

Truth be told, Katie fully intended to offer to do any chores the family might need done. Tavish insisted the family would not begrudge her the kindness she needed, but she hadn't experience with such charity.

During those horrible weeks between their eviction and Katie being given away in Derry, she and her family pleaded everywhere possible for shelter from the weather or a crust of bread. She would never fully forget one man she'd asked help of. He'd told her God took care of good girls. If she were starving and cold, it meant heaven was punishing her.

Katie had stood on his porch for what felt like hours, weeping. Her sister had been dead only three days, the guilt and grief of that loss still painfully fresh. What right had she to go begging kindness of others after doing such a terrible thing? That argument rang in her head even eighteen years later.

What right have you to be asking charity of these people?

"Is the dress too long for you?" Biddy sounded as though she stood just on the other side of the curtain.

"Only a bit." Katie closed her eyes tightly, doing her utmost to push away the memories. She'd find a way to repay their kindness, and then she needn't be indebted to any of them. "I'll be but a moment more."

She heard Biddy's footsteps retreat. Katie sat on the chest. Without looking at her feet, she peeled off her sodden stockings. Over the years, she'd developed quite a knack for changing her shoes and stockings without so much as glancing at her feet. She didn't need to look to know what she'd see. The skin would still be melted in twirling, twisted scars. She'd still be missing her smallest four toes and pieces of most of the others. 'Twas the only scar from those horrible months that wasn't tucked safely away inside.

She stood up. Best not keep the family waiting on her. She quickly finger-combed her wet hair. Her hairpins had all fallen out somewhere between Mr. Archer's house and the O'Connors'. There was no helping the state of things.

Katie pulled back the curtain and stepped out of the small bedroom. The O'Connors' two children were yet in the room, though they did little more than glance at her as she stepped out. In eighteen years Katie had seldom encountered children, perhaps only from across a room she was cleaning or playing in a park she passed when out walking. Between the Garrisons' wagon, the Archers' kitchen, and there in the O'Connors' home, she felt absolutely surrounded by them.

"There now. That doesn't fit too poorly," Biddy said, drawing Katie's attention to her.

Katie shook her head. "Not poorly at all." She was, in fact, rather grateful the dress was a touch too long. Her stockinged feet remained tucked out of sight. "I thank you for the stockings. They are quite warm, and my feet were mighty cold."

Biddy smiled at her husband. "Does she not sound so very much like home, dearest?"

"Aye, that she does." Ian tipped the newly repaired chair upright once more. "Joseph Archer caught Ireland in her voice within three words or so. I wondered if he'd send her off for it." Ian looked at her once more. "He didn't, did he?"

The reminder of her very short-lived employment didn't sit easily on Katie's mind. Being let go for no failing of one's own was not near so humiliating as being turned out for falling short of the expected mark. Still, she couldn't let this Irish family think a man who employed one of their own would do such a thing.

"He didn't send me off on account of my being Irish. I couldn't do all the work he needed me to do. So he felt there was little point keeping me on."

Tavish glanced her way a few times as he set glasses and plates out on the rough-hewn table. Ian's curiosity was no less obvious.

"So he sent you out into this rainstorm?" Ian asked. "That doesn't sound at all like Joseph."

Katie eyed the toe of her woolen socks, only to be struck by how little the stockings hid her misshapen feet. One could easily tell she hadn't all her toes and that those remaining didn't conform to their proper lengths. She shifted enough to hide them behind the overly long dress she wore.

"Let's lay out your things by the fire," Biddy said. "They'll dry much faster that way."

Katie nodded without looking at anyone and followed her. Biddy pulled a long bench up near the hearth and together they laid her clothes out a piece at a time. The room remained silent except for the sound of little Mary playing with her wooden horse. Were they all yet wondering over Katie's disastrously short time as Mr. Archer's housekeeper? She must have seemed remarkably pathetic to them.

"Let me pull this chair close to the fire as well," Biddy said. "You can sit there and warm up."

Katie shook her head. "The chair'll be fine where it is."

"Are you sure? Your hair is still wet, and you're shivering a wee bit. Closer to the fire is better."

Katie clenched and unclenched her hands, trying to work out even a tiny bit of the tension paining her in that moment. Closer to a fire was never better. Not ever. "If I might use the quilt Tavish pulled out earlier, I think I'd be quite comfortable."

"Of course. Of course."

Katie settled in, tucking her feet back as far they would go. The men returned to their work. Biddy checked on the simmering pot. Just as Katie began to feel the teeniest bit at ease, little Mary O'Connor, hand-carved horse in hand, came and stood in front of her.

Katie maintained what distance she could. She'd avoided children so long she didn't even really know what to do with one.

"Why were you in our barn?" Mary asked. "Are you a gypsy?"

A gypsy? What a conclusion to come to. Katie had assumed they'd all decide she was a criminal or a beggar. A gypsy!

"I do believe you're almost smiling." She knew Tavish's voice but hadn't realized he'd come over.

She didn't look up at him. The man made her insides jump about, a sensation she couldn't exactly call pleasant. "Gypsies don't smile," she told him.

"And even a wee joke there at the end. Impressive, Sweet Katie."

"Is she a gypsy, Uncle Tavish?" Mary looked quite intent on the answer.

Tavish's smile grew when he looked at his niece. "That is one of many things I intend to discover about the mysterious Miss Macauley."

"Are gypsies mysterious?" Mary spoke in an awed whisper.

He offered an exaggerated nod. He was so at ease with the little girl. Was that something a person learned, or was one simply born that way? Or was this more of Tavish's natural inclination to flirt?

Mary scampered off. Tavish kept where he was. He sat on the edge of the bench, his back to the fireplace, facing her. She kept herself pulled in under the quilt, remembering all too well the way she'd shivered at his touch. 'Twas not a safe thing to feel from a man she wasn't sure she could trust.

"So Archer truly let you go?"

"Aye, he did. A bit of bad luck, that."

He responded to her casual tone with a look of doubt. "Good show, Sweet Katie, but I'm convinced you're not so calm as you pretend to be."

"That only proves how little you know about me." Katie tipped her chin at the confident angle she'd perfected long ago. "I have learned well how to survive just this kind of difficulty these past eighteen years."

Tavish's brow creased, his head tipping the tiniest bit to one side. "You'll not be convincing me you're only eighteen years old."

"Are you calling me old, Tavish?" She speared him with a look.

He held up his hands in a show of innocence. "I said nothing of the sort."

"I am twenty-six. I can take perfectly good care of myself, thank you very much. So you can just wrap your mind around leaving me be."

"Twenty-six, are you?" No response to her declaration of sovereignty? "That's a perfect age."

She felt a tiny skip in her heart but firmly ignored it. "Perfect for what?"

"For you, Sweet Katie. The age suits you. Or it would, at least, if you didn't wear such a sour expression all the time."

Her hackles rose again. Why did he insist on needling her so mercilessly? "I only wear a sour expression when unpleasant people force their company on me. What say you to that?"

His answering smile was not the laughing, jesting one she'd seen so often that day. It was only half a smile, more in his eyes than on his mouth.

A twisting warmth started deep inside her at that expression. Katie looked away on the instant. She didn't at all like the effect he had on her.

"Tavish O'Connor, why is it you'll jaw the ear off any woman in your path?" Biddy stood not far distant, hands on her hips, eyeing her brother-in-law with a scolding look. "She's only just got herself warmed up the tiniest bit. Let the poor thing be, would you?"

"I am a horrible person, Biddy. Horrible." Tavish used a tone so humbly repentant not a soul would have believed it sincere.

A knock echoed around them.

"Michael," Biddy said to her son, "set your book down and go see who's at the door."

The boy could read. In all her years in Ireland, she'd not known a single lad from a humble family who could read even his own name. This America might not have warmly welcomed the Irish who'd come by the millions, but life had certainly changed for them there. Food, work, and learning. Such things were little more than dreams in Ireland.

Katie pulled the thick quilt closer around her. She was in out of the elements but didn't feel safe yet. Tavish disturbed her peace nearly as much as her uncertain future did.

She had survived crises before. She'd seen herself through the worst of difficulties. Surely she could handle this latest disaster. Surely she could.

Michael opened the door. There, the rain falling behind him, wind whipping in through the open door, stood Joseph Archer, wet to the bone.

He stepped inside, eyes falling directly on Katie. "You are a difficult person to find in a rainstorm."

Chapter Eight

Joseph's first reaction upon seeing Katie safe and whole was bone-deep relief. He had alternately pictured her wandering lost through the surrounding fields and floating face down in the dark river. Her hair hung in wet strings all around her face, and he was almost certain the ill-fitting dress she wore was not the one she'd had on at his home earlier.

Yet there she stood, not a hint of relief nor gratitude on her face for his having searched her out in this weather. If anything, she looked almost terrified.

"Come in out of the rain, Joseph." Biddy motioned him inside.

"Enter at your own peril." Tavish watched him closely, as if he suspected him of something underhanded. "The last person who came inside dripping like that was given a dress to change into. I don't particularly want to see you in ruffles."

That explained Katie's change of clothing. His relief at finding her unharmed was quickly subsiding. The foolish woman had dashed off in the rain, in the dark, in a place she had never seen in her life. Was she completely mad?

"I went to Thomas O'Connor's place," he said. "They hadn't seen you."

She offered no explanation but continued watching him with wide, uncertain eyes. How could she possibly be afraid of a man who'd dragged himself out into a storm simply to save her from her own foolishness?

He felt a tug on his wet coat and looked down to find little Mary O'Connor.

"Did you bring Ivy to play with me?" she asked.

"Not this time. She's at home with her sister." He patted her lightly on the head. Little Mary took her disappointment in stride and stepped back away again.

Joseph turned his attention back to the issue at hand: Katie Macauley and her harebrained ideas. "I really ought to be at home with the girls, myself, instead of riding out in the rain looking for a woman who hasn't the sense to stay put in weather like this."

He spoke more sharply than he'd intended. But he was cold and frustrated, and his patience had worn thin during the ride through the rain. Still, he wouldn't take back the accusing words. She'd brought him no end of trouble in that single evening.

"The sense to stay put?" She actually looked confused. "That's a fine thing coming from the man who tossed me out in 'weather like this.' I'd not have gone wandering around in rain and lightning and mud if you'd not dismissed me."

Her loss of position was his fault now? "I would not have dismissed you if you hadn't lied about being qualified for the job."

"I didn't lie about it. I only didn't realize everything you required."

He would not be blamed. "I was quite specific in my telegrams."

Biddy shooed the children, Finbarr with them, up the ladder to the loft. Joseph would have to apologize later for bringing this argument into their home.

"As I said before," Katie's tone had cooled some but not entirely, "I missed the bit about your daughters, and I'm sorry for that."

Missed it? That same foundationless excuse. "How could you possibly miss it? Did you even read my correspondence?" He was beginning to seriously doubt it. She'd been surprised by far too many things. How had he managed to hire someone with so little sense of responsibility? Rushing into rainstorms. Accepting a job without reading the requirements.

Katie's cheeks suddenly reddened, though she held herself at that defiant angle he'd seen again and again in the short time he'd known her. "The telegrams were read to me, sir." She took an audible and visible breath. "I don't know how to read." Her blush deepened.

An uncomfortable silence fell over the room. A knot formed in Joseph's stomach. He hadn't meant to embarrass her, but it had never occurred to him she couldn't read. She'd sent responses, answered specific questions.

"It seems whoever read you the telegrams did an unfortunate job of editing them."

"So it would seem." She held her chin high. Katie was as prickly as a hedgehog. "I have to depend on others, and that doesn't always turn out well. At times I get lied to. And sometimes I get thrown out in the rain for not being what people want me to be."

He stepped closer to her, shaking his head at her continued misunderstanding. "I didn't throw you out in the rain."

"You think I threw myself out, then?"

He held his hands up in confusion. "I have no idea why you left."

"You made quite clear that I was to take myself to the O'Connors and beg for their kindness. 'Fifth house down the road,' you said. ''Tis three miles or so,' you said. What was I to take from that except that you meant me to leave?"

He shook his head repeatedly, nearly at his wits' end with her. "I simply wanted you to know there was someplace you could go in the morning, when the weather had cleared. I know Thomas O'Connor and his wife well enough to be certain they would give you some idea of what you might do next."

He was a reasonable person, not the coldhearted villain she thought him. And, so help him, he'd been more patient with her than most people would have been.

"Then you didn't mean I had to leave right then?" She clearly still doubted it, though he hoped she was coming around a little.

"I can be demanding at times, but I'm not heartless."

Her unflattering evaluation of him stung more than he expected it to. Why should her opinion of him matter so much? He told himself to shake it off and see to the problem efficiently. He looked over at Ian.

"Do you have room for Miss Macauley here tonight?" She could come back home with him if her presence would burden Ian and his family, but he couldn't help thinking the night would pass more peacefully without her.

Ian nodded. 'Twas Biddy, however, who spoke.

"Tavish and Finbarr can sleep in the barn if they don't wish to brave the weather. We've room and food enough for a guest for the night." She held out to him a heavy wool blanket. "Wrap this around you for the ride back. 'Twill keep you a bit drier, at least."

He stood on the spot, undecided. He had brought Katie to Hope Springs. Her current predicament, though not precisely his fault, was more his responsibility than it was Ian and Biddy's. Joseph was not one to shirk his duties.

"Your girls'll be wondering what's keeping you," Biddy said. "They're a bit young to be left on their own for long."

They certainly were, and he'd been gone longer than he'd anticipated. He nodded to Biddy and turned back toward the door. A thought stopped him before he stepped out.

He looked over his shoulder at Katie. "Your violin is still in your—in the housekeeper's room at my house."

"I didn't want it to be ruined by the rain," Katie explained.

He nodded. "I'll leave it there. You can pick it up whenever you're able to."

Cool, wet air rushed inside as he opened the door. The weather, it seemed, hadn't improved. It would be a long ride home.

"Biddy, would you mind if the girls continue coming here during the day? I know you hadn't planned on it, but . . ." His eyes shifted to Katie but didn't stay there. No point placing blame for the mess he was in. He simply needed to address it and move on. "But circumstances aren't as favorable as I had anticipated."

"Of course, Joseph," Biddy answered. "We'll help in any way we can."

"Thank you."

"I am sorry this didn't work out, Mr. Archer," Katie said.

The door slowly swung closed behind him. "So am I," he said quietly.

He *was* sorry and not only because he was once again without a housekeeper. His disappointment ran deeper than he would have thought. Katie Macauley was a handful and a stubborn, easily offended woman, but he'd found her fire intriguing and, in a way, promising. Wyoming was a difficult place to live. Many couldn't survive such a harsh and trying life. He'd wondered what chance he had of keeping any Eastern woman there long but couldn't think of a better place to find a skilled housekeeper than his home city.

Katie was stubborn enough to make a real go of it, but he couldn't keep her on if she wasn't able to take care of the girls. He was back where he'd started.

"I am sorry too," he muttered again. "More sorry than you probably know."

Katie couldn't make sense of the past few minutes. What employer went haring off after a servant he'd fired? Fired *twice*.

"Well now, Sweet Katie, this is a first." Tavish stood at the mantle, near enough to be easily heard. "I can't say I've ever known Joseph Archer to chase after anyone in a rainstorm."

Katie wrapped her arms around her middle. "It is odd, is it not?"

"Very odd." Tavish didn't look away from the door Joseph Archer had walked out. His eyes narrowed, mouth twisted a bit.

"Should I be worried? Do you think he'll hold it against me?"

That pulled his eyes back to her. "No. I'm only worried about Ian."

"Ian?"

Tavish shook his head and sighed. "Poor man drove the Archer girls home in the rain, and no one came running after him. He must feel mighty neglected. He'll likely cry himself to sleep tonight."

"You're teasing again?" Katie had very little experience with someone who joked about everything.

Amusement shown in his eyes. "Would I tease about something so vital as my own brother weeping into his pillow?"

"I've a feeling you would and have." She eyed him knowingly.

"Do you consider that a character failing?"

Katie didn't know what to think of him. She didn't entirely trust him. How could she when she couldn't take seriously anything he said or did?

"I guess I know by the look on your face just what you think of me." For the first time since he'd met her, Tavish actually looked a bit offended. "You mean to present me a challenge, do you?" He stood straighter, shifting away from the mantle and closer to her. "I accept."

"I'd rather you just leave me alone."

A little voice called down from the loft above. "Have Mr. Archer and the gypsy lady finished their arguing, Ma, or do we need to stay up here longer?"

Ian and Biddy burst out laughing. Tavish was still looking at Katie. Had she actually offended him? Or did he think of her exactly as he'd said, as a challenge?

Katie pulled the blanket more tightly around herself as she sat once more in the seat she'd occupied before Mr. Archer's arrival. She refused to look up at Tavish. Did he truly mean to try and force her to like him, to trust him? She couldn't be the least comfortable with that idea.

Mr. Archer's visit had upended her too. Though he'd remained calm, she knew he was angry. She'd endured enough beatings, both physical and verbal, to know they always began with anger. Mr. Archer seemed a calm enough person. If she kept out of his way for as long as she remained in town, she might not find herself in trouble.

"I hope I don't sound as though I'm becoming too familiar," Biddy said, crossing to Katie's chair. "But I noticed Tavish and Joseph both called you Katie."

"I rather begged Mr. Archer to call me Katie after hearing how terribly he butchered my name."

"Saints above." Biddy looked tempted to cross herself. "The one time he took a stab at saying Macauley just now, I near died at how horrible it was."

"He'd apparently been saying it wrong to himself since my first telegram. He didn't even realize the name was Irish until I started talking."

Biddy laughed. Katie very nearly smiled herself.

"Joseph's pronunciation aside, do you prefer Miss Macauley or is Katie more to your liking?"

That was hardly a question worth asking. "Katie, to be sure. I've never been important enough to be called anything so formal as Miss Anything."

Biddy watched her a moment. Katie couldn't say just what Biddy was thinking, only that she was most definitely thinking.

"You're most welcome to sit with us at the table, Katie. But if you'd prefer sitting here where it's warmer, we'd not begrudge you that after the soaking you've had."

Katie only nodded. She would, indeed, prefer staying where she was, though not entirely on account of the warmth. She meant to keep a distance. From Tavish. From Joseph Archer. From everyone, just as she always had.

Chapter Nine

Katie had her own clothes on once more and those things she'd borrowed neatly folded by the time the O'Connors were up and about the next morning. She'd never been one for lying abed when there was a difficulty needing attending.

The family's routine was flawless. Each had a job and did it. Katie had thought she could find a way to help, but there seemed no need for her.

If she'd learned anything in life, 'twas that no one wanted a person hanging about who served no purpose. She took up her woolen shawl, dry after a night spent laid out near the low-burning fire, and wrapped it around her shoulders once more. Carpetbag in hand, she slipped out the front door, careful not to disrupt the family's work.

Tavish had told her the afternoon before that everyone in Hope Springs knew Joseph Archer. If everyone knew him, it stood to reason he knew everyone else. She didn't relish the idea of asking the same man who'd twice fired her if he knew of other jobs she might go seeking. Doing so, however, seemed her only course of action.

There was a saying she'd heard again and again in Ireland. "'Tis the humblest among us who can least afford to be proud."

A light shone through the Archers' dingy kitchen window as she made her way across the back porch. The family was awake at least. She steeled her courage and knocked. A long moment passed as she waited. She could hear movement just on the other side of the door.

Just as she made to knock again, the door opened. A harried-looking Mr. Archer stood in the doorway.

"I don't have time to talk, Miss Macauley."

"I've come for my fiddle is all," she answered. "I've no intention of disrupting your day."

He nodded quickly. "You'll find it in the same place it was last night." Mr. Archer turned back inside with no further comment, leaving the door ajar.

Katie stepped into the room, fully intending to be in and out quickly. But the chaos that met her eyes slowed her steps. She'd made some progress the evening before, clearing the table a bit, uncovering a space near the sink. It had all been undone in one night. What had the family been doing to make a mess so quickly?

Mr. Archer stood at the stove, adding kindling to the firebox. Pans and pots sat ready to be used, though nothing filled them. Biddy O'Connor had been nearly finished preparing their morning meal when Katie had left. Mr. Archer was only beginning his.

He might not want her about, but even a blind man could see he needed her.

She heard him mutter a word not many would say out loud. It seemed he'd already forgotten her there.

He opened and closed cupboards all around the kitchen, doing so with less patience as he went.

"Might I help you find something, Mr. Archer?" Katie asked.

He shook his head and continued searching.

"Are you certain? I took a good look about when I was here last evening. I might know where to find whatever it is you've misplaced."

"I haven't misplaced anything." He stood in the middle of the kitchen, brow deeply furrowed, looking about in obvious confusion. "I was only hoping to find a spare wooden spoon."

"You've lost your . . . wooden spoon?"

He shook his head. "I know where it is. I just don't want to wash it."

So many things became clear with that one sentence: the piles of dirtied dishes, the general state of filthiness, windows that looked as though they'd not been washed in months. She'd wondered how Mr. Archer had managed to make such a mess. If he regularly sought out a second spoon or pot rather than wash the one already out, he'd have quite a pile in no time at all. Perhaps he took the same approach to clothing and such.

"You don't care to wash your dishes, then?" Rather like a man, that.

"I don't have time. I still need to wake the girls, but I haven't finished their breakfast. Biddy will be expecting them soon." He pushed out a tight breath. Poor man looked done in, and the morning had only just begun.

"You go get your girls up and ready for the day. I'll see to your breakfast."

He was shaking his head before she'd finished her first sentence. "You don't work for me any longer, Miss Macauley."

"I far prefer being called Katie, and I'd consider it a kindness if you did so." She spoke with all the firmness she could muster. She'd quickly grown tired that morning of being useless to everyone. Here was something she might do, and someone who needed her, whether he was willing to admit it or not. "I've nowhere to be and no jobs of my own to see to at the moment."

He didn't give over in the least.

"I'd not be expecting pay, if that's what you're worrying about."

She set her carpetbag on the floor beside her fiddle. Mr. Archer would concede on the matter of breakfast if she had any say in the matter. Katie seldom felt needed, but when she did, she clung to it.

She crossed to the sink and dug about until she found the very thing Mr. Archer searched for. Holding it up for him to see, she said, "I'll have your breakfast ready in only a few moments. You'd best get your girls up and about."

"Miss—"

"*Katie.* And I'll have no arguing on the matter of breakfast. Unless, that is, you were displeased with the meal I prepared last night."

He shook his head. "It was the most edible thing we've had in this house for half a year."

Katie knew a moment of satisfaction at that. She might have known nothing of tending children, but she could certainly cook a meal. "Then I suggest you accept my offer graciously and see to your girls."

He hesitated. Katie fancied she could see in his expression the argument he waged with himself. 'Twould be a kindness if she simply forced his hand.

She moved enough dirtied dishes away from the water pump to slip the wooden spoon under it. She didn't look back at her one-time employer as she set to her scrubbing. Perhaps he'd see by the determined set of her shoulders that she'd quite made up her mind.

A silent moment passed before his sigh gave away his acceptance of her offer. "Thank you, Katie."

His gratitude threw her off a moment. She was unaccustomed to being thanked for the work she did. "You're welcome." Did he hear the uncertainty in her voice as clearly as she did?

He didn't comment on it but made his way back out of the kitchen. She set to work near frantically. How terribly incompetent she'd looked the night before. Though her dismissal was a decided thing, Katie wished to prove herself not entirely useless.

She found leftover soda bread from the evening meal and sliced it thin and even. Mr. Archer had already set out a small bowl of eggs and strips of bacon. Katie cooked up both, then browned the bread in the bacon drippings. 'Twas only one half of a true Ulster fry but would make a fine breakfast. The sounds of movement upstairs accompanied her efforts. The family would be down soon.

Katie pulled three clean plates from a cupboard—the last plates there.

Mr. Archer, despite his preference otherwise, would have to wash dishes at some point.

She did as she had the night before, clearing half the table by piling its contents on the other half. 'Twas somewhere between setting out the plates and placing forks beside them that the idea niggling in the back of her mind began to grow and blossom at a surprising pace.

She'd first heard of the housekeeping position some two months earlier. Even with the speed of the telegraph, these things took time. Mr. Archer couldn't have a replacement in Hope Springs in any fewer than eight weeks.

Her only shortcoming for the job was her inexperience with children. She could see to all the rest, see to it well, in fact. Biddy had readily accepted the girls coming by, quite as though she'd done so before.

Life had taught Katie to know perfectly well the arrival of an opportunity. She might be able to talk Mr. Archer into giving her work after all.

The table was neatly set by the time the girls and their father came down. Katie had the food ready and waiting for them. Mr. Archer's oldest, Emma, watched Katie with obvious distrust. Ivy, the little one, didn't look away from the eggs and bacon long enough to notice much else.

"It looks like real food," Ivy said under her breath to her sister.

"Katie was good enough to cook it." Mr. Archer pulled a chair out for little Ivy, helping her climb up. "You need to thank her for that."

They both offered a thank-you in near-perfect unison.

Mr. Archer looked over at her as well. "Thank you." The words were spoken with relief so thick Katie fancied she could see it hovering in the air around them.

Though she hated the thought of taking advantage of the poor man's desperation, she found a measure of reassurance in his sincere gratitude.

With the girls eating, the time seemed best for talking with him. If nothing else, he could ponder her suggestion over his meal, a fine edible meal she doubted he could produce on his own.

"Mr. Archer? Might I ask you a quick question?"

He turned to his girls. "You two eat, now. We're already late leaving for the O'Connors'."

The little ones tucked into their meal in earnest. Mr. Archer motioned Katie once more onto the back porch. She was not generally a superstitious person, but having been fired on that very spot once already, Katie couldn't help thinking her chances were dwindling.

"I'll not keep you long from your morning meal," she assured him. "I've had a thought I wanted to pass by you and see what your opinion was on it."

"Go ahead." Whether he was curious or wary, Katie couldn't rightly say.

"I noticed you've more to do than you've time to do it in." She told herself not to lose her courage entirely, as it seemed to be abandoning her in spades. "You said yesterday you mean to search out a replacement as I'm not quite what you had in mind. But, as you're needing someone until you find a replacement, I'd like to suggest you keep me on for a time. I can certainly put your house to rights and keep it that way until a new housekeeper arrives. 'Twould be a temporary arrangement only."

He shook his head immediately. "The girls—"

"I thought they might go to the O'Connors'," she added before he had a chance to fully reject her idea. "You meant for them to go there today, as I suspect they have before."

He turned to face her more fully, leaning his back against the closed door. "I am to pay you the enormous salary I promised so that you can do only half the job I hired you to do? Does this reduced work load still come with room and board?"

His tone was not promising in the least. Yet, he'd hit upon another of her pressing worries.

"I realize there'd be a reduction in pay. Likely in hours, too. Though—" She took a fortifying breath. Begging for consideration never came easily to her. "I haven't a place to live just now, so if it were possible to rent the housekeeper's room, only until you have need of it otherwise, I'd be appreciative."

She watched his expression change from thoroughly unconvinced to thoughtful. That, Katie told herself, was a good sign. He wasn't dismissing her out of hand.

"I could work here mornings and evenings, and a full day on Mondays for laundering," Katie said. She'd need the afternoons to search out other work. As she'd told Mr. Archer, this position was decidedly temporary, more so even than her sojourn in the town itself.

He mulled that over a moment. Katie held her breath.

"I'll pay you ten dollars and two bits a month, with the room and meals included," he finally said.

Ten dollars and two bits. Katie's heart stopped. She'd figured her salary at the rate Mr. Archer had written her. She would have been paid nearly twenty-one dollars a month.

"That is half the pay," Katie said quietly. She didn't mean to complain; the loss simply came as a shock. She'd depended on that salary to finish filling up her savings.

"You will have half the duties," Mr. Archer pointed out. "And half the hours."

"I understand. The salary is more than fair." And 'twas a far sight better than no salary at all. "I accept."

"Let us be clear, though, this is only until the new housekeeper arrives," he said. "And only if the O'Connors agree to continue taking the girls every day."

"Yes, Mr. Archer."

He gave a quick nod of his head and turned once more to go.

"One more thing, sir—that is, Mr. Archer." She doubted she'd ever grow accustomed to leaving off the usual sir. "As for the rest of the salary you would have paid had I been charged with the girls' care?"

"Yes?" The suspicion had returned to his tone.

"Seeing as Biddy would be taking on that work, assuming she accepts,

I thought perhaps she might take the portion of the salary I'm no longer earning."

His brows pulled together. Clearly he hadn't thought of that. "I'm not sure the O'Connors would accept payment for what they see as being neighborly."

"Perhaps not." She hoped he'd offer and hoped they'd accept. The O'Connors were far from wealthy, and the money would be helpful.

"Hmm." He looked reluctantly impressed. "That is very good of you. I'll offer and hope their Irish pride doesn't prevent them from taking me up on it."

"I thank you, Joseph Archer."

He left. Katie let out the breath she'd been holding. She had a job and free afternoons to fill with whatever other work she might find around town. 'Twas something of a promising beginning.

Chapter Ten

Tavish stood among his crops, eyes cast out over the lake at the back of his property and the distant mountains rising behind it. He had the best view in all of Hope Springs. The sky above was vast and clear. Yet, his thoughts weren't of the blue expanse above him but of the haunting beauty of a pair of deep brown eyes and the unexpected appeal of a stubborn and determined woman. He'd known Katie Macauley all of three days and had spent not more than a few hours in her company, yet he found himself thinking about her in the oddest moments.

"I refuse to muck out your plugged-up ditches, Tavish. So you'd best do something more than stand about with that idiotic expression on your face." Ian glared at him from the other side of one of those plugged-up ditches, shovel in hand.

He took up his own shovel and returned to the work of clearing debris washed into his irrigation canals by the heavy rains of two nights ago. "My thoughts were wandering, is all."

"Aye. I'd say they were wandering about as far as the Archer place," Ian threw back.

Tavish didn't acknowledge that remark in the least. He set to digging, leaving Ian to think what he would. His brother never had needed encouragement to offer his opinion.

"She's a fine-looking lass, I'll grant her that," Ian said. "But she'll not be easily won over."

Tavish tossed a shovelful of mud-plastered leaves and branches out of the ditch. "When did I say I wanted to win her over?"

"The last time you stood around staring at nothing was the week Bridget Claire moved to town, and we all know where that led."

Bridget Claire. Tavish didn't imagine he'd ever reach the point where hearing her name didn't strike some regret in his heart. If not for the fever that had claimed half the town and her with them, he'd have married her. *Darling, lovely Bridget.*

"Katie Macauley is—"

"A challenge?" Ian finished for him.

Tavish shook his head. "I was going to say a pill."

Ian sent another shovelful of muck out of the ditch. "You've a taste for sharp-witted and determined women, Tavish. Bridget, for all her sweetness of temper, could give you such a tongue thrashing at times. And we could all see you loved it. Teased her mercilessly you did, something you didn't stop doing the entire time you spent with Miss Katie. And, I'm thinking, you've a taste for brunettes."

Tavish pretended not to listen. His own musings about an attractive, fiery woman were one thing, but hearing his brother analyze the situation to death was another thing entirely. And bringing Bridget Claire into the discussion was not something he'd go along with.

"You know something, Ian? You sound just like a nosey old hen. Why don't you go put on one of your wife's skirts and bonnets and play the part to its fullest?"

"So have you called on Katie down at Archers?"

Not even thrown off the scent. Ian was a regular bloodhound, he was.

"I've plenty of work to do, and so does she." He thrust his shovel into the ditch blockage.

"We'll likely see her at church, as it is."

Tavish kept working, knowing Ian meant to prick him into a response.

His silence must have at last got his message across. They were back to work after a moment. Two more ditches were soon free of unintended dams.

Thoughts of Sweet Katie—he had to smile remembering how hard she'd worked to show him she didn't care for that pet name—only slipped in a few times. As he'd told Ian, she was intriguing, but she'd made her determination to dislike him abundantly clear. He'd enjoy teasing her when she came around but had no thought beyond. None.

Tavish's irrigation canals were finally clear and ready to run again. He and Ian walked down the road to Ian's farm to begin working on the clogged ditches there. Rain was ever a mixed blessing in Wyoming. The water was sorely needed, but the soil seemed to do nothing but run when wet.

Biddy cut them off as they passed between the barn and the house. "I've had a fine idea, Tavish."

The gleam in her eyes was too excited for Tavish's peace of mind, though he couldn't help a bit of amusement at seeing it.

"From the look of you, I'd say what you have in mind is more of a scheme than a mere idea."

She was undeterred. "Only wait 'til you've heard me out."

Ian chuckled low. "Send him out to the ditches when you've finished with him, love." He gave his wife an affectionate kiss before moving on.

Biddy spared a moment to watch her husband walk off, a look of contented happiness on her face. Tavish seldom envied his siblings' loving marriages, but every now and then he did wonder what it would be like to have someone look at him in just that way. Plenty of women blushed at him when he smiled. And there was a certain woman newly arrived in town who scowled at him regularly. None gave him anything resembling the fond gaze he saw on Biddy's face.

"So I had a thought earlier." Biddy was back on topic in a heartbeat. "I don't think anyone has stopped by the Archers' to invite Katie to the *céilí* tomorrow night. No Irishwoman alive could resist the lure of an Irish party such as we have here."

Tavish eyed her with suspicion. "And are you trying to say *I* ought to go extend an invitation?"

He thought he saw Biddy roll her eyes. "It's an absolute miracle any man ever wins a woman's regard. The lot of you are so hopeless at courting."

Tavish smiled. "Would it do a bit of good to tell you I'm not looking to win Katie's regard?"

She waved him off. "I saw the way you looked at her."

"And how, I beg you, did I look at her?"

"Much the way you looked at Bridget when she first arrived."

Again, talk had turned to Bridget. He shook his head firmly. "I've had this discussion with your husband already. I'll say this much, Katie Macauley is too stubborn by half and has made no secret of the fact that she doesn't much care for me. Amusing, certainly, but that's all it is."

He made to walk away, but Biddy's hand on his arm stopped him. "Tavish."

Saints, he hated it when she used that sympathetic sister voice of hers. Soon she'd be looking at him as one looked at an abandoned puppy.

"I'm not saying you're in love with her. You don't even know her."

At last someone was making some sense.

She, of course, wasn't finished yet. "But I've not seen you look twice at a woman these past four years. You flirt a bit and give them a smile meant to leave them weak in the knees. But I watched you watching Katie when she was here. That she's grabbed even a tiny bit of your interest isn't a bad thing, you know."

No, not *bad*. But not the sign from above his family wanted to make it.

"Would it hurt you to get to know her better?" Biddy asked.

"I suppose not."

"And—"

"Ah, begorra." Biddy always had an "and."

"—would it kill you to be a friend to her, welcome her, and see that she makes the acquaintance of others in town?"

He raised an eyebrow at that suggestion. "Don't think you're fooling me for a minute, Biddy O'Connor. 'A friend to her,' you say. I know the look of a matchmaker when I see one."

She shrugged. "A sister's allowed to hope, isn't she?"

"Katie Macauley dislikes me severely. And while I find that intriguing, I'm not crying myself to sleep over it."

Biddy's eyes took on a mischievous glint. "Did I also mention I fully intend to call on her tomorrow morning?"

Tavish groaned. Did no one in the family listen to him? "Don't get your hopes up, Biddy. I've a feeling Katie and I are destined to be nothing more than neighbors who ruffle each other's feathers whenever we cross paths."

Biddy smiled in a way that showed she clearly didn't believe a word of it.

He set his shovel over his shoulder again, ready to get to work and leave behind the gossip. "Am I to assume, then, you fully intend to throw Katie and me together, despite my objections and the fact that none of us knows much more than nothing about her?"

"I've a feeling about her, Tavish." Biddy tapped at her heart. "A feeling."

He shook his head at her female logic. She didn't know this stranger at all, and yet Biddy was already convinced of her goodness.

"I'll see you at the céilí, then." With that declaration, Biddy turned and walked back into the house.

Women always did seem to get the last word and the upper hand. An unsolvable puzzle they all were. Katie, perhaps, more so than most. She was half forged steel, half spun glass. And though he'd been kind and helpful and friendly, she'd declared him untrustworthy and thought him beneath her notice.

And the family wondered why he was not yet married.

Chapter Eleven

Saturday dawned earlier than Katie would have liked. She'd put in full workdays that week despite her arrangement with Mr. Archer. There was simply too much to do. Besides, she had no other job to be getting to.

In those few days, the kitchen cupboards were set to rights, the work-table scrubbed long and hard, and every dish in the house washed several times over. The girls thanked her dutifully after every meal, then threw her looks ranging from distrust to outright dislike. Mr. Archer took his coffee in the kitchen each morning before beginning his chores, and he spent those few minutes watching her as though he expected her to slip the silver into her apron pockets.

Katie kept her mouth shut and her mind on her work. What cared she if they disliked her? 'Twas but a job. And she didn't mean to remain in Wyoming forever. Work was her refuge. It had been nearly all her life.

Though Mr. Archer had taken his daughters to the O'Connor home each morning, Saturday brought a change in the routine. Shortly after breakfast, Biddy arrived at the kitchen door with her two children in tow.

"I can tell Mr. Archer you're here," Katie offered, unsure what she was meant to do. She thought she'd understood from her employer that he'd be walking the girls down the Irish Road as usual that morning.

But Mr. Archer appeared at her side in the next moment. "Good morning, Biddy. I wasn't expecting you."

"We decided to take a walk this morning. Michael hoped you'd let him tend to your horse," Biddy said. "You know how much he loves that animal."

Mr. Archer immediately turned his attention to the quiet boy hiding behind his mother's skirts. Michael O'Connor hadn't said a word the evening Katie had spent at his home. Finbarr hadn't said much, either. There was a bit of timidity in some members of that family.

But not quite enough in others.

Mr. Archer motioned Michael out toward the barn with a quick nod of his head. The lad moved so swiftly he nearly ran.

"When the time comes, he should consider ranching," Mr. Archer said. "He is a smart boy, and his talent with animals would serve him well."

"Aye, he may just do that." Biddy's smile was a fond one. "Now, Joseph, why don't you see to your work. I mean to stay here a bit, to let the girls play. I want to chat a while with Katie."

"With me?" The shock of hearing that loosened Katie's tongue. "Why would you wish to chat with me?"

Biddy looked from her to Mr. Archer and back again. "Why *wouldn't* I?"

Because no one ever has. But she couldn't bring herself to admit to it. Instead she stood mute and unable to look either of them in the eye.

"Miss Macauley is very quiet," Mr. Archer said. That Biddy winced at his version of Katie's name took some of the pain out of hearing it. "I can't imagine her 'chatting' with anyone."

He was right, but the picture he painted wasn't flattering. She'd had something of a friend at her first job in Derry. The other scullery maid in the house talked to her now and then, though she hadn't had much to say in return. And in Belfast she'd walked out on occasion with a very handsome jarvey driver. They'd talked, though mostly about his horse or carriage or her chores. 'Twasn't terribly personal, but she'd certainly chatted with people before.

Just because Mr. Archer thought it unlikely didn't make it impossible. Besides, a person who welcomed a bit of friendly gab might seem less suspicious to the man, less likely to go about pocketing his valuables.

"I'd enjoy a bit of a coze," she said, trying to look like she meant it.

"Really?" Mr. Archer clearly didn't believe her in the least.

Katie shrugged. "Why wouldn't I?"

His look was excessively doubtful. Had she only managed to make him more skeptical of her character? Perhaps she ought to turn that about, make him see it as a sign he'd been suspicious for no reason.

"You've admitted your very self that you know little about me, Joseph Archer. Perhaps I enjoy a chat more than you think I do."

"Hmm." It wasn't the sound of one convinced of another's reliability. "Enjoy your chat, ladies." With that he made his way out of the house and toward his waiting work.

"Go on and find the girls, Mary," Biddy said, shooing her daughter from the kitchen.

Katie returned to the sink and the pile of dishes that never seemed to go away. The very idea that someone stood nearby expecting her to make conversation only tied her tongue in ever greater knots.

"You hadn't come by," Biddy said. "I hope all's well here with you."

Katie nodded. "All's fine." She dried the plates one at a time with her dish towel.

"I'm pleased you've found some work. That was likely a worry for you."

"Aye." She slid the plates into the cupboard and began drying the pot she'd made the Archers' porridge in. Perhaps she should ask after Biddy's home or her family. But what would she ask? The children seemed well. Ian likely was, too, or Biddy wouldn't have left him at home untended to.

"Have you come to know the girls at all?" Biddy hadn't drawn nearer. Indeed, she seemed almost as unsure of Katie as Mr. Archer always appeared to be.

A straightforward and honest answer ought to help with that. "No, I haven't."

No further questions arose. Katie wiped down the counters and sink. A quick sweep of the kitchen would see that room tidied and ready for the day. She'd need to straighten the dining room next. Ought she to mention as much to Biddy? Was that a usual topic of conversation among people? She couldn't rightly say.

"Has Joseph been a good employer?"

Katie nodded before taking the broom from its corner. She looked up from her work when the silence grew surprisingly long. Biddy's usual smile had slipped noticeably. She watched Katie with a subtle expression of hurt on her face.

Katie paused in her sweeping. Biddy seemed to force a cheerfulness into her posture once more.

"I'm sorry for interrupting your work," she said, her tone a little heavy. "I'll not force you to talk with me when you've other things to be doing." She stepped toward the swinging door leading to the dining room. "I'll just go collect the girls, and we'll be off."

Katie realized with no small degree of surprise that she'd hurt Biddy's feelings. How had she managed that? She'd answered Biddy's questions, talked with her as she requested. In her inexperience, she must have done it wrong.

In the moment before Biddy slipped from the room, Katie called after her. "Wait, Biddy. Please."

Again that forced smile appeared on Biddy's face.

"I suspect I've offended you somehow. I can't say quite what I've done, but I hadn't intended to."

Biddy quickly shook her head. "No. Not at all. I can see you're not eager for company." Something in her tone added a "my company" to her words. She turned once more to leave.

"I hadn't meant to make you think I didn't wish for your company," Katie said. "I've no talent for making conversation is all. I have been a servant since I was eight years old. We were never permitted to chatter—'twas seen as a sign we weren't working hard enough. I've not learned how to truly chat with anyone."

"Did you really go into service at only eight?" It wasn't pity Katie saw in Biddy's eyes in that moment but something far closer to compassion.

"Aye."

The topic didn't end there. "How could your family bear to part with you so young?"

Katie might have been willing to confess to her lack of close companions, but she'd not admit her family had parted with her eagerly. "Circumstances required it, I'm afraid."

"Ah. The humble in Ireland have known a great many hardships these past years."

Katie nodded. Let Biddy think she'd been sent off strictly for reasons of poverty.

"I can't say I have your ability for cleaning and organizing," Biddy said. "The strides you've made in this room alone in only a few days are astounding. But I'm handy with a rag, and I'd greatly appreciate if you let me work alongside you in exchange for talking your ear off a bit."

"I cannot promise to make good conversation," Katie warned.

"Fair enough." Biddy's smile finally looked natural again. "And I'll do my best to ask you things you can't answer in only two or three words."

"I believe that might help."

"Five words that time." Biddy nodded. "That is progress, I'd say. Perhaps by the time we finish the dining room, you'll be up to six or seven."

"Let's not set our expectations too high." Katie allowed a little smile. Conversation didn't come easily, but she found herself almost enjoying it.

"I've a feeling, Katie Macauley, that you and I are going to become very good friends."

Katie had never had a close friend. She'd never wanted one. The few times she'd allowed herself to grow close to anyone, she'd been pushed away or left behind. She'd decided long ago that she simply wasn't the type to keep friends.

Biddy stayed for hours and hours. Katie fancied Biddy told her everything there was to know of her history, from the time her family left County Mayo during the last years of The Famine through her courtship with Ian while they both worked in a factory in New York. Katie also heard of their nearly ten years in Hope Springs. She listened with curiosity but stopped far short of sharing any of her own past.

Somewhere in the midst of her chatter, Biddy mentioned that the Irish families held a weekly céilí, a community party like those they'd known in their homeland. They played the music of Ireland and brought traditional dishes to share. Biddy said they even told stories, the blarney-filled tales that so captured a listener's attention. Katie was most certainly invited, Biddy insisted. Further, she said, Mr. Archer likely expected her to attend.

Katie found herself wanting to go, but she'd need to ask for the evening off. Men, she'd learned while working in kitchens over the years, were most amiable after they were fed. She'd best wait until he'd eaten.

She heard the telltale sounds of chair legs scraping in the dining room later that evening. The family, it seemed, had finished their meal. She stepped into the room just as Mr. Archer rose from his seat. The girls were only just disappearing into the parlor.

"Might I have a word with you, Mr. Archer?"

"Is something the matter?" Why did he jump so quickly to that conclusion? She'd not created any disasters at his house since securing her position once more.

"I only wondered if I might request the evening off. Biddy O'Connor invited me to a céilí tonight."

"I have no idea what that is." He was not one for making a person feel at ease in conversation.

"A party, Mr. Archer. Céilí is the word used in the old country."

He pushed his chair back up to the table, standing beside it with the air of one anxious to be moving along. "Ah, yes. The weekly Irish gathering."

"You've heard of it?"

"I have," he said. "I simply didn't realize it had a special name."

He didn't seem immediately opposed to the idea. That was promising.

"I know I'm supposed to work here mornings and evenings, so asking an evening off only a few days into the job is rather a lot to ask."

He raised a hand and cut her off. "You have already worked beyond the hours required of you. An evening off is not so presumptuous as you seem to think."

His words surprised her. After several days of pointed reminders that she wasn't being paid for her extra work, she'd have thought he wasn't counting the longer hours in her favor. An odd man he was, to be sure.

"And," he added, "I was more or less expecting you to attend. All the Irish in Hope Springs do."

"Then you don't mind if I go?" She wanted to be perfectly clear on that before hieing herself down the road. 'Twould be just her luck to return and find her things packed and waiting on the back porch, her job snatched away for a third time.

He shook his head and walked out of the room without further comment. 'Twas an easier thing than she'd expected.

Katie quickly saw to clearing the table, then slipped inside her room to tidy herself up. It would be a fine thing to hear the old tunes and stories.

She'd played a few of those songs on her fiddle for the Garrisons as they'd journeyed north from the train station but hardly ever in the months before that and not at all since arriving in Hope Springs. Her fiddle sat in a corner of her room, untouched. She hadn't had time to pick it up.

She missed her father every time she slid the fiddle beneath her chin. She longed for the sound of his expert playing, missed the peace she'd once felt at hearing his music fill their tiny house. More than anything, she missed the way he'd once smiled at her as though he loved her more dearly than anything.

"Go on with you, now," she whispered sternly to herself. "You've no right to miss what you don't deserve to have in the first place."

She wrapped her woolen shawl about her shoulders, closed the kitchen door behind her, and set off toward the bridge.

The sound of fiddles, tin whistles, flutes, and bodhráns led her to a tidy farmhouse several miles down the Irish side of the road from Mr. Archer's house. The fifth house on the left, she realized, which meant it was the home of Tavish and Ian O'Connor's parents. Katie smelled colcannon and bacon. The voices floating on the air rang deep with the tones of Ireland. She breathed it in, both soothed and upended. She longed for home, yet dreaded the memories connected to it.

Dozens upon dozens of people milled about. A group of musicians played together near the barn. Many of those gathered danced enthusiastically. A table sat spread with a great many dishes. Children eagerly stole sweet biscuits from the plates at the table's end.

Katie clasped her hands and watched it all unfold. With so many in attendance, she'd go entirely unnoticed. That was her idea of a perfect evening. No one other than Biddy would be expecting her. The night would be quiet and peaceful.

She believed that right up until the moment Tavish O'Connor and his teasing smile appeared at her side.

Chapter Twelve

Tavish nearly laughed at the startled look of alarm on Katie Macauley's face. He hadn't the slightest worry she was actually frightened of him. He'd wager she simply didn't know what to make of him. And, seeing as the feeling was entirely mutual, he found it endlessly amusing.

"Didn't your mother teach you not to sneak up on a person?" She didn't look over at him as she spoke. The stern set of her mouth didn't fool him for a moment. Katie meant him to believe her angry, but he didn't think she was as irritated with him as she worked to appear.

The woman could do with a fair bit of teasing, she could.

"You know, I don't think my ma ever mentioned that." He made a show of pondering the idea. "Perhaps we should go pull her aside and let her know you don't think too highly of her abilities as a mother."

For just a moment he saw panic flit across her face, quickly covered with an overdone look of scolding. "I knew you were trouble the moment I laid eyes on you."

"Oh, come now." He kept close to her side and smiled to himself when Katie inched further away. "Are you telling me when you first saw me sitting up in my brother's wagon that your very first thought was, 'That fine-looking Irishman over there is most definitely a rascal'?"

She kept her gaze on the crowd milling in front of her. Meant to not even look at him, did she? He would most certainly enjoy undertaking her introduction to the townspeople.

"So which of our fine Irishmen have you chanced to meet these past few days?" he asked.

Her chin rose more than a fraction. She'd certainly mastered the dismissively haughty look. "I've met hardly a soul, excepting you, and I can't say you'd fit on a list of 'fine Irishmen.'"

His chuckle at her well-turned response was joined by another amused rumble. He'd not realized until that moment that Seamus Kelly had happened past and overheard.

"I do believe you've been shown the door, Tavish," Seamus said with a grin beneath his ginger whiskers. "Aye, and kicked right on through it as well."

Tavish agreed with a nod. Katie had a way with set-downs. "This, Seamus, is Miss Katie Macauley, late of Mother Ireland. Though she's not told me exactly where she hails from, I'd wager Ulster."

"Ulster?" Seamus took off his green derby hat long enough to scratch at his head in an overly dramatic display of pondering. "It seems to me she has more than a touch of Dublin about her."

Tavish knew he would say exactly that. "You think everyone's a Dubliner. So which is it, Sweet Katie? Have I guessed right, or do the honors go to Seamus, here?"

Katie adopted a theatrically serious expression. She could tease and joke with Seamus but was all prickles with him? Tavish wasn't certain what to make of that. "Though it pains me to admit you're right about anything in this whole world, Tavish O'Connor—"

Seamus grinned at that. Tavish only just kept his own smile under the surface.

"—I was, in fact, born in County Donegal, directly in the heart of Ulster, and lived many years in Derry and Belfast."

Tavish began an exaggerated bow in acknowledgment of his own correct guess, a guess, if he were being honest, that had been helped along by

Biddy's quick summary of her earlier conversation with their newest Irish neighbor.

Katie, however, raised a hand to stop him. "'Tis with deepest sympathy for your friend Seamus, him of the impressive hat—"

Seamus tipped the brim of that very hat.

"—that I confess I've never been to Dublin nor set eyes on the Liffey. I hope that's something you can overlook and let me stay at this fine gathering."

A friendly word from Miss Prickles? It seemed she saved her stand-offishness and disapproval for him alone. He rather liked the idea of that particular challenge.

"You've gone and done it, you have," Tavish said to her under his breath, leaning in closer so as to be heard. Katie pointedly regained the distance between them. "Seamus is a Dublin man, born and raised in the Liberties. He'll likely claim you as kin, hearing you speak so highly of his town."

Seamus turned in the direction of the crowd and in a deep and booming voice called out, "Attention, my good people." He clapped, the sound echoing around them. The gathering grew still and listened. 'Twasn't everywhere the town blacksmith was also the resident entertainer. "We have here a fine Ulster lass who is newly arrived among us." He motioned back toward Katie.

Her eyes widened on the instant. Clearly she'd not expected to find herself the center of attention and didn't at all enjoy the experience. Biddy had apparently left out that bit, then. New arrivals always received a very warm welcome.

"If you were any sort of a gentleman," Katie urgently whispered, "you'd stop him."

"I might as well try stopping the rain, Sweet Katie." He felt certain she didn't appreciate the name he'd fashioned for her any more in that moment than she usually did.

Seamus continued addressing the group. The man never seemed quite as at home as he did when speaking before a crowd. "I do believe the lass deserves a song. What say all of ya?"

Cheers and applause answered his question. Seamus turned to the musicians. "What say you? Shall we play her a fine tune of welcome?"

The flute gave a quick, lively trill. Seamus turned back toward Katie, offered a friendly nod, and launched with enthusiasm into a tune the gathering knew well, though it had only lately come in to being.

> *In the merry month of June from me home I started,*
> *Left the girls of Tuam so nearly broken hearted,*
> *Saluted Father dear, kissed me darling mother,*
> *Drank a pint of beer, me grief and tears to smother.*

Others joined in the singing but held back on the dancing. Everyone knew the order of such things. Everyone, Tavish realized, except Katie.

"They are waiting for you, Sweet Katie," he said. "This is your welcome song. You are expected to start the dancing."

"I do not dance." She spoke firmly, her voice fair snapping with the declaration.

That reasoning wouldn't suffice. "You also told me that you don't smile, but I've seen hints of it my own self."

Katie shook her head, shook it with great emphasis, in fact.

"Refusing would offend them all." They'd likely see it as a sign of rejecting their offered friendship, in fact. "You're not dancing to say 'look how fine I dance.' You're saying, 'I thank you for the welcome.'"

That didn't appear to convince her. "I . . ." She glanced about, her eyes not resting on anyone but taking them all in quickly. "I made a promise many years ago not to dance until I—" Her brow knit, not with anger or frustration but something far closer to sadness. "I don't dance, Tavish. I don't wish to offend, but I do not dance. Not ever."

The song continued. Her words sat heavy on Tavish's mind. She'd promised someone not to dance, someone who seemed to mean a great deal to her. He could see by the pained lines in her face that the very idea of breaking that vow was ripping into her heart.

More and more eyes turned toward her expectantly. The time had come, it seemed, to trade his role of teasing companion to friend in a time of need. He'd undertake it for only a moment, he said to himself. He had no desire to get tangled up in any woman's troubles.

Tavish pointed a finger in her direction and made certain he smiled a bit. "You owe me for this."

His eyes roamed the crowd nearby. Who could be counted on to join him in his breach of etiquette? Ah, the very person. His littlest sister, though now a wife and woman grown, could always be counted on for a lark. He stepped up to her and held out his hand.

"Tavish?" she whispered urgently.

"I'll explain later, only go along with me in this."

Bless her heart, she followed his lead. He spun her out into the space set aside for dancing. He could see surprised looks on most faces in the crowd. As near as Tavish could recall, and he'd been attending the weekly parties for nearly a decade, no one had ever stepped out before the guest of honor.

He gave his family and closer friends pointed looks whenever their eyes met, silently telling them to join in. Slowly people began trickling out as well, taking up the dance. While he kept up the lively steps, he pondered just what to say in explanation. What had possessed him to step in for a woman so determined to dislike him?

The song continued as the dancing grew more general.

> *One two three four five*
> *Hunt the hare and turn her down the rocky road*
> *And all the way to Dublin,*
> *Whack fol la dee dah!*

As the song came to a fine and energetic end, the crowd applauded. Tavish's eyes found Katie. She looked braced for the worst, as though expecting to be thrashed or upbraided for refusing to dance.

Thrashed? For a dance? What had this woman been through? That she assumed she'd be mistreated tugged at Tavish's heart more than he cared to admit.

"Friends," he called out, "I think we owe our lovely new neighbor something of an apology."

Katie turned alarmingly pale. Tavish hoped she had the fortitude to stay standing during his explanation.

"We've grown so accustomed to greeting new arrivals with a dance that we've embarrassed our newest neighbor, I'm afraid." And now to formulate some acceptable reason when he himself had no idea of the whys of her refusal. "Miss Macauley is a bit shy of strangers and will need time to feel at ease enough among us to dance."

Shy of strangers. That wouldn't hold water. Katie Macauley didn't care for scrutiny, but she was hardly timid.

Everyone seemed to accept that reasoning. He'd have to apologize to Katie later for such a fabrication. She was, in that moment, surrounded by throngs wishing to make her acquaintance, likely all apologizing for making her uncomfortable with their attention. If she hadn't been shy of strangers before, she would be terrified of them after that.

Biddy, thank her kind heart, pushed through the crowd. She could be counted on to pull Katie out before her neighbors in their enthusiasm ran her off entirely.

"Good of you to take Miss Katie under your wing as you have."

Tavish didn't even have to look over to know 'twas Ian who spoke. He'd recognize the thinly veiled amusement in his voice anywhere.

"Your wife bullied me into it, if you must know." Tavish felt certain Ian wouldn't believe the half-truth. "Said if I didn't pay Katie particular attention, she'd tan my hide."

Ian's smile turned up a bit more. "I don't believe that for a minute."

Tavish shrugged, his eyes drifting back to where Katie and Biddy stood, heads together, chatting like old friends. Something Katie said drew a laugh from Biddy. Katie very nearly smiled. Very nearly. The change in her, with her eyes lit up and the weight that usually showed in her expression lifted, was captivating. What would she look like if she actually smiled? How might an evening spent with her go if she were in a laughing and teasing mood?

"A lovely colleen, she is." Ian apparently hadn't left yet.

"She is a mystery is what she is."

Ian only nodded. "Those are the best kind, brother." He slapped Tavish on the shoulder before heading off in the direction of his wife and her new friend.

Tavish considered joining them but thought better of it. While he found Katie enjoyably intriguing, he had no thoughts beyond that. Hovering about would only add to his family's speculating. No. Katie would have a far easier time of it if he made quite certain everyone knew there was no possibility of anything but friendship between the two of them.

Chapter Thirteen

Shortly after breakfast the next morning, Katie patted at her loose knot of hair, checking her reflection in the small mirror hanging in her room. The Archer family, she'd learned, attended church on Sunday mornings. She wasn't a religious person by any definition, but she could see the Archers hadn't remotely accepted her. Indeed they hardly seemed to approve of her. She thought it best to go along.

She straightened her cuffs. They weren't nearly as white as when first she'd made them upon arriving in America two years earlier. The dress was out of date and a touch worn, but it was the nicest she had. Both her work dresses were made of unexceptional brown fabric, more serviceable than pretty. This, however, was her fine dress, one reserved for rare occasions that called for something nicer. She'd chosen a sturdy fabric in a very light blue. It had held up to wear but wouldn't hold up to any fashionable scrutiny. The skirt hung full all the way around. Women of distinction wore their dresses narrower at the front now, with all the fullness in the back. Katie never had aspired to such heights of fashion.

She stepped back, pulling the front of her skirts up a touch. If only she could do something about the shoes.

She had none but her battered old work boots. Still, the dress hung nearly long enough to keep them covered. How she hoped no one would notice. She'd never had the means to own more than one pair of shoes. But worn-out shoes were a far sight better than the disfigured feet inside them.

She let the dress hang free once more. "It will have to do, Katie Macauley," she said to her reflection.

If the family threw her any scornful looks, she would simply do as she'd always done. She would hold her head high and pretend she cared not at all for their approval. Through countless insults and hurtful dismissals, she'd always kept her pain hidden. She could certainly continue to do so.

Katie smoothed the front of her dress and made her way to the parlor. The girls wore nearly identical dresses of lavender, white ribbons tied high on their waists. The most delicate of slippers encased their tiny feet. They might easily have been angels if not for their hair resembling two light brown bird's nests.

Mr. Archer stood with a comb in one hand and several white ribbons in the other, eyeing the girls with the look of one about to undertake a horribly distasteful task.

"You look quite lovely in your fine dresses, girls."

Katie smiled at the children. Ivy smiled back. Emma ignored her altogether.

"Katie." Mr. Archer sounded oddly pleased to see her. "Excellent timing."

She couldn't begin to imagine what he meant by that.

"The girls need their hair combed for church. Would you, please?"

"Comb their hair?" Had the man lost his mind? "You'll remember, Mr. Archer, tending to the girls does not fall to me."

He moved closer, an urgency in his face that seemed extreme considering they were only speaking of hair. "Biddy combs their hair during the week, but she is not here. I try every Sunday, and it never looks any better than this. They generally are both in tears by the time we're done, and I find myself cursing in a way unfit for children's ears. I would greatly appreciate your help."

He had lowered his voice, though Katie felt certain the girls could hear.

She spoke under her breath as well, mindful of nearby ears. "I have never combed a child's hair in all my life."

"You comb your own," he replied.

She folded her arms across her chest and eyed him. "You comb *your* own."

"My hair doesn't tie itself into impossible knots that nothing can undo short of a sharp pair of scissors."

With that declaration, chaos broke out in the room. The girls pleaded with their father, teary-eyed, not to cut their hair. They pulled on his arms, faces turned up to him in absolute panic. No matter that he assured them he wouldn't actually cut their hair, the girls would not be soothed.

"Please, Katie," he said over the noise.

That turned the littlest one's attention to her. She didn't speak, didn't plead. She simply looked at Katie with enormous, hopeful eyes. The poor child was convinced her father was moments from cutting off all her hair and that Katie was the only person who could possibly stop him. How could any person not feel affected by such a sight?

She could see to the girls' hair. It wasn't as though their father was leaving her solely in charge of them. Their well-being wasn't on the line. Katie could trust herself with that.

She held her hand out for Mr. Archer's comb.

"Bless you," he whispered.

His sincere gratitude touched her unexpectedly. A warmth grew inside, and it flustered her a moment. She covered her confusion by moving to the sofa and only looking at him out of the corner of her eye.

Mr. Archer dropped into a seat near the empty fireplace, relief and weariness etched into his features. 'Twas likely a hard thing for a man to raise two little girls on his own. No wonder, then, that he'd been willing to send off a housekeeper for lacking the ability to look after them. She felt an unexpected bit of urgency at that thought, a wish to help him even a little bit.

She set herself to the task of combing the girls' hair, opting to begin with the oldest, the one she felt more comfortable with.

"What are you wishing to do with your hair, Miss Emma?"

Katie's question noticeably surprised the girl. Likely she expected to have no say in the arrangement of her hair. She answered warily. "Mary's mother always makes two long braids."

Katie nodded. "Is that what you're wanting today? Or would you care for something new?"

She had Emma's full attention then. For once the girl didn't overflow with dislike. "I don't know about doing anything new. Papa might not approve."

Katie glanced at Mr. Archer. She hadn't thought to ask if he had rules regarding his daughters' appearance. He silently waved her on.

"We'll not do anything too grand," Katie assured her. "We'd not wish to distract anyone from their worshipping."

Emma nodded solemnly.

"We'll try something new. If you find it too much or you just don't fancy it, there'll still be time and plenty to make two braids and get to church on time. What say you?"

Emma looked downright eager despite herself. Katie could clearly see a war waging in the girl's eyes. No doubt her determination to dislike the new housekeeper stood at odds with her interest in a pretty hairstyle. Katie could appreciate the struggle. She herself knew it best to keep a distance from the family she worked for, being but a servant and one whose employment was only temporary. Yet, these two little girls tugged at her heart more than she cared to admit.

Katie instructed Emma to sit herself down on the floor in front of the sofa. Ivy had climbed on her father's lap, obviously quite content with the arrangement. A fine picture the two of them made. Ivy so obviously loved him, and he, in turn, treated her with great tenderness.

Slowly Katie worked the knots out of Emma's hair, being careful not to pull any more than was absolutely necessary. Knotted hair could be terribly painful.

Ivy prattled on about everything under the sky, from the cow in "Mary's papa's barn" to the peppermint sticks at the town mercantile. Her father listened without comment and without showing even a hint of boredom. Katie found herself fighting down a grin of amusement at his awe-inspiring self-control.

Two long, neat braids were soon formed on either side of Emma's head, falling directly over her ears and down in front of her shoulders.

Emma broke her minutes-long silence. "This is the same as always, just more in the front."

"Right you are, Miss Emma. The trick comes next, you see."

Katie took one braid and pulled the end back up to the beginning, making a single loop that fell just below Emma's ear. She tied one of the white ribbons Mr. Archer had given her around the very top in a neat bow. She repeated the step on the other side.

"Go see what you think," she told Emma.

How hard Emma tried to appear uncaring even as she moved directly to the mirror just around the corner in the entryway. Katie followed. She far preferred seeing Emma's first impression rather than trust the unreadable mask she'd likely put on afterward.

"Will it do, do you think?" Katie asked.

"I think so." Emma looked up at her, and Katie could see she was nervous. "Will Papa like it?"

Katie suspected Mr. Archer would be grateful for anything he didn't personally have to do with his daughter's hair. "That is a question best asked of him."

Emma nodded solemnly and stepped back in the parlor. Katie

watched her cross the room to where Mr. Archer sat. "Katie made me a new hairstyle."

"And she did a fine job," Mr. Archer said.

An almost painful longing entered Emma's eyes. "Do you think it's pretty?"

The reluctant hope Katie heard in the girl's voice struck deep in her heart. She knew that sound, knew the desperation behind it. She'd felt it herself nearly all her life. The child longed for her father's approval and love. 'Twas a heavy burden to carry in such a little heart.

"You are very pretty," Mr. Archer said.

Emma's expression warmed.

Mr. Archer mussed Ivy's still unkempt hair and looked across at Katie. "And do you mean to work the same miracle with this one's wild locks?"

Emma's face fell with her father's suggestion. Her little shoulders drooped.

"Actually," Katie said, "I think Miss Emma's style is so perfectly suited to her that we'd best name it Miss Emma's Sunday Hairstyle and reserve it special just for her."

Though he looked momentarily surprised, Mr. Archer followed Katie's lead. "You are absolutely right. No one could wear this style quite as well as Emma does."

In the next moment Emma's face transformed from the solemn expression she usually wore into a tentative smile. Katie couldn't remember having seen Emma smile once in the days she'd been there. She wondered in that moment if any father truly understood how deeply his opinion of his daughter mattered.

She liked her gruff and grumpy employer more in that moment, seeing him love his daughter the way he did. She liked him quite a bit more, in fact.

Mr. Archer's attention shifted to Katie. She fully expected to see something of approval in his face at having successfully tamed Emma's hair and the moment of happiness that had brought the little girl. Instead, his brow furrowed even as his lips pressed into a tight line. The man didn't look happy in the least.

Now what have I done?

"I need to go hitch the team to the buggy." He lifted Ivy from his lap and set her on her feet.

"Can I watch, Papa?" Emma asked. "I'll sit quite still and be careful of my dress."

Mr. Archer waved his oldest daughter in front of him and followed her through the door to the dining room. His steps echoed hard and determined.

"Sit here a moment, Miss Ivy." Katie motioned to the spot of floor Emma had occupied a bit earlier. "I'll be back directly."

Katie moved swiftly, following the path Mr. Archer had only just taken. When one's employer is so obviously put out with something, 'tis best to mend the trouble quickly.

"Mr. Archer? Might I have a brief word with you?" Chasing after him for a brief word had become something of a routine of hers.

He turned back. Tension remained in the faint lines around his mouth.

Katie stepped out onto the porch, crossing closer to him. Emma stood by the buggy, far enough distant to not overhear.

"Have I done something to upset you, Mr. Archer? You seem cross with me, and I can't determine just why."

"I'm not cross with you."

"You seem it."

He pushed out a breath. Katie thought she heard frustration in the sound. "I am not cross with *you.*"

"Who else could it be? You're not ever cross with the girls."

He leaned his forearm against the nearby porch post, his hand in a fist. His gaze had left her, though not an ounce of his tension had fled.

"Sir?"

"With myself, if you must know."

Katie couldn't imagine why. "Over what?"

He glanced at her for a fleeting moment. "Are you always this nosey?"

"Forgive me. I hadn't meant to pry." She stepped back a bit, reminding herself of the wisdom in not irritating the one who paid her salary. "If you're upset and I've played any part in that, I am sorry."

"It is nothing you have done." He tapped rapidly on the porch post. "I am sure it hasn't escaped your notice that Emma doesn't smile. She's not . . . She's not a happy child." The words seemed to stick in his throat as he spoke. "But she smiled just now, truly smiled, over something as simple as a new hairstyle."

"But why would that upset you?"

He pulled back from the post, his posture nearly rigid. "Because I don't know how to do that. I finally found something that makes my unhappy child happy, and it isn't even something I can do for her. Do you have any idea how frustrating it is to want something so badly and know you can't possibly have it? Do you have any idea?"

Katie's lungs tightened painfully. Had she any idea, he asked. His impossible wishes were nothing compared to hers. He wanted to make his daughter smile—that could be accomplished. Katie needed her sister's forgiveness. But the dead don't speak, and they don't forgive. She needed her father's love and approval, but what man could love one who cost him his home and the life of his tiny child?

"A great many people long for things they cannot have, sir," she whispered.

He didn't seem to find any comfort in her words. She hadn't expected him to. Mr. Archer stepped off the porch toward the buggy. Emma's longing gaze followed his every move. Could he not see that his daughter near worshipped him? She was a serious girl, to be sure, but at least in the company of her father, Emma didn't seem as unhappy as he feared.

"No, Mr. Archer," Katie silently said, "your wishes aren't impossible at all."

Chapter Fourteen

The church in Hope Springs sat at the end of the only road running through the town itself. Nothing stood behind the building, leaving ample room for buggies and wagons and horses. Someone had thought to erect hitching posts for just that purpose—several rows of them, in fact.

The arriving churchgoers kicked up a great deal of dust as they turned in the large field beside the church. Everything was dust and wind and dryness in Wyoming. How in the world did people farm in such a place?

A few of those making their way toward the modest church building looked familiar to Katie from the céilí the night before. Most she'd never before seen. What surprised her was the sheer number. Everyone living nearby must have come to services that morning. She looked back and forth from the rows of wagons to the building and began to wonder just how all the people who'd come would manage to fit inside.

Mr. Archer and the girls had already alighted, and Katie made to do the same. She slid to the side of her back seat and began to lower herself carefully down. Before she could make even the slightest progress, Mr. Archer held out a hand as if meaning for her to take it. A moment passed. She'd not expected the gesture nor knew quite how to respond to his offer of help. No employer, no man of means for that matter, had ever handed her down from a buggy.

Though she'd prefer to be left to herself, Katie opted not to make a scene over it. Mr. Archer had not shown himself the most patient of men. Refusing his offer of common courtesy would likely only shift his frustration to her. Katie set her hand in his as she negotiated the long distance to solid ground.

"Thank you, sir," she said. That look of scolding reminder entered his eyes once more, and Katie realized her mistake. "Mr. Archer," she corrected herself.

"I was a little short with you earlier, at the house," he said, the apology almost grumbled. Was he so unaccustomed to apologies, or only apologies offered to servants? "You don't deserve to have your head bitten off simply because I am realizing my limitations as a father."

"You say that as if you're a failure as a father."

"You would rather I lie?"

He truly believed himself a failure? "Your girls have a roof over their head and food on their table, and you haven't sold them into servitude. I'd say you're doing quite well."

"'Sold them into servitude?'" He looked almost as though he meant to smile. Apparently Mr. Archer thought she'd thrown that in as humorous exaggeration.

Katie cast her eyes about the crowd, hoping he'd think her attention had wandered. She didn't want to pursue the topic of fathers and the ways they might rid themselves of unwanted children. Her history and her secrets were hers alone. She'd not lay her soul bare for anyone.

Emma waved to another young girl as they approached the church building. "Hello, Marianne," she greeted quickly and quietly.

Little Marianne smiled back, obviously happy to see her friend.

Katie followed a step or two behind the family as they all made their way inside the church. She wasn't truly part of the family, and she hadn't a friend nearby to walk in with as Emma seemingly did.

A single aisle ran down the middle of the room, rows of pews on either side with space between the far ends of the benches and the windows on the side walls. Two doors sat on either side of the back wall with a single, long bench situated between them. 'Twas not the room itself that so surprised her, however, but the arrangement of the people inside.

The pews had already filled, with people standing by the windows. Those sitting on the right side of the room all wore something in a shade of green. The color adorned the ladies' hats, dresses, and shawls. The men's vests, shirts and, in a few cases, even their trousers were green. A person couldn't help but notice the pattern. The very same could be said of the left side of the room, except the color of choice was red. Katie looked from one side to the other. Nearly to a person, they wore their side's chosen color.

Katie saw many faces from the céilí but only on the right.

She understood then. The Irish sat to the right. Those who disliked the Irish sat to the left. So where, she wondered, did Mr. Archer sit, he who declared he had no part in it? She found him on the back pew, the only place in the room that could be declared neither right nor left. Suddenly the girls' lavender dresses became more than a pretty color for young girls to wear. They were neither red nor green. Katie was immediately grateful for the blue of her own dress.

In a flash of near panic, she realized the room had grown quiet and all heads seemed turned in her direction. She received smiles from the green side, curious looks from the red. A man, in the somber black of a clergyman, walked down the aisle from the front of the chapel toward Katie.

He smiled a very little and dipped his head a bit. "Good morning. I am Reverend Ford. You must be new in town."

"Aye. That I must be, indeed."

An audible gasp—one Katie thought a touch dramatic—emanated from the reds. The greens grinned with a great deal of triumph and enthusiasm. Her accent had obviously given away her origins.

The preacher's smile froze. "Well," he said as one intent on making the best of an unpleasant situation. "It is tradition to introduce new members of the congregation." He motioned toward the front.

"You mean for me to stand up there? Before all these people?"

He nodded patiently.

Katie didn't wish to make waves any more than she wanted to make a spectacle of herself. Neither did she wish to stand before them all in her threadbare cuffs and work-worn boots. "I suppose there's no avoiding it."

The preacher's smile grew more false. He gestured toward the front.

Katie sighed and nodded. "Best get this over with."

As she stood beside Reverend Ford, facing the room, her eyes found Tavish O'Connor a few pews back, sitting with his parents. She recognized Ciara Fulton, Tavish's youngest sister, and her husband nearby. Ian and Biddy weren't far removed. An older sister and her family occupied the pew behind Biddy's brood. What would that be like, to be so surrounded by family?

She let her gaze drift back to Tavish. Amusement twinkled in his eyes. He thought her predicament funny, did he? Katie set her shoulders and looked away. If she were to be embarrassed before the congregation, she'd not give Tavish the satisfaction of seeing her discomfited. She would rather he think her haughty than weak. She'd learned very young that people preyed mercilessly on the vulnerable.

"Friends." Reverend Ford spoke the word as though he wished he meant it. "We have a new member of our congregation." He looked at her, the same unconvincing expression of welcome on his face. "Tell us your name and where you join us from today."

He meant to make a point of her Irish roots. He meant to force her to take a side. Not only was she far from keen on being pulled into a feud, she might very well need a job from someone on the Red side of the room. Making enemies there was not wise.

"My name is Katie Macauley, and I come here today from the Archer farm, just up the road."

Amusement shown on the Irish faces, a touch of surprise on the Red.

"I meant"—the preacher's words emerged slow and a touch impatiently—"from where do you come to Hope Springs?"

"Omaha—'twas there I boarded the train that brought me."

Reverend Ford's smile slipped even as smiles appeared amongst the congregation. Even a few on the Red side of the room allowed themselves a wee smile.

"Perhaps I should take a simpler approach." The preacher clearly meant the words as a poor reflection on her intelligence. "We all would like to know if you come from Ireland."

Katie looked over the expanse of green and red. Did this town really require them all to stand up at church of all places and declare their nationality? She'd sworn to Joseph Archer that she would stay out of the feud. She meant it as much in that moment as she had when she said it.

"Before I answer, Reverend, might I pose a question to you? A matter of doctrine, as it were."

He pulled himself up proudly. "Of course."

She didn't allow her posture to slump in the slightest. "When I reach the pearly gates, how likely is it that God himself will have posted a 'No Irish Need Apply' sign thereon?"

The smallest splotches of heat began to form on his cheeks. "That is an odd question."

Katie nodded. "And might I say that, at least as it concerns attendance at church, so is 'Are you Irish?'"

If she weren't so thoroughly put out with the man, she'd have found his momentary blustering humorous. Reverend Ford recovered himself quickly. "Well, if you're Irish, then you belong over here." He pasted a smile on his face and motioned to the green side.

"You'll be forgiving me, Reverend, but I've never taken kindly to being told where I belong."

Katie kept her head high as she marched herself down the aisle, passing every pew without a glance. She looked neither to the Green nor to the Red but moved directly to the back and out the door without so much as a pause. She took the steps at twice her usual speed and made straight for the road back to the Archers' house. Let the town feud, if they wished. She meant to stay out of it.

Mr. Archer caught up to her before she'd gone far past the field where the horses stood waiting for their owners.

"I had a feeling you were going to run off," he said.

"I thought it best to get out of the building before I spat profanities at that man's head." She folded her arms across her chest.

"I told you staying out of this feud is almost impossible," Mr. Archer said.

That pulled her eyes back to his face. "I didn't come here to make enemies. Saints, I didn't even come here to make friends. I came to work. I came to earn the money I need to go home. That's all I'm trying to do. That's all. I'll not come to church and glare at my neighbor over the color of her dress. And I will not have some pompous, arrogant preacher—"

She bit off the rest of her remarks and turned away again.

"Will you at least wait long enough for me to get the buggy? It's a longer walk than you probably realize."

The offer surprised her. She'd fully expected to be scolded. "I thank you," she said, "but no. The exercise'll do me good. 'Twill give my temper a chance to cool."

He didn't leave. "Are you certain you want to walk all that way?"

She nodded. "Your offer is very kind, but I'm quite certain."

He hesitated a moment. What was the question she saw hovering in his eyes? He didn't voice it, didn't even hint at the reason why he lingered. She was but his employee, one who'd likely embarrassed him despite his not scolding her about it. If not for the way the town divided itself, she might have sat peacefully through the service and spared Mr. Archer the bother she'd caused.

She sighed. "I didn't realize the feud ran so deep as to touch Sunday worship."

"I did try to warn you," he said. "The feud touches everything, Katie. And though you did an admirable job of stepping around it in there"—he motioned back toward the church—"it will catch up with you eventually, and you will have to decide just where you stand."

Chapter Fifteen

Joseph suspected that first day that he'd hired no ordinary house-keeper. Katie Macauley seemed determined to prove him right.

The comments on Katie's expert handling of the town's preacher were plentiful, ranging from shock to admiration to wishes that more would stand up to Reverend Ford's dictates. Left unspoken was the fact that the preacher would not ask newcomers to take sides if the town hadn't in-sisted on dividing itself. Though Joseph didn't approve of the practice, he knew what had started it. The preacher had long ago grown tired of breaking up brawls in his church. Keeping the combatants separated had calmed things down considerably.

Katie had promised to stay out of the town feud. He'd heard her dec-laration but doubted her ability to carry it out. He'd seen the feud at its height. She hadn't.

She handed him his morning coffee almost the moment he reached the kitchen on Monday morning. Did she know the cup she'd given him was the one he preferred? He wouldn't put it past her to have discovered that. If not for her obvious discomfort with the girls, she might very well have been the perfect housekeeper.

The slightest hint of daylight coming up over the horizon drew him to the kitchen window. A soft blue lit the low eastern hills from behind. The small shrubs caught the tiny wisps of light.

"'Tis a beautiful sight, is it not?"

"I never grow tired of it." He stood gazing out, sipping at his coffee. The sunrises and sunsets were what had first bonded him to Wyoming. "There's nothing like it in the city."

"That there is true as a carpenter's corner."

He looked back at her. "Is that an Irish expression?"

"No, I can't say that it is. More of a Katie Expression, I suppose."

A Katie Expression. If anyone would have their own lexicon, she would. Katie did things her own way.

He turned again to the window, enjoying the sights of early morning. The silence between them was easy, comfortable. If things could always be that way, he would be more than satisfied having her there.

"Are you from the city, then?" Katie asked. He could hear pots clanging about as she began her morning work. "You talk as proper as any of the fine gentlemen I overheard in Baltimore."

"I lived my entire life there, actually, before coming here." *Before* eagerly *coming here,* he silently added.

"And what brought you out so far?"

He sipped and watched the sun continue to rise. Though few had asked him for specifics of his history, he wasn't averse to telling it. "I wanted to look out my window and see something other than rows and rows of houses. I wanted to live in a place that was quiet, where the air was clear. I wanted to see something real come from my work, something I raised with my own hands."

He'd wanted open space where his children could run and play and not feel as though the very city around them was closing in. He wanted to know his work counted for something other than an entry in a ledger.

"I've wondered since I came here," Katie said, "how anyone grows anything in a place where it never rains."

"It does rain sometimes." *Though not enough,* he acknowledged silently. "And we have water from the river and irrigation ditches already dug. We're far better off than most of the rest of Wyoming."

"Farms fail in other parts of Wyoming, then?"

He looked back at her. "Farms fail *here*." He'd known more than a few families who'd lost too many crops and were forced to move on. "I suppose the risk makes our little successes that much more satisfying."

She seemed to understand that. Had coming this far west been a risk for her? It likely had. And, he realized with a twinge of guilt, that risk hadn't precisely paid off. She was earning only half the salary she'd anticipated and, whether she realized it or not, had virtually no chance of finding other work.

"What did you do before you came out here?" she asked.

"I sat behind a desk in a tall building in Baltimore, day after day."

"You were a clerk, then?"

He shook his head. "I ran a company, one my family has owned since before the War for Independence. But I never enjoyed it the way my father did." He set his empty cup on the work table. "I wanted something different." Something his father hadn't understood in the least. Father questioned his decision right until the very end. Mother had questioned it as well. His late wife had railed against it at times. In uncertain moments, he himself wondered if he'd made a wise choice.

"So you gave all that up to come here?" The idea clearly baffled her as it had so many others.

"I still own a large portion of the company and, though I've left the day-to-day running of it to someone else, I do make a profit from its success." Although the generous income had failed to appease Vivian. His wife had missed her life back East too much to be at all comfortable in Wyoming.

"So a little extra income, then," Katie said. "That is a nice thing." More than merely nice, she seemed to find it a relief.

"Yes. So you need not worry about your salary. I can afford to pay you."

Her eyebrows shot up in surprised offense. "That was not my reason for asking, I assure you. I'm not so selfish as that. And I'll thank you not to go putting words in my mouth."

What little ease had existed between them vanished entirely.

"Why is it, Katie, that every conversation we have inevitably ends with you convinced that you ought to be thoroughly offended by some innocuous comment I've made?"

She planted her hands firmly on her hips and eyed him with much the same fire she'd thrown at Reverend Ford. "If I am a touch sensitive, Joseph Archer, it's only because you're so quick to condemn me. All I did was ask in a friendly manner about what brought you out here, and suddenly I'm a selfish, greedy woman who cares for nothing beyond getting paid."

"When did I say you were selfish or greedy? Did those words come out of my mouth and I somehow didn't hear them?"

She pointed a finger at him. "You needn't become sarcastic with me. I am not stupid."

Stupid? When had he said she was stupid? When had he even hinted at it? "And now we have come back to the part where everything I say is meant to insult you." He shook his head in exasperation. "I knew you were going to be difficult the moment you arrived here." He pulled open the door. "Lest you read any unintended criticism into my leaving, I need to go milk a cow and clean out a stall." He stepped outside.

As the door slowly swung closed, he heard her muttering to herself. "Isn't that just like a man? Gets the last word by running off to muck midden."

He poked his head inside once more. "Perhaps you'd care to tell me just what midden is."

In an instant her cheeks flamed and her eyes widened with surprise. Having at last claimed the upper hand in their argument, Joseph nodded crisply and stepped out once more.

He had the strangest urge to laugh. As it was, he smiled. If the uncertainty he'd seen flit across her face were any indication, his sharp-tongued housekeeper would be on the porch any minute intent on making a very humble apology. He was looking forward to that.

He turned to watch the door just as it pulled open. He crossed his arms over his chest and tried to keep down the smile he felt.

Katie caught sight of him and visibly started with surprise. "Laws o' mercy, Joseph Archer. You frightened me out of clear half my life, you did."

He could see that he had most certainly startled her. It was probably not very gentlemanly of him that he enjoyed the sight.

Katie pressed her open palm over her heart and took several quick, shaky breaths. "What in the name of Charlie MacMaster are you doin' standing here on the porch starin' at a door? Have you taken full leave of your senses?"

"Who's Charlie MacMaster?"

"That has nothin' to do with nothin', and I'll thank you for sticking to the topic at hand. You meant to frighten me, didn't you?"

He nearly laughed—the woman's words were almost impossible to understand. "Did you know your brogue gets very broad when you're angry?"

Katie plopped her fists on her hips and glared him down. "Well? You gonna tell me what you're about or am I to speculate on your lacking mental state?"

"'What am I doing?' I'm waiting for you, of course."

"For *me*?" His answer surprised her enough to take some of the air out of her sails.

"Though I'm not familiar with the exact phrase you chose, I am certain you implied that men, as a whole, are devious." He shrugged. "I assumed you wanted to apologize for that."

"Very well." Katie looked penitent, a little too penitent, in fact. "I am truly sorry that men are devious."

The woman was quick on her feet and witty besides. "You certainly avoided that apology. Isn't that just like a woman?"

Katie's posture relaxed by degrees. Though she was far from the verge of laughter, at least she didn't seem truly angry with him. He liked to think she had a sense of humor beneath her tough exterior.

"You'd be wise to speak kindly to a woman who means to do the washing today," she warned. "I may just let your clothes sit and fester until they stink enough to bring down the very heavens and let that be a fine lesson to you."

"As much as I would enjoy standing around talking about laundry, I do have chores."

"Might I ask you one more thing before you go wish the animals a good morning?"

Oddly enough, he didn't mind the delay in the least. When was the last time he'd had a good conversation so early in the morning? "If I said no, would it stop you?"

"Likely not."

He'd expected that answer.

"As I said, Mr. Archer, I mean to do the washing today, but I've not found a drop of bluing nor a single bit of laundering soap. Might you know where it's kept?"

Bluing? Laundering soap? He wasn't even entirely sure what those things were. "I haven't the slightest idea. We may not even have any. I've been sending the laundry out."

She seemed surprised to hear that. Surely she didn't think a man who couldn't keep his house clean had the time, energy, or expertise to do the family's laundry.

"Then I'll need to add that to my list, I suppose."

"You have a list?" Did he even want to know what her list entailed?

She looked tempted to roll her eyes. "A list of things I'm needing from town. You are ridiculously low on the most basic cleaning things. One would think your house hadn't been properly cleaned in months." She'd added a touch of dryness to her tone. It was clear to anyone with eyes that his house hadn't been properly cleaned in a very long time.

He stepped off the porch on his way to the barn. "Finbarr and I are going into town today. If you'll write down what you need, I'll pick it up."

She shuffled about uncertainly even as her color climbed higher. "Might I just tell it to you rather than write it down?"

He understood the difficulty in an instant. "My apologies, Katie. I'd forgotten you don't write." He could see he'd embarrassed her. That was badly done of him. "You are welcome to dictate a list, if you'd like. Or you could come along. We were planning to take the girls. They enjoy picking out sweets at the mercantile."

"Would I be expected to look after them?"

What was her objection to the girls? It seemed to go beyond mere discomfort. She was always very careful to avoid being left alone with them, even for the briefest of moments. "You would not be expected to tend them."

She nodded, her face registering immediate relief.

"Can I ask why you dislike them so much?"

"I don't dislike them at all," Katie said.

His gaze narrowed as he studied her. "Yet you are very insistent that you have nothing to do with them."

Her chin went up again. "I told you when I first came that I have no experience with children, and keeping a distance seems best for all of us."

He could clearly see there was more to it than that. He didn't think her objection to Emma and Ivy was personal, but he knew for certain it was deeper than a lack of experience.

"You make a good show of believing that, Katie. But there's more to it, I can see it in your eyes."

She grew instantly uneasy. Though his own curiosity pushed him to ask more, something in the near fear he saw in her eyes stopped him. There would be time to learn more about her. He found, in fact, he very much wanted to.

"Would you like to come with us to town?"

"Yes, I think I would." The change of topic seemed welcome.

"Then I'll offer you a friendly warning. Those living in town tend toward the Red side of Hope Springs' feud. They may not be very friendly."

"I'm not riding in to make friends, Mr. Archer. I only mean to get some few things I need."

He wasn't reassured. "Like I said, Katie, only a friendly warning."

Chapter Sixteen

A bit of Katie's heart ached watching Emma sit on the wagon bench beside her father as he drove toward town. The little girl longed for Mr. Archer's company, coveted it even. She knew that feeling so well, so deeply it hurt at times.

She herself sat in the wagon bed trying to concentrate on her duties so her mind wouldn't wander to her past. Ivy sat in the back as well, more than content with Finbarr's company.

They'd been in the wagon for some time, and Finbarr hadn't said much beyond a few quiet remarks to Ivy. Katie knew little about him, though she would have realized in an instant had she met him on the street that he was an O'Connor. He had Ian's coloring and Tavish's startlingly blue eyes.

"Why is it you never come up to the house for lunch with Mr. Archer?" Though Joseph Archer was a suspicious sort who showed himself inclined to be argumentative, he seemed fair-minded. "Surely he allows you time for a noon meal."

Finbarr nodded. His was an absolutely natural smile, nothing in it but contentment with life. "I bring my meal from home. That's part of our arrangement."

His American accent caught her by surprise. Only the slightest hint of

Ireland lingered in the background of his words, nothing more than the smallest twist to an occasional phrase. He'd obviously spent most of his life in this country, perhaps all of it.

Her first thought was how very sad that must be, not to have any memories of Ireland. But growing up amongst Erin's green hills and valleys wasn't Finbarr's past. His heritage, yes, but not his personal history. Would that be the way of things twenty, fifty years down the road? The children of those forced to flee the famine in their homeland would feel no special connection to Ireland.

Katie shook off the forlorn thought. She'd a lifetime of sorrow to be mulled over without adding a future of heartaches to it.

"Your arrangement?" she asked.

"I asked Mr. Archer when I first came to work for him whether I might collect a higher wage if I brought my own meal each day. Not a great deal higher, but a little."

"And he agreed to it?"

Finbarr nodded. "And it's made a difference. I've saved up quite a bit. Soon I'll have enough to buy the land he's holding for me."

What did he mean by that? Katie fully intended to ask him, but Ivy chose that very moment to lean dangerously over the side of the wagon. Katie reached for her, afraid she'd tumble over. Finbarr took hold of Ivy first and pulled her back.

"I only want to see the wheels." Ivy pouted at being pulled from her efforts.

"And suppose you lost your footing and fell under the wagon wheels?"

Ivy shrugged. "That'd kill me dead, I bet."

"It sure would. And I'd cry and cry," Finbarr said.

"And you wouldn't get to marry me when I'm all grown up." Ivy spoke quite matter-of-fact, as though their eventual marriage were a foregone conclusion.

"Exactly." Finbarr smoothed the girl's hair gently and then gave one of her messy braids a light tug. "So sit down before you topple over."

Ivy plopped herself back down and sat with her hands and chin resting on the side of the wagon, eyes on the scenery.

"You're betrothed, are you?" Katie quietly asked Finbarr.

He smiled back. "So she tells me."

"How old are you, Finbarr?"

"I've just turned sixteen."

The age suited him outwardly. Yet, he held himself like one older, wiser. "Those eleven years are quite a difference between the two of you."

The same good-natured expression remained on his face. "By the time she's old enough to truly be interested in the boys, I'll seem like an old man to her."

"Perhaps you'll even be married yourself." Katie tried to picture the lad grown with a wife and family. 'Twasn't too terribly hard to do. She simply thought of Ian, and the resemblance between them did the rest.

"Tavish is twelve years older than I am, and he's never married."

For a moment Katie felt bad for the prying she meant to do. Tavish O'Connor was a puzzle to her, one she thought on more than she ought. She wanted to understand him better.

"Why is that, do you think?" she asked Finbarr. "Seems to me some fair colleen would have set her sights on him long since."

"He had a sweetheart years ago. Bridget Claire was her name. He was going to marry her."

Katie pushed back an unexpected, ridiculous surge of jealousy. "What happened? Did she change her mind?" That seemed unlikely. Most women would think him quite a catch. Though she wasn't among them, she quickly added to herself.

Finbarr shook his head. Voice lowered, he explained. "She died of the fever, the same one that claimed quite a few others." He looked at Ivy with obvious discomfort.

Katie thought she understood. Mr. Archer was a widower. If she had to guess, Katie would say the late Mrs. Archer had been among those claimed by that fever.

Finbarr's attention shifted to Ivy more fully, she having inched her way closer to standing, even as she leaned further over the side again. "As my mother often says, Ivy, 'God is good, but don't dance in a small boat.'"

Katie grinned at the familiar Irish proverb. Ivy appeared less impressed.

"I'm not in a boat."

Finbarr pulled her into a brotherly embrace. "The principle's the same, dear. Don't tempt fate."

He kept her entertained through the rest of their short journey into town. Ivy laughed at the silly things he said, though he spoke so quietly Katie could hardly make out his voice. He had a way with Ivy and no denying. Katie couldn't remember ever knowing a young man his age with the patience to keep a five-year-old still and content. A remarkable lad he was, to be sure.

Katie's mind did not linger on Finbarr long but on his earlier words. Tavish O'Connor flirted and danced and teased like a man whole of heart and quite free of heavy burdens like those his youngest brother hinted at. Did he yet mourn Miss Claire? Or had he recovered from that loss?

She shook off the thoughts. Tavish O'Connor's past, present, or future had nothing at all to do with her.

Several people called out greetings as the Archers' wagon rolled past. Mr. Archer answered mostly with wordless waves. He pulled the wagon to a stop near the spot where the blacksmith and the mercantile stood on opposite sides of the road. Emma sat quite straight, looking like a proper young lady. Her gaze continually drifted to her father, though his attention was elsewhere.

Ivy stood in the wagon bed, motioning rather frantically toward the smithy. She tugged on Finbarr's hand. "I want to see the big fire."

Finbarr's eyes met Katie's. She bit back a grin at the exasperation she saw there.

With patience she suspected was simply part of his nature, Finbarr answered, "I don't think lingering near the blacksmith's fire is a good idea. Remember what we said about tempting fate."

Ivy's pout was monumental. Finbarr chucked her under the chin and smiled with a great deal of empathy.

During the course of the exchange, Mr. Archer had apparently alighted from the front bench, Emma with him. He stood at the back of the wagon. "Come down, Ivy." He held his arms out for her.

"I want to see the fire." She came very close to whining.

"Not today," Mr. Archer said. "Finbarr and I have some business to see to."

He set the little girl on her feet beside him. Finbarr had already hopped over the side. Katie made to hop down as well. Mr. Archer reached up for her, much as he had for Ivy.

"You needn't—"

"It's further down than you realize, Katie."

Did he think her no more capable than Ivy? "I am certain I can manage it, sir." She set out to do just that.

"If you insist on calling me 'sir' every time you're put out with me, I will start calling you 'Miss Macauley' every time I feel the same way." He speared her with a scolding look. "Now, if you would, *Miss Macauley*, allow me to help you down."

His butchering of her name, coupled with the prick her pride took at being spoken to almost as if she were a child, set her immediately against accepting his offer. "That will not be necessary. I can easily step down on my own."

"You can just as easily fall on your stubborn face."

Before Katie got out another word, Mr. Archer grabbed her about the waist and lifted her down to the ground just behind the wagon. The gesture surprised her enough to rob her of breath for a moment. He gave her a look that clearly meant he felt he'd won their short battle of wills.

The man had no idea how drawn out a battle that could be.

"I've found, Miss Macauley," Finbarr said in all sincerity, "when Mr.

Archer has his mind set on a course of action, it's best to go along. I've never known him to be wrong."

"He's not right about everything," Katie replied, just loudly enough to ensure Mr. Archer heard her. He took his girls' hands without acknowledging her remark, though she thought she saw his eyes flicker in her direction. "He's most definitely wrong when it comes to pronouncing my name. Perhaps, Finbarr, you might see your way to teaching him how to do the thing properly."

Finbarr grinned. "You don't care to be called Miss May-kuh-lee?"

He so perfectly matched Mr. Archer's dreaded version of her name that she couldn't help smiling. "I do like you, Finbarr O'Connor. Very much indeed."

With that compliment the poor lad turned a shade of red Katie'd rarely seen on anyone. She hadn't meant to embarrass him and took some comfort in seeing that his smile remained.

"I'm quite fond of Finbarr, myself," Mr. Archer said dryly, "but we are in something of a hurry."

Mr. Archer crossed the road, Ivy and Emma clinging to his hands. Katie followed a step behind, Finbarr next to her with his hands stuffed in his pockets, still flushed with embarrassment. Katie would have apologized if she hadn't been entirely certain that doing so would only make matters worse.

The front windows of the mercantile displayed goods of every imaginable kind, from foodstuffs to fabric to work tools. Katie's eyes lingered a moment on a very pretty bonnet trimmed in shades of blue. Her only bonnet looked quite old and plain in comparison. And when contrasted with the shiny, high-laced boots she spied in yet another display, her footwear looked downright pitiful. Katie tried not to be ashamed of her appearance, yet she'd always looked like a walking testament to the existence of poverty, and she thoroughly disliked it.

A sign sat in the window very near the display of shoes. Katie wished she knew what it said. Perhaps the mercantile was offering a fine price on boots. 'Twould be a good thing to know in case her beaten-up pair didn't last much longer.

"Do you read, Finbarr?" she asked quietly.

"I do."

For the briefest of moments she was amazed at that. That made two Irish children in this town, from beginnings as humble as her own, who could read.

"Would you mind telling me what the sign says just there in the window?"

Finbarr looked uncomfortable with the request. "That sign there?"

"I'd be greatly appreciative."

"It says . . ." His obvious hesitation made her wonder. "It says, 'Hiring. Inquire within.' And, then . . ." He cleared his throat, his eyes darting about.

"And then *what*?" Finding a place of business that was openly hiring was something of a miracle.

"It says that . . ." His face went as white as it had red a moment earlier.

'Twas Joseph Archer who finished for him. "It says, 'No Irish need apply.' And that is meant most sincerely."

"Oh." She'd wager the shopkeeper had sat on the Red side of the church room the day before. "Are the Irish allowed inside at least?"

"Yes."

Katie looked at Finbarr. He offered a tiny nod of agreement, though he still fidgeted in obvious discomfort.

"Perhaps I'd best tell you my list and wait out here."

"Suit yourself," Mr. Archer said. "If it sets your mind at ease, though, I have never known the Johnsons to turn away a customer. They won't offer to be your dearest friend and are more likely than not to vaguely insult you, but they will take your business."

Katie pondered a moment. She'd be on her own once Mr. Archer replaced her. If she had any chance of surviving in this town, of making a living there, she needed to be able to make her own purchases.

A chime rang as Mr. Archer opened the mercantile door. He held it, and his girls stepped inside. He watched Katie with a question in his eyes.

"I am no coward," she said to him, her chin held at a determined angle.

"I never said you were."

Katie stepped through the door he held. The girls had already moved directly to the glass jars of sweets displayed near the counter. Mr. Archer made his way there as well, though he kept his gaze on the shop proprietor.

"I have a list of things I need," Mr. Archer said, pulling a paper from the pocket of his trousers and unfolding it.

Katie hung back, away from the counter. She would see to her purchases after Mr. Archer had finished with his. The girls yet stood eyeing the sweets. Katie would likely have done the same at their age if she'd had the opportunity.

"I have some business at the smithy," Mr. Archer said to the man behind the counter. "Have Joshua load those things into my wagon."

"Certainly, Joseph."

If Katie didn't already know her employer had a great deal of money, the way the shop owner scraped and bowed would have told her as much.

Mr. Archer turned to his daughters. "Here is a penny." He handed Emma the coin. "You can each pick a sweet for yourselves. Then sit on the bench by the door and wait, understood?"

The girls nodded, eyes wide with anticipation as they searched the jars with renewed enthusiasm.

"You won't mind if I leave you here?" he asked Katie.

"Perhaps if you gave me a penny as well, I'd fancy the idea a bit more."

He didn't seem to appreciate her attempt at humor. The man was grumpy as could be.

"I'll be across the road at the blacksmith's," he said.

She nodded. He hesitated a moment before slowly leaving. Was he so worried she couldn't look after herself?

Katie stepped up to the counter. She'd show Mr. Archer and Finbarr and all the others that she could handle a frosty welcome from the town merchant.

"A very good morning to you," she said to the proprietor.

He didn't reply but continued straightening cans on the shelf behind the counter.

"I'm needing to make a purchase. Is it you I'd be talking to about that?"

The man didn't even look at her. He couldn't have stood more than ten feet away. She knew he could hear because he'd spoken at length with Mr. Archer.

The door chime sounded. The shop owner looked up from his cans, and he smiled warmly at whoever had walked inside.

Katie glanced back. A woman stepped toward them, looking the very picture of loveliness in a soft-yellow dress trimmed in white lace two inches wide at the very least. She wouldn't have been out of place as the lady of any of the fine houses where Katie had worked.

"Mrs. Archibald," the proprietor greeted, his voice smooth as velvet. "So pleased to see you." His was an accent Katie didn't recognize in the least. The words he spoke came out long and lazy. All she could say with certainty was he didn't hail from Ireland nor from Baltimore.

"And you, Mr. Johnson." The woman spoke with refinement. "Have I come at a bad time?"

"Not at all," he replied. "I haven't any customers to see to."

Hadn't any customers? Katie knew for sure and certain he'd heard her declare her intention of making purchases.

"Begging your pardon, Mr. Johnson. I do believe it is my turn."

He looked at her for the first time. His smile remained in place, but his eyes had lost all hint of a welcome. "Patience, miss. I'll get to you." He turned back to Mrs. Archibald, she of the fine yellow dress. "And what brings you in today?"

"Your wife told me you've received a shipment of ginghams."

"We have. I'll show them to you myself."

They spoke so pleasantly, with no sign that they'd treated anyone poorly, despite Katie's standing directly beside them.

If she were to have any chance of completing her business, she'd simply have to press her point. "My order will take but a moment, Mr. Johnson," Katie said. "And I feel I must mention again, I was here ahead of Mrs. Archibald."

She received another patronizing smile. "Wait your turn, I will get to you as I promised I would."

"But it *is* my turn."

The door chimed again. Two more women stepped inside, neither of whom looked at all familiar to Katie. She listened a moment to the chatter between them. They weren't Irish or at least didn't sound it.

"I'll be with y'all in a moment," he said to the newest arrivals. "Just as soon as I've pulled out the ginghams for Mrs. Archibald."

He meant to leave her out completely. She'd been standing there before anyone else arrived, and he meant to skip right over her. What a maddening man! He and the preacher clearly embraced the same approach to courtesy.

Katie stepped back up to the counter, facing Mr. Johnson head on. "Have you no desire to sell something to a paying customer?"

Mr. Johnson looked at the others in a way that spoke of quiet but exasperated amusement, before returning his gaze to her. "A paying customer would have money. Do you have money?" She could hear the laugh he didn't quite hold back.

"You misunderstand. These items are for Mr. Archer's household. He would be paying for them."

Mrs. Archibald's hmph was so loud it was likely heard in the streets of Dublin. "Isn't that just like the Irish? She came here intending to charge someone else for her purchases."

She made Katie sound like a regular sneak-thief. "But these are his purchases, in a manner of speaking." Surely these people could understand something so simple.

The two newest arrivals looked more than a touch uneasy at the conversation, though neither stepped into the fray.

Mr. Johnson crossed his arms over his chest and eyed Katie as if she were an absolute menace. "Mr. Archer was already here and made his purchases."

"I've come for a bottle of bluing, a scrub brush, and a cake of soap— all household items. Mr. Archer brought me with him so I could get them from your mercantile."

"He didn't say anything about his housekeeper making purchases." Katie half expected Mr. Johnson to pat her on the head and send her out to play. "We do not allow our valued customers to be cheated."

Infuriating man. "If I wished to make free with my employer's money, don't you think, Mr. Johnson, I'd choose to spend it on something far fancier than cleaning supplies?"

"What I *tink* is that you had best keep quiet and stop bothering folks."

Tink instead of *think.* Katie'd heard that particular mockery of the Irish pronunciation enough times not to think it a particularly impressive display of wit.

"Pardon me a moment, ladies."

He motioned for Katie to step a bit to the side. She did so. The gaze he turned on her was sharp and piercing. She recoiled despite her determination to appear courageous.

"You are expecting me to simply hand you goods you don't intend to pay for and which Mr. Archer didn't request." He lowered his voice to a whisper. "I would not allow a filthy Irishwoman to buy a half-penny's worth of goods on credit. So you would do well to keep quiet and out of the way where your kind belongs."

The entire room went silent in that moment. Katie heard nothing beyond the echo of the words he spat at her. Mr. Johnson stepped back to his other customers, quite as though he'd not uttered such a hateful, stinging rebuke. Katie blinked a few times.

Filthy Irishwoman.

In that moment she felt eight years old again standing before the staff in Derry as the housekeeper told them all every mistake she'd made, every way in which she'd failed in her duties. She'd been horrified and humiliated then.

There, in Johnson's mercantile, with the shopkeeper and the women standing about, Katie knew she couldn't, in that moment, bear more ridicule.

Chapter Seventeen

Tavish waited outside the smithy's while his horse was reshod. His eyes were firmly fixed across the street on the mercantile. Katie had gone inside with Joseph Archer and his girls, but her employer had left her there some minutes earlier, crossing to the smithy to have a replacement piece for a bridle forged. No Irishman in Hope Springs could feel the least bit at ease knowing one of his countrywomen was facing the very Red Mr. Johnson on her own. That Katie likely didn't realize the kind of man she was dealing with only added to Tavish's worry.

When Joseph didn't emerge from the smithy to return to the mercantile, Tavish knew something had to be done. If one thing could be counted on where the town merchant was concerned, it was that he'd not keep a civil tongue in his head simply because his Irish customer was female.

Tavish crossed the road and moved directly inside the mercantile, setting off the bell that announced a new arrival.

"Good morning to you, Mr. Johnson." He hoped the shopkeeper heard the warning buried in his tone. "Good morning, ladies."

Mrs. Archibald didn't return the greeting; he hadn't expected her to. Only the Archibalds hated the Irish as much as the Johnsons did. The other two women offered him small smiles, one even blushing a bit. He was used to the women, whether they sided with his countrymen or not, taking note of him around town. It meant nothing at all in the end. The Red Road citizens wrote him off quickly as just another Paddy, and the Irish citizens knew he wasn't interested in love.

Katie had slipped further back from the counter, not looking at anyone. Perhaps he'd been worried for nothing. She might not have even attempted to interact with any of them.

"Katie?" Tavish whispered upon reaching her side.

Her attempt at lack of interest failed utterly. Those beautiful brown eyes of her were filled with absolute misery, a look of surprised hurt still lingering there.

"Merciful heavens, what did they do to you?"

"I'm fine." The words shook a tiny bit.

Clearly something had happened. He should have come in sooner. "Mr. Johnson is the reddest of Reds hereabout, as are the Archibalds. You can't tell me either of them treated you kindly."

"Oh, he smiled and spoke sweetly enough."

Every Irishman in town knew and despised that smile of Johnson's, so patronizing and full of thinly veiled hatred. "His smile makes you feel sick to your core, does it not?"

Katie nodded. She took a deep breath but yet looked unsettled.

"I'd be guessing you also discovered that the Irish are expected to keep quiet and give way to any other customers who might wander inside."

"Aye."

Tavish very nearly pulled her into an embrace right there in the mercantile. He knew the misery she was experiencing and wished with surprising force he could wipe away some of the pain he saw.

"And we can't buy anything on credit, despite the fact that the rest of the town can. And he often charges us more for the things we buy than he charges those on the Red Road."

"We hadn't gone as far as prices." She appeared to calm by degrees. "I stopped trying to make my purchases after he . . . after . . ."

Tavish stepped closer and lowered his voice. "After he *what*, Sweet Katie?"

She didn't answer. Her gaze fell again. After the fire he'd seen in her so many times, Tavish hated seeing her beaten down.

He placed two fingers under her chin and raised her face again. He only allowed himself a moment to consider how pleasant the simple touch was. "After what, Katie?" he asked again.

"He called me a 'filthy Irishwoman.'"

Tavish froze, not with shock—Johnson said such things often—but with anger.

"He called you that to your face, he did?" Tavish had always been the first to argue in favor of keeping the peace, of not resorting to violence. But he had to work hard to keep from marching to the counter and belting Johnson so hard he'd need every shovel on the Red Road to scrape him up off the floor. "Joseph Archer's a blasted fool leaving you here alone like he did. He knows what Johnson is."

Tavish leaned in close so he could lower his voice and still be heard. That she didn't pull away as she had again and again at the céilí told him how much her time at the mercantile had upended her. Were she entirely unaffected, she would have given him a firm shove and a thorough scolding.

"Listen to me, Katie Macauley. If ever that fool of a man you work for sends you in here again without so much as a soul above the age of nine to support you, don't wait around for Johnson to spew his venom. You march yourself directly to the smithy. That's Seamus Kelly's establishment, and there's nearly always an Irishman or two about the place. Any one of them'll stand by you as you deal with our local"—Tavish shot an angry look in the direction of the counter, but he refused to speak out loud the word that first came to mind—"shopkeeper."

Katie looked hesitant, unsure. "I've no wish to make more trouble. I'm new to town and only passing through in the long of it. Stirring things up is not at all what I wish to do."

He allowed himself a fleeting moment to ponder her "only passing through" comment. Did she mean to run off, then? The question stirred up too much confusion inside him. He'd best stick to the immediate issue.

"They wouldn't come storming in with shillelaghs or any such thing. They'd keep quiet and peaceable but near to you. Johnson keeps the insults to a minimum when he's outnumbered and when he's dealing with men instead of women."

Her shoulders dropped. "Your Hope Springs has proven a mighty disappointment."

"Don't say that, Katie. We—"

The door chimed.

"Oh, saints preserve us," Katie muttered, glancing at the door.

Tavish followed her gaze. Joseph Archer had finally returned.

"He'll be expecting to leave," Katie said, "and I haven't made my purchases yet."

"Do you want me to explain to him?" Tavish offered. He couldn't countenance the thought of her being pushed around by yet another man in this town. She'd endured enough that day already.

Katie didn't pause even a moment. "I fight my own battles."

There was the fire he'd missed along with her trademark stubbornness. "Might I say, just because you can doesn't mean you have to."

"A woman alone *always* has to, Tavish. It's the way of things." Katie moved back to the counter where Mr. Archer stood talking to his daughters.

She had backbone, he'd give her full credit for that. And though that same fierceness had often been directed at him, he admired it. He hung back a bit but within hearing range. He wouldn't allow any of them to insult her.

"Ivy wants a peppermint," Emma was saying. "I've decided on a butterscotch."

Johnson was as outwardly friendly and cheerful as he always was with the Red Road while his attention was on Joseph. "Did Joshua get your order into your wagon?"

"He did. However, when I asked after Miss Macauley's items, he indicated she hadn't made any purchases." Joseph sounded rather more curious than upset. "When I left here a few minutes back, Miss Macauley was your only customer. It strikes me as rather odd that she hasn't purchased anything yet."

"When you returned I meant to ask if she was authorized to charge purchases to your account or if you had any restrictions."

Katie raised an eyebrow at that. It was, no doubt, not at all the real reason she hadn't been permitted to make her purchases.

"I was only being careful with your money, Joseph," Johnson said.

"You are aware that Miss Macauley is my housekeeper, are you not?"

"Yes, of course." Mr. Johnson was all deference and respect.

"Then you may consider her authorized to purchase in my name any items she deems necessary to do her job."

Joseph had taken her side. Tavish felt some relief at that and an unexpected bit of jealousy. He'd come in to help her and support her, but Joseph would likely walk out the hero in her eyes.

And what do you care about that? She's nothing but a difficult and troublesome woman. And intriguing. And unexpectedly adorable.

"How am I to know which of her purchases are for your household and which are for her?" Mr. Johnson asked.

Joseph Archer leaned against the counter, his gaze firmly on the shop owner. "She will tell you."

He meant to send Katie back into the lion's den, then? Tavish would have to make certain the Irish knew to keep an eye out for her when she was in town.

"If that is what you wish me to do." Mr. Johnson seemed convinced the path was not a wise one. "I will see to it you receive an accounting of all her purchases."

Joseph waved the suggestion off. "That will not be necessary."

On more than one occasion Tavish had felt infinitely grateful that Joseph Archer had maintained his neutrality in the feud. He alone could appease both sides, as he'd done during the horrible fever and several dry seasons when fire threatened to take out the entire town. He felt a bit of that gratitude again in that moment.

"Now, ladies," Joseph said, "I trust you will not mind if Miss Macauley completes her business. She has been here for some time, and I am in a great hurry to be going."

The two most recent arrivals nodded and offered brief words of agreement.

"Of course, Joseph. We wouldn't wish to delay you." Mrs. Archibald was all kindness and sweet words with Joseph Archer.

Tavish thought for certain he saw Katie roll her eyes.

"Rather transparent, that one," he whispered from directly beside her. "All sugar with some and spitting fire at others."

"I think it helps that Mr. Archer's a fine-looking man."

He grinned. Her comment was too pointed to have been anything but a barb directed at him. "Well now, that fair puts me in my place, does it not? Seems to me I've some competition to be worrying over."

"Now you're just being ridiculous."

He had, in fact, meant to be teasing, but discovered with some surprise that he did wonder if anyone else was vying for her good opinion. The "anyone *else*" part of that thought struck him. Was he trying to win her regard?

Right there in the mercantile he realized he was interested in Katie Macauley, intrigued by her, already well on his way to pursuing her. When had that happened?

At some point during his reverie, Katie and the Archers left the mercantile. She hadn't even bade him farewell. He might be pondering pursuing that maddening colleen, but she clearly could take him or leave him.

Tavish slipped outside as well, catching up to them as Finbarr was lifting Ivy up into the wagon bed.

Joseph stood at the front wheels and spoke as Tavish arrived. "Thank you for going in after Katie. I hadn't realized Johnson would give her trouble, not when she was making purchases for my household."

"She's Irish, Joseph. The Johnsons and the Archibalds will give her trouble every moment she's here, no matter who she is working for." He hoped the warning would make Joseph think twice before leaving her unsupported with Red Roaders.

"That is more true than it ought to be." Joseph shot a quick look in the direction of the mercantile. "Still, I thank you."

Tavish nodded. "We've learned to look out for each other where the Red Road is concerned."

Joseph climbed onto the wagon's bench. Only Katie remained on the ground.

"I thank you, too," she said. "'Tis a comfort to know not everyone hereabout thinks of me as a fil—"

"Don't say it, Sweet Katie." He interrupted her, not liking even to think of such a thing being spat at her. "You don't need to hear those words again."

"'Twas a pleasure seeing you again, Tavish."

He smiled. "And here I thought you didn't like me."

"When did I say I did?"

He tipped his head thoughtfully. "Still trying to decide, are you?"

She shrugged. "I'm giving it some thought."

Tavish handed her up into the back of the wagon. Was she truly thinking on it? He watched her as the wagon rolled away down the street. Her gaze remained on him as well.

If she hadn't made up her mind about him just yet, it seemed to him he'd best do what he could to tip her opinion in the right direction. And then figure out what she meant by "only passing through."

Chapter Eighteen

Katie scrubbed so hard at the laundry that afternoon she swore the sheep that gave its wool to make the blankets found itself cleaner than it had been at dawn. Whether her fervor came from an intense dislike of laundry or the horrible morning she'd had, Katie couldn't rightly say. Either way, the Archers would be wearing the cleanest clothes in town.

She entertained for one fleeting moment the idea of asking Finbarr to write out on the back of all Mr. Archer's shirts, "Laundering by Katie." 'Twould be a fine way to spread word about town that she was looking for a bit of side work.

As she hung the last of the Archers' laundry on the line, Katie eyed her red, cracked hands. She'd seen laundry maids at the great houses where she'd worked. Their hands were always raw and often bleeding and increasingly scarred with every passing year. Katie had spent some time at a wash bucket. She'd forgotten how unpleasant a task it was. Perhaps working as a full-time laundry maid was not her best option.

Now that is your vanity talking, she told herself. *You'll take whatever work you can find and be grateful for it.*

She set the large laundry basket on the back porch. The day had begun to wane, and she'd best see to the family's evening meal. It wouldn't help her at all to be fired from the one job she had. Again.

Before she'd set a single foot inside the house, she heard the sound of horse hooves approaching at a very leisurely pace. A moment later, the animal came into sight, with the Archer girls seated on its back. Tavish led the animal, a stunningly beautiful bay mare, at a slow walk, glancing back at the girls a few times as he approached the barn. Ivy grinned from ear to ear. Emma even looked tempted to smile.

What a puzzle Tavish O'Connor was. He teased and flirted like an expert, yet in the mercantile that morning he'd been sincerely attentive, concerned for her. He'd been kind and gentle. And there he was, taking time out of his day to bring two little girls home and treat them to a horseback ride. If that weren't sufficiently confusing, the man was handsome enough to set even her guarded heart fluttering.

"Do you see these impressive horsewomen I have here, Katie?" Tavish called out as he tied the horse's lead to a post.

"Aye. They've the finest seats I've seen in many a year. Quite natural in the saddle, they are."

Emma's chin came up a notch. Katie had quickly realized the girl fretted a great deal. She wished to be seen as competent, elegant, and beautiful, by her father especially. The tiniest of compliments gave her a needed ounce of confidence.

Ivy so painfully resembled Katie's own poor sister. Emma's deep uncertainty and quietness put Katie firmly in mind of herself. Nine and five the girls were. Very near the ages she and Eimear had been.

During Katie's moment of distraction, Tavish had helped each of the girls down and walked with them to the porch where Katie stood. Did he mean to leave her solely responsible for them? Katie slid back into the shadows near the kitchen door.

Tavish pulled two wrapped bits of butterscotch from his pocket and handed them to each of the girls. "Don't tell your father I gave you sweets so near to dinner," he whispered.

Ivy took the treat eagerly and plopped it in her mouth. Emma, ever the responsible young lady, slipped hers into the pocket of her pinafore.

The girls sat on the edge of the porch, Ivy's jaw working fiercely at her mouth full of sugar.

"A fine animal you have there, Tavish."

"Aye, that she is. As fine a horse as ever I've ridden. She's made me quite the envy of the territory. Not a month goes by that someone doesn't offer me a fortune for her." Tavish leaned against the house near where Katie stood.

"And yet you don't sell her?"

Tavish shook his head. "When a man finds such a treasure, he doesn't part with her for anything." His was a flirtatious smile if ever Katie had seen one. The protective, empathetic man from the mercantile had stepped away, it seemed, and the Tavish Katie'd come to know was back once more.

Finbarr came out of the barn, his eyes almost immediately settling on the girls.

"Your brother there is a fine young man," Katie said.

"He's by far the best of us all."

"Now that I believe."

Why was it the man always grinned when she attempted to put him firmly in his place?

They both watched the lad quietly sneak up on Ivy, who hadn't noticed his approach. He grabbed Ivy around the waist and spun her about. The girl's giggles filled the yard.

"Are you going to miss me 'til tomorrow, Ivy?" He held her draped over one shoulder.

She laughed so hard her words came out in spurts. "Not. One. Bit."

"I think you know the punishment for fibbing, dearie."

Ivy wiggled in his grasp, still giggling. Katie glanced at Tavish, wondering what he thought of the scene. A grin as wide as the River Foyle split his face.

"Are you going to say it?" Finbarr asked.

Ivy shook her head. Finbarr made quite a show and a great bit of noise expressing his wounded feelings against the backdrop of Ivy's obvious enjoyment of the performance. He set her down on the porch next to her sister and squatted down in front of them.

He pointed a theatrical finger at Ivy. "Someday, wee'un, you will miss me and then you'll wish you'd told me so."

"Are you going somewhere?" Emma asked.

The smile he offered her held far less teasing in it than the one he'd bestowed on Ivy. "No. But there'll come a time when I'm not working here day after day and being big brother to her. Ivy'll have to admit she misses me then." He tapped Ivy's little nose. "Won't you?"

Ivy shook her head, and Finbarr laughed. True to form, Emma didn't join in their revelry.

"I will miss you," she said, with a touch of real sorrow in her words.

He chucked her under the chin. "I'll be back tomorrow, sweet girl. I'll see you then."

"And even when you aren't coming here every day, you'll still live nearby." Emma phrased the statement almost as a question.

"And you can come visit me when I'm quite fancy in my own home." He pulled one of her braids and stood.

Katie liked the boy. She wished even more in that moment that any one of her older brothers had been nearby during the horrible months before Eimear died. Surely an older brother would have watched out for them both, would have comforted her the many times she'd been scared and alone.

"Are you walking back with me, Tavish?" Finbarr asked from the edge of the porch.

"Go on ahead," Tavish answered. "I've something to ask Katie, here, and I don't mean to do it with you standing there listening."

He meant to ask her something? She hated that her heart pounded at the thought.

Finbarr waved to the girls before beginning his walk home.

"You've something to ask me?"

"I've come upon a rumor that you've decided Hope Springs is a disappointment," he said.

"A rumor? I told you that my own self just this morning."

"Ah." His look of dawning realization was a touch overdone. "That just might be where I heard it."

"What does all this have to do with whatever it is you mean to ask me?"

"I am meaning to ask if your afternoon is free Friday."

That sounded almost as if he was asking her to spend an afternoon with him. "Free for what?"

He chuckled at that. "Ever the wary one, aren't you?"

Katie didn't care to be laughed at. Tavish and his thick black hair and heart-meltingly blue eyes could take his mocking and go.

She reached for the kitchen door, intent on leaving him out on the porch to tease his own self. His hand covered hers on the doorknob. A tingle immediately started where his fingers touched hers. She pulled back. Her mind knew full well to be careful where a handsome, teasing rogue was concerned, but the rest of her was far too aware of him.

"If I promise not to tease you too mercilessly, would you go for a bit of a drive with me on Friday?" he asked. "Not even as a social engagement, mind you. I thought you might enjoy seeing a bit of Hope Springs."

"You wish to take me on a tour?" Katie didn't mean to become attached to the place, but finding a few reasons to like the town would be nice.

"A small tour," Tavish said. "And maybe a wee bit of gazing into each other's eyes and whispering sweet nothings."

She skewered him with a look of scolding rebuke, one he couldn't possibly mistake for encouragement. "Absolutely not."

He didn't look the least surprised. Indeed, he looked even more amused than before.

"Perhaps we'll just keep to the tour for now," he said. "What say you?"

She hesitated. A day off from her work would be nice. Perhaps she'd even learn enough of the town to decide what she ought to do next. 'Twas Tavish's company that made her waver. She enjoyed him, most of the time. But he also made her very nervous. And she couldn't be certain he didn't mean to tease and gaze and whisper just as he said.

"Come now, Sweet Katie. You might even enjoy yourself."

"That's doubtful," she muttered. "Now what about that possibly made you laugh? I meant it, you know."

He just shook his head. "You're a tough one, Katie Macauley. But I mean to talk you round to enduring me at the least. Take a ride with me. I'll be a perfect gentleman, my word of honor."

An afternoon away from her endless list of chores would be nice. But only if Tavish behaved himself. "A *perfect* gentleman?"

The devilishly handsome grin he produced was not terribly reassuring, yet there was sincerity in his eyes. "You'll hardly recognize me I'll be so well behaved."

Oddly enough, Katie believed him. "I suppose I could spare an hour or two."

She heard his almost silent laugh. "I'll come by Friday about noon, if that'll do for you."

Katie nodded. A simple drive was all it would be. A chance to see the town and nothing else. She stepped inside the house without pausing even to watch him walk away. He'd likely take that as a sign she was hiding how much she fancied him. She didn't. Not at all.

She fancied him so little, in fact, that she continually reminded herself she didn't care for him while she prepared the family's evening meal. The silent conversation continued even as she set the table. She could admit to being curious about the man but nothing more. And it was only curiosity that made her heart hammer and her hands shake a wee bit when she thought of spending an afternoon with him. Curiosity and nothing else made her wonder just what it would be like to have Tavish O'Connor gaze into her eyes as he'd teasingly threatened.

You see how it is with me, Eimear? I tell myself no heart flutters and no attachments, and still my mind runs away thinking of the blue-eyed devil. Except Tavish didn't truly seem like a devil. A tease and a flirt, yes, but not a bad man underneath it all.

Besides, an afternoon seeing Hope Springs wouldn't turn her thoughts to love or tender attachments, even if Tavish did flirt mercilessly. Katie knew it to be the truth: she simply needed a chance to lodge that fact more firmly in her mind.

Perhaps if she got the Archers started on their meal, she could pull down the wash while they ate. That would free up her evening enough that she might sneak away with her fiddle. She'd not played since coming to Hope Springs. She needed the music, needed the calm it brought her.

Katie stood near the door connecting the dining room to the kitchen as the family sat down to their meal. "Is there anything you're wanting that's not out?"

"No. Everything looks fine." Mr. Archer wasn't one for flowery words of praise, though he had once complimented her on the coffee she made.

"Very good. I'll just be slipping out to take the laundry off the line." She turned and pushed on the swinging door.

"Aren't you going to eat?"

At the moment Katie would gladly skip a meal to get a moment to herself. "Aye, after I've brought in the wash and a couple other things."

He shook his head. "Sit down and eat, Katie."

"In here?" She'd never in all her life eaten with the families she served.

"Would that be so awful?" Mr. Archer seemed surprised at her insistence.

"Not awful, simply . . . odd."

"I think you would adjust." He motioned to an empty seat on the other side of Ivy. "Join us."

"Truly, I'll have a bite later in the kitchen when I've a moment."

The man looked entirely unmoved. "Sit. And eat."

Several responses jumped to her lips. But seeing that the girls were taking in the exchange with wide eyes and unflagging attention, Katie settled on holding her chin a touch high and leaving without further comment. Let the man make of that what he would. She might be a servant, dependent on a wage, but she was a woman grown with the right to her dignity. Being ordered about like a child was something she'd not endure.

Frustration pricked at her as she crossed her spotless kitchen. Absolutely spotless. Not that Joseph Archer had noticed the miraculous progress she'd made in only a week. The parlor and entry hall weren't perfect, but they were a far sight better than they had been. How could he complain about her eating schedule and not even notice the work she'd done?

And why did she care that he hadn't noticed or thanked her or seemed properly impressed? She'd never longed for acknowledgment from any of her other employers.

Katie pulled open the back door only to have it pushed closed once more. For a moment she couldn't account for such an odd thing. Her mind, however, quickly pieced the mystery together. Mr. Archer stood behind her, his arm reaching out past her shoulder, hand flat against the door. She'd been so lost in her thoughts she'd not even heard him catch up to her.

Katie kept her back to him and folded her arms in front of her. "Have you come to order me about some more?"

"Order you about?" Though Katie knew Mr. Archer had to be standing almost touching her to have reached the door from behind her, the nearness of his voice still startled her. "If I've learned anything about you over the last week, it's that you do not respond well to being told what to do."

"People've been doing just that since I was eight years old, as if being poor and forced to work for my keep somehow made me lack-witted. I'm not dull nor foolish nor incompetent nor—"

She swung around to face him, determined to make her point, but her words faltered. Turning about put her very nearly nose to chest with

Mr. Archer. She hadn't expected that. Didn't care for it, in fact. Katie put as much space between them as she could, only to find her back pressed to the door behind her.

He didn't seem to notice her discomfort. "I never said you were any of those things. I only wanted you to eat."

"And I mean to eat." She held herself with utmost dignity. "Just as soon as it suits my plans."

He lifted his exasperated gaze to the ceiling. "You are so stubborn."

"Aye, that I am. Stubborn enough not to die of starvation, as I've proven once already in my lifetime." Guilt twisted in her to hear those words fall from her mouth. She'd survived The Famine but not out of stubbornness. She'd lived only because her sister had not.

Mr. Archer crossed his arms in a perfect imitation of her own stance. Katie couldn't say if the change made her want to smile or simply open the door and run. "Miss Macauley—"

She cringed. *May-kuh-lee.* Who in heaven's name pronounced it that way?

The tiniest glimmer of a smile touched his face. "You'll have to teach me how to say your surname correctly." He even sounded a little bit amused.

"I'm no miracle worker, Joseph Archer."

That glimmer grew, though not by much. He had brown eyes. She'd not noticed that. They'd only ever looked dark before. Until that moment, standing so close to him, she'd only thought of his appearance in the simplest terms. Dark eyes. Lighter hair. Of a common height for a man. He was beginning to seem like a real person, more than merely the man she worked for.

"I suppose something catastrophic will happen to the laundry if it is left on the line while you eat?" he pressed

Katie had every intention of eating something quickly after she'd seen to some chores, but she hadn't time for a full sit-down meal, not if she were to grab a minute alone with her music. "It will set me behind schedule. I have something I need to do this evening, but I mean to finish my work first."

He didn't reply, neither did he move away. He stood, studying her. Katie couldn't say if he meant to yield or was simply taking a moment to formulate more arguments.

"Please, Mr. Archer."

"This is something important to you?" He sounded as though he already realized the answer to his question.

"Yes, sir."

His gaze grew more pointed at her slip.

"Mr. Archer," she corrected.

He let it go without further objections. "But you will eat?"

"Yes."

While he didn't actually say anything, she saw in his face the moment he decided to leave her to her task. She offered a small nod of gratitude. He moved silently back into the dining room.

Though she knew herself free to go about her work, she remained with her back pressed to the door, hand on the knob beside her. She hadn't expected that of Mr. Archer. No employer of hers had ever cared if she ate or slept or rested. Yet, the same man who rarely had a word for her during the day, who grumbled a great deal more than any person ought, seemed to concern himself with her welfare.

The contradiction stayed with her as she pulled down and folded the laundry. She thought about it as she washed the Archers' dishes and scrubbed out the sink. Her mind had not yet moved on even as she ate her own hurried meal. The moment she took the handle of her father's fiddle case in her hands, however, those worries quieted, slipping back to the furthest reaches of her thoughts.

Katie stepped out the back door, fiddle firmly in her grasp. Under her other arm she held a blanket, one old and worn that would not mind an evening spent in the outdoors. The night had grown dim and a touch chill. She set her eyes on the clump of trees she'd decided upon earlier.

The wind blew across her path, pulling her skirts hard against her legs. She clutched the blanket and fiddle to her and pushed on. The evening was far from silent, though what noises she heard were too distant and too garbled for identifying. How very unlike the constant roar of the city.

Katie stepped beneath the canopy of branches. The air turned cooler. The trees grew near the bank of the river that wound its way around Hope Springs and past Mr. Archer's fields. A person would be hard pressed to cross the river without the help of a bridge.

She spread her blanket beneath the trees and sat overlooking the river. The sun dipped lower on the horizon, the sky filling with the blazing colors of sunset. 'Twas a perfect setting for a quiet evening of music.

She opened the fiddle case, her eyes falling on the familiar instrument. She tightened the hairs of her bow, then took up the fiddle. She closed her eyes and pulled the bow across a string.

"Too low," she whispered.

One string at a time, Katie tuned the fiddle just as her father had taught her—she kept her eyes closed and listened, shutting out every other sound. She always found the act of tuning deeply satisfying. Here was one trouble she knew how to fix. Few other problems could be seen to so quickly and disposed of so easily.

Katie sat with her fiddle tucked under her chin, bow in hand. How she missed her father. She'd not heard a single word from him since the day he left her in Derry. Mother wrote now and again, her words written out by their priest. Katie'd had those words read to her, even dictated letters in return. But Father never sent so much as a second-hand greeting.

Someday she would give him back his land and home. She would show him the headstone she meant to purchase for Eimear's grave. He'd see it all, and he would love her again.

"And I'll do it all, Eimear. I'll do it all even if takes my entire life long."

She needed a quick-paced tune, something to lift her heart. With the first measures of "Reel Du Goglu," her uncertainty gave way.

Here was home.

She played through "After the Sun Goes Down," "Paddy McFadden," and many other tunes she'd never learned the proper names of. Jigs ran into reels, which gave way to airs and waltzes. She played until every joint in her left hand ached and the tips of her fingers pained her. Far too much time had passed since she'd last spent more than a few short minutes playing. Her fingers weren't used to it any longer.

The music took her back across time, before Baltimore, before Belfast, even before Derry. In her mind Katie could perfectly see the hearth in her childhood home and her family gathered around. William, her oldest brother, had left before Katie had any memories of him. But she could picture Danny and Brennan sitting there during the short time before they'd followed their brother to Manchester and the promise of work and wages and food to eat. Their faces grew more vague with every passing year, but she remembered their being there. Her clearest memories were of only Mother and Father and Eimear sitting with her around the fire.

She stopped in the midst of "The Irishman's Choice," suddenly too overcome to play on. Emotions waged a war inside her. Loneliness, homesickness, and the joy of happier times mixed and melted together. Her throat thickened.

Try as she might, Katie could no longer picture her family together. She saw only her mother's tired face, her father's smile replaced with defeat. She saw Eimear, pale and thin. Then she heard from across the years the tune Father had always played at the end of each evening.

She took up her bow once more. She hesitated only a moment before allowing the plaintive strains of "Ar Éirinn" to step out of her past and fill the air around her. She felt herself very much as she'd been all those years ago when hearing her father play late into the night. 'Twas as if she again lay wrapped in a quilt tucked safely in bed, blissfully unaware of the pain that lie ahead of them all, free of the guilt she would carry the rest of her life.

As the last note died out over the river before her, Katie opened her eyes once more. The sun had long ago set, the fields cast in deep impenetrable shadows. She held her fiddle to her heart.

"I miss you, Father," she whispered. "Do you miss me, I wonder?"

She would see him again one day, she'd vowed to herself she would. She'd see him again and tell him how sorry she was for all the wrong she'd done, for the pain she'd caused him. And she would play "Ar Éirinn" just for him. Between the tune and the restitution she meant to make, he just might welcome her back.

She would be home again at last.

Chapter Nineteen

Katie and Biddy sat on the Archers' front porch Thursday afternoon taking turns at the butter churn and chatting about nothing in particular. Katie had developed something bordering on a talent for pointless gabbing, though she'd never done it before coming to Hope Springs. She found she enjoyed having someone to talk to.

"I've thought of something I can do when this job isn't available any longer," she said.

"Have you?"

There was something very comforting in knowing her new friend cared enough about her to be excited on her behalf.

"Well, as near as I've been able to tell, no one else in Hope Springs is looking to hire on household help."

Biddy shook her head. "No one else can afford it. The ranchers out at the edges of the valley might be able to, but I'd not go there if I were you," she added quickly. "They're single men, every last one of them, and not terribly well mannered or civilized."

Katie had heard all that herself. "I was thinking more along the lines of, well—" She found herself reluctant to confess her idea. What if Biddy laughed? What if she truly was a fool for even considering such a scheme? "I thought I'd start something of a business."

Such relief surged through her when Biddy didn't scoff. "What sort of business?"

Katie could breathe again. She had a supportive and listening ear in her new friend. "I haven't many talents," she said. "I can clean and I can bake, but that's it."

She wiped beads of sweat from her forehead. The day was hotter than any she'd yet experienced in Wyoming. A breeze blew, the only relief from the heavy summer air.

"So I thought I might try selling baked goods." The idea was young, and Katie wasn't fully sure of it yet.

Biddy's eyes grew wide. "A bakery? Wouldn't we be the fancy town?"

"I don't mean a full bakery like in Baltimore or Belfast or any of the big cities."

"Katie! Katie!"

She turned at Ivy's voice. For reasons she couldn't explain, the littlest Archer girl had become increasingly friendly over the past week. Despite her efforts to keep a distance, Katie couldn't seem to manage it.

"Watch me, Katie. I can run so fast!" Ivy's dress whipped hard against her legs as she ran with all she was worth the full length of the front of the house. Apparently finished with her demonstration, the little girl dropped dramatically to the ground, lying on her back with her arms and legs sprawled out.

Katie looked over the porch rail at Ivy. "I hardly even saw you pass by, so quick were you there and gone."

"I. Told. You." Her gasps for breath made the words choppy.

"Where did you learn to run like that?" Katie asked as she continued churning.

Ivy put a hand up to her eyes to block the sunlight. "Finbarr showed me. He says you have to watch where you're going and then run like the banshee is out to get you."

Katie smiled at that. Irish children would run for their lives at such a thought.

"What's 'the banshee'?" Ivy asked. She hadn't yet pulled herself up off the grass. "Finbarr made it sound scary."

"The banshee is an ill-meaning spirit," Katie warned. "'Tis said the banshee will lead the unsuspecting into dangerous paths until they're hopelessly lost forever and all time."

Emma arrived at the porch's edge in time to hear Katie's words. Ivy seemed quite excited at the idea of a horrid specter, while Emma didn't appear to like the possibility in the least.

"Then Finbarr wasn't merely teasing us?" Emma asked.

"He was teasing you, sure enough. But tales of banshees have been around since before St. Patrick himself. Finbarr hardly made it up."

Emma's mouth twisted in thought. "Why do boys do that? They say things they know will scare us just to tease."

"I have known Finbarr nearly all his life," Biddy said. "He teases the girls he's fond of. All the O'Connors do. My Ian, when we first met, called me Itty Biddy. 'Twas his way of teasing me."

"Truly?" Emma looked unmistakably hopeful. "You think Finbarr is fond of . . . us?"

"I most certainly do," Biddy answered.

Katie watched closely as Emma pondered that. Part of the little girl's puzzle fell into place in that moment.

"Poor thing's in the throes of first love," Biddy whispered.

"Aye. I didn't piece it together until this very moment."

A look of absolute empathy entered Biddy's eyes. "She's been sweet on Finbarr since she was Ivy's age."

"Does he realize as much?"

Biddy smiled and nodded with emphasis. "Poor little thing doesn't realize she's too young to catch his eye."

Ivy scrambled back to her feet. She waved enthusiastically to a wagon just making the turn at the fork in the road, this one destined for the Red side of things. Katie hadn't met many people from that side of town, none she'd care to meet again at the very least. Still, the young family in the wagon offered a friendly "good afternoon" and returned Ivy's wave without hesitation.

So Katie waved as well. They looked shocked and didn't return the gesture. Apparently waves between roads was as forbidden as sitting together at church.

"Tell me about this bakery you're opening up."

Katie shook her head. "Nothing so grand as that. Only bread, and perhaps cakes for special occasions."

Ivy ran alongside a pony cart as it turned toward the Irish Road. The little girl giggled, drawing a grin from the driver. Katie recognized him from the céilí, one Ryan Callaghan from Cork. Biddy waved, and he tipped his hat in return. The Red Road family hadn't even acknowledged Biddy sitting there.

"'Tis a complicated place you're living in, Biddy."

She laughed lightly. "Aye, but isn't every place?"

A great deal of wisdom lay in those words. "Troubles follow us wherever we go, it seems."

Biddy nodded again. "But you don't see a view like this one everywhere you go." She motioned out over the sprawling horizon just in front of them.

Katie had quickly come to appreciate the stark beauty of the area. "That you don't."

A wagon crossed over the bridge. Ivy darted out as she had with the previous passersby. She drew too near for Katie's peace of mind.

"Don't run out in the road, Ivy dear!" she called out. "You'll get yourself run down, you will!"

Ivy's shoulders dropped dramatically, as though Katie had single-handedly ruined her entire life.

"So you can really make a living selling bread?" Biddy asked.

There was the difficulty. Katie wasn't sure she could. "I can't rightly say. I don't know the proper way to figure those things. I hope so."

"What'll happen, Katie, if you can't?"

She paused in her churning and rolled her sore shoulders. "I've no other ideas. If this won't work, I'll have to consider going back to Baltimore."

"Pompah!" Little Ivy's voice carried across to them.

Mr. Archer came around the corner from the direction of the barn, apparently on his way to the porch. What had brought him there? Generally during the day she saw her employer only at lunch time.

He didn't come up the steps but stopped just on the other side of the porch railing. 'Twas to Biddy he spoke. "Finbarr has finished his work for the day. I'll take you both back in the wagon, if you're ready to go. It would save you the walk."

"I thank you, Joseph. My sister-in-law is watching my little ones so I could have a good gab with Katie, here. But I'd best go relieve her."

Mr. Archer nodded and turned to walk back the way he'd come. Biddy stopped him.

"Have you a moment, Joseph, to think on a problem?"

"Of course."

Of course? Was this the standoffish, grumpy Joseph Archer Katie had come to know?

"You may have heard that our Katie, here, has found herself with only half the pay she'd come to Wyoming expecting."

"Biddy," Katie said urgently under her breath. Her friend didn't so much as pause.

"She's needing to find work after her heartless employer tosses her out to make way for her replacement."

"Biddy."

"She's to be thrown into the hedgerow, you know. Had you heard anything like that, Joseph?"

Something very much like laughter shone in the back of Mr. Archer's eyes. Katie found she couldn't look away from the sight. 'Twas an unexpected change in him, one she liked very much indeed. He seemed a regular, approachable sort of man in that moment.

"I had heard that, actually," he said. "Katie still spends her afternoons here, so I'd guess she hasn't found secondary work."

"Alas, no." Biddy shook her head, her lips turned down in an expression of utmost sorrow. Her antics were enough to nearly bring a smile to Katie's face. If not for Joseph Archer's presence and her uncertainty about his opinions, Katie might even have laughed. "But she does have an idea," Biddy added.

He was looking at her now. "Do you really?"

"Just the beginnings of one," Katie replied. "I'm sure you've more important things to spend your time on, though."

He didn't take the excuse she handed him. "What is your idea?" He leaned against the railing.

"I thought of starting a business." The idea sounded ridiculous spoken out loud to someone who actually knew about such things. "It's likely a foolish idea."

"What kind of business?"

"Baking bread and such." She quickly added a bit of explanation. "Not a fancy bakery with its own building, just me and a stove."

"How much would you charge for your goods?"

Katie couldn't believe he was taking her idea seriously. "I never learned to do proper ciphering. I don't have the first idea how to figure prices."

"But I do." Mr. Archer smiled at her then. Truly, fully smiled.

Katie felt a rush of heat steal over her face, something she hadn't anticipated in the least. He stood too close to have missed the rising color in her cheeks. She couldn't account for it and had no idea what he would make of it.

"There now," Biddy said. "I knew Joseph could help. If anyone hereabout would know how to get a business off and running, Joseph would."

Katie hadn't entirely shaken off the impact of his smile. She did manage to give him what she hoped was a grateful look.

"Running a business takes a lot of investment, in time and money," he warned. "Do you have savings you could tap into to purchase supplies?"

She did, indeed. An old biscuit tin tucked under her bed held several rolls of pounds and dollars saved over eighteen years. She could not, however, spend it all. "I do have some."

He nodded. His expression had turned contemplative. That he hadn't dismissed her idea offhand was comforting and encouraging. But she missed his smile, brief as it had been.

"I had planned to go into town on Monday," Mr. Archer said. "I can check the cost of the goods you'll need. We can use that to determine your prices."

"Thank you for that, Mr. Archer."

Something of his earlier smile reappeared, though not quite as bright as it had been. Why didn't he smile more often, she wondered.

Mr. Archer turned toward the yard and called out to his daughters playing there. "Climb in the wagon, girls. We're taking Finbarr and Mrs. O'Connor home."

As the Archers made their way out of sight, Biddy paused beside Katie. She squeezed her hand. "I knew just as soon as I met you that we'd be friends, Katie. With this bakery, you'll not have to run off looking for work elsewhere."

"Don't get your hopes too high yet," Katie answered. "I can't say any of my plans have worked out too well over the years."

Biddy pulled her into an embrace. Katie froze. She'd not been hugged in years.

"I'll be optimistic for the both of us, Katie. As the saying goes, 'Hope springs eternal.'"

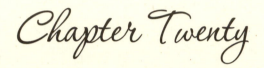

Chapter Twenty

Joseph sat at the kitchen table on Friday finishing his lunch. His thoughts were firmly on Katie. More often than they should have been, his eyes were on her, too. She sometimes wore a painfully heavy look on her face while she worked. He could see her thoughts were thousands of miles away and that those thoughts weighed on her. She'd worn much the same look the night before.

She'd excused herself just as soon as she cleared the table, insisting she had something important to see to. Joseph sat on the back porch and listened to the sound of violin music floating over the river. He knew Katie was the musician. Her talent was awe inspiring. He wanted to ask her where she'd learned, how long she'd played, why it meant so much to her that she would skip meals in order to play. He'd thought of her plan to sell bread and thought it a shame she couldn't make her living playing music. Her talent was absolutely wasted in a town like Hope Springs.

Katie Macauley was a puzzle. She had a fiercely independent nature yet at times seemed painfully unhappy in her self-imposed seclusion.

He set his plate and fork on the worktop beside the sink as he'd taken to doing after his midday meal. Though Katie didn't always talk to him while she washed the dishes, she did sometimes. He liked spending those moments in conversation with her. He looked forward to it all morning, if he were being honest.

"Did you ever have anything to eat last night, Katie?" It was, perhaps, not the most sophisticated beginning to a conversation.

"I'm afraid it slipped my mind," she said.

He didn't like the idea of her missing meals. Though he knew better than to say as much, she'd been too thin when she arrived, her face showing clear signs of having gone too long without regular, filling meals. That hint of gauntness hadn't left her yet.

"Katie."

"No need scolding me. I have had two meals already today."

He'd learned within the first few days that she took offense easily. Joseph wasn't sure if that came from past hurts or simple mulishness. His curiosity about that had only grown.

"Is there a reason you are so opposed to the idea of eating with us?" he asked. If she would only sit down to meals with them, as their last housekeeper always had, he would know she was getting the nourishment she needed. "I assure you the girls are well behaved at the table, and I generally refrain from scraping my teeth with the tines of my fork."

"Servants do not take their meals with the family they serve." She spoke with utmost finality.

"Our last housekeeper took every meal with us." He had fully expected his new housekeeper to do the same.

"I've heard the girls talk of your last housekeeper." Katie gave him a look of exasperation. "They rather thought of her as a grandmother, I'd say. She was family to them. I am a stranger who arrived at the doorstep not two weeks ago. The situations are hardly the same."

Joseph had never been one to be so easily distracted, though, especially from such an enormous mystery as she was. He'd more than once spied a deep-seated pain in her eyes. Yet her determination and fire spoke of an inner strength he couldn't help admiring.

"You are accustomed to large households, where the servants far outnumber those they work for and the two worlds never intersect and seldom collide." Joseph himself had grown up in just such a household. "Life isn't like that in Wyoming. Towns and houses are too small to be divided up that way."

"You're telling me Hope Springs hasn't divided itself along very real lines, are you?" The disbelief in her tone couldn't have been more apparent.

He leaned against the worktop, warming to his topic. Here was the reason he enjoyed her company. Her conversation was intelligent. She had the confidence to state her opinions even if those positions differed from his own. It was a far sight better than trying to keep up a conversation with a quiet sixteen-year-old.

"In a place as large as Baltimore or Boston or New York," he said, "the Irish and those who fervently dislike them can be entirely at odds, and yet the city doesn't come to a halt over it. For the most part the two sides keep to themselves and don't interact any more than necessary. That cannot happen here. We are too near and too few to avoid being part of each other's lives."

"You'll forgive me, sir, but being part of anyone's life is not on the short list of things I mean to accomplish." She washed the plate from his noon meal, her movements quick and expert. "I told you I didn't come here to make friends."

"You seem to be Biddy O'Connor's friend."

The tiniest hint of a smile briefly touched her lips. What a difference it made in her countenance. She looked younger, lighter, happier. He very much liked seeing the change.

"Biddy didn't give me a choice," she said. "She is my friend, no matter how I might feel about it."

That most certainly sounded like an O'Connor. They had to be the most determined people Joseph had ever met. Fortunately for the Red Road, the O'Connors hadn't taken up the feud in earnest. If they ever decided to jump into the fray, there would be no stopping them.

"You asked me a few days ago what brought me west," he said, still standing nearby as she washed dishes. "I've been meaning to ask you the same thing."

"I came here for a job."

She crossed a continent for something that was plentiful back East? "Were there not enough jobs in Baltimore?"

"For someone of my age and nationality, there were none that paid near as much as this one was supposed to." She set herself to drying the dishes, going so far as to all but turn her back on him.

He felt a twinge of guilt at that. She had lost half her expected salary. He couldn't say what else he might have done, though.

"To leave behind the life you had there and the people you knew, to pull up your roots. That is drastic in the extreme."

"I had no roots in Baltimore." She spoke very matter-of-factly, but the declaration was an odd one.

"Your telegram said you had been working there for two years." Surely she'd put down some roots in two years.

"'Twas just a place I worked." Katie dried her hands on the dish towel and walked away.

His curiosity propelled him forward. "If this job hadn't come to your attention, you'd be working there still. Surely you meant to eventually make it your home."

"Baltimore would never have been my home any more than Belfast or Derry was." Her voice rose with each word, her tone growing more crisp. "There's only one place that will ever be home to me, and it was certainly not Baltimore."

She didn't even look at him. He could see her take each deep, difficult breath. His wish for an invigorating conversation had taken them down paths difficult for her to travel.

"Where is home, Katie?" he asked gently, knowing that was what pricked at her.

The briefest of moments passed in silence. She stood perfectly still as though too pained to even breathe.

"Home is a tiny place few people have ever heard of." Her own voice lost a bit of its edge. He even heard emotion there, something he'd found she tried very hard to hide. "I haven't been there since I was eight years old."

"Surely in that time you've earned enough to pay for a return journey." She had left Ireland only two years earlier. In the more than a decade between leaving her little town and leaving her homeland altogether, she could easily have amassed what she needed to go back. Ireland was not that large.

She pushed a strand of loose hair out of her eyes. Sadness filled her bearing. "I have some debts to pay before I'd be welcomed back."

"Debts? But you were only eight years old. How can an eight-year-old become so indebted she can't earn the price in nearly twenty years?"

He couldn't comprehend such a thing.

"The Famine was a desperate time, Joseph," she said quietly. "People did things they weren't proud of in order to survive."

He could easily picture her as a tiny, overly thin child trying to stay alive during the horrors that had gripped Ireland. But what could a child have possibly done to render her unwelcome in her own home?

"You don't think your family and neighbors would welcome you back after two decades? Whatever you did, they must realize you were only a child." And they likely missed her as much as she obviously missed them.

Katie shook her head. "Some things cannot be forgiven. All I can do is put right what I am able to and hope it is enough."

"I have my doubts they meant for you to go in the first place."

Suddenly her eyes were snapping again. What had he said to so quickly earn her wrath? "My father gave me away, Joseph Archer. He handed me over to strangers and never once looked back. He most certainly 'meant for me to go.'"

He'd done it again—insulted her without meaning to. He reached out, not sure what he might do other than apologize and offer her some sort of reassuring pat on the arm or squeeze of the hand. She stepped back out of his reach.

"Don't think you understand my life when you know nothing of me," she flung at him. "Yes, I crossed a continent for money. I left my country on the promise of money. You may call that greedy or self-serving or any number of things, but money is the only way I will ever be allowed back home, and I mean to see to it that happens, whether or not it meets with your approval."

His approval? Did she really think he'd undertaken this conversation from such a position of superiority?

A quick rap sounded on the kitchen door. Neither of them moved to answer it. They stood just as they were, watching each other.

A second knock broke the silence, this time from the front of the house.

Joseph pushed out a small, tense breath. "I'll answer the door."

"No," she immediately cut in. "A proper servant answers the front door for her employer."

"You know I don't care about all that."

"But *I* do." Frustration emanated from every inch of her. "I don't have many skills, Joseph Archer, but I know how to be a good servant. So long as I am working here, I would ask that you allow me to see to my duties properly."

She didn't wait for his response but marched herself directly toward the dining room door, no doubt headed for the front of the house.

Did she have any idea how much he hated feeling like they were enemies? Too many conversations ended in an argument. Too many interactions felt like a tug of war. He'd come to enjoy her company right up until those moments when things inevitably fell apart between them.

He pulled open the back door. Seeing Tavish O'Connor standing there didn't improve his mood.

"Hello, Tavish."

"Good afternoon. Is Katie about?"

He'd come to call on Katie. Thinking about it, that was the only thing that made sense. Tavish would have gone to the barn if he'd come looking for him or Finbarr.

"Katie went to answer the front door," Joseph said, stepping aside so Tavish could come in.

"I can tell you who she'll find there. Bob Archibald was pulling up just as I was."

Joseph muttered a few choice expletives under his breath.

"My thoughts exactly," Tavish answered. "Archibald's not one for making neighborly calls out of nothing but friendliness."

"Honestly, I'm surprised he's taken this long to make a formal complaint," Joseph said.

"You think he's come about Katie, then?" Tavish asked.

"I *know* he's come about Katie."

That sobered Tavish considerably, something Joseph understood well. Katie had come into the town's mess unknowingly, ignorantly, yet she would bear much of the brunt of it all.

"Shall we go save the fair damsel from the bloodthirsty dragon?" Joseph asked.

Tavish looked momentarily surprised. "We're to be allies, then?"

"For the moment, at least." Joseph could even smile a bit at the thought. He and Tavish had never been enemies in the true sense of the word, but neither had they been friends. "We have a fair maiden to rescue."

Tavish walked with him from the kitchen. "You realize, of course, Katie has likely slaughtered the dragon on her own by now."

"That would not surprise me in the least."

They reached the front entryway in time to hear Katie tell Bob Archibald, standing yet outside the door, that if he meant to be a stubborn mule, he could very well stay out on the porch, but she'd not waste another minute holding the door for him.

Joseph stepped up beside her, acknowledging his visitor with a nod of his head. "Good afternoon, Bob. What can I do for you?"

Bob's expression could not have been less friendly as his eyes roved over Katie. Joseph felt a very real urge to slip her behind him and stand as something of a shield. But, though Bob was vocal in his dislike of the Irish, Joseph had never known him to actually harm a woman.

"I see you still have this Paddy here," Bob said, dislike heavy in every syllable.

Joseph looked him in the eye. "There's no one here named Paddy."

"You know perfectly well I mean this Irish girl." He motioned at Katie with his stubbly chin, hatred dripping from his words.

Joseph glanced back quickly at Tavish. He hadn't needed the reminder, apparently. Tavish pulled Katie away from the door and to his side. Joseph turned his attention back to Bob.

"A few of our families saw her and another of her kind sitting on your porch yesterday," Bob said. "They were acting as though they were the queens of the place."

Joseph had seen Katie and Biddy on the porch himself. There had been nothing high and mighty about their behavior. "You know a lot of queens who churn their own butter, do you?"

Bob's mouth pulled in a tight line, anger snapping in his eyes. "You can make light of it all you want, Joseph, but we see what's going on here. You have two Irish working for you, and your house is crawling with their kind. For years you've sworn that you will not take sides, but we have reason to doubt that lately. We won't stand for it, Joseph."

Joseph stepped onto the doorway and looked down at his neighbor. "Are you threatening me?" He pushed the words out through his tight lips.

"I am warning you. We'll do what we must to keep the Irish in their place."

"Then let me issue a warning of my own. I have told both sides of this petty conflict to leave me out of it. Should either group"—he threw a look back at Tavish before turning his glare on Bob once more—"bring their war to my doorstep, there will be consequences. And I think this town knows full well that I am capable of following through with that promise."

He saw Bob blanch the slightest bit and knew his threat hit home.

"Now I suggest you go back home and tend to your crops and your family and quit worrying about my employees. Is that clear?"

Bob gave a short, quick nod. His obstinacy had not fled entirely, though. "I would suggest you tell that girl of yours to warn her people not to get too above themselves. We know how to bring them back down."

He slammed his battered hat on his head and stormed off the porch and down the path.

Joseph forced himself to close the door calmly. He hated having to make threats against the people he considered his neighbors. The fact that he technically owned the land they all farmed was his only bargaining chip. Only the reminder of his position convinced them to leave him out of the mess they'd made of their lives.

He yet stood facing the door with his back to Katie and Tavish. "I don't know what you had planned for this afternoon, but you might consider talking with the Irish Road instead."

"You think Mr. Archibald was serious in his threat?" Katie asked.

He turned back to look at them. Katie was obviously surprised. Tavish wasn't in the least.

"He was serious," Joseph answered. "The only real question is how far the Red Road will take that threat."

Worry creased Katie's brow. As much as Joseph disliked seeing her upset, he felt she needed to know the truth of the situation. Tempers might very well calm and nothing serious would come of it. But history had shown the embers might just as easily be fanned into a fire.

"Do you mind, Katie, if we postpone our drive?" Tavish spoke with a somberness born of too much experience with such things. Joseph knew he had taken Bob's warning to heart. "I think it'd be best if we go talk to my Da."

She gave a slow nod. "I'll fetch my bonnet."

Tavish and Joseph remained after she slipped into the back, both of them still looking in the direction she'd gone.

"Ian and I said she'd start a war in Hope Springs," Tavish said. "I honestly thought we were exaggerating."

Joseph sincerely hoped things didn't reach that point. "If your father can talk with the Irish Road before Seamus Kelly stirs them all up, we might avoid the kind of violence we've seen in the past."

"I don't know." Tavish shook his head. "I don't think the Red Road is as upset about having another Irishwoman in town so much as having one *here*. She's crossed the boundary of where we're generally allowed to be. So long as she is living and working here, I don't believe the Red Road will simply let that pass without responding."

Joseph paced away from the door. "I can't just throw her out. She doesn't have any family. She doesn't have anywhere to go. I can't imagine any of the Irish families are hiring housekeepers."

Tavish followed him into the parlor. "None of the Irish could afford to."

He stopped at the tall parlor windows, looking out but not really seeing. "She is thinking of selling bread to make a little money. I haven't told her this yet but, seeing as she could only really sell to the Irish half of the town, I don't think she would ever make enough to live on."

"You think the Red Road will manage to run her out of town, then?"

He looked back at Tavish, recognizing the mixture of anger and worry on his face. Joseph felt the same thing himself.

"Like you said, the Red Road will not be appeased so long as she is living anywhere but the Irish Road. I am sure plenty of families would be willing to take her in, but I know their financial situations better than anyone. None of them can afford another mouth to feed."

Tavish shook his head. "Katie wouldn't take charity anyway."

She certainly wouldn't. Further, Joseph knew she'd only come to Hope Springs to earn money. If she left his employ, there would be no extra funds to add to her savings. She would leave for certain. He'd known her not quite two weeks and yet already found the idea of her leaving unsettling. But if she stayed in his home, the town would be thrown into battle again.

"I'll see if my Da can't keep the Irish tempers from flaring. Maybe that'll buy us a bit of time."

Joseph nodded. He held out a hand to Tavish, who took it and shook.

"You and I haven't always been friends," Joseph said, "but I think we can count each other as allies in this."

Tavish nodded. "I'll go see if Katie's ready to be off. And Ian'll likely come by and let you know what's been decided."

Joseph stood alone in the parlor a moment, weighed down and tired to his core. He'd come to Wyoming for peace and calm but had somehow landed himself in a firing range. Staying out of the conflict grew harder each time tensions flared up in the town.

This time was worse. He worried what the Red Road might do to Finbarr out of spite. He worried even more what they would do to Katie. She was seen by both sides as something of a symbol of their conflict.

"Joseph?"

His heart clenched at the sound of his name on Katie's lips. She'd never called him simply "Joseph" before. It echoed around in his mind, settling as warmth in his chest. He hoped his reaction didn't show on his face when he looked over at her.

She crossed to where he stood, looking up at him. Her threadbare bonnet framed her apologetic face. It was little wonder, really, that he felt drawn to her. She was fire and sweetness, determination and beauty all in one.

"I am sorry I've brought you trouble so quickly. You did warn me how it would be, and I didn't listen, not really."

Joseph shook his head. "This isn't your fault. The town has been this way for a decade."

Her brow creased in concern. "Once my bakery is up and running and you're not employing me any longer, the Red Road will leave you out of this, won't they?"

He didn't have the heart to tell her things couldn't possibly work out as easily as she hoped. Too often he'd seen pain and worry in her eyes. For just a moment he wanted to see hope win out. "They're only worried that I'm taking sides. Once your situation has been settled, I'm certain they'll calm down."

"I'm beginning to realize what a chance you took allowing me to stay. I don't want you to regret it."

Joseph reached out and brushed his hand along her cheek. It was an impulsive gesture and an inadvisable one. But he couldn't help himself. "I don't regret it, Katie. Not at all."

Color stained her cheeks. She didn't step back or pull away. He thought she even leaned the tiniest bit into his touch. The urge to pull her to him and kiss her smiling lips grabbed him without warning. For a moment he couldn't think of anything else.

Sanity won out in the end, but only just. He let his hand drop back to his side and managed something of a casual smile.

"Tavish is probably waiting for you."

She nodded mutely.

"You probably shouldn't keep him waiting."

After another nod, she turned and left the parlor. Tavish would have the pleasure of her company for the afternoon. A great deal of that would likely be spent discussing the tensions in Hope Springs and formulating plans. But even in the midst of that difficult topic, Tavish would get to spend time with her, talk with her, enjoy her smile.

Joseph recognized his gnawing of jealousy for what it was. He wanted to be the one sitting at her side, the one she saw making plans to help her. Tavish would be the hero, and he would be her indifferent employer, the one unwilling to jump into the fight. She would have no idea that his neutral position and the ability it gave him to negotiate with both sides was all that had saved the town from destroying itself many times over.

He flexed the fingers of his right hand, remembering all too well the feel of her soft face as he'd touched her. It wouldn't do. He was her employer. She worked and lived under his roof without a single relative about to look after her. She was a young, unwed woman living in the same house as a young, widowed man. There was a certain inherent vulnerability in her position.

"You are her employer," he firmly reminded himself under his breath. "So long as that is true, you have to keep your distance."

He would do all he could silently and out of view to keep the peace for her sake as much as his family's, but no hint of his affection for her would ever show in his face or deeds.

There were some lines that simply could not be crossed.

Chapter Twenty-One

Katie sat in the elder O'Connors' home listening in on the hastily called family meeting. All the O'Connor children, except Finbarr, and their spouses sat discussing Bob Archibald's earlier threats and just what ought to be done about it.

She slumped down in her chair feeling all sorts of a fool. Ian and Tavish had warned her that she'd cause problems in town. Joseph had warned her. Even Biddy had hinted at it. She hadn't believed any of them, not really.

Joseph hadn't given her the scolding nor the "I told you so" she thoroughly deserved. He'd been kind and understanding. His touch had been so gentle and tender. And entirely unexpected. Heat spread through her at the memory.

Biddy took a seat beside her and squeezed her hand. "Chin up, Katie. 'Tisn't nearly as bad as it likely seems."

"Mr. Archibald said the Red Road would 'do what they must.' And he said it in such a way—" Katie felt unsettled all over again at the thought. "He was so angry."

"This is nothing we haven't dealt with before." Biddy didn't look overly shaken. Katie took some comfort in that.

"You think your family can calm things down, then?"

"Certainly."

But the expressions on every other face weren't nearly as comforting. Katie had only ever seen Mr. O'Connor smiling. At that moment, though, his mouth was pulled in a tight line, his eyes narrowed beneath his creased brow. Katie heard none of the lighthearted banter they'd shared at the céilí.

"We'll need to get around and talk to the others before Seamus Kelly spreads his own ideas on how to handle it." Thomas Dempsey, husband of the O'Connors' oldest daughter, spoke with such wariness Katie knew Seamus Kelly must have caused difficulties before.

"I'd say watchful waiting is best," Mr. O'Connor said. "And showing the Reds that our Miss Katie is looking to leave Joseph Archer's employ."

That caught Katie's attention. "I what?"

"You told Biddy that your situation at Joseph's is temporary. Is that still true?"

"Aye." Katie nodded. She'd accepted that she'd be leaving, but the idea felt almost wrong all of a sudden. "Though I won't be leaving for another two months or more. He'll not have a new housekeeper for at least that long. And I've no other means of supporting myself."

Looks of hesitant relief passed over all their faces.

"We just need word to spread down the Red Road that your position at Joseph's is not permanent." Mrs. O'Connor nodded again and again as she spoke. "But it's equally important that the Irish know you're not turning tail and running."

"But if I were to go entirely, wouldn't that calm everything? The Red Road couldn't complain then." She didn't like the idea of leaving immediately but couldn't help wondering if, at least in the long run, it might be the right answer.

Clearly no one else thought so. Katie looked from one of them to the next, wondering what about her suggestion had them worried. She was, after all, really only passing through on her long road home.

Biddy answered for them all. "The Red Road has managed to run a few of the Irish out of town. If they manage to force you out—you who have stood up to them already and found employment with a man they're desperate to call their ally—they'd see that as a sign they could push out the rest of us. They'd only be encouraged to try that much harder."

Katie let that thought roll around in her mind a moment. "So if I stay where I am, the Red Road will declare war. But if I leave town, they'll come after you still?"

"Aye," Mr. O'Connor nodded. "That about sums it up."

What would happen when she eventually left? She had no intention of staying forever.

The discussions continued. Biddy leaned in and whispered. "'Tis a shame to spend your afternoon like this. I know for a fact Tavish, there, planned to take you on a picnic."

A picnic. The idea fluttered about within her. "I've never been on a picnic."

"Haven't you?"

Katie shook her head.

"Well, it would have been a treat, let me tell you. He even had his mother pack up your meal so it'd be edible. Tavish hardly cooks, you know. Takes a lot of his meals with his parents or siblings. We take pity on the man, seeing as he can't make anything apart from eggs and frying up a bit of meat."

Katie looked over at Tavish. He sat deep in discussion with his family. He'd meant to treat her to a picnic. Though he teased and flirted a great deal, she couldn't say he wasn't thoughtful. "This picnic seems to have been a great deal of trouble to go to."

"Aye, but worth it to him, I'm certain."

Katie nearly laughed at the conspiratorial look on Biddy's face. "You're playing matchmaker, are you?"

Biddy shrugged, quite obviously holding back a grin. "Only saying what I'm seeing."

"You think he fancies me?" She filled her voice with all the doubt she felt.

"I think he's beginning to."

Katie looked over at him in the exact moment he looked up at her. Tavish gave her one of his smiles that never failed to make her heart pound a bit.

"Now what say you to that?" Biddy whispered.

Katie lowered her eyes and shook her head. "I say men are too confusing for any woman's good."

Biddy only laughed. "Put on your best smile, Katie dear. One of those 'confusing men' is headed directly for you."

Sure enough, Tavish reached her side in the next moment. He spoke to Biddy first.

"You and Mother have been assigned to go speak to a few of the ladies up the street."

Biddy seemed to have been expecting that. "We're to go begging for patience, then?"

Tavish nodded. Biddy moved to her mother-in-law's side.

"What've you been assigned to do?" Katie asked.

"I have been given the very trying task of spending the afternoon with a certain mischief maker newly arrived from Baltimore."

Mischief maker. "That would be me, then?" She tried to sound unbothered by how they all thought of her.

Tavish gave her an apologetic look. "A poor choice of words, I'm afraid." He held a hand out to her. "Will you give me a chance to redeem myself, Sweet Katie?"

"I told you not to call me that." She objected more out of embarrassment than true indignation.

He sat down next to her in the seat Biddy had vacated. "Does the name really bother you?"

"It doesn't make a lick of sense is all." She dropped her gaze to her clasped hands, hating that she was about to admit a failing in herself. "You can't honestly say I've been 'sweet' to you." *Or to anyone else.*

"I've a feeling, Katie, that underneath it all, you really are sweet."

She vaguely remembered her mother calling her "sweetie" when she was a little girl. She even thought the endearment might have suited her once. But she'd not been that way in a very long time. Not since The Famine. A sweet little girl wouldn't have refused to save her family's home. A sweet little girl wouldn't have cost her sister her life. She might once have been tender and loving, but life had made her hard.

In that moment, she hated that about herself.

"Katie?"

She took a deep breath. Until she had composed herself again, she wouldn't look up at him.

"Saints, I didn't mean to make you cry."

She shook her head. "I don't cry." Emotion burned at the back of her eyes, even shook a bit in her voice, but there were no tears.

Tavish slipped his hand around hers. Katie held fast to him, finding an odd, unsettling kind of comfort in his touch.

"I've not made a very good start of it, but I hope you'll still spend the afternoon with me."

The house sat quiet and empty except for the two of them. The entire O'Connor clan had gone out to talk with their neighbors. Katie sat there, her hand in Tavish's, taking in the peace of that moment.

Perhaps in his company she might find some respite from the worries always at the back of her mind. For that one afternoon she could pretend to be carefree.

She looked up at him and offered a smile that felt a touch uncertain. "I've never been on a picnic."

He sighed a bit dramatically. "Biddy told my secret, I see. What a bunch of gossips I'm related to."

"She also told me you didn't cook a single bit of the picnic fare, a promising thing, seems to me."

Tavish chuckled quietly. He stood and pulled her up with him. "Never mind my cooking skills. I've picked out the second finest view in all of Hope Springs."

"*Second* finest?" She followed along willingly. That he still held her hand went a long way to soothing her tumultuous feelings. Her heart skipped about, to be sure, but his company mostly proved calming, reassuring. She'd never have guessed as much having seen what a shameless tease and flirt he was.

"Aye, the *second* finest view in town. I have to save something to build up to."

"You mean to spend another afternoon with me?" She liked the idea very much indeed.

He tipped her a crooked smile and wiggled his eyebrows, a sight that made her smile in spite of her general tendency not to.

"There's that smile I've been waiting for," he said.

Two men had touched her in a matter of a couple hours. Yet, how different her reaction to the two. Joseph's touch was confusing, upending. With Tavish, she simply found her smile growing along with her sense of contentment.

So which was preferable and which was best avoided?

They walked down the road, back toward his house, but didn't turn in there. He led her up to a humble house situated not quite directly across from his. He waved as they passed. From the front window, a silhouette waved back.

"Whose house is this?" Katie couldn't make out the person inside.

"My Granny Claire's," he answered. "When I asked if I could shamelessly use the view from the back of her land to impress a certain hard-to-impress lass, she agreed rather eagerly."

Katie had met Mrs. Claire, a woman who couldn't have had fewer than eighty years to her credit. She hadn't realized until that moment that Mrs. Claire was Tavish's grandmother.

He walked with her past the house and out among the fields. He held her hand in one of his, their picnic basket in his other hand. "How am I doing so far, Sweet Katie?"

"How are you doing at what?"

He looked across at her, the twinkle in his eyes as evident as ever. "In general."

"'Tis hard to say, Tavish. You *are* sort of gazing into my eyes. If you start whispering, you'll be breaking every promise you made to me about this outing of yours." Light replies and hints of laughter came easier with him than they ever had before. 'Twas like the weight of life lifted for just a moment.

His gaze grew more intense. "If you didn't have such beautiful brown eyes, Katie, I might be able to look away more easily."

Heat crept over her cheeks. "They are quite an ordinary shade of brown, as you well know."

But he shook his head. "They are nothing of the sort."

"Flattery, Tavish?" She leveled him a look of reprimand.

"I swore off longing glances and whispered words, Sweet Katie. I said nothing about compliments."

They stopped near the banks of the same river that ran past the Archer farm and the town itself. The buildings of Hope Springs were distant enough to be small but near enough to add color to the view. Hills stretched out beyond the town. Above, the sky was an uninterrupted swath of clearest blue.

"This is only the second finest view?"

Tavish laid out a woolen blanket on the rough ground at the water's edge. "Aye. Someday I'll show you the finest."

"'Someday'?" She sat on the blanket, though not directly beside him. She wasn't yet that comfortable with him. "Seems I should tell you now, I'm only passing through this town. Add up enough tomorrows, and you'll have run right past someday."

He gave her a quizzical look. "You're not really considering leaving, are you?"

She was more than considering it. Leaving was an unavoidable even-tuality. "I've always intended to go back home, to find my family. I only came here to earn what I need to go back."

"To Ireland?"

How could an Irishman sound so shocked at that? "My family is there."

He looked almost troubled. "I don't think you realize it, Katie, but you've become a rallying point for the Irish here. You're like a promise of possibilities." His usually jovial expression had disappeared behind a look of earnestness. "You're the first of any of us to live off the Irish Road. You've crossed a boundary no one else has managed. And you stood up to Reverend Ford like a regular warrior."

Katie had never blushed so much in her life as she did when Tavish took to complimenting her. "That was a fit of temper, not an act of heroism."

Tavish leaned closer until she had no choice but to look directly into his intense blue gaze. "I'm not going to say the Irish have been saints in all this, but we've taken more than our share of beatings. Then you arrived, strong and determined and refusing to be cowed by any of it. Word is you're even looking to start your own business, to make your own way."

"But that's not—"

"Katie." He took her other hand. "Sweet Katie. You have no idea what you've given your countrymen here in this tiny corner of the world."

"What have I given them?"

"Hope."

Chapter Twenty-Two

Katie's thoughts roamed all over creation that night as she sat in the corner of the Archers' parlor seeing to the family's mending. She smiled at thoughts of the pleasant afternoon she'd spent with Tavish. Thoughts of the Red Road's threats hung about as well. Perhaps louder than that, even, was Tavish's insistence that she had become a point of pride for the Irish there, a reason to look on their own future with optimism. Katie didn't want to be anyone's banner.

Watching the Archer girls pass an evening with their father only refreshed in her mind how desperate her need for home truly was. The girls sat on either side of him on the sofa. Ivy listened to her father reading aloud. 'Twas a child's fairy tale, from what Katie gathered. Her own father had told her many such tales of banshees and fey ones and leprechauns. She cherished the memory of those moments.

Emma sat reading a book of her own. Nine years old and she could read. At nine, Katie had been scrubbing floors and pots and dreaming of going back to a home that no longer existed.

As if sensing Katie's gaze, Emma looked up at her. Had someone told her the day she arrived that seeing distrust in the face of either of the Archer girls would prick at her heart, Katie would never have believed it.

Yet, she didn't like the fact that she worried the girl as much as the girl worried her.

"Are you enjoying your book?" she asked from her chair just off to the side of the family.

Emma nodded.

"What's the story about?"

"A boy in Holland," Emma said, voice as quiet as ever. "He and his sister want new skates, but their family is too poor."

"Does he get a job, then?" That was always her father's solution. When money grew tight, another of her brothers left to find work.

Emma held the book open against her. "They both already have jobs, but there still isn't money for skates."

Katie knew that situation well. Every cent she earned, she saved. There'd never been fancy things like skates, not even a ribbon for her hair that wasn't second-hand.

"Have you read the book?" Emma asked. "Do you know if Hans gets his skates?"

Katie had never read a book in all her life. "I haven't. But he seems like a fine lad. I'd like to think everything will turn out well in the end."

Emma's expression turned earnest. "He works hard, and he's nice." Her brow creased even as her arms tightened around the book. "Like Finbarr, except Hans lives in Holland and Finbarr lives here."

Bless the child's heart, she certainly fancied Finbarr O'Connor. "You'll have to tell me how the story ends."

Emma nodded and took up her book once more. What must that be like, to take any book or paper in her hand and be able to read it, to know just what it said?

Katie let her mending sit unattended in her lap. "Where did you learn to read, Emma?"

"My papa taught me."

A fortunate girl she was. Katie looked over at Ivy, leaning so carefree against her father as he read to her. Two happy, healthy girls, free of the hunger and pain and fear she'd seen all around her as a child.

Joseph closed the thin book he'd read to little Ivy. He pulled her closer, resting his cheek against the top of her head.

She'd once sat cuddled against her father on quiet evenings such as that. Love and pride shown in his eyes while he'd taught her to play the fiddle. She'd once had a measure of the happiness she saw in the Archer family. Saints, but she wanted that back.

"Papa? Is Holland near Ireland?"

Joseph answered Emma without pulling away from Ivy in the least. "Holland is much closer to Ireland than we are. Both countries are in Europe."

That brought Emma's attention back to Katie. "Have you ever been to Holland?"

Katie set aside her mending entirely. "I have only ever been to Ireland and the United States."

"Papa has been to Ireland," Emma said.

Katie hadn't heard that before. "Truly?"

Though he yet held little Ivy in his arms, Joseph's attention was on Katie. "My company does business in Belfast."

Belfast? "When were you in Belfast?"

He gently stroked Ivy's hair as she leaned against him, her eyes closed. "My family went several times when I was young. I was last there twelve years ago."

Katie quickly counted backward. "*I* was in Belfast twelve years ago. We might've crossed paths."

He smiled at her a bit. She did like his smile. It softened his entire face and sent a shivery warmth straight through her.

"I think I would have remembered you," he said.

What a great deal of smoke that was. "A plain servant in plain clothing?"

"*Plain?* I don't believe that."

"Bless your lying tongue, Joseph Archer." She picked up her mending again. "But fourteen was something of an awkward age for me."

The remnant of his smile tipped. "I was twenty-one, which was an awkward age for me."

"Now there is something I don't believe." She could easily see him as a young man, his light brown hair combed to utter perfection, those deep, piercing eyes of his not missing a detail, little or great.

He shifted, lifting Ivy into his arms. "I ought to take this little one up to her bed. Emma, you too."

Emma rose but didn't immediately follow them out of the room. She stood just in front of Katie. "I'll tell you how the story ends."

"I would like that, Miss Emma."

Emma watched her unwaveringly. She held her book to herself in one arm, the other arm hanging at her side. Katie had the very real urge to reach out and touch the girl. For once, she followed the inclination. She slipped her fingers around Emma's small hand.

"You aren't the way I thought you would be," Emma said.

"I'm not?"

Emma shook her head. "I thought you would be old."

Katie smiled at that. "I thought your father would be old too."

"And . . ." Emma hesitated. Katie lightly squeezed her little fingers, hoping to encourage her. "And I thought you would be cross, but I think now you might be nice." Emma gave her the tiniest of smiles.

Katie returned the gesture. Emma was a sweet, sweet girl indeed. "You'd best head up to your room, Miss Emma. Your father'll be waiting for you."

Emma nodded and moved swiftly from the room, not looking back to where Katie watched her go. The girl kept quiet, pulled into herself, her very feelings hidden from the world. When she did venture to reach out, 'twas only with heavy hesitation and such a great deal of worry that she'd be hurt by it. Was poor Emma as lonely as Katie so often was?

She rose from the chair and walked to the fireplace. Katie had dusted the many frames and trinkets set on the mantle every day since her arrival. Some were photographs of the family and the late, beautiful Mrs. Archer. Other frames held sketches of Baltimore and of the landscape around Hope Springs. The collection told quite a story of the Archer family.

What would we have put on our mantle if we'd had one, Eimear?

Perhaps Father's pipe might have sat there. If the mantle shelf were deep enough, they might have put his fiddle there, as well. Those two things always brought her father to mind: music and the smell of pipe tobacco.

Katie closed her eyes, thinking back. Her brothers didn't leave behind anything when they went one by one to Manchester looking for work. There'd been nothing of them in the home but memories and longing.

Mother had a small glass bowl, given to her by her own mother. They'd never used it. Mother always feared something would happen to it, so she'd kept it put safely away. Katie remembered sitting on the dirt floor near the cupboards, looking at the beautiful glass bowl and imagining how fancy they'd all be to actually use it. She'd imagined her grandmother and what she must have been like. Katie loved that bowl. She would have put that bowl up on the mantle beside Father's fiddle.

She would put Eimear's doll on her mantle too, if she had one. The ragged plaything had never left Eimear's hands, not even at the very end. Her sister died with it in her arms and was buried with it there still.

Someday, Eimear, when I'm back home again, I'll find something of yours, something that makes me think of you, and I'll put it out, just like this—she lightly fingered the trinkets on the Archers' mantle—*so everyone who comes around knows who you were.*

Joseph came down the stairs in the very next minute. "The girls are in bed."

Katie struggled to pull her mind to the present. Though she looked at the Archers' treasures on their mantle, 'twas Father's pipe and Mother's bowl and Eimear's doll that filled her thoughts.

"Are you unwell, Katie?"

"Forgive me." Her voice sounded steadier than she'd expected. "I fear I'm a bit distracted this evening."

Katie turned away from the mantle and offered a quick nod, hoping the gesture looked businesslike. Joseph watched her, his eyes seeming to take in every inch of her face.

"I know that look, Katie, and it is not one of distraction." He took a single step closer to her, his expression changing from pondering to one of concern. "I saw that very look in the mirror for a long time after my wife died." He spoke gently, softly. "Who are you missing?"

The question pierced her. Each beat of her heart pulsated pain in her chest. *Who are you missing?* She'd lost every person she cared about in one way or another those first eight years of her life. No one had truly mattered to her since.

Who was she missing? The only truthful answer was "everyone."

She settled for a half-truth. "I simply get lonely sometimes."

"You said this morning you haven't been home in eighteen years. When did you last see your family?"

"Eighteen years ago."

The answer clearly surprised him. "What? Not any of them?"

She shook her head. Her heart dropped clear to her toes as the enormity of her loneliness struck her anew.

The empathy in his expression could not be mistaken. Joseph Archer had known loss and heartache.

"I am sorry for chastising you about this earlier today," he said. "You were right—I didn't understand at all."

No one understood, really. She hadn't a soul to share her struggles with. Even those who'd lost loved ones wouldn't understand the added pain of having been responsible for that loss. Just thinking about it brought her spirits low.

She jumped at the first change of subject that came to mind. "I wondered if I might ask you something about the bread I mean to sell."

A bit of wariness entered his expression but not enough to be truly worrisome.

He guided her to the chair she'd sat in earlier with a light hand on her back, just the way Katie had seen distinguished gentlemen do when walking beside fine ladies. She couldn't say if she felt flattered or terribly out of her element. One thing was certain, that brief touch had the same effect as the earlier brush of his hand along her cheek: utter bewilderment. Her thoughts flew into disarray, her insides twisting in knots of uncertainty.

Why did he affect her that way? She knew the pounding heart and swimming thoughts for what they were. He was young and attractive. She enjoyed his company when he wasn't on his high horse. She absolutely adored the way he loved his daughters. It all pointed to one thing. Her heart had become aware of him, no matter how ill-advised such a thing was, no matter how ridiculously misguided.

"What is your question, Katie?"

Her question? In that moment she had far too many questions even to ponder.

She pulled herself together. 'Twas hardly the time to be examining her foolish heart, though she did make a close study of him. His demeanor was entirely businesslike. No signs of attachment or deeper feeling showed in his expression. He was perhaps less gruff than he'd been those first few days, but he was hardly sick with love for her.

Katie scolded herself for even thinking it. She wouldn't deny that she felt drawn to him. But letting that pull grow to any kind of true attachment would be foolish. He was a man of wealth and consequence. She was a servant, nothing more. A servant in his house, even. That, she decided, was the reason his kind gestures overthrew her calm so quickly.

"Katie?"

Ah, begorra. Why could she not focus the tiniest bit? "My apologies, Mr. Archer." She couldn't bring herself to call him Joseph again, except in her own mind. "My thoughts seem to be wandering all over without asking my permission first."

He just shook his head and watched with his usual calm patience. No. This was not a man losing his heart to a servant.

She set her mind to the matter of her business. It seemed the town feud would explode if she didn't find work outside of the Archer home. She had no ideas beyond her bread.

"I'm grateful to you for offering to help me plan my baking business, and I hate asking more of you, but I've stumbled on a difficulty I can't think my way around."

She'd spent the evening trying to create a watertight plan. To increase her savings for returning home, Katie had decided what she needed to do to find better paying positions, how to make what she had last so as not to spend any more than necessary. Even the trip to Wyoming had been well thought out, weighing the cost of the trip there and back against the money she expected to make. Saving enough to return home had taken a lifetime of planning. She wouldn't approach her one chance at income in Hope Springs any less carefully.

"What is your difficulty?" Mr. Archer asked.

"Depending on cost, I can likely pay for the supplies I need. But I've no place to bake the bread."

"You can bake the bread here."

That he didn't hesitate set her mind at ease. She'd been reluctant to ask such a thing if he weren't entirely supportive of the idea.

"I thank you for that. I know it isn't a very long-term answer to my troubles. Once you have a new housekeeper, I'll be out on my own, which worries me a great deal. There are no ovens in ditches."

He laughed at that. Katie saw no humor in it and gave him a look that told him as much.

He held up a hand. "I'm not laughing at you. I just enjoy your 'Katie Sayings.'" His smile stayed. "'No ovens in ditches.' That is my favorite so far."

"Never mind how I said it. The truth's the same. I need a great many things if I'm to give this bread business a go. And I hadn't realized until this afternoon just how much depends on my success."

He gave her an apologetic look before resuming a serious demeanor. "Are you feeling pressure, Katie?"

She sighed and nodded, her shoulders slumping despite her determination to remain strong.

"I just don't want to fail." Too many people depended on her success. 'Twas a feeling she wasn't accustomed to. She'd been alone for so very long.

Katie brushed a loose tendril away from her face. Her hair always gave up all efforts at control by the end of the day. 'Twas a fitting unraveling for such a flustered moment.

"I'm a little worried I've taken on more than I'm capable of seeing to."

Joseph leaned forward with his arms on his knees. He looked her in the eye. "As my good friend Ian O'Connor would say, 'Big men are not the only kind that can reap a harvest.'"

Katie felt an instant grin at the familiar Irish proverb. A smile appeared on Joseph's face as well. He really had a lovely smile, one she'd do well not to think on too closely.

"Best be careful there, Joseph Archer. You're beginning to sound like an Irishman."

He shook his head. "All I have to do is say 'Macauley' and any *actual* Irishman will know the truth."

She liked him better when he smiled; he was far less intimidating. "I'm more and more pleased you didn't fire me a third time, Joseph."

"And I am pleased you are calling me Joseph."

She hadn't realized she'd let the name slip. To her relief, he didn't seem upset. "You prefer it even to 'Mr. Archer'?"

He nodded slowly. "I am finding that I do."

That put her mind at ease. She'd not need to worry about slipping on his name again. "Joseph it is, then."

He rose abruptly, as if he'd suddenly grown uneasy. "I will see you in the morning, Katie."

"Good night, Joseph."

He looked back at her just once. He offered no spoken farewell but simply nodded and stepped out of sight into the stairwell.

Katie put her head in her hands. *You'd best watch yourself, foolish woman. He's not a man for you. Servants have their place and wealthy men have theirs, and the two don't ever meet.*

Chapter Twenty-Three

Katie hadn't come to the céilí, and she wasn't at church Sunday morning. Tavish stood in the churchyard worrying over that. He hadn't seen her since their picnic. He thought the afternoon had gone well. But then she had essentially disappeared. That seemed like a strong argument against her enjoyment of their outing. Unless she was ill or worried. Perhaps he'd scared her off by talking of the Irish Road's hopes for her.

Tavish stopped Joseph in the field beside the church as he approached his buggy, both his daughters walking beside him. "I didn't see Katie at church today," he said.

Joseph nodded. "She insists she will not set foot in a church run by a 'raving hypocrite.'"

Tavish grinned at that. "Sounds just like something Katie would say."

"Yes, she's a spitfire." There was an undeniable fondness in Joseph's eyes.

Tavish immediately bristled, though he kept the reaction hidden. How far did that fondness go? Did Katie feel the same way?

"How is she doing as your housekeeper?" He tried to make the question sound casual, all the while watching closely.

"My house is very clean." Joseph offered nothing beyond that. He lifted Ivy up into the buggy.

"Katie is a fine woman," Tavish added.

"Yes, she is."

Tavish could tell he was being sized up. And by the narrowing of Joseph's eyes, he recognized Tavish's intent as well. They stood, eyeing one another for several long and silent moments. Tavish had not intended to pursue Katie in the least. Now, it seemed, he had a rival.

Joseph Archer was infuriatingly difficult to read. Was it confidence that kept him so at ease? Joseph did have the advantage. Katie lived in his house. He could see her, talk to her every day. Joseph was wealthy, with the air of class and money about him. Tavish had none of those things. And though Katie had warmed to him a bit, he didn't yet feel she'd entirely shed her wariness of him.

"Men." Reverend Ford arrived beside them with his usual look of condescending friendliness. "A good day to you both."

Tavish managed a half smile for the man. Sometimes he wondered how the preacher kept his position when so few in the town cared for him.

"Joseph, I noticed that housekeeper of yours didn't come to church today."

That housekeeper. The preacher's tone clearly dismissed Katie as no more important than a bit of farm equipment or household goods. Tavish clamped his jaw shut to keep from letting into the man.

Emma Archer, still standing beside her father, spoke up before anyone else could. "Her name is Miss Macauley." The little girl managed precisely the reprimanding tone the correction required.

Reverend Ford bristled a little at being corrected by a child. Joseph lifted his daughter into the buggy without scolding her. Tavish gave her a covert wink, bringing the tiniest smile to her eyes.

"Miss Macauley does not choose to attend services?" The preacher would not be deterred.

Would Joseph repeat Katie's exact objection to the preacher? Part of him hoped so, but the more logical part of him knew that doing so would likely cause trouble for her, and, in turn, all the Irish in Hope Springs.

"Miss Macauley is an employee in my household, not a slave or a child. How she chooses to spend her days is entirely her decision."

"Yes, but everyone in Hope Springs attends church." The reverend clearly found Katie's absence inexplicable.

Another voice entered the discussion. "Perhaps she is a papist." Mr. Johnson's Southern drawl never failed to grate on Tavish. He had no gripe with Southerners as a rule, only with Mr. Johnson and his hostility toward his Irish neighbors.

"I had thought of that." Reverend Ford nodded pointedly. "It would be a shame, certainly, if she did prove to be one of those Catholics."

In a moment of horrible timing, Seamus Kelly arrived just as the preacher made that observation. "You forget that many of your faithful attendees, many who contribute to your donation plate every Sabbath, consider themselves 'one of those Catholics.'" The look Seamus gave the preacher was nearly belligerent.

Though Seamus was generally the most cordial and friendly of fellows, his was precisely the quick-fire temper that had earned the Irish in America a reputation for being rabble-rousers. Add to that his enormous blacksmith's build, and there was little about him that spoke of peace and calm.

Considering the real and recent warning from the Reds in town, a scuffle could easily lead to bigger problems.

"Keep calm, Seamus," Tavish muttered under his breath. "A church-yard is not the place to start a fight."

"I'm not the one startin' anything."

Mr. Johnson drawled, "Isn't it just like the Irish to argue with a man of the cloth?"

"Are you calling me a heathen?" Seamus growled.

Reverend Ford stepped between the men, holding up his hands in a show of peacemaking. "Certainly we can get along with one another on the Lord's Day."

Mr. Johnson's smug satisfaction would push even a saint to brawling.

Tavish couldn't blame Seamus for wanting to belt him. Tavish himself had wished it many times over in the years since Johnson's arrival. But it was hardly the time or place.

Tavish stayed close to Seamus's side, keeping his voice low so as not to be overheard. Seamus wouldn't take kindly to being corrected in front of his nemesis. "Be the bigger man, Seamus, and just let this go. The Reverend's objection to Catholics is known to us all. You can't start a new fight over old news."

"Who's saying this grudge isn't a new one?" Seamus's eyes narrowed as he glared down the merchant. "They made it new when they threatened our Miss Katie."

Mr. Johnson tsked loudly. "That is the look of an Irishman itching for a fight." He shook his head, a condescending smile turning his lips. "Isn't that just their way?"

Bob Archibald arrived in just that moment, taking a strategic position beside Jeremiah Johnson. Now the fat was truly in the fire. If Seamus didn't step down, there'd be a full-fledged brawl.

Tavish locked eyes with his fellow Irishman, hoping an unspoken message would pass between them. *Don't let them prick at you,* he silently told the man.

Something of Tavish's words and look must have penetrated Seamus's thick skull and fiery temper. His posture relaxed a bit.

Then Bob Archibald opened his fat mouth and nearly undid it all. "So, Joseph, I see you kept that Irish girl of yours at home where she belongs and not here making trouble."

Seamus's mouth drew into an argumentative line. A few others from the Irish Road who stood near enough to hear took on angry expressions of their own. Tavish himself felt a burning need to turn around and pound Archibald into the ground. *That Irish girl of yours.* He spoke of Katie as though she were a child or a slave, one who belonged to someone the way an animal might.

He kept his hands unclenched only with a great deal of effort. His eyes shot to Joseph Archer. If the man didn't say something in Katie's defense, he would, and he knew himself well enough not to trust he'd say it entirely with words.

Joseph kept calm as ever, not the least ruffled nor bothered by their difficulties. He stood leaning against the side of his buggy, casual and un-concerned. "Miss Macauley," he said, "works in my home, nothing else. What she chooses to do with her Sunday mornings is her decision to make and hers alone."

Johnson flicked an invisible bit of dust from the collar of his suit coat. "Seems to me we discussed the general dissatisfaction with that arrange-ment."

All eyes, and there were a great many gathered around, both Irish and Red Road, turned to Joseph. 'Twas not the first time his loyalties had been questioned, nor was it likely to be the last. Joseph pulled away from his buggy enough to stand at his full height. Nothing in his expression changed from his usual look of casual detachment.

"I can't imagine any of my neighbors would wish me to go without a housekeeper while waiting for my new one to arrive."

"So you don't mean to keep her on?" Seamus asked.

Tavish knew the looks of concern on the Irish faces for what they were. If Joseph was bending to pressure from the Red Road, they would lose their most important ally. Their *only* ally, truth be told.

"I mean to do what is best for the running of my household. Now, if all of you insist on beating each other to a pulp, I would hope that, out of consideration for Reverend Ford, you will choose to do so away from the churchyard."

How Joseph Archer managed to bring looks of guilt and discomfort to the faces of the crowd with no more criticism than those words held and without the slightest change of his own expression, Tavish didn't know.

A murmur of consent wove its way through the crowd, though the more hotheaded on both sides didn't disperse. Tavish caught Ian's eye as he worked to convince the Irish gathered around to be on their way.

Lance Goodwin appeared to be doing the same amongst the Reds. How long before the few voices of reason were not enough? They'd be back to fighting in the streets.

Tavish stepped to where Joseph was climbing into his buggy. The man was the only one with enough influence on both sides to put a stop to it all.

"You mean to ride off, then, with the arguing still going on?"

He didn't look at all ashamed. "This is not my fight, Tavish."

"So long as you're living here, it's your fight."

Joseph shook his head. The man was so mule-headed. He could keep the peace if he chose to. He could cool tempers. But he only ever did so *after* things were out of control.

"Are you prepared to watch your Irish neighbors starving this winter because Johnson won't let them buy the food they need to survive? He's done it before, and you know he'll do it again."

Joseph looked over at Johnson and Archibald glaring at Seamus Kelly and Damion MacCormack. Those four would tear each other's limbs off if given half a chance.

"Johnson did that in retaliation for Kelly charging the Red Road twice what he did the Irish for his blacksmithing," Joseph said. "If Kelly keeps his prices fair, I don't think things will come to that."

Was the man so blind? "Seamus's prices were raised in response to the mercantile overcharging the Irish for every single purchase any of us made. And that was done in response to an argument like today's. If you'd step in and help put an end to it now, while it's small, we could avoid all that hurt and suffering."

For that bit of logical argument, Tavish received a look of wearied impatience. "It isn't as little as you make it out to be. The Red Road feels threatened. I think you and I both know why."

Katie.

Tavish hated the feud as much as Joseph did, but it absolutely burned him how the man could be so blasted calm about it all the time. More often than not he turned a blind eye to it. Yes, Seamus's ridiculously high prices for the Reds were revenge, pure and simple. But compared to the devastation the mercantile could wreak, a mere blacksmith had little power. And that tiny bit of retaliation was about all the Irish had. Until Katie. She'd not been brought low by her unequal status. She'd risen to the occasion.

Joseph drove off. Between Ian and Da, they'd managed to talk down the Irish, leaving the Red Road no one to argue with at the moment. The combatants were dispersing, but not without flinging looks of contempt at one another. 'Twas a scene they'd played out before. These little disagreements would grow in frequency and duration. The tension would grow to retaliation. But with any luck, that wouldn't lead to the violence it sometimes had.

"I hate to see this starting up again," Da said, shaking his head at it all. Tavish's father had bemoaned the fighting from the very first, never taking up the arguing personally. "I suppose we couldn't avoid it for long."

The crowd made its way out of town. Biddy had likely taken the children and Ma home to avoid the arguing. The preacher had retreated to the church porch. Tavish and his brother and father were the only ones left in the now deserted yard.

"Seems we'd best figure what to do regarding Katie before next Sunday," Da sighed. "We might have Reverend Ford crossing himself like 'one of those Catholics' if the town keeps going at each other's throats."

"You blame this on Katie?" Tavish took immediate exception to that.

He received identical smiles of amusement from his father and brother.

"Taken a shine to her, hasn't he?" Da asked Ian, a teasing glint in his eyes. "Stand down, Tavish. We're none of us blaming Katie. But she's crossed a line no Irish have managed around here. What happens next could change how this town's future plays out."

"That's a lot to ask of someone who's only been here a couple weeks." Tavish wiped a trickle of sweat from his forehead, the heat of the day not helping his mood.

Ian slapped him on the shoulder. "We should save the Red Road the trouble and run her out of town ourselves."

He heard the laughter in Ian's voice and knew he'd not kept his budding interest in Katie a secret. "Do that, and I'll run *you* out of town."

Tavish climbed into Da's wagon, as did Ian. Da set the horse in motion, and slowly they rolled out of town. Joseph Archer's home came into view. Tavish shook his head in frustration.

"Joseph means to let Katie go," he said. "That will encourage the Reds, you can be sure of that."

"Give the man a little credit, Tavish." Ian always was quick to defend his friend. "Katie herself said the job didn't entirely work out, and that was before all the troubles down the other road. But she won't be forced out of town completely. That's the crucial thing."

Not forced, he hoped. And yet she'd said she meant to leave on her own eventually. They had to find a way to keep her in town long enough for him to change her mind on that.

"Did Biddy tell you about her bread-selling idea?" A worrisome idea, that. No one could argue against Joseph's business sense, and he didn't think Katie could support herself on the income she'd bring in.

Ian nodded. 'Twas Da who spoke, though.

"The Irish are rallying behind her, whether she wants them to or not. If she fails, it'll be like we've all failed. They remember too well two winters past when we watched our neighbors suffering, starving almost like they had in The Famine. Everyone's been living with that fear in the back of their minds ever since."

Tavish hadn't forgotten that hard winter. Johnson hadn't relented until a half-dozen Irish families were forced out. Would he take that same line until Katie had no choice but to leave in defeat as well?

"I don't know about you, lads, but I'll buy every loaf I can afford if it'll keep her here and give the Irish in town a reason to hold their heads high." *And give me reason to think she might stay for good.*

They continued over the bridge in silence. The road stretched out in front of them, home after home of families he knew well, cared about. They'd come from all across Ireland, driven from their homeland by starvation and desperation. He hated the thought of anything happening to them. But neither did he like the burden they were placing on Katie's shoulders.

"Do you think our Miss Macauley is up to the challenge?" Da sometimes seemed able to read his very thoughts.

Tavish didn't have to even think. "If anyone can stand up under this kind of weight, Katie can. But we've lost too many battles to think this'll be an easy one."

He'd first been drawn to her by those eyes and by her determination to hate him. But he was pulled back time and again by her fire and spirit. The softness he saw in her heart, the tenderness she worked so hard to hide, held him almost spellbound.

Not since Bridget had a woman fascinated him so. She had been very much like Katie, an intriguing contradiction. She too had been equal parts fragility and tenacity. He'd adored that about her. Now here was Katie Macauley, tugging at his heart like he'd not expected to experience again. How could he even think of losing the chance to know her better? He'd do whatever he must to see to it she stayed.

Chapter Twenty-Four

Katie awoke in a panic. She smelled smoke. She tossed back her blanket and threw her legs over the side of the bed. Her heart raced in her chest. Smoke meant fire.

She rushed out the door into the dark kitchen. Where had the smell gone? She'd never find the fire if she couldn't smell the smoke. The oven seemed the likeliest place. Had she checked before going to bed that the embers had burned down in the firebox? She couldn't remember.

Perhaps she hadn't been keeping the stove clean enough. A fire might start in the pipe, or under a stove lid where grime and grease dripped and collected. Maybe she hadn't cleaned as thoroughly as she thought.

She stumbled through the dark room, unable to truly see anything. She bumped hard into the end of the work table. Stepping around it, she slammed her knee into a chair.

The pain didn't slow her. She had to find the fire. She had to find it before it was too late.

A pile of kindling might have been left too close to the stove. A rag left too nearby could catch as well. Katie couldn't be certain she hadn't done something careless.

Her hands followed the edge of the table all the way to the far end. She felt through the darkness until her fingertips brushed the iron stove.

The cold iron stove. Cold, not hot. Cold. Still, Katie pulled open the door to the firebox. 'Twas dark inside. Not so much as a glow of embers.

"No fire," she whispered over the sound of her pounding heart. The words penetrated her foggy mind. There was no fire.

She didn't smell smoke, she realized. Not any smoke at all. She hadn't, in fact, since waking up. Relief and exhaustion took a quick and merciless toll. She rested her forehead against the front of the oven. Tension coiled tight inside.

Eighteen years and the mere thought of fire still terrified her. A moment's contemplation would have told her she'd dreamed the smoke. She always dreamed of fire when something in life was worrying her more than usual.

But she'd not stopped to think through the possibility she had been dreaming. Instead, she'd stumbled through the dark in her nightgown and bare feet, convinced the entire place was coming down around her in flames.

"What a fool you are, Katie Macauley," she quietly scolded herself. "A frightened fool."

A sliver of light spilled across the floor. "Katie?"

Had she woken Joseph? She didn't think she'd made so much noise.

"Why are you kneeling at the stove?" he asked.

How utterly humiliating. "Would you believe I'm offering homage to the gods of baking?"

"No."

Katie sat back on her heels. One deep breath didn't calm her enough. She took another. Confession seemed the best course of action. Otherwise he'd think her the greatest looby ever to walk the earth. "I thought I smelled fire, but I must have dreamed it. I couldn't remember if I'd properly seen to the stove before retiring for the night."

"So you rushed out to check?"

She nodded. When she looked at him to offer another apology for disrupting his sleep, she noticed he was still dressed, though his collar hung looser than usual, his shirttails untucked, boots and socks removed. Yet, his hair remained tidy.

"What are you doing up so late, Joseph? Are you feeling unwell?"

He set the lantern he carried on the table near them and lowered himself, squatting beside her. "You come tearing out of your room in complete darkness to bow to the stove, and you are wondering if *I* am feeling unwell?" He raised an eyebrow, but something in the gesture felt almost like a smile.

"Are you teasing me?" It wasn't his usual way, but she felt certain he was doing just that.

"You seemed to need it."

Katie dropped down to sit. 'Twas an odd thing, sitting on the floor talking to her employer in the middle of the night. Nearly as odd as the tiny skip in her heart at his lingering almost-smile.

"Dreams can seem too real at times, can't they?" He watched her closely.

"Sometimes life is too real as well."

He nodded, slowly, watching her.

Her attraction to him hadn't lessened in the short time since she realized it was there. Sitting about with him would not be comfortable.

"I am sorry to have caused such an uproar," she said, getting to her feet. "I'll just slip back into my room again for the night, and we can forget all about this."

"Are you certain you weren't hurt? I heard you bump into something."

Katie shook her head. "I'm fine, I assure you. I'll just—"

His eyes had grown enormous, staring in what looked like horror at the floor. "What happened to your feet?"

Saints, she hadn't even stockings on. Her misshapen feet were bare and there for the scrutinizing. There in all their ugliness. "Nothing, Joseph. 'Tis nothing at all."

In one swift motion, he stood and took hold of her arm before she could take even one step in the direction of her room. His gaze broke away from her feet and landed firmly on her face.

"That is *not* 'nothing.'"

"Then it is none of your nevermind, is what it is." She hated that he'd seen her mangled scars. Hated that a handsome man who had captured even a bit of her heart, no matter that he didn't return any of those feelings, saw such a horrid piece of her past.

"Katie—"

"This didn't happen here tonight, so you needn't concern yourself over it." She would escape one way or another.

He didn't release her, didn't pull his eyes away from her face. "Have I not earned even the smallest bit of your trust, Katie?"

To her surprise, he sounded hurt. To her even greater surprise, she felt bad for it. Katie never opened her life to anyone. Not anyone.

He took her hands in each of his. He likely meant it as a gesture of comfort. Tavish had done the same the day of their picnic, and she *had* found a sense of peace and calm in his touch. With Joseph she was more nervous than anything else.

"You have trusted me to help you start your bakery. You've told me how much money you have saved to invest in it. You are moving ahead based on the numbers I have given you. Can you trust me with more than mere numbers?"

She owed him a lot for all he'd done for her. Refusing even a tiny explanation seemed unfair.

"My feet were burned in a fire," she said quickly and quietly.

She couldn't be certain whether she saw pity or compassion in his eyes. Neither sat particularly well in that moment.

"And?" He clearly knew there was more.

She'd not speak in any greater detail about the fire. But she knew he must realize the fire hadn't cost her several toes and pieces of the rest. "I lost a few bits to frostbite."

Katie looked him in the eye once more, silently challenging him to expect more information from her than that. His kindnesses didn't require her to humiliate herself.

"Will you come sit with me a moment, Katie?" The request was made with such quiet gentleness, she found she could do nothing but nod and allow him to guide her with the lightest pressure on her arm. Twice in but a few days she'd confessed something to him and then been invited to talk about it. It was not Katie's idea of a comfortable chat. And yet, somehow, his attentiveness only endeared him to her further.

She wasn't in love, not by any means. But she *was* fond of him, and that worried her a bit.

He led her into the dining room. He set his lantern on the table, illuminating the room. Papers sat in neat stacks on the table, a chair pulled out sideways, as though someone had risen quickly.

Joseph held out a chair for her, pushing it in after she sat. She'd never grow used to being treated like a lady of refinement, yet he insisted on helping her down from buggies and guiding her about with a genteel hand on her arm or back. That, if nothing else, drove home how mismatched they were and just how wise she would be to tuck her fondness firmly away.

"I have a feeling," he began, his tone wary, "you will either ignore me completely for this, or bash me over the head with the nearest thing you can find, but I am going to chance it. Do your feet pain you?"

At one time the pain had been unbearable. "They only ache when the weather changes or if my feet are overly cold."

His brow creased, and his eyes bored into her once more. "The amputations do not appear to have been done very expertly."

A fine way to say her feet were a horrid sight.

"I can see I have offended you. That was not my intention," he said.

He laid his hand on hers for a brief moment. They were rough and callused but warm and gentle. She suspected there was more to Joseph Archer than the unapproachable man of means she'd labeled him when they first met.

"I was only worried that your feet hadn't healed as they should," he added. "You are on your feet all day, Katie. If that causes you pain—"

"It doesn't." She couldn't remain entirely angry with him when he seemed so genuinely concerned about her. "The toes weren't removed by a proper surgeon," she confessed, though reluctantly. "So I realize they don't look neat and tidy."

"A country doctor, then?"

She shook her head. "Servants don't warrant the cost of a man of medicine." She'd been working in the kitchen in Derry a matter of days before Cook realized her toes were frozen beyond saving. She hadn't made herself useful enough yet to excuse the price of a doctor.

"Then who undertook it?"

"A blacksmith." She spoke the words in little more than a mutter. Those moments had been locked away and out of reach for a reason.

"A blacksmith?"

"I do not ever talk about this, Joseph. So if you mean to badger me, I'll just march myself back to my room."

He held up his hands in a sign of defeat. "Just give me your word that you'll tell me if you are ever in too much pain to—"

"My feet haven't pained me in a long time." But the subject still did.

He clearly meant to say more.

"What is it that has you up so late?" Katie indicated the stack of papers, hoping for a change of topic.

"You, actually."

"I am sorry for all the noise earlier. I couldn't see the table."

But he was already shaking his head. "Not that. I was going over the figures I gave you. I want to give your bakery the best chance of success I can."

All these papers, the late hours, were on her behalf? "You truly didn't have to do that."

"I know. I wanted to." He looked suddenly uncomfortable. His lips moved wordlessly a moment, as though rethinking what he meant to say. "I want this to work for you."

"Tavish said the Red Road and the Irish are all waiting to see if I fail or succeed, that failing would likely mean they'd start fighting again." She could see the confirmation of it in his eyes. "I'd really rather not fail."

"I'd also really rather you didn't." He picked up a stack of papers, eyes focused on the sheet on top. "I think we've settled on the right price per loaf. That can be adjusted if need be. We have to balance your need for a profit margin with the price your customers will be able to pay but still keep demand high enough for a viable business."

Katie raised an eyebrow. "And people say the Irish don't speak English."

His smile reappeared. "You'll have to forgive me for that. When I get started talking business, I tend to run away with myself."

Katie propped her elbow on the table, leaning her head against her upturned hand. "You said you left behind the world of business because you didn't like it. Sounds to me as though you secretly do."

He shook his head. "I liked business; I just didn't love it. When I can use what I learned about business in the context of something I do love, I can't help a little enthusiasm."

'Twas the most animated she'd seen him. "Something you do love? Like farming?"

He nodded.

"And bread now, apparently," she added.

He seemed to catch her teasing. "I am growing increasingly fond of bread."

"Perhaps you'd be willing to translate all that you said about cost and demand and such."

"Gladly. A lower price will sell more loaves, and the more loaves you sell, the more money you'll make."

"Ah. Now that I understand."

Joseph stacked his papers once more. "Finbarr and I can get your supplies as soon as you're ready to get started. I think the O'Connors have already begun finding you customers."

"Biddy said as much when she dropped off the girls this afternoon."

"You'll simply have to recruit the rest yourself."

Katie nodded. "I can do that."

"I believe you could do anything you set your mind to, Katie."

The praise both warmed and embarrassed her. "I'll say good night, then, Joseph."

He followed her to the dining room doorway with the lantern in his hand. "So you don't run into the table again," he explained.

He is a kind man, more so than I'd ever have guessed. She'd been abrupt with him before. At the door to her room, she turned back to look at him.

"I'm sorry I snapped at you when you asked about my feet. It wasn't an unreasonable question considering how shocking they look."

He kept near the table, his lantern only dimly lighting the room. "Is that why you are so careful to keep them hidden, so people won't ask questions?"

She nodded. 'Twas the reason exactly.

"Then I won't ask about them again."

"Thank you," she whispered. His earlier questions had already filled her mind with blacksmiths and crude cutting instruments and pain she never could seem to forget entirely.

"And, Katie?" He still didn't come nearer, though he watched her closely. "I hope you know that I won't tell anyone what you've told me in confidence."

"I know you that well by now, Joseph. You're trustworthy, I'm certain of it."

"Trustworthy is exactly what I am attempting to be," he muttered. He shifted about a moment before taking a step back. "I should let you get some sleep."

"Yes. Good night, Joseph."

He nodded as though not entirely aware he did so. Then, quick as a heartbeat, Joseph Archer was all business again. "And a good night to you as well, Katie."

He moved with determined stride to the table and retrieved the lantern. 'Twas the last she saw of him before quietly closing her door.

She leaned against it and told herself to breathe. Memories of fire and cold and pain had dealt her a blow. Joseph's kindness was both a balm and a prick of added uncertainty. She'd once thought him an indifferent employer, the kind of wealthy man who cared little for those beneath him.

But in the moments he'd talked with her, listened to her with such compassion and gentleness, she'd begun to see him in a different light entirely. Joseph Archer was a good soul and a loving man, and Katie could no longer deny she liked him very much indeed.

Chapter Twenty-Five

Katie fully expected to have to go around begging people to buy her bread. She'd opted to start small, not offering cakes or tarts or anything fancy until she had a good number of regular customers. But before she could go up and down the road asking who might be interested, her Irish neighbors came to her. Many asked to be added to her delivery route before even inquiring after her prices.

Her orders filled two large baskets with fresh baked loaves, far more than she'd have ever imagined. Biddy drove her out to make the deliveries in a cart lent them by her father-in-law. The O'Connors' eldest daughter had happily agreed to look after Biddy's children and the Archer girls.

"Nearly every house on the Irish Road ordered from me, it seems."

"Don't sound so surprised," Biddy said. "You're a groundbreaker for your neighbors. They've no desire to see you call it quits on account of having no customers."

Again and again Katie had been told how much depended on the success of this idea of hers. She couldn't at all be comfortable with it.

"I'm worried these families are spending money they do not have on something they do not need."

Biddy shook her head with sharp emphasis. "If the Red Road can drive you out, Katie Macauley, you who have shown more fire and determination than any one of them has encountered here, they'll not hesitate to up their efforts at driving us all away. Your fortitude is something we most certainly need."

"I've never been a hero, Biddy."

She received no sympathy, no reprieve. Biddy skewered her with a look. "Seems to me it's time to rise up, then."

Biddy, she'd discovered, knew how to read and write and had made a list of her stops. She made each delivery and received her eight cents in return and, without fail, a word of gratitude and encouragement. 'Twas an odd thing to be thanked by someone who was buying goods from her. She owed them her gratitude, not the other way around.

"If I take on any more orders, I'll have to add a second baking day." Katie pulled out her second basket of bread as they continued their deliveries.

"We'll have you baking every minute of every day if we can possibly manage it. Part of your success will be not needing to work for Joseph any longer."

To her surprise, Katie felt a twinge of regret at the thought. "Joseph Archer is a good man," she said. "The best I think I've ever worked for."

"Oh, aye. That's true as heaven. He's been a grand friend to my Ian. If not for this infernal feud, they'd be as close as bark on a tree."

"The feud keeps them apart? But I thought Joseph stayed out of it."

"He does." Biddy pulled up at the next house. "Being the closest of friends with an Irishman would hardly be a neutral position, now would it?"

Katie didn't climb down right away. "He lets his insistence on staying out of the fight come between him and a friend?"

"Don't judge him too quick or harsh. Joseph's in an impossible situation."

She didn't understand. He'd *chosen* his position.

"Go deliver your loaf, Katie. We can talk as we drive on."

Again she hadn't a chance at the door to even begin her own

thank-you before receiving a sincere one herself. She was yet shaking her head at the oddness of it when she slid back onto the seat beside Biddy.

"You'll forgive me the history I'm about to tell you, Katie, but you won't understand unless you know how all this began. I promise to keep it brief, though I cannot guarantee to tell it well."

"A tale told truthfully is always told well."

Biddy smiled at that and drove on. "While my husband's family and I were all working in a factory in New York, word came to the owner that a friend of his was looking for able-bodied people willing to work in exchange for land. This friend had purchased thousands of acres, an entire valley far off in the West, but the land was useless without canals."

Katie had often heard since her arrival that canals and irrigation were the only reason farming was even possible in Hope Springs.

"My father-in-law grew up in the countryside of Ireland, a man of the land. He never was happy in the city."

Katie's heart cracked a bit at that. Biddy might just as easily have been speaking of Katie's own father. She'd seen him die by bits in the weeks after they lost their home and land. The few letters she had received from her mother painted a picture of Father's life in Belfast. It was nothing but hard work and living day to day. She heard no joy in Mother's description. For that reason as much as any Katie worked and saved so fiercely every penny she earned. Someday she would give him back his land.

"So the entire family left New York," Biddy continued. "I was married to Ian by that time, though only just, and we came as well. Most of Ian's siblings came along. Between all of us, we dug enough canals to earn for ourselves two hundred acres, hardly enough to support us all. The other families that came on the promise of land received about the same."

Farms too small for those depending on them. 'Twas the Irish countryside all over again, the very situation that left them vulnerable to starvation when a single crop failed.

"The man eventually grew anxious to move on and wished to sell his land but refused to part with it in pieces. He wouldn't divide it and sell the parcels to the O'Connors or the Kesters, who lived here at the time, or any of the others here in the valley. He meant to hold out for the entire sum at once."

"But who could possibly afford to buy thousands of acres?"

Biddy gave her a significant look. "Who indeed but a wealthy young businessman from the East looking to start a new life?"

"Joseph."

Biddy nodded. "He bought the entire valley and enormous swaths of grazing land beyond. Then he began selling it in family-sized parcels to those looking to farm. He sold larger parcels to those looking to ranch."

"So everyone bought their land from him?"

"He was offering a livelihood to people poor as the earth itself. Not a soul among them had enough money on hand to buy two hundred acres outright. They're buying their land from him on time. He holds the notes to nearly every farm in Hope Springs."

Biddy pulled the cart to a stop yet again. Katie had another delivery, though she dearly wanted to sit and hear the rest of the tale.

Upon returning she didn't need to breathe a single word. Biddy continued on without prodding.

"There's been Irish hatred in this country ever since the first of us arrived desperate and starving on its shores. We came as a matter of survival and discovered far too many in America would rather we had died along with the millions back home who'd done just that." 'Twasn't bitterness in Biddy's voice but an aching sadness. "Many jumped at the opportunity to have land in a valley with irrigation and natural sources of water in a place as dry as Wyoming. But so very many of those who came brought their hatred of the Irish with them, and they infected the others. They'd point down our side of the road and tell their newly arrived neighbors that, if not for 'those filthy Irishmen,' the town might have been home to 'good, deserving Americans.'"

Katie had heard those arguments all over Baltimore. Never mind that the Irish fought in America's Civil War. Never mind that Irish labor built the railroads. They were considered a scourge that needed to be driven out. They were despised simply because they looked a bit different, played music that sounded a bit different, and spoke in a way that landed a bit odd on American ears.

"Joseph holds the note on nearly every farm in this valley," Biddy continued. "He once confided in Ian that staying out of the feud was every bit as much a wish for peace as it was a matter of being ethical. He owns homes and land on both sides of the argument. To take one side over the other would be crossing a line for him."

Katie had never thought of it that way. Of course, she'd had no idea of his true position. "He's a landowner." The word sat sour in her mouth. She knew all too well the monster a landowner could be.

"A heavy word, that, for anyone who has lived in Ireland."

Katie nodded.

"I suspect he hates being put in such a position," Biddy said. "But his ownership of the area is a bit of leverage no one hereabout can overlook."

"He holds it over their heads."

"No, quite the opposite in fact. He has been known, during difficult years, to accept late payments or partial payments or barters, none of which he is required to do. He has helped people survive here who wouldn't have otherwise. Dragging him into the feud, everyone understands, might very well forfeit any claim they might have on his mercy."

"That sounds so . . ." How did she even explain what struck her so wrong in that? "It seems terribly heartless."

Biddy shook her head. "In our darkest days, there was no one—*no one*—but him who could stop the fighting. It wasn't just that he hadn't ever taken sides but that he held power over both sides equally." Regret filled Biddy's voice. Katie listened with hardly a breath breaking her concentration. "I've seen him broken by it, Katie. He's sat by our fireside, head in his hands, telling my Ian, 'I didn't come here to be the ruthless businessman. I didn't come here to lord it over my neighbors. This was supposed to be a peaceful place.'"

Katie knew she'd seen a glimmer of that the first day she knew him. In the moment he'd realized she was Irish, a frustrated tiredness had washed over him. He knew she would cut further away at the peace he'd not managed to find.

"Don't judge him too harshly, Katie. He keeps himself apart from his neighbors because we give him no choice. He knows if he left, the town would kill each other. And he knows if he ever took sides, there would be no one left to stop the fighting."

They made several deliveries in silence. Katie tried to digest what she'd heard. The accusations she'd thrown at Joseph that first day haunted her. She'd accused him of harboring hatred toward the Irish, of being petty in his dismissal of her. But he had been right all along. She'd brought to his doorstep the very trouble he worked hard to prevent.

The second basket was empty and the cart turned back in the direction of Biddy's home before Katie took up another topic. Theirs had been an outing for heavy conversation.

"Why is it Joseph and Tavish don't get along?"

"Honestly?"

Katie let her tone turn dry enough for humor but not offense. "No, I'd rather you lie to me."

Biddy smiled for what seemed like the first time all afternoon. "The two of them are mad jealous of each other, though neither would ever admit it."

"Jealous?" Katie wouldn't have guessed that. "What is it they envy in the other?"

Biddy lightly laughed. "If we make too many of these journeys every week, you'll have me spilling every secret I know." Still, Biddy indulged her. "I am sure you've been given ample opportunity to discover Tavish is a flirt of the first water."

Katie grinned. "I have, indeed."

"But you've not yet seen that he is the hardest working man you'll likely ever meet." A sisterly fondness touched Biddy's expression. "He was among the first to buy land from Joseph. He knew just what parcel he wanted, but he wasn't content to take up farming purely for feeding himself and any family he might have. Tavish planted berries."

"Berries?" She'd certainly not heard that.

"He knew there were no berry farmers anywhere near here, perhaps none in the entire territory. Yet berries grew wild, so he felt certain they could be cultivated. He has worked himself to the bone in the years since building on that dream. He bottles preserves, cordials, and, though we don't mention it to the preacher, some of the best berry wine you'll taste anywhere."

Katie was impressed. It seemed Joseph and she were not the only business-minded people in town.

"Tavish has eager customers all over the territory, south of the railroads, even. His crops are as good, perhaps even better, than anything found back East. He can ask an impressive price for what he produces." Biddy guided the horse around a rut in the road. "Yet, for all Tavish's work and long years of saving, he still lives in a one-room house on a farm he does not yet own outright. All his work has not gained him a drop of water in the ocean of wealth Joseph was handed at birth. I think that is a hard pill for Tavish to swallow."

"I can see how that would be difficult."

Biddy flicked the reins. "And Tavish puts that same tireless determination into calming tempers and arguments among the Irish. He wants so much to see this feud put aside. He's often spent all night long talking sense into some stubborn, hotheaded Irishman, only to have the lot of them at someone's throat again in a few days' time. That would wear on any man. I think he envies Joseph's ability to stay out of it, because he knows that is impossible for him."

"What does Joseph envy in Tavish, then?" The scale seemed decidedly tipped in Joseph's favor.

"Tavish has an easy and effortless way with people. He makes friends almost without trying. He hasn't a bit of shyness about him. Tavish is quick with a smile or a quip. People are drawn to him."

"Joseph doesn't strike me as shy."

Biddy shook her head. "No, but he strikes everyone he meets as standoffish."

Katie could solve that riddle. "Likely because he *is* standoffish."

Biddy laughed right out loud. "Aye. Standoffish. Grumpy. Often everything but sociable. Part of that is the result of his need, his determination, to keep out of the town argument. He needs to be in a position to help, but that means he is often lonely. He sees friendships and connections come so easily to Tavish, and I suspect it eats at him."

Biddy pulled the cart to a stop at her father-in-law's house.

"Do they know how the other feels about them?"

"I doubt it. Men can be terribly thickheaded."

'Twas Katie's turn to laugh at that.

Biddy put an arm around her shoulders and squeezed, a gesture that had become surprisingly commonplace between them. How quickly they'd become friends. "You just keep in mind what I've told you when next you see those thickheaded men. Know there's more inside than they let on."

"That's true of all of us, I daresay." Katie had her share of complications and secrets.

She thought on it all as she made her way back to the Archer home. These two men she'd come to care for were so mired in the feuding, though in drastically different ways. Both had told her they believed she could make a difference in it. She and her bread could help.

That, she found, was as strong a motivation as the promise of enough money to one day go home.

Chapter Twenty-Six

Two hours after the start of the céilí Saturday night, Katie was doubting the wisdom of coming. The words of gratitude offered to her at every turn were overwhelming. What would happen to these people if her venture failed? They had come to see so much more in it than a few loaves of bread.

Katie breathed a sigh of relief when the company gathered about the fire, sitting as families to listen to the stories. Though she enjoyed a bit of blarney, she didn't care at all for open flames. And she was feeling acutely the weight of her neighbors' faith in her.

Where was Tavish when she needed someone to tease her from her heavy mood? He'd not come to the gathering. Katie told herself she cared little, that she hadn't been counting on his company. She didn't believe a word of it.

With the attention of the gathering firmly rooted elsewhere, Katie thought it best to take her leave. She'd return to the quiet of her own bedroom and get an early start on her night's sleep. She had to be up in the morning to cook the family's breakfast and see to the girls' hair before they left for services.

As she walked away from the party, her thoughts returned to Biddy's startling revelations. Hope Springs had caught itself in a complicated web.

She'd come to know the families there. They were good people. Good people who seemed so very trapped.

The homes down the Irish Road were generally dark during the céilí—no one was at home after all—but a light shone under the door of the barn Katie was steps from passing. She counted back from the elder O'Connors' house where the party was always held. She had passed the oldest sister's house first, then Ian and Biddy's. This, then, was Tavish's home. From the look of things, he was in his barn.

Why hadn't he come to the céilí?

She ought to continue on, go about her own concerns without bothering him. But she'd missed him more than she'd expected to. Katie stood on the road facing his barn for long, drawn-out moments, debating.

"What would you have me do, Eimear?" Talking to her sister had seen her through many difficult times. But in that moment, knowing she had no one but her long-dead sister to turn to, the conversation only drove home how very lonely she was. Even with every Irish family in town greeting her, she felt alone.

She stepped off the road and onto the path leading to Tavish's barn door. She needed a friend.

Katie rapped lightly on the door before opening it the tiniest bit. She stepped inside but didn't immediately see anyone. "Tavish?"

From the far reaches of the barn, hidden in a shadow, echoed a voice. "Is that you, Sweet Katie?"

Tavish stepped out into the light cast by a lantern hanging from a peg on the center post of the barn. He held a metal bucket in his hand.

"I thought I'd come by and see where you lived," Katie said.

Tavish's smile tipped. "This here's the barn, dear. I live in a house like a right regular person."

Ah. There was the teasing she'd missed. "Do you, now? I'd heard rumors you were born in a barn."

"Why is it you aren't at the céilí?" he asked.

She came the rest of the way inside, stopping not far from the post where the lantern hung. "I might ask you the same thing."

"I haven't finished my chores." He set his metal bucket down beside the cow stall. "The workday never ends during harvest."

"I thought harvest wasn't for another month or more."

"For the sane farmers, yes. For those of us raising berries, which I might point out is only me, this is the busy time." He stood with one hand on the door to the stall. "Would you like to stay a bit? Talk to me while I finish?"

"I would, actually."

"'Actually,' she says, as though it's a great shock that anyone might enjoy chatting with me."

"Aye. It is something of a shock. Seeing as I haven't chatted with you in nearly a week now, I can't quite recall if it was an enjoyable thing or not."

"Oh." His eyebrow arched and his mouth opened in a wide circle, even as laughter twinkled in his blue eyes. "Could it be you've missed me, Sweet Katie?"

"Not at all."

"Not at all?"

She shook her head. He matched the movement precisely. After a moment, Katie was fighting a smile.

"Perhaps a wee little bit." 'Twas more of a confession than she'd meant to make. "But only a wee bit. And only because there hasn't been anyone else to talk to."

"Your very last choice, was I?" The cow lowed in the stall behind them, pulling Tavish's attention away. "Hush, you troublesome beast. I'll get to you in a moment." His was a look of sorely tried patience. "The cow's rather fond of me."

"Someone ought to be."

His laughter rang out again. "I'm right pleased you dropped in, Katie. You've brightened my day already."

Was he sending her away? She'd begun to enjoy talking with him.

"Put away the puppy dog eyes, dear. That wasn't a good-bye."

"I wouldn't want you to neglect your cow." Katie thought she managed not to sound overly anxious to stay. "She'd grow terribly lonely."

"I'm about to go talk sweet to her, I am. She'll be fine enough." Tavish took a three-legged milking stool off its hook near the stall door. He leaned a touch closer to Katie, lowering his voice. "If you stick around long enough, I'll come back out and talk sweet to *you*."

Katie just smiled. Though she'd never tell him as much, she would enjoy hearing a few sweet words from him. She felt happier in his presence than nearly any person she knew.

He raised an eyebrow in surprise. "No objections this time?"

She shrugged. "Best see to your chores, Tavish."

"I haven't a fine seat to offer you," he said. "But a woolen blanket set on the pile of straw just there would make a comfortable spot."

Katie glanced over at the straw. "Would I offend your friend by sitting on her next meal?"

Tavish picked up his metal bucket once more and opened the stall door. "Hay is for feeding the animals, Sweet Katie. Straw is for them to lie down on."

Too much time had passed it seemed since her days on a farm. Katie hadn't remembered there was a difference between the two.

"You'll find a pile of blankets in the corner not far from the straw."

Katie nodded and searched it out. She took the thick, gray blanket on top and spread it out on the straw. Behind her she could hear Tavish speaking in low tones to his cow, though she couldn't make out his words. She looked around as she sat herself down. This barn was not the monument to crippling poverty she'd seen time and again in Ireland, the working men bent under the weight of want and struggle. Here was a measure of prosperity in the hands of a man who obviously took pride in what he'd built for himself.

She thought of Biddy's words a few days earlier. Tavish worked hard, tirelessly even. The barn was nothing fancy but was sturdy and cared for. Katie liked knowing that about Tavish.

A moment passed before she realized someone was speaking her name. A moment more and her mind wrapped around the obvious.

"I'm sorry, Tavish. My thoughts were wandering."

"Wandering far, it would seem." Katie could hear him, though she could barely make out his silhouette through the slatted stall wall that separated them.

"I was only thinking that my father would very much have liked a barn such as this."

"He was a farmer, was he?"

Tavish sat on the stool beside the cow. Katie could see enough to tell that much. And she could hear the still-familiar sound of milk splashing into a metal bucket. She found an added measure of comfort talking to someone she didn't have to look in the eye. It was almost like talking to her own self.

"He *was* a farmer," she answered. "Until The Famine."

"Aye." 'Twas a sound of complete understanding. Tavish's family had themselves fled Ireland during the height of The Hunger. "The Bad Times drove many people from farming. I suspect your history has a landlord in it somewhere."

"It seems every poor Irishman's history involves a landlord," Katie said, then thought on Joseph and his role in this valley. She liked knowing he at least tried to be fair-minded and merciful. "We hadn't money enough to pay our rent. The landlord sent his agent along with the local lawman to our home late at night after we'd gone to bed."

"In the middle of the night? I'd imagine your father argued against that."

"He wasn't given the chance." Katie breathed deep, telling herself she'd not be overcome by yet more memories. "They came with torches and set fire to the roof. They didn't even wake us first."

The milking stopped. Tavish muttered a Gaelic curse, the very one Katie had heard from her father that night.

"Something woke Mother. The fire must have been burning for some time. The whole roof was glowing, and the smoke so thick I could hardly see the rungs on the ladder when I climbed down from the loft. She and Father grabbed blankets as we rushed out. I—" She'd been given charge of Eimear. She nearly said as much to Tavish, but the words would not come. Katie hadn't admitted to a living soul since leaving Cornagillagh that she'd ever had a little sister. She'd run with Eimear to a tree at a safe distance from the burning house and told her strictly to stay put. Then she'd turned back. "I went back inside."

"Begorra, Katie! What were you thinking?"

"I went back for my father's fiddle." She'd been foolish to do so, but she'd also been panicked, frightened clear out of her mind. "He played it every night. Every night. Leaving it behind would have . . . would have felt like leaving a bit of him behind to burn up in that house." Her throat thickened and her heart ached at the thought of those terrifying moments. "'Twas foolish, I know, looking back, but I had to. He played that fiddle every day. He taught me to play on that fiddle. I simply couldn't leave it there."

"You're fortunate you got out with your life."

Every time she allowed her thoughts to dwell on that night, Katie swore she could smell burning thatch again. It filled her even as she sat there in the calm of Tavish's barn. Once more she felt the heat of the fire. She ran with bare feet across the dirt floor, glowing embers dropping like shooting stars from the roof above. Her eyes stung. Her heart punched a fearful rhythm against her ribs. Katie grabbed the fiddle from its usual place beneath her parents' bed. For just a moment she'd thought to climb under there as well to escape the fire raining down.

She ran, fiddle case clasped to her. Thatch dropped in burning heaps on all sides of her. Mounds of it covered the only path out. So she ran through the fire itself. The flames seared her feet and set the back of her nightgown smoldering. Huge clumps of the roof came down as she rushed out of the house. The heavy thatch blew cinders and smoldering bits of itself out the open door in an enormous explosion of sparks, knocking her to the ground.

She'd lain there, crying as she listened to the merciless crackle of fire consuming her home, gasping for air as pain radiated from her feet and legs and back. She'd saved her father's fiddle, but the deed had left deep scars.

"Is that the same fiddle you had when we rode into town with you?" Tavish asked.

"Aye. The same."

He'd begun milking again. The rhythmic thwank of each stream of milk set a soothing tempo her heart tried to slow enough to meet. 'Twasn't rushed nor forceful but quiet and constant. Katie focused on the sound.

"Do you carry it as a reminder of your father or as something to play?"

Katie hadn't given it a lot of thought. She hadn't allowed herself to. "Both, I suppose." She did, in fact, think of her father every time she played.

She wove her fingers together, setting her clasped hands on her lap. Though she'd shared more of her history lately than she ever had before, the telling hadn't grown easier. "My father was a fine fiddler. One of the best in all of Donegal, many swore."

Tavish stepped out of the cow stall and poured his bucket of milk into a tall, metal can sitting not far distant. He crossed close to where she sat and leaned against the nearest stall, facing her. "Did your father give you the fiddle because it meant so much to you?"

Katie tried to take in a breath, but it stuck. Father hadn't given her the fiddle as a token of her bravery or her love of the music he played on it. He hadn't given it to her in memory of the hours he'd spent teaching her to play.

Truth be told, he hadn't given it to her at all.

"I'm sorry, Katie." Tavish sat down beside her. "I should have realized speaking of his fiddle would make you miss him."

If only that was what weighed on her heart. It seemed every memory of home and family came tinged with regrets and guilt.

"I have my grandfather's pocket watch," Tavish said. "He gave it to my oldest brother when we left Ireland, and my brother gave it to me."

Katie grasped at the change in topic, hoping her mind would make the shift as well. "That was kind of Ian to give it to you."

"Ian?" His brows pulled in before understanding dawned in his eyes. "I'd forgotten you never knew Grady. He and Patrick, the brother just younger than me, were soldiers with an Irish regiment from New York. They both died at Gettysburg."

"I've heard tell of that battle. 'Twas said to be fierce beyond imagining."

"Aye. Both sides suffered heavy losses," Tavish said. "Our family alone lost two. Mr. Johnson lost a brother. I suspect that's part of the reason he hates us so. Johnson hails from the South; his brother fought against the Irish regiment in that very battle."

She leaned her head against his shoulder as they sat side by side. "Losing a family member brings a person such pain."

He took her hand in his. What Katie wouldn't have given to have received from her parents even a fraction of the sympathy she felt from Tavish in that moment.

"Now I have Grady's watch," he continued, "which was my grand-father's. I miss them both, but having something that belonged to them, something real I can hold in my hand, makes them feel closer, somehow. Probably the way your father does, having something he gave to you that means so much."

He compared her father's fiddle with his brother's watch. Little did he know how painfully different the situations were. Tavish came by his treasure rightly.

"My father didn't give me his fiddle." She pushed out the confession. "I stole it."

"You what?" Clearly he thought she was joking.

"He took me to Derry for my first job, and while he was talking with the housekeeper, I nipped off with his fiddle and hid it behind some flour sacks there in the kitchen where he'd not see it." She rushed the words so she'd not lose her courage. Confession, she'd heard said, was cleansing for the soul. She'd not thought she would ever be willing to confess this. "Father had a great many bundles that day, and I thought he might not realize right off that he was missing something."

She glanced up at Tavish, a little nervous at what she'd see there. The smile had entirely disappeared from his face. "Did he notice?"

"I imagine he did eventually." She lifted her head from his shoulder once more. He likely didn't appreciate the contact any longer. She'd just admitted to being a thief, after all. "I think he knew where it was, but it wasn't worth coming back for."

"You said he played it every day. I can't imagine he'd not come back looking for it."

She felt tears building behind her eyes. She never cried. Not ever.

"Katie?"

"He loved that fiddle. Not a day went by he didn't open the case and take it out. I know he knew I had it. I know he knew. He could have come for it. He could have come back for—" Emotion choked off the word that would have come next. *Me.*

She hadn't taken the fiddle because she wanted to play it nor because she wanted it for herself. In her desperation she'd taken it out of fear she'd never see him again. Stealing his fiddle meant he would come back.

But he never did. His utter silence after Eimear's death, his willingness to give her away to a stern-faced housekeeper, had hurt. But knowing not even his beloved fiddle could make him come back and see her again had broken her utterly.

"How old were you?"

"Eight."

"You were only a child."

"No one was a child after The Famine." Her lungs squeezed tighter with every breath. "We were nothing but cobbled-together pieces of the children we once were."

Rather than pull away, he'd begun rubbing her hand between his. "I suspect, Katie, there's a great deal you hold inside from that time."

"Too much," she whispered.

One of his arms slid around her shoulders and pulled her close once more. Katie melted against him, welcoming his warmth and his embrace. She'd expected him to toss her out upon hearing she was no better than a thief. Instead, she was offered comfort. She'd received no embrace, no comforting touch after the fire, nor on any of the long and miserable nights they passed in cold and hunger afterward. Neither of her parents spoke a word to her in the days after Eimear's death.

"I mean to give my father back his fiddle someday."

"I've a feeling," Tavish said, "he'd be far more grateful at having his daughter nearby than his fiddle."

"I want him to be." She made the confession quietly, almost afraid to speak her misgivings out loud. "I want him to see I'm not the selfish person I was then."

Tavish kept his arm around her, rubbing her arm with his hand. "There's not a soul on earth who would think you selfish."

Selfishness was her besetting flaw, the part of herself she'd worked hardest to overcome. 'Twas that shortcoming that had led to the worst mistakes in her life.

"I can see you think I've no idea what I'm saying." He turned the tiniest bit, enough to look more directly at her. "Let me give you my list, then. You talked Joseph into paying a bit of your salary to Ian and Biddy for watching his girls, knowing they could use an extra dollar or two. I suspect you're the one who works magic with Emma Archer's hair every Sunday."

She looked up at him. "You noticed that?"

He smiled. "She's so proud of her fanciness. I think the whole town's noticed how she's brightened up over it."

Katie's heart warmed at the thought. "Sweet Emma. I wish I could do more for her."

Tavish tipped his head, eyeing her a bit pointedly. "That's not the wish of a selfish person, Katie."

"Well, I do try not to be." She could even smile a little. "But you're talking of little things. Tiny bits of kindness don't make up for an all-consuming flaw."

He watched her, his brow creased as though sorting out a great mystery. "You truly think of yourself as selfish?"

"I know the things I've done and the person I've been." So many pieces of her past told her what she was.

He touched his hand lightly to her face. "And you need your father to tell you otherwise?"

"I hurt him, Tavish." Pain and regret sat heavy on her heart. She'd wronged her father in many ways, cost him so very much. "I need to know that he sees a change in me."

"My Sweet Katie, you've a far more tender heart than you let on when first we met."

That was the truth and no denying. She'd kept a lot about herself hidden for years. 'Twas safer, easier that way. "I might turn that around and say you are a vast deal less obnoxious than *you* let on when first we met."

She felt him chuckle. "Seems we've been a good influence on each other," he said. "Maybe if I'm a very good boy, you'll come sit in the straw with me every Saturday."

"Anyone hearing you say that who didn't know just what you meant might think we were misbehaving."

He leaned in close, lowering his voice. "You mean like gazing into each other's eyes and whispering sweet nothings to each other?"

She smiled. "You've been threatening to do that for some time now."

"Not *threatening*. Promising." He lightly touched the tips of his fingers to the underside of her chin, tipping her face up toward him once more. "You know something, Katie Macauley? I love that smile of yours. 'Twas well worth waiting to see it, you know."

His thumb brushed just below her lip. She closed her eyes, aware of nothing beyond the tiniest whisper of his touch. Her pulse pounded a rhythm she felt through every inch of her.

If she'd wondered before whether or not her heart was in jeopardy, she knew in that moment it was in very real danger.

"I think I'd best be heading back to the Archers'," she whispered with some effort.

His thumb stilled but remained lightly touching her. The briefest of moments passed before he answered. "That is probably wise."

His hand fell away from her face. Katie kept her eyes closed, hoping her heart would slow again. She felt him move on the straw next to her and his arm around her shoulder fell away. With him no longer touching her, Katie could regain control of herself.

She opened her eyes and glanced warily up at him.

"I do know how to behave, I assure you," he said with a small smile. "Come, then." He took hold of her hand as he stood, bringing her to her feet with him.

He released her hand as soon as she stood. Katie felt more than a little relief at that. She'd likely have gone too weak in the knees to stand if he'd kept as close to her as he'd been.

"I'll walk with you back to Archer's," he said.

"Are you afraid I'll lose my way?" Her attempt to lighten the conversation felt forced even to her own ears.

Tavish grabbed the lantern as they passed it. "No. I think it's a good thing for the cow to see I have other females in my life besides her."

"Cows do have a tendency to become far too full of their own importance." The ridiculous topic helped release her tension. How she'd needed him again and again the past years to lighten her burden when it grew too heavy to bear.

"Ah, there it is again. I have sorely missed that since I last saw you," Tavish said, pulling the barn door closed behind them.

"Talk of cows?"

He chuckled. "No. That rare smile of yours. 'Tis a sight, I'll tell you that. And I mean to see to it you pull it out often."

"I'd be greatly appreciative if you did."

"Well, then, how about I strike a deal with you, Sweet Katie. Since you were good enough to share something of your history with me, as we spend our walk to the Archers', you feel free to ask me a few prying questions. We'll even up the tally that way."

"Prying questions, you say." Katie thought on it a moment. "Do you prefer your soda bread in farls or loaves?"

His eyes darted in her direction, amusement and confusion in his expression. "I have no idea."

She'd wondered if he would know that term. "Did your mother cook it for you in triangles or circles?"

"Triangles."

Interesting that farls were the preferred style in Ulster. "Are you from Ulster, then?"

"Aye. County Antrim. We'd a farm not far from Larne. Out in the countryside."

Memories flowed over her fast and thick. "There's nothing quite like the Irish countryside. We had shades of green there I don't think even exist here."

"If there are shades of green here that aren't actually shades of brown, I'd be very much surprised."

He did have a way of bringing out her smile. She'd nearly put back the emotions that had grasped her while reliving that terrible fire. "I think I heard your family's been here in Wyoming ten years."

He nodded. "And eight years in New York City before that."

Eighteen years, then, since they left Ireland. "Was Finbarr born in America?"

"That he was."

Thoughts of Finbarr turned her curiosity another direction, to a very quick conversation she'd had with the boy during her one and only trip into town. "I heard you had a sweetheart many years ago, that she was taken by the same fever as the late Mrs. Archer."

His expression grew noticeably strained. "Many people died of that fever. It was a bad time for Hope Springs."

They kept walking, but Tavish didn't speak more. She'd never seen him close off so quickly and so entirely. Clearly his memories of his lost love still weighed on him, much like her memories of Eimear and father and the fire.

Katie slipped her hand in his and walked at his side. She knew the pain of loss and loneliness. There'd be no pressing him for further discussion, no adding to his weight. She simply walked with his hand in hers, grateful they had each other's company on a night that had unexpectedly held difficult topics and confessions.

She had little experience with such things, but she began to suspect this was exactly what it meant to have people in one's life who cared about each other. They talked through burdens and walked at each other's side. 'Twas something she knew in that moment she wanted very much indeed.

Chapter Twenty-Seven

"I've such a problem, Biddy, you've no idea." Katie slumped onto the bench of the wagon beside her friend. 'Twasn't the most elegant of hellos.

Biddy set the horse in motion. "Tell me about this terrible problem of yours."

For a woman who never told another soul about things even as small as a sore throat or a poor night's sleep, she'd become a regular budget spiller.

"I think I'm falling in love."

Biddy, the troublesome creature, smiled as though she'd been told the funniest of stories.

"There is nothing funny about love, Biddy O'Connor."

"I'm not laughing at the idea of love. I'm laughing at *you*."

Troublesome, troublesome, troublesome. Why, then, did Biddy's words trigger a smile inside? Of course, she'd no intention of letting Biddy see that smile until she'd ribbed her a bit. "A fine friend you are, laughing at my pain. Would you care to say now that my bread is dry and Donegal is the lowliest of counties? Or did you mean to save those stabs for a bit later?"

Biddy frowned dramatically. "A terrible friend I am. And yet, I'll not apologize for laughing at you. 'I'm falling in love,' you say, as though you're making a grand revelation." Biddy clicked her tongue. "You've been treading that path for a while now."

The wagon rolled over the bridge leading to the Irish Road.

"But I didn't tell you the whole of it. I'm falling in love with *two* men. At the same time, Biddy."

Biddy nodded. Katie did not believe her friend, for all her confidence in her observations, had realized *that* bit of Katie's dilemma.

"Joseph and Tavish, am I right?" Biddy spoke far too calm for one who'd been brought into the confidences of a very confused woman.

"How did you know?" She could imagine few things worse in such a situation than everyone and their barn rats knowing the state of her heart.

"Little things." Biddy shrugged a shoulder. "A bit too much curiosity when Joseph's name comes up. The way the tension in your shoulders relaxes when Tavish sits near you." She pulled the wagon to a stop at the very first house. "And the fact that they're the only bachelors you've spent any amount of time with since coming to town." Biddy tapped at her head. "Quick thinking, I am."

"Quick thinking and troublesome."

"Go deliver your bread. We'll discuss the mess you're making of your heart as we go."

Smiles and deliveries went hand in hand, but Katie had to force the latter in that moment. Just as soon as she'd climbed back onto the bench, she took up the topic again.

"What am I to do? Falling in love is not at all what I came here for."

Biddy flicked the reins. "You can't plan love the way you do a meal. It happens when and where it will."

Not very considerate of it. "And what's a woman to do when she's served up two of those meals and isn't sure she wants either one?"

"Is that truly what you're debating? Truly?"

Tavish was next on Katie's list of deliveries. Love had not only a poor sense of timing but a horrid sense of humor to go with it.

"I never meant to stay here. How can I even consider love if I'll be gone in a few years?"

Biddy's teasing slid away on the instant. "A difficulty, that is. I don't think you can fully open your heart until you can open your mind to new possibilities."

Biddy could have made a living creating new proverbs with the number she'd tossed out during that ride alone.

"Even if staying were an option—" Katie had very briefly entertained the idea in the quiet hours of the night "—what am I to do with *two* of them? I know enough of these things to know that's not how it works."

They'd reached Tavish's tidy little house.

"Run on up, Katie. I'm certain Tavish would be happy to help you make your mind up."

Katie snatched up the loaf and shot Biddy a look of warning. Bared her soul, she had. Confessed her worries and feelings, she had. *Might just as well have saved yourself the trouble and confessed to a mockingbird.*

Tavish was not home; he never was when she made her deliveries, being a farmer with work to do. But, as was his custom, he'd left her something on the porch alongside the towel she always wrapped his loaf in. On a previous day she'd found a length of ribbon almost exactly the same shade of blue as the dress she wore to the céilí each week. This time 'twas a small bucket of plump, ripe raspberries.

'Twas no wonder she'd fallen for him. In all reality she hadn't stood a chance. A rather underhanded thing for fate to do to her.

Biddy noticed the bucket almost the instant Katie sat in the wagon once more. "Those are prize berries you have there, Katie. Takes a fine sort of man to think of such a thing."

"I might've guessed you'd cheer for Tavish."

Biddy reached across and squeezed her hand. "No, my dear friend. I am cheering for *you.*"

She groaned in frustration. "Then why won't you help me and give me a bit of advice? I don't know anything about fancying a man or how to tell if that fancy is something more."

They rolled on down the road, a weekly occurrence for them. The ever-present Wyoming wind sent swirls of dust on ahead. Katie had come to relate to the tiny dust devils, all turned about and traveling a road full of twists.

"Would you care to hear how I first knew my Ian was in love with me?"

Katie reached into her basket to pull out the next loaf. "Is that how a woman goes about deciding if she loves a man? Figuring out first if he loves her?"

"Saints, no. It does help a wee bit knowing where a man stands. But in the end, you love whom you love."

Biddy drove along, quite at ease with handling the horse and wagon. How long, Katie wondered, did learning such a thing take? She'd very much like to be able to drive herself.

"Tell me about Ian."

A fond and affectionate smile immediately crossed Biddy's face. "We worked at the same factory in New York, but at different times of the day. He arrived in the dark of morning and left early in the evening. I arrived near noon and left in the dark of night.

"We'd known each other but a few weeks when Ian began coming to the factory after I ended my day to walk me home. He said he couldn't be easy at the thought of me walking alone at night. The man had to be back there to begin his day not many hours after he came to see me safely home, yet he did it night after night."

A kind and thoughtful thing.

"He worked long and hard every day, and I am certain sleep was near about the most precious thing in the world to him at that time." Biddy's eyes positively shone. "A man who will give up something precious to himself for the sake of a woman most certainly loves her."

Katie couldn't imagine any person making such a sacrifice for her. "How do I know if what I'm feeling is anything more than interest?"

"One word, Katie. 'Time.'"

Chapter Twenty-Eight

Joseph moved quietly behind Emma, not wanting her to know he'd followed her. She'd sat in the parlor with such a look of determination on her face for several long moments before clasping her book to her and walking from the room.

Emma stood in the doorway of the kitchen. Katie was working inside but didn't notice her visitor.

Joseph silently willed Emma to say something. She kept quiet so much of time, but had brought herself that far.

"May I sit in here?"

His relief at hearing Emma speak up disappeared beneath his worry over Katie's answer. She'd never hidden her discomfort with the girls.

Katie looked surprised but didn't hesitate more than the length of a breath. "You certainly may."

Emma stepped inside. "I'm trying to read my book, but Ivy won't stop talking."

Joseph silently laughed from his place just out of sight in the dining room. Ivy always had been a talker.

"The kitchen is very quiet," Katie told Emma. "You're welcome in here anytime."

Tension slipped from his shoulders. Katie hadn't rebuffed his sensitive little girl.

Emma walked to the table and sat, laying her book open upon it. She held herself so stiff and proper. Joseph wasn't sure why. Emma didn't run and chase like the other children in town. She didn't laugh with them or take part in their games. He saw a loneliness in her that broke his heart.

Katie checked on whatever was cooking in the oven. The aroma was mouthwatering. Though his housekeeper hadn't proven perfect by any means, she most certainly could cook.

"Is this still the story about the boy with the skates?" Katie asked.

"I'm not a very fast reader." Two spots of color spread over Emma's cheeks. Joseph was ready to jump to her defense.

"I didn't mean it that way, Miss Emma. Why, you must be a very fine reader to be making your way through such a long book as that."

Emma fussed with the corner of the book cover. "Papa reads longer books."

He stopped himself from speaking out. Emma was so very hard on herself. He had told her many times that she didn't need to be. If only Katie would say the same thing, maybe Emma would begin to believe it.

"Someday when you're quite grown, you'll be reading books every bit as long as his. Maybe longer, even."

A whisper of a smile touched Emma's face. Smiles from her were rare as diamonds. Katie managed to bring that out somehow.

"Have you any objections to a wee snack while you read?"

There was no mistaking Emma's eagerness. Joseph shook his head in amusement. For a woman who professed not to know anything about little girls, Katie had certainly hit upon the best tactic.

She pulled down the cookie jar and set two cookies on a small plate. Then she poured a glass of milk from the pitcher in the cooling cabinet.

"Do I have to give one to Ivy?" Emma asked when the plate was set beside her.

"This is a reading-in-the-kitchen treat. As you're the only one reading in the kitchen, I'd say it's yours and yours alone."

"Thank you, Katie."

She lightly touched Emma's shoulder. "You're quite welcome, Miss Emma."

Emma turned silently to her reading, seemingly content with the arrangement. She'd been anything but happy with Katie's arrival a month earlier. Emma had come as close then to throwing a tantrum as Joseph had seen her in some time. Suspicion had turned to tolerance and, it appeared, nearly to acceptance. Even Katie seemed more comfortable. Joseph thought he saw fondness growing between them.

He had sent word back to Baltimore inquiring after new applicants for the housekeeper's position. The longer Katie was there, the more torn he felt about that. She ran the house with a quiet precision that, in all honesty, rather amazed him. Their meals had never been better. The girls were coming to like her. He liked her too, probably a little too much.

She was a perfect fit. Almost. If Katie stayed, the Red Road would be up in arms. The feud would flare on the instant. He'd known from the moment he realized she was Irish that she couldn't stay permanently.

"What do you do at the Irish parties?" Emma asked.

Katie set what looked like a tart on the windowsill. "We dance and sing and play music."

She had Emma's attention entirely. Would Emma enjoy dancing and music? Joseph hated not knowing for certain.

"The Irish are terrible fond of telling stories," Katie added as she crossed the kitchen toward the door of her room, "so a great deal of tale-telling goes on as well."

"The Red Road has barn raisings," Emma said. "They do a lot of those same things, but I don't remember any storytelling."

Katie leaned around the door frame, having just stepped into her room. "That's because the Irish are a great deal too fond of hearing themselves talk," she said with a grin.

Emma smiled back. "I know some people who aren't Irish who talk a lot as well."

"Perhaps we aren't nearly so different as we all think."

Joseph leaned against the doorframe between the dining room and the kitchen. He hadn't been hiding, really, but decided there was no point pretending he wasn't listening. Emma saw him there. He gave her an encouraging smile.

Katie stepped out a moment later, wrapping her woolen shawl around her shoulders. "Do you need anything before I go, Miss Emma? Another biscuit, perhaps?"

Emma shook her head, a few crumbs lingering on her lips. "We call them cookies."

"You know, I've heard that since coming over. I can't say I've grown used to it yet."

Joseph knew the instant Katie saw him there. A hint of worry followed close on the heels of surprise in her face. "Why, Joseph!" She actually seemed a little alarmed. "How long have you been hovering there?"

Did she think he would find something to criticize in her treatment of his daughter? "I only just arrived."

A deep pink stained her cheeks, and she wouldn't quite look at him. "I'm for the céilí, unless you're needing something, of course."

He shook his head.

Emma spoke again. A few short weeks earlier she had been quiet as a mouse. "I think that is your prettiest dress."

Katie set an affectionate hand on Emma's arm. "Thank you, Emma. I know it's not terribly fine, but it is my favorite."

She fussed a bit with the frayed cuffs. The tip of one worn boot, peeking out from beneath the full skirt of her dress, was quickly tucked out of sight again. His mind filled in that moment with the memory of those feet, mangled and broken. It was little wonder, really, that the haughty superiority of the preacher, the threats from the Red Road, and the prospect of losing her job hadn't undermined her determination. She had clearly endured far worse.

"Thank you for the . . . biscuits, Katie." Emma looked back at him, clearly unsure if he disapproved of her treat. He tried to look encouraging.

Katie squeezed Emma's hand in her own. "You're welcome to read in here whenever you'd like, and I'll be most certain to find you a treat whenever you do."

Emma smiled, something she'd begun doing more often. Joseph distinctly heard her whisper to Katie, "It's almost as if we're secret friends."

Secret friends. His Emma had a friend, one who had to leave whether Emma realized it or not. Katie could not continue living and working there.

"I will see you in the morning, Miss Emma." Katie pulled the door open. She looked back at him. Her gaze pulled him. "And you, Joseph. I'll see you in the morning as well."

The door closed behind her. No matter how well she'd come to fit in among them, she could not stay. Not because she'd insisted she was unqualified. Not because the town would object.

So long as she worked for him, he couldn't allow himself to be anything other than her employer. Hiding his growing feelings for her was necessary but frustrating to no end. Joseph would go absolutely mad if she lived under his roof much longer.

***

"Bless you, Katie Macauley. You've brought us a tart!" Mrs. O'Connor accepted Katie's offering with more excitement than it warranted.

Still, Katie enjoyed it. A lot of time had passed since anyone fussed over her. "They're your son's raspberries."

"Ah, now." A teasing glint entered the woman's eyes. "Your baking and his berries? Seems the two of you make a fine team."

Biddy, standing at Katie's side, wrapped an arm around her shoulders. "I've been trying to convince her of that since the day she arrived."

"It's a blush I see stealing across our Katie's face." Mrs. O'Connor grinned. "Seems she's coming to believe you more than she once did."

"The two of you are trouble." Katie laughed through the declaration.

"Trouble, she says." Mrs. O'Connor shook her head. "No, aye, says I. We're merely talking and gabbing." Mrs. O'Connor exchanged an obvious wink with her daughter-in-law. "Why don't the two of you go enjoy yourselves?"

"Oh, won't we just?" Biddy slipped her arm through Katie's. "And we might even find ourselves a certain berry farmer wandering about in need of a few sweet kisses."

"Trouble, says I." Katie tipped a weighty look in Mrs. O'Connor's direction and received a shooing away in return.

She and Biddy walked arm in arm, smiling at the familiar faces they passed. Such a feeling of family filled the gatherings, a welcome closeness Katie had not felt in eighteen years.

"I should warn you," Biddy said, "the O'Connors aren't likely to stop giving you grief over Tavish. They were the same way with Bridget Claire years ago."

Bridget Claire. Tavish's dead fiancée. "I asked him about Miss Claire once, but he wouldn't talk about her."

Biddy nodded in immediate understanding. "He never does. Not with anyone. 'Twas a hard thing for him, watching her grow ill and die. In fact, you're the first woman he's shown any kind of preference for since her passing. The entire family is grateful to see him coming back to himself again. And, what's more, they like you, every last one of them. Tavish, of course, more than the rest."

Tavish did seem to like her company. Katie flattered herself he might *more* than like it. But her thoughts were too muddled in that area for her to think beyond the moment.

"So don't fret over the O'Connors' teasing," Biddy added. "They don't mean any harm by it."

"You say 'they' as if you're not even more guilty than the rest of them."

Biddy laughed and squeezed Katie's arm in her own. "Only because I like you even more than they do."

Eloise MacCormack joined Biddy and Katie in the next moment, along with two other women. "How are you, Katie?"

"Grand altogether," she answered.

"We were wondering something and hoped you wouldn't mind us asking you."

Katie pushed down the wariness she felt at that. Her Irish neighbors had always been considerate in their inquiries. "You can ask, though I may not answer."

Smiles touched all their faces. Eloise moved ahead with her question. "We've been adding a few numbers together, and we're a little worried, Katie."

They did, in fact, look concerned. "What's weighing on you?"

"You sell your bread for eight cents a loaf," Eloise said, "but when we make our own, it costs a bit more than that. Are you losing money on this, Katie?"

Here were people who'd been strangers to her but a few weeks earlier, and they were worrying over her future. Not since she was a child had she mattered that much to anyone.

"Joseph Archer figured the sums. I'm not growing rich by any means, but I do make a bit of money."

That didn't seem to put their minds at ease. "You're certain?" Eloise pressed. "At the Irish prices, even baking is expensive here."

"Irish prices?" Katie hadn't heard of anything quite like that.

"Aye." 'Twas Biddy's turn to look a touch confused. "The Irish are charged a higher price for basic things at the mercantile. Flour, sugar, molasses."

"Joseph Archer bought all my supplies."

Amazed glances flitted between them all.

"Then you likely paid the Red Road price." Eloise's eyes grew wide. "Mr. Johnson wouldn't dare cheat Joseph Archer."

Red Road prices. Irish prices. What kind of place was this?

Rose McCann, who'd come over with Eloise, set a hand on Katie's arm, looking up hopefully into her eyes. "My husband's birthday is Monday week, Katie. I'd meant to bake a cake special for it. But at the price you buy your supplies, it'd cost me less to buy the cake from you. Would you consider it?"

What could she do but agree? Expanding beyond bread was absolutely necessary. Though she hoped more loaves would be sold each week at some point, Katie knew her profits hadn't yet covered what she'd spent starting her business.

"And had you considered offering a proper brown bread?" Eloise asked. "I can't tell you how I've longed for a brown bread like we knew at home. If anyone could make it the way our grannies did, it'd be you."

Brown bread. Katie's heart filled with home at the mere thought of it. "Might be tricky finding wheat ground to the proper coarseness."

Eloise waved off that objection. "But if you could?"

"I'll see what the mercantile offers and give it some thought," Katie said.

The women made their way back amongst the partygoers. Katie mulled over what they'd said.

"Tavish told me Mr. Johnson overcharges the Irish, but I hadn't realized he did it as a regular practice."

"Aye," Biddy replied. "'Tis one of the reasons far more Irish families than Red have had to give up on living here."

They walked together toward the chairs and benches set up around the empty fire pit. There was not a fire that night. Katie was relieved to see it.

"Does Mr. Johnson charge more out of spite or as a means of driving the Irish away?"

Biddy frowned at the question. "Both, I'd guess. 'Tis hardest on us in the winter. We depend a lot more on what we can purchase."

"Like bread at a good price?" Katie still could not comprehend how she could be selling bread at a profit to herself but at a price lower than her neighbors could make their own.

"Word will spread fast that buying your bread will save money, money that could be used to buy other things our families need. I daresay you'll quickly be filling orders for soda bread and brown bread and daily loaves. There aren't enough of us to make you rich by any means. But I'd say we'll keep you busy."

Katie had spent so much of her life focused on how to make more money, how to save faster. She'd not done so out of greed but a desperation to return home. Until Biddy had pointed out that she likely would make very little as the Irish baker woman in town, Katie had hardly given it a thought through all their conversation. She would be doing a service for families who needed it. She could give them the tiniest reprieve from the weight of an injustice.

"Perhaps you might offer tarts at a price for special occasions," Biddy said. "I swear the entire gathering near drowned themselves drooling over it as you walked to the food table."

They sat in two chairs side by side where the partygoers always gathered for stories.

"Rose did say something about a cake for a birthday." Katie tried to not worry about whether her friends could afford fancy offerings when they needed her to save them money on something as basic as bread.

"We don't have such treats often, mostly at céilís and special times."

"I'll have myself a regular bakery before too long." Katie liked the sound of it. To be an independent woman of business would be something indeed. She could leave Joseph's employ and calm the rattled nerves of the Red Road. Better than that, even, she'd be helping these people who had welcomed her as a friend, some, like the O'Connors, who even treated her like family.

Emma's voice jumped into her thoughts. *It's as if we're secret friends.* "Does Emma Archer have many friends?"

Biddy didn't bat even an eyelash at the sudden change in topic. "She and Marianne Johnson are quite the matched set, peas in a pod, they are. But other than Marianne, Emma hasn't really any chums. She tries so hard to be such a proper little lady, and she's so quiet on top of it. The other girls think she's putting on airs."

"Aye. I've seen that in her myself. But where do you suppose she gets that from? Joseph can be grumpy, but I've not seen him act quite so . . . I guess proper is the closest word to what I'm trying to say."

"The word you're looking for is snobbish." Biddy threw Katie a look of mingled amusement and irritation. "And before you object, I'm not saying Emma is, but she comes across that way. Vivian Archer, Emma's late mother, was as snobbish as they come. She went to great lengths to make quite clear she hated everything about this place. She walked about looking down her nose at everyone. We were none of us civilized enough or sophisticated enough for her tastes. Everyone in town could tell she tolerated us but disliked the necessity of it very much." Biddy quickly crossed herself. "I oughtn't speak ill of the dead."

"Then why don't you speak of the living? We can say all the unflattering things about them we want."

Biddy laughed at that. "Emma doesn't speak of her mother often, but when she does, 'tis always of a lady who was sophisticated and proper. She remembers her being quite a fine lady. The rest of us, however, remember her as quite a—"

"Pill?" Katie finished for her.

Biddy's face filled with mischief. "May she rest in peace."

"May she, indeed." Katie kept a straight face, though she felt sore tempted to laugh.

"You're trouble, you are." Biddy leaned her shoulder against Katie's, giving her a friendly nudge. "We'd best choose a different topic, else I'll be at my rosary all night."

"Aye. A living topic, I'm guessing you're wanting."

Biddy tapped on her lips, eyeing Katie thoughtfully. "You know, that Tavish O'Connor, he's quite alive, I hear."

"Oh, no, you don't. Then I'll be all night at my rosary—coveting my neighbor's brother-in-law, I'd be."

Biddy burst out laughing. Katie laughed along, right until the moment she realized that Tavish stood but a few feet away, watching her with a look of utter amusement on his face.

Heat stole across her cheeks. How long had he been standing there listening to her gossip like a dairymaid? She slouched low in her chair and muttered, "Ah now, if that doesn't just burn it all."

Chapter Twenty-Nine

"A pleasure seeing you as well, Sweet Katie." Tavish shot Biddy a questioning look. Why did he get the feeling he wasn't entirely welcome?

"Your timing's near about as good as an unwound pocket watch," Biddy told him.

"Interrupted a good gab, did I?"

"You may well say that." Biddy's tone was too exaggerated to hold any actual scolding. "I've not seen my friend Katie since Thursday, when we drove up and down the road delivering bread at such a speed you'd think the banshee was nipping at the horse's hooves. I'm needing a more leisurely coze just now."

Katie smiled at that. Tavish loved the sight of her smile. She'd seemed so irritable the first day or so that he'd known her, so quick to spit nails. He liked her fire, but he adored the moments when she softened.

"I don't know that those were the fastest deliveries ever made," Katie said, "though we *were* a bit rushed if you go to that of it."

"Heavens, Katie." Biddy wrapped an arm around her shoulders and gave her a tight, friendly squeeze. "There are times I swear you sound like Ireland herself. I can't remember the last time I heard someone say 'if you go to that of it.'"

While he agreed, Tavish hadn't come to discuss Katie's turns of phrase.

"Though I risk getting my ears boxed for interrupting again, I haven't seen Katie in a week, I haven't. So find some reason to give your seat over to me for a piece, would you?"

"Would I? Would a duck swim?" Biddy tossed back.

Katie pushed against Biddy's shoulder with her own. "Who sounds like Ireland now?"

Biddy stood. She gave them both a terribly conspiratorial glance. "Have a fine coze you two." Then, as she passed him, she whispered a bit of advice. "Don't drag your feet, Tavish. She's beginning to wonder."

What did she mean by that, exactly?

He took Biddy's vacated seat.

"The word around the céilí is a certain town baker woman brought a fine raspberry tart to share," he said. "And, to hear tell, the tart is made of quite the plumpest and finest berries, which makes clear just which farm they came from."

"I stumbled across a basket of berries while making my deliveries, and I stole away with it before anyone could stop me." Katie's attempt at a devious look was entirely ruined by the smile in her beautiful brown eyes.

Tavish settled back in the chair, at home for the first time all week. Again and again he'd cursed his early harvest schedule. He'd thought of her every single day but hadn't a moment free to call on her. He'd had to settle with leaving the coins for her bread beside a bucket of his finest berries on the porch. She'd baked the tart with those berries, and he noticed she wore the ribbon in her hair he'd left for her at the last delivery.

"I've been meaning to thank you, Katie," he said.

"Thank me for what?"

"For being a friend to Biddy. Though I can't say why, she's not had a close friend in all the years we've been here. The entire family is grateful to you for that bit of kindness."

Katie shook her head. "You say that as though it were a great act of selflessness to accept her friendship, when I know it is not."

He hated the picture she carried around of herself. "You're still convinced you're a horrible person, then?"

"Not horrible, only—" Her forehead scrunched in thought. "Only not as good a person as I'd like to be."

"Who among us is?"

"But I'm working on it." Katie seemed to speak as much to herself as to him. "I've a few things yet to do before I can feel satisfied with the person I am."

Things to do? He watched her closely. "Like returning your father's fiddle?" He lowered his voice, remembering she'd spoken of that in confidence.

Katie nodded, a heartbreaking earnestness in the gesture. What other weights did she carry in her heart?

"I've a feeling it'll mean very little to you," Tavish said, "but even with that mark on your record, I think you're far from being the greedy person you're convinced you are. More important than having your father see that, you need to see that about yourself."

He knew the instant she decided to change the topic. Her entire expression underwent a transformation from deeply thoughtful to light-hearted. "I've not seen you about lately."

"I hope you know I've not been avoiding you." He not only accepted the new direction for their gabbing but appreciated it. He wanted her to know the reason for his absence, that he wasn't staying away on purpose or not thinking about her.

She smiled and some of his worry lifted. He hated that he couldn't seem to lighten her as easily as he managed with others. She needed it more than any other person he knew.

"I may have been young when we left our farm," she said, "but I remember what harvest time was like. You've likely hardly slept, let alone had time for socializing. I had my doubts you'd even come tonight."

"I do miss a great many céilís in July and August." He had a feeling he'd feel that loss more acutely that season. "And I spend the fall making preserves and listening to my female relations telling me what I'm doing wrong in the undertaking, and I help my brother and brothers-in-law with harvesting their fields. Come October, I'm running deliveries all over the territory and beyond, trying to beat the snows." He grew tired just thinking of the relentless schedule ahead of him.

"Then 'tis little wonder your family despairs of ever seeing you married off. Sounds to me as though you haven't time at all to be courting."

"Hmm." Tavish leaned in so close he could smell the flowery scent he'd come to associate with her since their picnic by the river. Could she hear how hard his heart had begun pounding? "Is that a complaint or an invitation, Sweet Katie?" he whispered.

Her gaze locked with his. They were near enough to each other he could see her eyes turn a touch foggy. Her expression turned nearly blank. Each breath came slow and long. If he hadn't been entirely convinced that kissing her would undo every bit of progress he'd made at getting past her barriers, he'd have done so without wasting a single moment.

"I'm sorry, what was your question?" Katie's voice sounded hushed and jumbled.

Tavish's gaze remained on her face, though he didn't move the slightest nor answer. He couldn't look away from that dreamy expression she wore. He also had no idea, himself, what question he'd asked.

A third voice jumped in. "Seems to me a lad ought to kiss a lass when she looks at him that way."

Tavish nearly laughed out loud. Leave it to Granny Claire to say just that. Katie smiled despite the color creeping across her face.

"Good evening," she said to Granny.

"Good evening kindly."

Though Tavish vaguely remembered that old country way of returning a greeting, only his granny still used it.

He stood and helped her into the chair on Katie's other side. Many of the chairs and benches gathered around the empty fire pit were filling. The storytelling would begin soon.

He lightly kissed his grandmother's wrinkled cheek. "I missed visiting with you at the céilí last week."

She patted his face the way one would a small child, something she'd done these many years. "A sweet half-truth, that. I'll wager you weren't pining for any female company but this sweet lass's, here." She nodded with her head in Katie's direction.

"Ah, but when I didn't come to the party, Katie came to see *me*."

At Granny's curious look, Katie rushed to clarify. "On accident."

Tavish laughed heartily. *On accident.* What a delight she was when wary and stubborn.

"This one'll keep you humble, Tavish, no mistakin'. A handsome man needs that in his life near about as much as anything else at all." Granny emphasized the declaration with a firm nod. "So"—she lowered her voice to an overly loud whisper—"go sit next to her again, will you? Storytelling's a good time for a little snuggling."

"Is there anything you need, Granny, before I have me a 'little snuggling'?"

Katie colored up adorably.

"Get on with you." Granny laughed and shooed him away.

Tavish settled in once more. He grinned at Katie.

"Watch yourself," she warned him.

Adorable, and no mistaking. Was it any wonder he'd missed her so much over the week since he'd seen her?

In the midst of the circled chairs and benches, Seamus stood and spoke in a roaring voice. "Now do you know what I'm going to tell you." A typical beginning to a very tall tale.

The gathering hushed quickly, eager eyes turned in his direction.

"Not many years back, a lass and a lad were wearing out their soles walking up and down the roads of . . ." He offered the crowd an overdone look of contemplation. "Bless me if I can't bring to memory just which county they were walking about in."

Knowing their cue, the listeners immediately filled the air with suggestions, no doubt naming their own home counties.

Tavish cupped his hands around his mouth and made his own enthusiastic suggestion. "Antrim!" To Katie he said in a tone of utmost seriousness, "There's no county can equal Antrim."

Katie raised an eyebrow before calling out in her most carrying voice, "Donegal!"

She must have spoken at precisely the right moment. Seamus pointed in her direction. "It *was* County Donegal, now I set me mind to it. Over the craggy roads of Donegal this lad and lass were walking."

He wove his tale in the traditional broad and expressive way.

Katie turned to Tavish. "There's no county can equal Donegal."

"Aye. Quite full of their own importance over there, they are." He pulled his features into an overdone look of disapproval. "Nothing like the fine people of Antrim."

She smiled just as he hoped she would. A teasing remark, a sincere compliment, and she colored up and smiled sweetly. Finding little ways to please her was becoming a favorite pastime of his.

He hoped Joseph Archer was wrong and that her baking would prove sufficient to support her. Otherwise, she'd likely leave. Life without Sweet Katie Macauley didn't bear thinking about.

Chapter Thirty

Katie nearly doubled her bread orders over the next two weeks. She baked twice a week, alternately making her deliveries on foot or gratefully accepting Biddy's offer to drive her about on those days when she was able.

She knew as long as she lived she'd not forget the look on Rose McCann's face when she delivered an iced cake for her husband's birthday. Her eyes grew wide. Absolute joy filled her smile. The McCann children looked as though they'd been granted full access to a candy shop. Katie couldn't remember the last time she'd brought someone happiness so easily.

She'd also had an order for a berry tart and a loaf cake. Joseph had helped her determine the lowest price she could charge and still make a small profit. Katie struggled with charging her neighbors above her cost. She needed something to live on, but she wished she could simply give them the lower prices she paid at the mercantile. The Irish had been pushed and starved and driven from their homes enough times in the past without such cruelty following them there.

Katie came inside after gathering vegetables from the small family garden just behind the barn late one morning to find a folded bit of paper stuffed under the kitchen door. Someone had written a word across the front, though Katie couldn't say what the word was. She flipped it around in her hand a few times, trying to decide what she ought to do with it.

Any note left for Joseph would have been brought to the front door. Even then, she couldn't imagine anyone in Hope Springs communicating with *him* that way. They came to call when they had something to say.

The note, she felt more and more certain as the day went on, was meant for her. She even unfolded it, despite the pointlessness of that. It wasn't a long note. But a few lines of words.

Who would leave a note for me? She wondered that again and again. The Irish who knew her well were full aware she couldn't read. Perhaps one of the other families?

But as she made her next round of deliveries, no one inquired after a note they'd left, no one seemed to be expecting anything from her. 'Twas then she began to worry a bit. If an Irishman hadn't left the paper, then someone from the Red Road must have.

She kept the note in her apron pocket, wondering over it as the days continued to pass. If someone from the Red side of the argument had left her a note, 'twasn't likely to be a friendly bit of conversation. Part of her wanted to know what it said. But another part of her dreaded the knowing.

Worse, yet, people had begun watching her. Not people she knew but strangers. Katie was acquainted with every Irish family in town. The people who'd taken to staring her down whenever she was out of doors were unfamiliar. She knew in her increasingly wary heart that these were Red Roaders keeping an eye on her and doing it in a way that left no room for doubt as to their ability to keep close track of all she did.

Katie didn't like it one bit.

Tavish seldom came around to see her, almost never, in fact. She understood the absence; a farmer was quite busy during the growing and harvest months. She didn't expect to see him, yet she found herself watching. He would read the note to her. She could have someone to talk to.

She stood in the lingering heat of late afternoon, pulling laundry off the line. If only the town would quit pitting themselves against each other.

Even with those worries, she was happier in Hope Springs than she had been since leaving home. If not for the feud, she'd not hesitate to believe she could live contentedly there until returning to Ireland. And even if the returning took years longer than she'd originally planned, the thought of a delay didn't panic her as it once had. She actually looked forward to the promise of time spent there. Without the fighting, Hope Springs would be almost perfect.

"I've heard a certain baker woman is in need of a few berries."

She looked up from folding the girls' bedding. "Berries, is it?" She dropped the precisely folded sheet into her laundry basket. "I've not seen you in nearly a week, and it's berries that finally bring you round?"

Tavish set his bucket of berries down beside her basket, a look of amused surprise on his face. "I'm beginning to suspect, Sweet Katie, that you're a touch put out with me."

She was, a bit. She'd seen only the tiniest glimpses of him over the past fortnight. That he hadn't even come to the céilí the last two weeks quieted any worries she'd had that he was avoiding her specifically. Still, she saw no reason to tell him as much. 'Twould do him good to work a bit at keeping her good opinion. She suspected he didn't have to work hard at it where most people, most *women* especially, were concerned.

"I've not a had a moment to myself." His tone was apologetic enough to speak of actual regret but not so thick with it to convince her he entirely believed her show of offense. He was teasing her as he always did.

Katie shrugged and turned back to the laundry, pulling one of Emma's dresses from the line. "You might at least have stopped by after services yesterday and said a quick 'Good day. Fine to see you. Must be off.' Would it have killed you to do even that?"

She didn't turn back but could hear he'd come closer. "I couldn't do that," he said. "See, you weren't at church, and I don't speak to heathens on the Sabbath."

"That had best be a comment made in jest, Tavish O'Connor." She sent him a look of warning over her shoulder.

Far from appearing penitent, Tavish's lips turned up in a lazy smile. Her heart flipped about at the sight.

"Now why don't you—" She stopped short, snapping her head in the direction of the not-too-distant road.

"Katie?" Tavish sounded understandably confused.

She motioned with her head toward the wagon slowly lumbering toward the Red side of town. The wagon's occupants watched her as they passed.

"I swear I can feel them looking before they even come into view," she said, something of a shudder sliding through her. "The Red Road's taken to staring me down when I'm out of doors. They don't say anything, don't truly act threatening, they just . . . watch me."

Tavish's eyes were fixed on the wagon as it picked up speed just past the edge of the Archer farm. "How long have they been doing this?"

"The last week or so." She didn't like it but wasn't entirely certain the Reds meant to be hostile. They might just as easily be checking to see if she yet worked for Joseph Archer, to see what she was doing and where. "It seems whenever I am outside—laundry, washing windows, any of those things—someone from the Red Road passes by, and they always slow down and watch me."

The strangeness of such pointed scrutiny had quickly given way to discomfort. She didn't like their staring at her, and she worried over their reasons.

"This only happens here?" Tavish asked.

Katie tried to busy herself with the laundry, but the disquiet in Tavish's tone increased her own tension. "I am only ever here or down the Irish Road. I've never seen any Reds down there."

His gaze returned to the now empty stretch of road visible from the side yard where the clothesline hung. Katie let her eyes follow his. There was something quite unnerving in knowing half the town kept such a close watch on her.

"And"—she pulled from her apron pocket the note she'd kept

there—"a few days back, this was left at the kitchen door. I don't know for certain it's for me, but I suspect it is."

Tavish took it from her and nodded immediately. "'Tis your name written on it."

"Again, I'm only guessing, but I suspect it's from the Red Road."

His expression grew instantly tight. He unfolded the note and made quick work of reading it.

"Have you told Joseph about this?" Tavish asked, his words clipped.

"Not yet. I kept hoping they would stop or I would find out why they were staring at me." She shook off the tension coiling inside.

"Where might we find Joseph about now, Katie?"

She set the last piece of laundry in the basket. "We don't need to bother him with this immediately."

"You blasted well should have bothered someone with this just as soon as it began." He held out a hand to her. "Let's go track him down."

"He's likely out in the fields," she warned. 'Twould be a long walk and no guarantee they'd find him.

He took quick hold of her hand and tugged her in the direction of the waving grain out beyond the barn. He didn't keep her hand in his, but he did walk close to her side. His company had generally been enjoyably friendly. But since the céilí two weeks earlier, when he'd sat at her side throughout the storytelling, giving her again and again a look she could only interpret as keen interest, Katie'd found herself a touch jittery around him. 'Twas as if her heart quite suddenly realized it was in danger.

She'd told Biddy some weeks past that her heart was being tugged by the two men in her life. But having Tavish flip it clear around with a mere glance was worrisome. She could not fall fully in love with a man whose home was here.

"Why did you not come tell me the Red Road's been harassing you?" Tavish asked. "Or Biddy at least. She would've seen to it someone knew what was going on."

"They haven't truly been harassing, only keeping a close eye." So Katie had been telling herself.

Tavish held up the note she'd given him. "'Tis more than that, Katie. 'Tis far more than that."

She had no answer to such a declaration. The note, as she'd guessed on her own, was not one of friendliness. Tavish's tense posture and tone made her wonder just how threatening the words were.

They made a slow walk along the side of the field, glancing down each row as they went.

"I know the two sides don't get along with each other, but I've not seen anything too alarming yet. There hasn't been outright violence."

"A couple years back," Tavish said, "the Irish children were physically prevented from going to town for school for several weeks until the Red Road was convinced to stand down. The windows of the mercantile have been shattered a time or two. Though no one knows just who did it, even the Irish admit it likely wasn't the Red Road. Animals have been let loose down both roads."

Katie moved the smallest bit closer to him. She didn't at all care for the picture he was painting. "And you think I should be worried about being barred from town or windows in the house being broken?"

"No one would dare attack Joseph Archer's home."

She swallowed against the thickening in her throat. "But you think they might attack *me?*"

"That is a risk I'd rather not take." He glanced down yet another row. "Joseph," he called out.

Sure enough, they'd found the man they were searching for. He seemed more than surprised to see them. After a few words with Finbarr, Joseph moved swiftly to where she and Tavish stood.

"Is something the matter?" He clearly could sense the answer to that.

"I feel silly, Tavish," she murmured. "They've not actually done anything."

He was unmoved by her reluctance. "They've given you reason to worry, Katie. That *is* something, and it needs to be addressed."

Joseph looked from one to the other, brows knit, mouth turned down in a slight frown. "Someone is bothering you?"

Bothering me? The phrase fit in its lack of urgency. She didn't like that she'd pulled him away from his work for something as ridiculous as "people are looking at me and sending me unfriendly notes I cannot even read."

He was still watching her expectantly.

"It's nothing terrible."

Tavish jumped in immediately. "Do you have a bit of time, Joseph, to talk this over?"

The men exchanged looks Katie couldn't translate, except that they came to some kind of agreement. Joseph turned back toward the field and, cupping his hand around his mouth, called out to Finbarr that he would be down by the house.

They began walking in that direction. Katie felt terribly foolish. "This wasn't worth leaving your work."

Joseph addressed Tavish, not acknowledging Katie's objection. "What has happened?"

"The Red Road has taken to staring Katie down. She said when she's outside doing her work and any Reds pass by, they slow down and watch her pointedly."

She walked alongside them, mutely shaking her head again and again. Joseph was a busy man, one for whom she'd caused enough difficulties already, and he was forced to listen to complaints that people were looking at her. Ridiculous. Embarrassing, if she were fully honest.

"Do they say anything?" Joseph might have been asking either her or Tavish.

Before she could answer, Tavish did. "No. They just move down the road unnaturally slow and watch her every move."

Joseph pulled off his wide-brimmed hat and wiped sweat from his brow, his mouth in a straight line. Tavish's expression matched his almost perfectly.

"And this happens often?" Joseph asked.

"Apparently every time she's outside and any of them pass by."

The men's longer strides were quickly outpacing Katie's shorter ones. "And," Tavish continued, "it seems someone left this note for her on your back door a while back."

He handed it over to Joseph. 'Twas *her* note and she still had no idea what it said. Joseph didn't seem inclined to tell her any more than Tavish had.

They'd nearly reached the yard behind the house. Neither man had even looked back in her direction for several moments.

"If either of you need *me*," Katie said dryly, "I'll just be over here folding laundry and waving to my slow-moving neighbors."

They both turned in her direction practically in unison. Tavish's lips turned up a bit. Joseph looked a little more contrite.

"We've been cutting you out, haven't we?" Tavish motioned her up to where they'd stopped. "Come on, then. We'll let you talk, word of honor."

"How long has this been happening?" Joseph asked.

She untied the work apron she'd not taken off when they set out to find Joseph. "The better part of two weeks."

"Two weeks? And you didn't tell me?" Joseph didn't sound at all happy about his ignorance.

"She didn't tell anyone."

Katie set her apron over the wood railing of the back porch. "Seeing as I had no idea what the note said—still don't, if you go to that of it—I didn't realize there was anything more to their watching than a collection of nosey neighbors. Does the note say they mean something by all their staring?"

"It's vague," Joseph answered, "but it isn't very friendly."

The note wasn't the only thing being vague. Katie looked to Tavish, hoping he would share a bit more.

"The note was unsigned and said, more or less, that our kind belongs on the Irish Road and nowhere else. It further promised that the Reds would not rest until you were either where you ought to be or gone from town entirely."

Katie didn't like that at all. "And that is being vague, is it?"

Tavish shrugged. "They didn't say what they meant to do about it."

Joseph jumped back into the conversation. "If I had to guess, I would say what they mean to do is make Katie uncomfortably aware of the fact that they know exactly where she is at all times."

"By staring at me." She'd been a bit unnerved by the scrutiny before. Realizing what the Reds meant by it increased her discomfort tenfold. "But what am I to do about it except ignore it until things are more settled? That is just what Mr. O'Connor said when Mr. Archibald made his complaints. We endure the endurable to keep the situation from getting out of hand. So long as there's no danger of violence, I'd prefer to let it lie."

Tavish moved closer, looking her directly in the eye, his expression earnest. "You're here every day, *alone*. There's danger in that if the Red Road is already up to mischief."

Katie knew that well. She'd not truly recognized how alone she was day to day until the first time she'd felt the prickle on the back of her neck from a wagon of Reds watching every breath she took. And yet what could be done? She knew perfectly well how very busy everyone was. They hardly had time to sit about keeping an eye on her and her troubles.

"What can be done?" She looked to Joseph.

He didn't answer immediately. He rubbed at the back of his neck, shifting from one foot to the next. His eyes scanned the empty yard. Katie distinctly heard him mutter a strong word. "I don't like the idea of you being harassed when no one is here with you. But I really don't think making it an issue at this point would be wise."

He paced away a few steps.

"We could have someone from the Irish Road here every day, just by asking," Tavish said. "Not one of us would like to see anything happen to Katie."

Joseph shook his head. Katie knew immediately why.

"The Red Road would see that as an act of aggression." Joseph paced back again. "Clearly"—he held up the note—"they would calm down considerably if Katie wasn't living off the Irish Road. But I can't have another housekeeper here in any less than six weeks, and even that is optimistic."

Katie's heart dropped. She wasn't taking in more than a fraction of the income she needed to support herself without her housekeeper's salary. Yet her replacement was nearly on her way.

"Joseph, might I bend your ear a piece?"

He opened and closed his mouth several times in quick succession, pure confusion pulling at his features.

Tavish chuckled. "She wants to talk with you a bit, Joseph."

Katie smiled in spite of her worried heart. She looked over at Tavish. "Sometimes I think no one speaks English around here but us."

He winked at her. She quickly pushed down a little leap in her heart. Her situation required her attention more than did her budding attachment to a certain blue-eyed Irishman, especially one she didn't see often enough to be at all certain of his feelings for her.

"Might I talk with you?" she asked Joseph again.

He nodded, so she led him a few paces away. She could see Tavish was surprised that the conversation was meant to exclude him. She'd have to explain afterward that the topic was a business one.

"You said it'd take at least six weeks more to have a new housekeeper here," Katie pushed right into her topic. "I know the Red Road has given you grief over my being here, but so long as they realize you're working on a replacement, they'll likely be appeased."

He watched her without comment. She hoped that was a good sign.

Before she asked her favor, she needed to give him her best arguments. "I've been doing some figuring, and I'm bringing in less than fifty cents above what I'm spending each week on my baking. I came to Hope Springs expecting two hundred dollars a year, and I accepted when it was cut to one hundred. But, as near as I can tell, where I am now, I'll only make about twenty dollars in an entire twelvemonth."

She could see her figuring wasn't in error. Joseph didn't disagree with her numbers. More than that, he looked concerned.

"I cannot possibly rent a room and pay for the use of someone's oven and the fuel to heat it, as well as feed myself on twenty dollars a year, Joseph. It can't be done."

He quickly shook his head. "Your business is young. You'll gain customers over time."

She had thought of that. "That argument won't hold. The town is small, and I can only sell to half of it."

An overly warm bit of wind blew hard against them both. Tavish yet sat just out of hearing range, watching the conversation closely. Katie kept all signs of her growing worry tucked out of sight. She'd already come across as vulnerable to them, with the Red Road staring her into fits of discomfort and leaving her notes of warning. She'd not add to that by breaking down over this.

"You're saving them money," Joseph said. "Eventually the Irish families will buy every loaf they eat from you."

"Eventually, perhaps. But I have to figure 'now.' And the reality is, I haven't the money to support myself yet." Katie clutched her hands in front of her, attempting to keep herself calm. She was about to ask an enormous favor and wasn't at all comfortable with it. "I hoped you might delay bringing in a replacement, even just for an extra month or two, so I'd have time to save a bit of my salary to live on while I'm waiting for things to turn around."

She could see resistance in his face and rushed on before he could voice it.

"I'm a hard worker, Joseph, and I've done good work for you."

"Of course you have. I'm not faulting your work."

Press on. Press on. "I know the Red Road is unhappy, but it would only be a bit longer."

"The Red Road's displeasure is great enough already." He turned away, to pace, she'd guess.

Katie stepped around him, keeping herself in his line of sight. Hopefully she'd be harder to argue with if he had to do it to her face. "They have already accepted that you need time to bring someone new here. A little delay would be understandable."

But he was shaking his head. "The Red Road has made perfectly clear they are running out of patience. They will not be easily convinced to wait out a further delay."

"They'd believe it coming from you, Joseph. And we could make absolutely certain they were aware of my efforts to find a new situation on the Irish Road. That would keep things calm, I'm certain it would." It simply had to work. She didn't know what else to do, how she'd live.

"That might be," he conceded. "But the answer is still no, Katie. I need a new housekeeper, and I need to get her here sooner rather than later."

If he thought the Red Road would accept the delay, why was he so anxious? "You said you had no complaint with my work."

"I don't." But he wasn't looking her in the eye.

"Then your complaint is with me, personally?"

He started to say something but shut his mouth firmly. He turned away again.

"Then it's me you want gone, not simply the trouble an Irish employee is bringing you?" As painful as the idea was, it made sense. He hadn't tossed Finbarr out. She had come up short in his estimation somehow.

"I think it would be best for everyone if I had a new housekeeper as soon as I can get one here." He spoke quietly but firmly.

The words sliced through her with all the devastating precision of a knife. She'd worked tirelessly in his home. She'd expertly seen to the mess she had been handed. In the weeks she'd been there, she had started to feel like an accepted part of their family life. Had she misunderstood so entirely?

"You'll not even grant me a couple of extra weeks? A few days, even?"

He shook his head no.

Katie's throat tightened painfully. With effort, she managed to speak. "I'll set myself more earnestly to finding a new situation." She took a quick breath and set her shoulders. "Now, if you'll excuse me, I have laundry to take in."

She quickly spun about, making certain her face was entirely hidden. She pressed her lips together hard, trying to breathe calmly through her nose. Each step took effort. He wanted her to leave as soon as possible. She'd thought herself more a part of the family's life than that. She thought she'd become valuable to them.

Something hurt deeper than even those realizations. Perhaps she had something of the answer she'd been searching for with him. The tiny bits of affection she'd sensed sat firmly on her side and hers alone. Katie pushed the thought away fiercely. Evaluating her pain never made it go away.

She pulled clothes off the line, folding them in jerky movements. Fear for her future mingled with regret at her abrupt dismissal. And she yet had the Red Road's animosity to deal with.

She told herself 'twasn't anything near as bad as the many crises she'd passed through. Still, pain clenched her chest.

"Katie?" Tavish's whisper came from directly behind her.

She hadn't heard him approach. His hands clasped her arms just below the shoulders. She kept a distance between them, not ready to let herself trust him or any other person she'd come to care about. In that moment, trust meant vulnerability, and she'd been hurt enough already.

"Everything will work out in the end, Katie. You'll see."

"How can you know that?" She wrapped her arms around her middle, holding herself against the worry building inside. She had no such surety of a happy ending. Few things in her life had "worked out in the end."

She felt him kiss the top of her head. She closed her eyes and pushed out a tense breath, slow and deliberate. This man, who often teased her mercilessly, was showing himself capable of remarkable tenderness.

She turned enough to lean her head against his shoulder, though she kept her arms around herself. His arms slipped about her, and he pulled her close.

"I grow so tired of everything falling apart," she whispered.

Tavish rubbed her back in slow, gentle circles. "Well, you've a great many people who'd happily help you put those pieces back together."

Chapter Thirty-One

An odd mingling of hope and desperation drove Katie through the next week. She continued to bake all the day long on Tuesdays and Thursdays, filling every order that came her way. The late hours of night and earliest moments of morning found her scrubbing and cleaning and working at the housekeeping duties that wouldn't fit between the kneading and rising and baking.

Come Friday night at the end of her first month of bread deliveries, Katie could hardly piece two thoughts together. She stood at the kitchen sink scrubbing out the pan she'd accidentally burnt the Archers' dinner in. Her mind cried out for rest, her body aching and complaining right along. She'd not slept more than four hours in any of the nights that week.

More than her exhaustion weighed on her. Joseph Archer had hardly spoken a word to her since refusing to grant her any extra time to find a different roof to live under. Truth be told, they were both doing a fine job of avoiding each other. She didn't tell him that Red Road folks were coming by in bigger numbers, taking even more time to watch what she did. She didn't tell him how much it hurt that he wanted to be rid of her so quickly and so entirely.

Someone down the Irish Road would take her in. Someone would accept a mere pittance in exchange for giving her a roof and an oven. She worked very hard to convince herself of that. 'Twas her only hope for a future in Hope Springs, something she wanted more and more all the time.

What am I to do, Eimear? I don't want to be living in the ditches again. The thought haunted her more with each passing day.

Katie scrubbed ever harder at the pan. The work made her feel eight years old again, working in the kitchen in Derry, trying so hard to do the work set out for her despite her exhaustion and the pain of the house-keeper's beatings. In her thoughts she'd pleaded with her father to come back for her, hoping he'd somehow hear her silent begging all the way to Belfast. She'd spent those early nights wrapped in a thin wool blanket under the scullery table, crying in her loneliness. How often Eimear's tiny, angelic face had entered her thoughts in those quiet, still hours of night.

"'Tis your fault she's dead," Katie had told herself night after night. "No one will weep for you but your own self."

In time the tears had dried, but the ache remained. Only when weariness or worry stacked too high before her to see any glimmer of light beyond did she feel the need again to cry.

She'd reached that point the night before. Overwhelmed by exhaustion and a deep, deep loneliness, she dropped into a chair in the kitchen and wept. But with the morning had come the necessity of pulling herself together again and hiding her pain as she'd learned to do so long ago. Joseph didn't want her around. Tavish didn't come to see her. She would have to carry this burden on her own shoulders.

Katie turned her attention to Emma, reading at the work table as she'd begun doing most evenings.

"Are you wanting another cookie, Miss Emma?" Katie had trained herself to say cookie instead of biscuit, though the word still sounded odd to her ears.

Emma shook her head. "No, thank you."

The girl was lonely, painfully so. For that reason as much as any other, she welcomed Emma to the kitchen and saw to it Emma knew she liked having her there. She hoped the new housekeeper would see that need in Emma and give her the kindness and attention she needed.

"You seem to be nearly finished with your book. Have you enjoyed it?"

"I have." Her words were often oddly formal and correct for one so young. That likely hadn't helped her make friends. Children who sounded like adults often didn't fit in either world. "Papa ordered another book for me in his last telegram to Baltimore. That was almost a month ago. He said it should arrive in a week or so."

"It is a fine thing your father taught you to read." She set Emma's plate and glass down in the sink beside the soaking pot.

"Papa said reading is a gift."

Katie nodded. She could hear Joseph saying that. He had something of a philosophical bent, a quiet wisdom. She would miss that when she left. He might not have liked the idea of her staying, but she'd come to love working in his house.

"My father told me music was a gift." She remembered out loud.

Emma slipped the ribbon she used to mark her place in her book and closed it. "Do you like to play your violin?"

"I do."

Emma's face creased in confused concentration. "But you don't play it anymore."

She hadn't, in fact, played in some weeks. But how did Emma know that?

As if hearing the question Katie didn't speak, Emma went on. "You used to sit out by the river and play. I opened my bedroom window, and Ivy and I listened to your music."

She'd had an audience and never realized it. "I hope I didn't keep you awake."

Emma shook her head. "The music was pretty."

"Thank you, Miss Emma." Katie took a seat near her, too tired to continue standing.

"One of the songs you played made me think of my mother." Emma made the admission in a quiet, hesitant voice, as if unsure how Katie would react to it.

Katie laid her hand gently on Emma's where it rested on the table. "Did it, now?"

Emma nodded. "I listened to it and closed my eyes. I could see her dancing in a beautiful gown. She was very pretty."

"I know." Katie squeezed the girl's fingers. "I've seen her portrait on the mantle and the little photograph you have of her in your bedroom. She was beautiful."

Emma lowered her eyes and pulled a bit into herself. "I don't remember her as much as I used to."

"Oh, sweet child." Katie slipped her other hand beneath their clasped ones, encircling the small hand in both of hers.

Emma looked at her again, her face filled with pleading. "Would you play that song for me?"

"Of course I will. Do you remember the tune at all?"

Emma shook her head. "But I would know it if I heard it."

"Come, then." Katie stood but kept Emma's hand in hers. "We'll stumble on it if we put ourselves to the task."

They walked into Katie's room. She motioned for Emma to hop onto her bed while she pulled out her neglected fiddle. The task of tuning would take but a few moments.

"Was it slow or fast?" she asked as she adjusted the strings.

"Somewhere in the middle, I think."

Katie nodded, though the answer wasn't very helpful. "Did it have a sad sound to it, like a song that would make a person cry, or was it happy, something to make you cheerful?"

Emma pulled her legs up in front of her and wrapped her arms around them. "A little bit sad."

So likely not a jig or a reel. An air or a waltz, perhaps.

"What do you say I play some tunes, and you let me know when I've hit upon the right one?"

Emma nodded.

Katie began with "Achill Air." But it wasn't the tune Emma wished for. She played through "Forneth House," "Irish Lamentation," "Gaelic Air," and "The Gentle Maiden." At the end of each, Emma shook her head. None was the song she wanted to hear, but she didn't stop Katie's playing. Instead, she settled in, snuggling into the corner of the bed. Katie made herself quite comfortable at the head of the bed.

The plaintive notes of "The Dawning of the Day" brought sadness into Emma's eyes, but not the recognition that would have accompanied the tune she waited for. Katie had chosen more lamenting songs, as those best fit Emma's description. But she disliked the way they'd depressed Emma's spirits.

She let the tune end early and moved immediately to a quick and vigorous rendition of "The Irish Washerwoman." Emma sat up straight in her surprise. A smile crept across her lips, growing as Katie played each verse faster than the last. When finally Katie could play no faster and had to end the song, Emma was grinning. 'Twas Ivy, however, who spoke.

"That was my favorite of all of them." She sat in the doorway, her legs crossed and her head resting against in the doorframe.

"How long has Ivy been sitting there?" Katie asked Emma, she having a better view of the door.

"For a few songs. May she come sit here as well?"

"Certainly."

Emma waved her sister inside. Ivy stopped at the bedside, wide eyes turned up to Katie. "Will you play a song we can dance to?"

How could Katie help but smile at the girl's eagerness? "What kind of dancing were you wanting to do?"

"Spinning and hopping." She emphasized her words by acting them out. The littlest Archer never seemed to stop moving. So different she was from Eimear, who'd been quiet and still even before illness and hunger laid her low.

"Spinning and hopping, is it to be? I believe you're needing a reel, then."

Katie herself had danced to "Úna Bean Uí Chuinneagáin" when she was no older than Ivy. 'Twas an old traditional Donegal tune.

Ivy took to the music in an instant, dancing about Katie's room with a broad grin on her face. After a moment, Emma slid off the bed and took up the dance as well.

The girls spun about, hands clasped. Katie smiled to watch them, even as an aching loneliness settled once more in her heart. Might she and Eimear have danced that way had her sister regained her strength?

"Another! Another!" Ivy clapped her hands together in excitement.

Emma grinned and giggled. Katie couldn't say she'd ever heard Emma laugh. The sound alone was worth battling her own exhaustion to keep playing.

"More spinning?" Katie asked.

Both girls nodded eagerly. They danced about to "Cailíní Ard a' Ratha" but began to tire partway through "The Foxhunters Jig." Katie slowed the tempo again with "Celia O'Gara." Both girls settled back on the bed, curled up at the foot of it, listening.

She could hardly countenance how much she'd feared being around the girls. She'd quickly come to treasure them. If only Joseph would let her stay a bit longer.

Katie's arms had long since begun to ache. "I'm sorry we didn't find the song you wished for," she said to Emma, keeping her voice low. The girls were nearly asleep.

Emma didn't open her eyes. "We can try again another time."

Katie leaned back against the brass headboard and let her arms and fiddle rest at her side. Though she'd played herself nearly to exhausti Katie was grateful to have taken up her instrument again.

"Will you play one more?" Emma asked.

"Certainly."

There was nothing for it but to play the song she always finished with, the tune her father had played every night as she'd fallen asleep.

Katie breathed out the tension in her. She set her fiddle once more beneath her chin and closed her eyes. The very first note of "Ar Éirinn" took her back through time as it always did. Brennan, Danny, Mother, Father, and little Eimear all danced in and out of her thoughts. Their faces were not so firm in her memory as they'd once been. She could no longer recall the sound of her brothers' voices nor the color of their mother's eyes.

What things had they forgotten about her? Did they remember her at all?

The tears she'd fought all day fell hot and wet down her cheeks. Well she understood Emma's heartache at realizing she'd begun to forget someone so important to her as her mother. If she hadn't taken so long to earn the money she needed, her family could have been together again, and no one would have been forgotten.

Joseph stood in Katie's doorway, watching the tranquil scene. His girls had fallen asleep to the sound of Katie's music. They were at ease with her, happy and content in her company. Yet, while the girls slumbered peacefully, tears rolled down Katie's face. He stepped inside, unsure what he could say or do. She likely wouldn't welcome him, as it was. They hadn't parted on the best of terms the last time they truly spoke.

conversation several times, wishing he had tuation without hurting her feelings. The ng on an extra month or more, his entire s mind trying to stay indifferently friendly. But telling her so was entirely out of the

opened her eyes. A look of dismay crossed

her face. Clearly she didn't want him there. He searched his mind for an appropriate explanation and a parting comment.

Katie didn't say anything. She didn't insist he leave or scold him for coming in the first place. She silently set down her bow and swiped at her cheeks, the movement quick and embarrassed. Perhaps she was more uncomfortable with her tears than with him.

Joseph crossed to the head of the bed. She looked miserably unhappy. He pulled a folded handkerchief from his pocket and held it out to her, but her tears only picked up pace.

"Please take it," he said quietly.

She accepted his square of linen and dabbed at her wet cheeks. They'd hardly spent a moment in the same room over the past week. The air around them radiated their mutual discomfort. Joseph had no idea how to get back what little ease they'd once had with each other. Confessing the entire reason for letting her go would likely only make things worse. He'd seen for himself how naturally she'd turned to Tavish O'Connor in her moment of disappointment.

He would content himself with doing what he could to help her. He reached for the bow and took it up along with her fiddle. He set the instrument carefully in its case, left open on her dressing table.

Why was she weeping? He'd seen her upset and frustrated and, at times, noticeably emotional. But he'd not once seen her cry.

"Did the girls upset you?" He hoped they hadn't.

"No. They're such sweet little angels."

He sat on the edge of the bed beside his sleeping daughters. "Am I to assume, then, you're no longer deathly afraid of these 'sweet little angels'?"

She smiled a bit at that. He hadn't spied so much as a hint of a smile from her in days. Seeing it eased some of the weight he carried.

"I was never afraid of them," Katie said, "only afraid I'd break them or misplace them or something."

She wiped another tear from her face with his handkerchief. They were falling slower but hadn't stopped. The girls hadn't upset her. Then what? He didn't think she would have hesitated to tell him if he had caused her tears. The only other possibility was the music.

"Is it the song that makes you sad or is it playing the song?"

She sat silently thoughtful a moment. "Both, I suppose."

She pulled her legs up next to her. The girls yet slept at the foot of the bed. Joseph shifted so he faced her more directly. Did she have any idea how much he worried about her, how much he'd missed talking with her the past week?

"My father played that song every night." She blinked hard several times, likely trying to stop the tears that still gathered in her eyes. "I would fall asleep listening to it."

"Does the song have words?"

"Aréir is mé téarnamh um neoin . . ." The words drifted off, a look of uncertainty on her face as her eyes met his. "The lyrics are Gaelic." She said it as something of an apology.

"That wasn't English?" He knew he didn't have the O'Connors' knack for teasing and joking. She did seem to appreciate his attempt, at least. "What do the words mean?"

"I don't know that I can translate word for word." Katie pinched at her lower lip, her brow furrowing.

Joseph fought back a smile but found doing so hard in the face of how appealing she was when thinking so hard.

"'Tis the story of a man who falls in love with the woman of his dreams."

He doubted she had any idea how fully she'd captured his attention with that brief description.

"But they can't be together," Katie continued. "So he loves her in silence. He won't even whisper her name in order to spare her the pain of a hopeless love."

A hopeless love. He let his gaze drift away from her face. "What keeps them apart? Does she not love him in return?"

"I believe their circumstances prevented it. Perhaps their families would not have approved, or she was promised to another."

"Or perhaps something about their situation made it impossible," he said. That scenario struck far too close to home. "That is a sad song, Katie."

"But it was so beautiful when my father played it." Her voice filled with longing and the real sound of emotion bubbling again. "I'm sorry to have turned so weepy tonight. I only ever cry when I'm tired."

He shook his head. She didn't need to make excuses for her very understandable tears. She'd made clear her music made her think of her father. "Being separated from family is a difficult thing. Do you ever write to them, or they to you?"

"On rare occasions. I've had word from my mother a few times since we were separated. Their priest in Belfast writes her words down. She even wrote once while I was in Baltimore."

He knew she'd lived in Baltimore over two years. Had she truly only heard from her mother once in that time? No wonder she always seemed so lonely.

"Have you written to them since you came here?"

"No."

He watched her a moment, debating. An offer hovered in his mind. But would she appreciate it? "Would you like to write to your family?"

"Perhaps someday," she answered.

She'd told him her goal was to return home, yet she didn't wish to send word to her family. What had happened between them?

"Tell me if you decide to send a letter. I'd be happy to write it out for you." He couldn't imagine the frustration of illiteracy. He did, however, know the difficulty of waiting months for a reply to a letter sent so far away. "Actually, I could send it as a telegram to be mailed from Baltimore. The letter could reach Belfast in less than a fortnight."

Her eyes opened wide and something like eagerness lurked just beyond reach. He was immediately grateful he had made the offer.

"Thank you, Joseph. I'll consider it."

He couldn't extend an invitation to work there longer. He couldn't. The man in her song might have kept silent, but Joseph was certain that man didn't have to live under the same roof as his unrequited, impossible love.

He rose to his feet. Late night conversations in her bedroom were not the best method of maintaining his sanity.

"I should take the girls up to their beds. They are worn out from all the dancing, it seems."

Katie smiled. "You watched them, did you?"

"From just outside the door. I can't remember the last time Emma laughed." He lightly stroked little Emma's hair as she slept. He missed the lighthearted child she'd been before Vivian died. "Thank you for giving her a reason to smile."

"She's such a sweet girl. I only wish we'd found the tune she wanted to hear. We'll have to try again, I suppose."

Joseph looked away from his daughter to her. "You would indulge her again?"

"Of course I would." She looked fondly at Emma. "The music made them both so happy."

Joseph lifted Ivy from the bed and held her to him with one arm. Emma took a little more doing, but in a moment's time he held both his daughters in his arms. At the door, he turned back.

"Have a good night, Katie." He wanted to say more but knew better.

"And you as well," she answered.

He stepped out into the dim kitchen. The girls lay heavy against him. He looked back only once in the direction of her door. He'd found a woman who loved his girls. She had a tender heart and undeniable strength. If only she could forgive him for insisting she couldn't stay. If she never left, he'd never have a chance to win her over.

Chapter Thirty-Two

Katie welcomed the smells and sounds of the céilí the next evening. The atmosphere of friendship enveloped her. Life had changed for her here. It had changed for the better.

Biddy and Ian both greeted her as she walked among her Irish neighbors. Tavish's mother and father did as well. Mrs. Claire offered a "good evening," to which Katie replied, "Good evening kindly," bringing a smile to the old woman's face. So many welcomed her, asking after her health and her business, praising her bread and the way in which she'd managed to undermine the unjust practices at the mercantile. They were kind and accepting.

Yes, life had certainly changed for the better.

"What is this here, my friends?" Seamus's voice carried in the relative quiet that followed the end of a song. He stood not too many paces from Katie. "I see our Miss Macauley has brought with her a fiddle."

Katie froze. She'd not meant to draw attention to her instrument but merely to sneak in on a song or two. There'd not been time to bake anything. Her music was all she had to offer them that night.

"Do you play that fiddle, Katie?" Seamus asked, a very Irish twinkle in his eyes.

She hid her embarrassment behind a cheeky retort. "I'm not such a fool as to carry it about simply for show, the way one would a fancy green hat."

A few laughs and noises of enjoyment emanated from the crowd.

Seamus tipped his green hat to her. "We'd like to hear you play. Would you do best on a slow bit, or are you up for a jig?"

"I can hold my own."

"Oh, can you now?" He looked equal parts doubtful and intrigued. "Perhaps ya'd like to play a piece for us."

Play by herself before all these people? 'Twas not at all what she had in mind. "Perhaps you'd care to get started, and I'll join in."

Seamus shook his head. "That's not how it works, I'm afraid. You play us a piece, and we'll pick it up from you. That way, you see, we don't outpace you."

The town certainly had proven set in its ways. First she'd been expected to dance, then declare her origins in church. She'd managed to wriggle her way out of those obligations. Katie couldn't figure a means of avoiding playing for them all.

"Do you know 'The Donegal Reel'?" she asked.

A man seated amongst the musicians, Thomas Dempsey she knew his name to be and a son-in-law to the O'Connors, nodded and looked around at the others.

"Here I go, Eimear," she murmured.

She slowly opened her fiddle case, worried at the shaking she sensed in her hands. Would she even be able to play? She pulled out the bow and tightened the hairs just so. The musicians offered her a note to tune by.

If only Father were there beside her. He could play any song ever thought of, at any tempo, in any key. He'd sat beside her many times as she'd played. She would have welcomed his encouragement just then, as well as the chance to show him how far she'd come, how hard she'd worked to learn to play well the fiddle that had meant so much to him.

Katie set her fiddle under her chin and took up her bow. She knew "The Donegal Reel" well and knew it to be a fine song for dancing, besides being quite a thing to listen to. If she could play it well for this crowd, she'd have no reason to feel ashamed of her ability.

She took a breath and began. As always, the music took hold in an instant. The notes flowed and jumped and trilled. Though she didn't close her eyes, her vision filled with Cornagillagh and Father and the people who'd played the songs of Ireland when she was but a tiny child.

She'd played for some time before realizing the others had not joined in. She focused once more on her surroundings, confused that she yet played alone. Her bow stilled. Everyone stood watching her.

Had she done something wrong?

Katie lowered her fiddle and looked around. No one was even dancing. That had never happened at any céilí she'd attended. Her face burned with embarrassment. She knew she hadn't played poorly. Why, then, had she been left to play alone?

"Why did you stop?" Until he spoke, she'd not realized Tavish was there. He'd played least in sight for days and days, so she'd not expected to see him that night.

Katie looked over at him, knowing her humiliation must have shown.

"No one else was playing," she explained quietly. "I'm not certain why."

"Sweet heavens, Katie." He shook his head. "They were all too blown down by you. I don't think any of us have ever heard your equal."

She looked about. Had they truly been impressed?

"Finish the song, will you?" Seamus said, amongst murmurs of agreement from the others.

Katie shook her head. "I don't care to play for people, not all by myself."

"We'll play with you," Thomas Dempsey offered, taking up his penny-whistle once more. "We were only amazed, is all. Play a spell with us. 'Twould be a shame for you to put away your fiddle so soon."

She hesitated. Tavish took her hand in his and led her quite easily to where the musicians were gathered. She stood just a bit apart from the others.

"Couldn't I stand in the back?"

"Just play like you did a minute ago," he said. "You'll fair knock 'em all down."

She pushed out a tense breath. "This isn't at all what I had in mind when I thought to bring my fiddle."

He kissed her fingers before releasing her hand. A man ought not do that to a woman who needs steady hands to play. She watched him make his way back into the edge of the crowd.

"'The Donegal Reel,' now," Thomas Dempsey instructed the musicians. "Follow Miss Macauley's lead. And keep up—if you can."

Katie set her instrument under her chin once more and began playing the tune from the beginning. The pennywhistle joined first, with the others taking it up over the lines that followed. She breathed a sigh of relief as the dancing began again and her efforts faded in with the others.

She remained among the musicians for several songs more, grateful they'd chosen tunes she knew. Seeing the joy that dancing or singing along to the music brought her neighbors made her smile. She'd learned to care for these people who'd been strangers to her not two months earlier.

Katie's eyes fell on Tavish again and again. He didn't dance with anyone but stood nearby, watching her with such a smile on his face as made her heart melt inside. She had to force her thoughts away from the kiss he'd given her hand and the all too vivid memory of his embrace but a few days earlier. Thinking on either moment would likely leave her too shaken even to play.

After a full half-hour, Katie's fingers protested. She'd asked a lot of them during her time with the girls the night before. As the last strains of "The Little Beggarman" died out, she lowered her fiddle. She offered a quiet thank-you to the other musicians and made to step away.

"One more, Katie!" Seamus Kelly called out before she'd moved far. "Give us one more."

"One more!" someone else shouted.

Katie looked to the musicians. She saw only smiles and encouragement. Perhaps she could play one more.

"Something fast or slow?" she asked.

Thomas Dempsey spoke for the lot. "Slow. Show 'em how a Donegal fiddler can play anything at all."

Slow? The first song that always came to mind was "Ar Éirinn." But she couldn't play that tune without tears spilling from her eyes. She searched her mind for others that might do without breaking her to pieces.

She settled on "The Dear Irish Boy." Within a measure or two, understanding and approval touched the faces of most gathered around. The plaintive tune was an old one and familiar.

Thomas Dempsey joined with his pennywhistle, but the others merely listened. Oddly enough, this time she didn't long for the rest of the instruments. The simplicity of the duet added to the beauty of the song.

The air came to its close. Katie held her fiddle to her and mouthed a silent "Thank you" to Thomas Dempsey. He nodded in return.

"I'd say you broke everyone's hearts with that one, Sweet Katie."

She looked up at Tavish, suddenly at her side. "I haven't played that tune in years. I can't even say what brought it to mind."

"Well, you'd best think of a few more. They'll likely not let you come back next week unless you have your fiddle with you." His usual teasing grin held a note of tenderness that went straight to Katie's heart. He'd enjoyed her music, and that touched her deeply.

A tiny voice reached her ears in the very next moment. "Katie, that was the most beautiful song ever, ever!"

Katie spun about in shock. "Ivy Archer, what in heaven's name are you doing here?"

Had the girl followed her? How had she not noticed the child? Ivy was too young to be out alone. She might have become lost or wandered off.

Katie lowered herself to Ivy's level. "Listen to me, love. Your father'll be out of his mind with worry. You ought not have—"

"But Pompah said we could come listen to your violin."

As those words sunk in, Katie's entire frame froze. "Your father's here?"

Ivy nodded.

Katie lifted her eyes and glanced about the gathering. She didn't need to look long. For the second time that night, the entire group had gone still and quiet. Until that moment she'd not even wondered why another song hadn't begun.

There in the midst of the céilí, the most Irish thing that happened in Hope Springs, stood the one man who had sworn to avoid anything that even resembled taking sides.

Joseph Archer.

Chapter Thirty-Three

Tavish was not often at a loss for words. But Joseph Archer standing in the midst of a céilí was not a sight he was at all prepared for. The way Katie's eyes lit up when she realized Joseph stood there wasn't terribly comforting either.

"If everyone stares Joseph down like they are, he'll turn tail and go." Katie sounded decidedly displeased at the possibility.

"You can't fault them for being a touch shocked," Tavish answered. "Seeing anyone at a céilí who isn't Irish is . . . Well, it's never happened once in the ten years I've been here, I'll tell you that much." And Tavish suspected Joseph hadn't come out of a sudden burning desire to study Irish culture.

Ivy tugged Katie in Joseph's direction. Katie, in turn, tugged Tavish in that direction as well. He hadn't been forgotten; that was promising. He kept at her side as the littlest Archer girl pulled her to the center of everyone's attention.

"You've come to the céilí, then?" she said to Joseph.

"The girls wanted to hear you play." He looked around at the gathering.

Everyone still watched him, likely as thrown by his appearance as Tavish was, though for decidedly different reasons.

He spoke to Tavish next. "I hope we aren't ruining the party."

You're full ruining my *party.* But Tavish shook his head. He knew Katie would want the Archers to enjoy themselves. 'Twas only his own jealousy that made him reluctant to welcome the first of their non-Irish neighbors to the weekly gatherings. "Everyone is welcome at a céilí."

"Oh, Pompah!" Little Ivy still held Katie's hand, even as she eyed the gathering with unmistakable eagerness. "This party smells so good!"

Katie smiled at that. How Tavish loved her smile. Perhaps it was the rarity of it.

"They've scones over on the table," Katie told Ivy. "Have you tried one yet?"

Ivy's eyes grew wide. She shook her head no.

"Do you mind if she has one, Joseph?"

Joseph. How long had they been on a first-name basis? Tavish watched them both but saw nothing really beyond perhaps a friendship.

Joseph motioned his daughter on. "Go ahead, Ivy."

She ran the moment the words left his mouth.

"But don't take them all," he called after her.

"A fine thing it is that you've come," Katie said. "A fine thing."

Tavish inched a bit closer to her, keeping a firm eye on Joseph Archer. He took some comfort in knowing Katie had not shown a preference for her employer. But then, she'd only shown the very beginnings of a preference for *him* the last time they were together.

"A person can't help but love a céilí." Katie looked around at the gathering before turning her gaze once more to Joseph Archer. "There are so many fine things to eat, and the music'll make your heart dance inside you."

"The music we've heard already has been . . ." Joseph's voice trailed off, as he searched for the right words.

Tavish, for the first time that evening, felt some kinship with the man. How did one describe a talent like Katie's? She surprised him at every turn.

"I wasn't horrible, then?" Though Katie laughed as she posed the question, there was some uncertainty in her tone.

Tavish opened his mouth to heap well-deserved praise on her, but Joseph beat him to it. "After last night's concert and this evening's, I have to wonder what I'm doing having such a talented musician cleaning my kitchen."

Last night's concert? Katie played her music for him? That thought sat in his mind about as peaceably as a summer storm.

She smiled hopefully. "Did you really think it was good?"

"Good?" Tavish shook his head at the inadequacy of the word she'd chosen. "I think you need to search out a bigger word than that."

Joseph nodded. "I've attended concerts in the finest halls of New York and London, and what I have heard you play would have shamed most of those musicians and thoroughly impressed the rest."

Tavish had always thought Joseph a reticent and ineloquent man. Yet, that compliment far outshone what he himself had managed. But then, he had never attended concerts in fine music halls nor heard any professional musicians play. He couldn't offer a compliment like Joseph's; he hadn't Joseph's history or privilege.

"I do wish my father could hear your words," Katie said. True regret laced her tone. "He often despaired of me ever learning to play well."

"Your father would not despair of it in the least if he had the pleasure of hearing you." Joseph smiled in a way that did not strike Tavish as anything near indifferent.

Tavish set a light hand on Katie's back, a gesture he knew was possessive but one he felt driven to make. He'd seen the very real hurt in her expression during her conversation with Joseph Archer a few days earlier. He'd seen her smile at the sight of Joseph there at the party. Her feelings weren't entirely evident. But Joseph, at least, ought to know Tavish's interest in Katie wasn't casual.

"Are you certain we're allowed to be here, Papa?" Emma asked. "We don't usually . . ." Her eyes took in the crowd with obvious misgivings.

"Tavish," Katie whispered, looking up at him. "Do you think Finbarr might be recruited to help with Miss Emma?"

"I'll see to it." He'd recruit the entire céilí to do her bidding if she wished it.

Ian's Michael passed by in that moment, saving Tavish from having to actually leave Katie's side. He motioned the boy over.

"Fetch Finbarr over, will you?" he whispered in the lad's ear and received a nod in response.

He leaned in close to Katie once more. "Michael will fetch Finbarr," he told her in a low voice.

The smile of gratitude she gave him lit up the entire night. A man would do a great many things to see a woman look at him in just that way.

"Anything else you're needing, Sweet Katie? The moon, perhaps? A few stars? Just ask, and they're yours."

"All I need is for you to stick close by and keep me from panicking."

Stick close by. And she thought this a favor she need beg of him? He'd already planned to do just that all night.

"I rather feel like I'm hosting a dignified visitor and desperately hoping he'll like Ireland." Katie shook her head, apparently finding her own explanation rather lacking. "This isn't even Ireland, and Joseph's a neighbor, not—" Again she shook her head. "I fear I'm not making a great deal of sense."

He took her hand in his. He felt the effect of that simple touch clear to his heart. "It made perfect sense, darlin'."

Color touched her cheeks. An encouraging sign, that.

Joseph Archer's eyes had stopped darting about the crowd and settled, as near as Tavish could tell, on Katie's hand entwined in his. Tavish hadn't intended to make an overt statement of his intentions but thought it best that Joseph knew where things stood.

An uncomfortable silence settled over them all. Katie seemed particularly worried about the newest arrivals, but she didn't make any move to pull her hand from his. Joseph kept his eyes off the two of them. Emma glanced about in heavy uncertainty.

Into the awkward moment came Finbarr. "Michael says I'm to come see you, Tavish."

"Aye. There's someone here I thought you'd like seeing." He motioned in the little girl's direction.

A grin split Finbarr's face in an instant. "Why, Emma! Have you come to join our party?"

She nodded shyly, her countenance pale except for deep spots of color on either cheek.

Step in, Finbarr. Katie would be more at ease if she knew Emma was looked after.

"Would you like to come sit with my friends and me?" Finbarr offered. "The storytelling's about to start. I think you'd enjoy hearing the tales."

"May I, Papa?" She sounded near ready to beg.

Joseph gave Finbarr a stern look. "Are these stories proper?"

"They are, Mr. Archer. I promise you."

"And you'll keep an eye on her?"

Katie jumped into the questioning herself. "And won't let her too near the fire?"

Tavish squeezed her fingers. He knew her history with fire and understood her caution.

"I promise you both," Finbarr said. "I'd never let anything happen to Miss Emma. Not anything."

"Please, Papa?"

Joseph gave her a brief smile and nodded.

Finbarr held his hand out to her. Emma's eyes grew wide. Slowly, uncertainly, she slipped her small fingers into his larger hand. Tavish would have to remember to thank the lad after the céilí. He'd done a fine thing for Emma and Katie as well, whether he realized it or not.

Finbarr smiled at Katie. "Make sure one of these two asks you for a dance."

Tavish grinned. There was another reason to thank Finbarr. Though Katie didn't dance, and Tavish didn't mean to ask her, he liked that the idea of it was planted in her mind.

"Maybe I'll ask *you* for a dance," Katie threw back. "What say you to that?"

"Not a chance of it." Suddenly Finbarr had an Irish brogue as wide as their da's. "I've a lass on me arm, in case ye hadn't noted it. I mean to keep her there, not go dancin' with the first strange woman what asks me."

"Aye, get out of here, Finbarr, before this 'strange woman' belts you one."

He laughed as he left, but before he moved far, his attention was back on Emma.

"A good lad, that one," Katie said, watching him go.

"He is." Tavish and Joseph spoke in almost perfect unison. He could see Joseph found it no more amusing than he did, though Katie seemed to enjoy it.

Ian stepped up to Joseph's side. Tavish was glad to see him. Maybe his brother would take Joseph on a tour of the party. Tavish couldn't seem to get so much as a moment or two alone with Katie.

"Good to see you here, Joseph," Ian said.

"I hoped I would be allowed in even if I can't say the name of the thing."

Ian smiled broadly. "Speaking Gaelic isn't necessary to attend."

"That's good." Joseph shook his head. "I'm still working on saying Macauley."

Ian winced, eliciting a laugh from Katie. She didn't laugh often enough. Hearing her do so had become something of a life goal of Tavish's.

"Be certain to have yourself a bit of the black pudding Mrs. O'Connor set out," Katie said. "And Liam Desmond brought cider everyone has been raving about."

"Cider and black pudding." Joseph looked at least a little interested. "I can honestly say I've never had that particular meal."

"We'll have you eating like an Irishman in no time, you'll see."

Tavish rubbed the back of her hand with his thumb. He'd done just that during the last céilí they'd attended together. She had let him hold her hand for a while during the storytelling. The simple touch eased his growing concern over Joseph Archer. Katie wouldn't allow it if she were truly interested in someone else. Would she?

"Pompah! Pompah!" Ivy rushed to her father's side, a generous bit of powdered sugar on her face. "They have cookies. Can I have a cookie?"

"May I have a cookie?" he gently corrected.

Her face twisted in confusion. "If you want one."

Katie laughed at that, bringing Joseph's eyes back to her again. Tavish kept hold of her hand, all the while feeling like an idiot for being jealous. Katie hadn't shown an attachment to Joseph. Why, then, was he so convinced he had competition?

"I think you'd best take the girl for a biscuit," Katie said. "I know how fond your daughters are of them."

Ivy pulled her father to the sweets table. Katie looked toward the fire.

"We don't have to sit near the flames if you'd rather not," Tavish assured her.

She shook her head. "I was actually searching for Emma, though I know Finbarr will take care of her. I worry, is all."

Tavish slipped her arm through his. He walked with her toward the back row of benches. "What are the chances, do you think, of Seamus telling his 'a lad and a lass were out walking' story?"

A twinkle lit her eyes. "No chances about it. I've heard that tale every week since I arrived."

A commotion back by the house pulled both their attention in that direction. People were rushing about, their voices raised.

"What in the blazes? Wait here a moment, Katie."

She flung a look of annoyed defiance. "Why would I do that? If there's trouble, I'd rather help than sit about wringing my hands."

He'd moved no more than a few paces toward the growing crowd when he heard the sound of a horse crying out. They weren't near the barn. 'Twas odd for the animal to be anywhere near the back door of the house.

He caught sight of the bucking and jumping creature, and his mind froze.

"That's your horse, Tavish," Katie said.

It was, indeed. "But I walked here. Ériu was in her stall in my barn."

Tavish pushed his way through the crowd. He pieced the mystery together quickly. 'Twasn't the first time an animal had found its way down the Irish Road during a céilí. The Red Road had long since adopted it as a preferred bit of mischief. He couldn't say, though, just what had his very even-tempered mare so skittish.

"Tavish." Katie sounded worried.

"We'll get her back home, don't you fret."

She shook her head frantically. "No, Tavish. Something's happened to her tail."

He snapped his head back to look. Ériu's tail was but a stub.

"You don't suppose it's been docked, do you?" Katie kept up with his rushed pace.

He couldn't even answer. If the Red Road had burst into his barn and maimed his animal, he'd have real difficulty not going after them all himself. The O'Connors had always been the peacemakers on the Irish Road. But to hurt an animal—he couldn't abide that. Especially not a gentle creature like Ériu.

Tavish placed himself between his frantic horse and the crowd. He tried talking to her, but doubted Ériu could hear him over the other voices. Ian and Da were doing their level best to get everyone back. Until the animal calmed, distance was best.

Tavish checked to make certain Katie hadn't come too close. Saints, if she were hurt . . .

Michael rushed to his side, a rope in hand.

Katie hurried toward them. "Michael, don't get too close." She tried to make herself a shield between the lad and the horse.

Tavish set a hand on her shoulder, all the while keeping an eye on his horse. "Michael is better with my horse even than I am." He spoke swift and firm, easing her backward. "But *you*, Katie, are making me nervous."

"Me?"

"You're putting yourself in danger."

Michael slipped around the barricade Katie had made of herself. He'd tied the rope into a makeshift bridle. Tavish kept Katie on his other side, but he couldn't watch her and Ériu at the same time.

Where's Biddy? He found Joseph Archer first.

"Joseph," he called out. The time had come for setting aside rivalries. Katie's well-being was on the line.

Joseph moved quickly through the crowd, eyes darting between the horse and him. "Has the tail been cut off fully?"

"I don't know." He nudged Katie toward Joseph. "But this lass here's determined to get herself trampled. Keep her back, will you?"

Joseph nodded. Though Tavish wasn't keen on leaving her in his hands, he had to see to his horse. And Katie's stubbornness was legendary enough to make him wonder if she'd step away on her own.

He and Michael took a full half hour, calming and roping the horse. While Michael spoke to Ériu, Tavish checked her close. Ériu had what looked like rope burns on her neck and hind quarters, no doubt from being held captive while her tail was assaulted. He cursed long and expertly before turning his attention to the animal's tail.

Let it just be the hair. Just the hair.

"Is it docked, Uncle Tavish?"

He set a gentle hand on Ériu and forced himself to look closely at the remains of her once long, thick tail. He pushed out a breath. "They've only cut the hair."

Michael nodded and rubbed at the horse's nose. "Still, she'll be miserable without a tail to swat the flies."

Something the Red Road knew well. The act was one of warning, a reminder that they could do worse.

The céilí had broken up. Everyone had left, no doubt to check their own animals. The Irish had lost animals over the years, either set loose in the middle of the night or, as had happened the last time the feud heated up, shot right in their own barns.

"Help me get her back to the barn," he said to Michael. If he concentrated on the horse, perhaps he'd keep himself from storming down the Red Road himself.

Michael led the horse with all the skill of a born horseman. Tavish kept at Ériu's side, just breathing in and out and telling himself to stay calm. Pounding any Red Roader he could find would hardly keep the peace, though it might do his anger a bit of good.

Da stood at the roadside. Tavish knew the look of simmering tension in his father's face. He likely wore the same one.

"Go home, Tavish," Da said. "Sleep this off. We'll have enough tempers to calm on this road without yours being tossed into the mix."

"You really think we can keep Kelly and those of a mind with him from retaliating?"

Da only shook his head. "We've a fight coming, son. Without a miracle of some kind, we've a fight coming."

Chapter Thirty-Four

"This is one point on which your stubbornness will not outlast my determination." Joseph stood at the back door, blocking Katie's path out.

She was thoroughly put out with him.

"If you're wanting to eat tonight, Joseph Archer, I suggest you get out of my way. I've deliveries to make, and time is tight." She glared at him, an oversized basket of loaves propped on her hip. "Now quit fussing like a granny and let me go make my deliveries."

"Not on your life."

"Joseph." She muttered his name in complete frustration.

He didn't budge. "You will not be going out alone, Katie. Not even just down the Irish Road. The Reds crossed that border when they cut the tail of Tavish's horse." He set his jaw. "And they are already upset with you."

Katie knew all that. She was well aware her presence had started this latest feuding. Being stared at for nearly a month certainly kept her situation fresh in her mind.

Joseph took her basket from her.

"You won't be stopping me from going," she warned him. Katie'd known the moment she left the céilí that giving up on her Irish neighbors was not an option she would consider. The enormity of what they were trying to stand up under had finally begun to sink in.

"I know." He set the basket on the table and turned to face her. "All I am asking is that you wait until I am done for the day so I can go with you."

That wouldn't do. "They know I make deliveries in the afternoon. Pushing that back will convince them I'm scared."

"You should be scared, Katie. *Cautious* at the very least."

She paced to the sink. She'd been tense all Sunday and through laundry the day before. Being outdoors, knowing someone nearby had attacked an innocent animal and that same person was likely among the crowd who stared at her, made for a long and worrisome day. But her neighbors, for better or for worse, looked to her as something of an example of strength. She had to live up to that.

"I'm the first Irish to cross that bridge, Joseph. I've lived off the Irish Road. I've started my own business, one that doesn't depend on the Red Road." She didn't know how to make him understand what that meant. "I saw something on the faces of my neighbors on Saturday. I don't mean fear or worry. I saw defeat, Joseph. Things've hardly begun to get bad, from all the whispers I've heard, and they already know they can't win."

Biddy had made her out as some kind of battle banner. But Katie hadn't understood until the céilí. The Irish needed at least one person, one instance in which they weren't the ones defeated.

Joseph moved to where she stood at the sink. "I don't want you giving up, Katie. I don't want the Irish losing the hope you have given them. But there is no way on God's green earth I am letting you walk out that door alone."

There was no mistaking his inflexible tone. Behind it Katie heard real concern.

"I suspect you know something you're not telling me."

He rolled his shoulders, taking a tense breath. "The mercantile has noticed a drop in sales. Johnson has tracked that to fewer Irish buying basic things like flour and sugar and—"

"Baking ingredients." Katie knew what Joseph was getting at. "So Mr.

Johnson is angry with *me* because he doesn't dare sell *you* those things at the 'Irish price,' but the Irish aren't buying because they can get their bread from me at a better price."

He nodded slowly, with emphasis. "And he is not happy about it."

"You think he'll come after me?" Her heart thudded.

"The fact that I cannot guarantee he won't is reason enough to ask you to wait until someone can go out with you."

He'd given her pause. But she didn't want the Irish to feel they'd lost already. She needed to make her deliveries on her usual schedule. "Tuesday is Biddy's laundry day, so she can't go about with me."

Joseph didn't grant her reprieve at that. "The O'Connors' youngest daughter, perhaps?"

"She is helping Tavish make preserves today."

He nodded. "So Tavish won't be available, either."

"No."

Joseph rubbed at his mouth and chin. "What about Finbarr? I realize he's only sixteen, but he would be one more person, one more set of eyes."

"You don't need him here?"

"I do. But I need him with you more."

Katie laid a hand on his arm. "Thank you for that, Joseph."

He set his hand on hers. "Just promise me you'll be careful. Make some kind of arrangements for your next deliveries."

They stood there a moment, his hand pressed to hers. "I am sorry so much about Hope Springs has disappointed you," he said.

"Not disappointed." She found she meant it. "Life is different here from what I expected, but I'm happy here. And I haven't been happy in a very long time."

He gave her fingers a squeeze before stepping away. To her surprise, she missed having him there. He didn't make her heart jump about in the way Tavish did. He didn't draw an immediate smile from her, nor fill her with warmth at the very sight of him. But she missed his company almost the moment he walked away.

Joseph took up her basket of bread. "Let's go track down Finbarr."

She followed him out, wondering all the while what her different re-actions to the men meant. Did Tavish tug at her more because she cared for him more? Perhaps. But then, what did she know of such things?

They reached the barn. Finbarr was inside. Joseph said nothing be-yond "Will you help Katie make her deliveries?" Finbarr agreed without a moment's hesitation.

Joseph handed the basket over to Finbarr. "Keep a weather eye out."

"I will." Finbarr was not fazed in the least by his employer's heavy tone. He carried her basket out of the barn.

"I thank you again for sending Finbarr with me," Katie said, staying back a moment.

"You're welcome." His tone was more than a touch distracted, though his attention seemed fully on her.

She stepped to the door.

"Katie?"

"Yes?"

He didn't move closer to her, but neither had he looked away. "I'm glad you've been happy here."

"Glad enough to let me stay on?" she asked.

"You know I can't do that, Katie."

Disappointment stung at her, but she hadn't truly expected any other answer. She nodded silently and slipped from the barn. She'd come to love his little girls, and she felt at home with his family despite the difficulties with the Red Road. She would miss that when her replacement arrived. But, she told herself, she wouldn't be far away. And living on the Irish Road would be a fine thing.

Finbarr walked companionably with her down the road, carrying her basket wherever she needed him to without a word of complaint. Her deliveries ran quickly and smoothly.

Things changed at the senior O'Connors' house. Mr. O'Connor stood in his yard talking with members of the Scott, O'Donaghue, and

Flynn families. Even from a distance, Katie could see they were not having a light, friendly chat.

"Trouble, it is abrewin'." Finbarr could certainly manage a deep, rolling brogue when he put his mind to it.

Katie approached the group warily.

"Seamus has a good point, O'Connor," Mr. Scott said as Katie drew within hearing distance. "We have turned the other cheek so many times the entire road's grown dizzy from spinning about. The Red Road crossed our bridge on Saturday. They could've killed your son's horse."

Mr. O'Connor didn't let that assertion stand. "Injured, perhaps. But I don't think the animal would have been killed."

"I, for one, am tired of making excuses for the Reds," Mr. Scott said. "*They* come after *us* every time. Every flare-up of this feud has been started by them."

"I'm asking only for patience," Mr. O'Connor said. "We're approaching winter too quickly to risk the kind of trouble Johnson gave us the last time we retaliated."

Mr. Flynn nodded along with him. "But how do we convince everyone their patience will pay off in the end?"

Mr. O'Connor pulled Katie up next to him. He kept an arm about her shoulders. "Because, lads, we finally have one of our own who has taken the Red Road on and come out victorious. She's shown them what we're capable of. She's shown them we've backbone enough to stand up to them. And, most important, she's done it without getting into this feud, without warring with the other half of this town."

All the men watched her. Katie would have found their attention unnerving but two months ago. In that moment she simply returned their gaze, not shrinking in the least. She'd become a part of this community. She'd found a way to help.

"If our Miss Katie can make a success of herself with the odds so stacked against her, surely the rest of us, with land of our own, with each other's support, can as well. And we can do it without going to war."

While doubt still hung in their faces, Katie also saw an easing of tensions. She suspected they didn't want to be neck deep in conflict again. Had the town ever managed to avoid that?

"Kelly'll make a fuss," O'Donaghue warned.

Katie gave them all her brightest smile. "Perhaps if I brought Seamus Kelly a fine berry tart, he'd be so terrible pleased, he'd forget all about marching on the Red Road."

Finbarr grinned at her, the breadbasket still in his arms. "I don't think Tavish's entire crop could make enough tarts to keep Seamus Kelly's temper in check."

Thank the heavens for Finbarr O'Connor. Chuckles rippled through the group.

Mrs. O'Connor waved to Katie from the porch. She pulled the O'Connors' loaf from the basket and hurried over.

"Good afternoon to you, Katie."

"And to you. I have your bread."

Mrs. O'Connor raised the loaf to her face and took a deep breath through her nose. "Delicious."

"Well, I'm not the town baker woman for nothing."

"Indeed not." Mrs. O'Connor gave her a fond look. "I don't believe anything about you being here is 'for nothing.'"

Katie glanced back at the men still deep in conversation up the path. "I am apparently here to save everybody. I can't say I'm entirely confident in that. Though I fully mean to do my best, I can't say it's a role I'm at all suited to."

Mrs. O'Connor leaned against the porch post, her eyes on the men as well. "The more important the task, the more likely it is to be accomplished by one who seems too small for the burden. Big men are not the only kind that can reap a harvest, Katie."

"Aye, but they make shorter work of it."

Mrs. O'Connor nodded sagely. "But if it's got badly, it'll go badly."

Katie felt a smile return to her face and her heart. "Are we to exchange old-country proverbs, now?"

For that she received a conspiratorial wink. "I know a great many of them, I assure you." She motioned Katie back toward the road. "Get on with you now. I know you've work enough to do. Let my husband talk down the tempers. You just keep showing our people what it means to keep your shoulders back and your head up."

Shoulders back and head up. Life hadn't entirely broken her yet. She could stand tall under this newest burden.

Before she'd taken so much as a single step off the porch, a shout pulled everyone's attention to the road.

Ian drove his wagon at a quick clip toward the spot where the men stood. "To town, Da!" he called out. "Quick, now."

"What's happened?" Mr. O'Connor hadn't moved, but his expression showed concern.

"A fire."

The words sent a chill down Katie's spine.

"Fire at the smithy's. Kelly's fit to tear the town to the ground searching for the one responsible."

"Reds." Mr. Scott's eyes hardened. "Has to be the Reds."

"We don't know that." But Mr. O'Connor seemed a bit suspicious himself.

Ian had reached the group. "While we're all standing here debating, Seamus is likely belting everyone in sight. Tavish is holding him back for the moment, but we all know that won't last."

The men climbed in the wagon and in a trice were rushing back up the road.

"Do you think the Reds set the fire?" Katie asked Mrs. O'Connor, still standing on the porch. She didn't like the idea of people going about setting things aflame.

"'Tis hard to say. Seamus Kelly's never had a fire get out of control before. But, on the other hand, a blacksmith is always at risk of such a thing happening. On yet another hand, the Red Road is plenty mad enough just now to do something hateful."

"That is a great many hands."

"Aye." Mrs. O'Connor nodded gravely. "And a great deal of trouble."

Finbarr came up the path to where they were speaking, still holding Katie's basket. He, too, looked troubled.

"Will Seamus Kelly really go about swinging his fists, even not knowing who might have set the fire?" Katie asked. "Not knowing if it was even done by anything other than bad luck?"

Mrs. O'Connor nodded slowly.

"That seems a foolish thing to do."

'Twas Finbarr who answered. "But Seamus Kelly is not one who's likely to die of wisdom."

Mrs. O'Connor gave him a half-hearted scold. Clearly she agreed. And more clearly, still, the lad was repeating what he'd heard said before.

"I'll walk with you to make the remainder of your deliveries," Mrs. O'Connor said. "I think it'd be best if Finbarr tells Joseph what's happened."

"Mr. Archer likely already knows," Finbarr said.

"Even so." Mrs. O'Connor gave her youngest son a pointed look. "'Tis the beginning of more troubles, and well we know it. It's best Joseph prepares himself."

Finbarr silently nodded. He set Katie's basket on the porch steps and hurried off.

Katie's heart had lodged itself clear in her shoes. *The beginning of more troubles.* If trying to burn down a man's business, the very means by which he fed his family, was the mere *beginning* of troubles, the feud was likely to grow bad indeed.

"Is this all my fault?" she asked, despite not entirely wanting to hear the answer.

"No." Mrs. O'Connor gave her an empathetic look. "This has been brewing for years. You're only the latest excuse."

"And, it seems, I'm to be the saving grace as well." They walked slowly down the path back to the road.

"We've put a great weight on you, haven't we?"

Quite a task they'd handed her. Katie's list of past failures sat heavy in her thoughts. She had let people down before. She'd fallen monumentally short of the mark.

She couldn't bear to cost these people so much.

Shoulders back. Head high. "I only hope I don't let you down."

"We've faith in you, Katie Macauley. You'll not disappoint a one of us."

Chapter Thirty-Five

"Why, Katie Macauley, what brings you round here?" Mrs. Claire asked the question with such an eagerly hopeful look.

Katie was instantly glad she'd chosen to visit on her way to the céilí. The dear woman had taken a spill the week before, and Katie worried about her. "I've brought your bread."

"Ah." Though Mrs. Claire tried to hide it, Katie saw the woman's face fall.

"If I'd not be bothering you," Katie quickly added, "I'd like to visit a moment."

"And why would a young lady with admirers waiting for her down the lane want to sit and chat with an old woman?"

Katie could hear the loneliness behind Mrs. Claire's words. "For one thing, I love hearing you talk of the old country, but you're never given a chance at the céilís. Too many people there who're fond of hearing their own selves speak."

Mrs. Claire smiled at that. "That's true as the day is long." She pulled the door open all the way. "Come in out of the wind, dear. I'll not turn away a visitor, especially one who's not coming out o' pity."

"Pity?" Katie offered a very overdone scoff as she stepped inside. "You're a customer. I'm here out of pure greed."

Mrs. Claire's laugh did Katie's heart good. Mrs. Claire looked pale and worn and older than she had before. Katie hated seeing it.

"I don't suppose you mean ever to tell me who it is that's paying for my bread three times a week." Mrs. Claire had been attempting to force the information from Katie from the first loaf she'd delivered.

"Not a chance of it." Katie set her fiddle case down near the door and looked about. "Shall I put your loaf by the stove?"

"Aye. That'll do." Mrs. Claire shuffled, cane in hand. She lowered herself into an old rocking chair. A cool breeze came in through the slightly open window, as did the not-too-distant sounds of the céilí.

Mrs. Claire hadn't a proper kitchen like the Archers but something of a lean-to attached at the far end of the house. Katie's heart sank at what she saw there. Dishes sat awaiting a good washing. The narrow table needed cleaning. 'Twas not the months of neglect she'd first come across at the Archer home, but rather the week Mrs. Claire had spent since her fall unable to see to her own housekeeping.

"Just set the loaf down wherever you find a spot," Mrs. Claire instructed from her chair by the window. "I'll not keep you longer than need be."

"Oh, I'm not in any hurry." Indeed, Katie meant to stay until she had things straightened a bit.

"You can't tell me you aren't anxious to spend the evening with Tavish, now."

"'Twould do him good to wonder why I'm not rushing to his side. The man doesn't exactly rush to mine, I'll have you know."

Mrs. Claire nodded as she rocked. "Far too sure of his welcome, I'll wager. He's never had trouble catching the lasses' eyes, you know."

"Oh. I know it well enough. Handsome and charming and quick with the sweet words. He knows just exactly how to make himself agreeable."

"Someday, though, some sweet colleen'll have him wrapped about her finger, and he'll not quite know how to win her over. She'll expect more than a twinkling eye and a roguish smile when they happen to be together." Mrs. Claire's smile spoke of fondness and humor. "He'll have to make quite an effort then."

Speaking of efforts, Katie needed to find a way of cleaning Mrs. Claire's home up a bit without offending the dear woman. Her eyes fell on a tin of Pratt and Montgomery Tea—anyone from Belfast would recognize the tin immediately—and an idea struck.

"How in heaven's name did you come across this?" She held the tin up for Mrs. Claire to see. "I've not seen Pratt and Montgomery Tea since leaving Ireland."

"M' daughter lives in Belfast. She sent me the tea for my last birthday, she did."

"A fine gift, that." Katie set the tin back but straightened a few things around it as she did. "Your daughter lives in Belfast, does she? In which part?"

Katie kept Mrs. Claire talking. She asked questions about her daughter and grandchildren. She even shared stories of her own time in Belfast. And she worked as they visited. She washed the dishes and cleared the table.

Just as Katie reached for the broom, a knock sounded at the door. "Who might that be?"

"'Tis Tavish. I can see him standing at the door." Mrs. Claire watched through the window. "He's waving to me. Do you think we should let him in?"

Katie found herself firmly in the mood for a bit of teasing. She crossed to the doorway and sent a grin in Mrs. Claire's direction. "Who are you knockin' on the door?" she asked in her most foreboding voice.

"Katie?" Tavish sounded surprised.

"You don't sound like a 'Katie' to me," she called back. "You sound like an unrepentant mischief maker."

Mrs. Claire's shoulders shook with silent laughter. The woman looked twenty years younger in that moment.

"If you don't let me in, dear," Tavish said, "I'll show you just how much mischief I can make."

Katie could see Mrs. Claire was enjoying this as much as she.

"I assure you, I'm quaking in my boots at *that* threat," Katie said through the door.

Tavish appeared at the open window in the next moment. He raised an eyebrow at Mrs. Claire sitting there. "I've a feeling you're encouraging her, Granny."

"I'm only agreein' with her. Takes some work to be afraid of a lad who calls himself 'Katie.'"

Tavish shook his head. "I'm beginning to think introducing the two of you was not the wisest thing I ever did."

Mrs. Claire exchanged a knowing look with Katie. "'Tis good when a man can admit he's not very bright."

Katie pressed the back of her hand to her mouth to hold back a laugh. Mrs. Claire didn't bother keeping her amusement hidden.

"The two of you together are trouble, and no denying it."

Katie moved to the window. "Good evening there, Mr. Katie."

He shook his head, smiling at her. "You gonna let me in, darlin'?"

"Keep calling me darlin' and I just might."

Tavish shifted so he looked directly through the window at her. "Open the door, Sweet Katie."

She shrugged and glanced at Mrs. Claire. "What say you? Should we let him in out of the wind? Or should we leave him there to ponder just how to sweeten us up a bit more?"

"I suppose we'd best let him in." Mrs. Claire sighed as if terribly put upon. "He's such a wee little thing, he's like to blow away with the slightest gust."

"And that would be a full tragedy, it would," Katie said dryly.

Tavish dropped his head into his hands. Katie and Mrs. Claire laughed.

"The door's not locked," Katie said. "Let your own self in."

In the next instant, Tavish stepped inside, eyeing them both warily. "Are the two of you through teasing me, then?"

"I make no promises," Katie answered.

Tavish leaned down and kissed Mrs. Claire on the cheek. "How is life treating you today, Granny?"

Mrs. Claire patted his face. "Better and better."

"Precisely how I'd feel if Katie were spending an evening with me." Tavish winked.

Katie felt her face flush.

Mrs. Claire began rocking again. "And how would you feel if she talked your ear off, hoping to distract you while she slyly set herself to cleaning your house?"

"I wasn't fooling you, then?" Katie should have known.

"'Twasn't yesterday I was born."

Katie moved back toward the kitchen. "I'll just sweep up, then, and not worry about finding a way to keep you from noticing."

"I shouldn't let you." Mrs. Claire shook her head. "But pride is only friend to a fool."

Katie took up the broom and set to work once more.

"Seems Katie and I are thinking alike," Tavish said to Mrs. Claire. "I stopped in to see if I could chop you some wood. Looks like rain again tonight, and the air might grow chill."

Mrs. Claire's shoulders drooped a bit. "Growing old is a hard thing, it is."

"Aye," Tavish said, "but 'tis a difficulty too many are denied the privilege of enduring."

That perked her up a bit. "Keep your philosophizin' to yourself, Tavish O'Connor, and get to work on that firewood."

He passed Katie on his way to the back door. He tipped a crooked smile at her. "And how have *you* been?"

She swept as she spoke. "Busy I've been. Busy and worn. But it's best to leave the bad tale where you found it, so I'll not stretch it far and wide."

"But you're well?" he pressed. "And no one's threatened you or made trouble?"

She shook her head. "No more than usual. I'm watched all the time. And the Red Road comes by the house often to ask Joseph how much longer I'll be overstepping my rightful boundary."

"And you're not leaving Joseph's property alone?"

"No." Though Katie rarely had reason to leave the Archer farm, she did, at times, feel as though she were imprisoned by its boundaries. There was some safety to be found there, but she was chafing under the limits of it. "Has anyone yet solved the mystery of that small fire at the blacksmith shop?"

Tavish leaned against the frame of the closed door in the makeshift kitchen. "It's impossible to tell if the fire was set intentionally or merely a bit of bad luck. Far too many of our countrymen are determined to believe it deliberate and to exact some form of revenge."

"And the Reds?" Katie could easily imagine how such a small thing could grow bigger than them all. Blame and vengeance rarely led to clear-headed decisions.

"None have admitted to anything, though they aren't exactly weeping over the damage to Seamus's establishment."

Katie paused in her sweeping, her mind too burdened for anything but thinking on their troubles. Hers was the only other Irish business. 'Twas no wonder they so desperately needed to see that she hadn't given up. If she and the smithy were both brought low, it would be a blow to the Irish confidence indeed.

"No more of this heavy talk, now," Tavish said. "Tonight's a céilí night. There'll only be smiles and light hearts this evening."

She tossed him a challenging look. "And who's to make certain of that, I'd like to know."

"Are you doubting the joy of my company, darlin'? I think you know full well that you shouldn't."

"Just how would I know that when I've had so little of it lately?"

He chuckled. "We'll remedy that tonight, sweetheart." And he slipped out.

"That is a man who knows just exactly how charming he is." Katie looked to Mrs. Claire. "Seems a dangerous thing to me."

"'Tis only dangerous if the man himself is dangerous." Mrs. Claire rocked slowly, her look a little more contented, if not entirely happy with the world. "Excepting my own sweet, departed husband, Tavish O'Connor is the very best of men."

Katie swept out the corners around the stove. She'd do as thorough a job as she could. "The very best, is he? And you're not a little partial to your grandson?"

"He's not my grandson."

Surprise stopped Katie on the spot. Not her grandson? "But he calls you Granny."

"He was engaged to my granddaughter Bridget before the fever took her."

Katie wondered why she'd not made the connection. Their last names were the same, after all. Then again, Tavish had never spoken to her of his late fiancée, so she really knew very few details about her. "I am sorry you lost your granddaughter."

"She and her brother and her parents—my son and his wife—and my dear husband all died within two days of each other."

Katie's heart ached at the thought of so much pain. How much she hurt at losing but one member of her family. This woman had lost five in a matter of days. She'd been even more alone in life than Katie.

"I'll tell you, I fully expected Tavish to cut the connection between us. But he still calls me his granny and treats me with such love and kindness as some don't receive even from their own kin."

For all his teasing, Tavish was proving himself a man of dependability and kindness. "Anyone can see how much he loves you."

"Perhaps I'm stepping beyond myself," Mrs. Claire said, "but I might say those same words to you, Katie."

The dustpan she held hit the floor with a clank.

Mrs. Claire laughed long and heartily. "You weren't expecting that, now were you?" She pressed a hand to her heart as she kept laughing and rocking. "And that there is the look of a woman plagued with uncertainty."

"I'm not plagued." She swept up the scattered dust. "A bit bothered, yes, but not plagued."

"Leave the floor be, Katie, and come sit with me a piece."

She pulled a spindle-legged chair up next to Mrs. Claire's rocker. "Is there something I can do for you other than the floors?"

Mrs. Claire patted her hand. "I do thank you for the work you've done, but just now I'm wanting company more than a clean house."

"Don't give me that pitiful face, you old schemer." Katie could have laughed at the dramatic look she was receiving. "It's not company you're wanting but a chance to tease me about Tavish."

"Perhaps a little." Mrs. Claire leaned a touch closer. "Mostly I want to know what it is you're uncertain about, your own feelings or his?"

Katie laid one arm over the back of her chair and turned to face Mrs. Claire a little more. "There was a time I'd not have believed a word he said to me. All he ever did was tease." Heavens, she'd not even liked him at first. "But I've come to know him better."

Mrs. Claire nodded. "And now when he tells you he cares, you believe him."

"Aye."

"Then it's your own feelings that you remain uncertain of?"

"No. I'm well on my way to being in love with him." Likely more than simply "on her way."

"But I can see you hold back." Mrs. Claire studied her. All at once her ponderous gaze filled with understanding. Her brows shot up, her mouth forming a small circle. "Aye, now that does make a great deal of sense." She nodded. "Joseph is a complication, is he not?"

Heavens, had she been so obvious? "I—"

"Don't go fretting, dear. I doubt anyone's pieced it together." Mrs. Claire's sharp gaze narrowed on her. "I can see you're trying to decide where your heart truly lies."

Katie nodded. "I do like them both. They're fine men and kind, and I enjoy their company. And Joseph's little girls—"

"You don't marry a man for his children, dear."

Marry? When had things moved to *that* point?

Mrs. Claire laughed deep and loud. "Frightened you a bit, did I?" She laughed all the more as she rocked back and forth. "You'll forgive an old woman for giving you advice after advice, but I'll tell you, sweet lass, both Joseph and Tavish are fine men, and you'd do well to give your heart to either one of them. But take time to sort it all out. An important decision should never be made in haste."

Tavish came inside in the next moment, his arms full of firewood. "There is a storm brewing outside, and no mistaking." He set a load down in the basket near the stove.

Katie couldn't look up at him. She'd been too tossed about by Mrs. Claire.

Tavish dropped the rest of his armful of wood at the fireplace. "How long has your back door been catching?"

"I'd say things've been sticking for some time now." Mrs. Claire gave Katie such a look of mischief. "And isn't that a terrible thing, Katie? To have so much that's *sticking?* Not moving in any useful direction. Terrible, terrible."

"Stop it," Katie muttered but found a smile creeping up from deep inside. She peeked over at Tavish. Did he have any idea his granny was teasing her about him?

About him and Joseph Archer. She really did need to straighten her heart out.

Tavish brushed dirt from the wood off his hands. "Would you mind if I come by on Monday morning and plane it properly?" Apparently he'd not noticed his granny making mischief.

"I'd be appreciative if you did what you could to straighten things out." Mrs. Claire actually wiggled her eyebrows at Katie.

Tavish finally seemed to catch the undercurrent. "Have I missed something?"

"A few of the windows stick too." Mrs. Claire suddenly took up his topic of conversation.

Tavish looked from one to the other but finally shook his head. "'Tis likely the change in weather. I'll check them all on Monday."

"That is very good of you, Tavish."

"'Good of me'?" His denial was humorously overblown. "I'm only after doing this so when you're dead, your ghost won't haunt me."

Mrs. Claire laughed, her sweet face wrinkling in the happiest of lines. How easily he pleased his granny, a woman who was not actually his kin. 'Twas little wonder Katie loved the man. His was a kind and giving heart.

"I don't know what that look is, Sweet Katie, but I like it."

She crossed to where he stood by the fireplace. He took her hand between his.

"You're a good man, Tavish O'Connor." Perhaps the best she'd ever known.

His smile turned amusedly doubtful. "Says the woman who sat with a vicious hatpin in her hand the entire first two hours she knew me."

"You noticed that, did you?"

"I noticed everything about you." He cupped her face with his hand. "I noticed you were scared half out of your mind." His thumb brushed her cheek. "That you listened to what we said, but pretended you didn't. That you had the deepest brown eyes I'd ever seen in all my life." His eyes crinkled at the corners as his smile grew. "And that you hated me on sight."

She *had* hated him. She'd thought him arrogant and untrustworthy and a man best avoided. How very wrong she'd been. Katie leaned against his shoulder. There was such immediate comfort in his nearness.

"Well, now." Tavish wrapped his arms around her. "This is a fine way to spend an evening."

She closed her eyes and committed the feeling of the moment to memory. His embrace was warm and gentle. And, heavens, he smelled good.

From her rocking chair Mrs. Claire called out, "Just in case either of you were wondering, I have me eyes closed firm and tight. So if you're wanting to undertake a fine bit o' kissing, you'll not have an audience to fret about."

She felt Tavish laugh. "Well then, Katie. How about a 'fine bit of kissing'?"

He raised her hand to his lips, putting her frayed cuffs right in her line of sight. She tried tucking her hand away, but Tavish didn't let go. He pressed his lips to the back of her hand, then smoothed her sleeve and cuff as though they were of the finest silk and lace.

"You'd be beautiful in anything, Katie. Don't be weighed down by it."

Katie leaned her cheek against his, pressing her hand to the other side of his face. She could hardly think for the pounding of her heart. "You are a good man, Tavish. Your granny was right on that score."

Tavish kissed her forehead, lingering over the gesture. Katie simply sighed. Mrs. Claire had been right on another score; she had, indeed, fallen in love with Tavish O'Connor.

The matter of Joseph Archer was another thing entirely.

Chapter Thirty-Six

Katie looked happier. Joseph didn't know what had changed in the past two weeks, but she smiled more. Worry remained in the back of her eyes but didn't weigh her down as it once had. Perhaps she hadn't heard about the shoves and insults some Irish and Reds had exchanged a few times since Seamus Kelly's fire. She would fret all the more if she had. He worried they had all put too much store by her bread-baking success in Hope Springs. She would likely think any setback would be disastrous for everyone.

She'd stopped asking about keeping her job, but he was certain she still thought about it.

Joseph hated that. He had already offered the position to a qualified candidate in Baltimore. He expected her acceptance to arrive any day, and the woman herself to follow shortly thereafter. But he knew Katie didn't have anywhere to go yet. He'd had to bite his tongue again and again to keep from giving in and saying she could stay.

Tavish came by now and then, talking with her in the kitchen. Though he felt like an idiot, Joseph couldn't keep himself away from the kitchen while Tavish was there. He knew he was acting out of pure jealousy, but Tavish had every advantage. Katie wasn't living under his roof.

He wasn't paying her salary. He didn't have to worry that the slightest show of interest would ripple as whispers and aspersions on her character.

Joseph couldn't make his own case so long as she was still his housekeeper. There was an ethical line there he simply couldn't cross, not to even mention the rumors that would start. But he wasn't about to sit back and let Tavish claim her entire regard by default.

He came in from the fields late in the afternoon almost three weeks after the Irish party he'd attended. No one had named names, but everyone knew the Red Road was responsible for cutting the tail of Tavish's horse. And though no one could be as certain as they were in the matter of the horse, Joseph fully suspected the blacksmith's fire was no accident. He hoped this round of feuding would prove different from those in the past, that tempers wouldn't flare to the point of widespread violence.

Biddy and Katie were sitting on the porch as they often did.

"Is this a ladies-only gathering, or am I allowed to join you?" Any of the O'Connors could have come up with something more clever than that. Joseph had never been particularly adept at casual conversation.

Katie looked up at him, a welcoming smile hovering on her lips. She couldn't be entirely indifferent and look at him that way. There had to be some degree of affection behind it.

"Come sit," Biddy instructed. "We're only gabbing."

He sat down on the porch steps, facing the yard and his giggling daughters. They had blossomed since Katie came. Even Emma ran and jumped and laughed like a little girl ought to. It was nothing short of a miracle.

Joseph was grateful to see them outside. "Should we ruin their fun by reminding them how soon the snow will come?"

Biddy shook her head immediately. "I am trying not to remind *myself* of that."

"Does Hope Springs get a great deal of snow, then?" Katie looked from Joseph to Biddy and back again.

Joseph laughed. *Does Hope Springs get snow?* He'd had no idea what snow really was before moving to Wyoming.

"We were snowed in for only four months last year," he said.

"What?" Her eyes grew wide. "In your houses?"

"No," Biddy answered. "Snowed in to the valley. Only a few weeks of that saw us unable to visit each other."

Katie's lips twisted in thought, an expression she wore often. Whether or not she realized it, Katie was a thinker. That was one of the first things that had drawn Joseph to her. She possessed a keen intellect, an absolute must in a woman.

"'Tis no wonder, then, the town is at each other's throats so often," she said. "I'll likely be climbing the walls by the end of the winter."

"You'll grow more accustomed to it with each passing year," Biddy said.

Katie gave her a half-smile. "So by my third or fourth winter, I'll not be the least surprised to see snow piled to the rooftops?"

Her third or fourth winter. Joseph liked that she'd begun talking of being in Hope Springs for years.

Katie's gaze shifted to him, tension pulling at her mouth and eyes. "Will the snows be bad enough I won't be able to make my deliveries? Begorra, Joseph." Her words came faster and higher. "In a few more weeks my bread will be all the income I'll have. If I can't even walk down the road—" A shaky breath cut off her words, evidence of the panic she'd kept all but hidden for weeks.

He missed the smile she'd worn only moments earlier. Tavish would tease her; Joseph had personally seen that happen many times in the last two weeks. He didn't have Tavish's ability in that area. But he could try.

"If only you had a friend with a sleigh." He shook his head, even rubbed his chin. Dramatics weren't really his style, but he tried. "That would be a very good thing, I would imagine. If only . . ."

Katie's tense shoulders eased noticeably. "You don't happen to have a sleigh, do you, Joseph Archer?"

He leaned back on his elbows, legs stretched out over the porch steps. "I do so happen."

"And you do consider me a friend, don't you?"

Friend? He cleared his throat. "'Friend' isn't the word I would use."

He could see his mistake instantly reflected in her face. "I didn't mean 'friend' exactly," she said. "I . . . I realize I'm only your servant. I didn't mean to sound overly familiar."

Joseph looked over at Biddy. "My words didn't sound the way I meant them to, did they?"

"I certainly hope not."

"Don't fret over it." Katie's lack of concern sounded forced. She stood. "I should probably . . . check on the stew I have in the oven."

Joseph reached up and took her hand. "Don't go, Katie."

He'd made a mess of what should have been a friendly conversation. He never had been good at such things. If she would only listen long enough for him to try to extricate his foot from his own mouth, he might undo the damage he'd done.

He tugged on her hand. She lowered herself onto the step beside him. Her look of uncertainty held a bit of fear.

"I truly didn't mean to presume upon your kindness," she said. "I know I only work here."

He might be obligated to keep the depth of his feelings hidden, but he would not allow her to think she was nothing to him but a servant.

He leaned in to speak to her. She looked ready to jump out of her skin. He felt much the same way but probably not, he was forced to admit to himself, for the same reason.

"I don't want you to think I don't like you." He lowered his voice. Biddy sat close and he didn't want to admit to even as little as he was about to if she could hear every word. "I do like you, Katie. We all do," he quickly added. "When you move on, we'll . . . we'll miss you."

He propped his elbows on the stair behind him. "Have you found a place to live yet, down the Irish Road?"

"I've asked around, and no one has a room to let or an oven they don't mind letting me use for hours on end, day after day. By the time I pay for a room and food to eat and the use of someone's oven, I'll be out of money. I simply don't have enough left after paying for baking supplies."

He held the words back. So many times he'd been on the verge of tossing out his own sanity and chances for winning her over and rashly offering to let her remain. Katie turned a bit and leaned against the railing. She didn't raise her eyes to his again.

He knew what she needed—the security of a place to stay in the long term—but he couldn't give it to her. She was miserable and worried. And he couldn't help. Sitting there, helpless, was not an option. Joseph stood and moved away.

"Uncle Tavish!" Mary O'Connor's squeal of delight filled the yard.

Katie looked up immediately. Joseph could have cursed, no matter that he was in mixed company. He had never before set himself to compete with Tavish O'Connor in anything remotely social. Tavish would win.

Seeing Katie light up at Tavish's arrival drove home a painful realization. Tavish had likely won already.

Tavish grabbed Mary about the waist and tossed her into the air, catching her easily in his arms. She giggled and grinned. He whispered a quick request in her ear before setting her back on the ground.

Mary ran over to the steps and spoke to her mother, using that air children adopt when reciting something they've committed to memory. "Uncle Tavish says that he'd be much obliged if you wandered off a bit so he could sit by Miss Katie and whisper sweet words to her."

Tavish grinned. Mary couldn't have delivered the message better. Biddy shot him such a look of scolding. 'Twas Katie's smile, though, that filled his vision. Heavens, but he'd missed her over the past few evenings.

A man knew he was truly caught when a woman filled his thoughts when they were apart.

"Seems to me I'd best wander about." Biddy's tone fell somewhere between a sigh and a laugh. She walked down off the porch, whispered, "Be good" to him, and made her way out to where the children were playing.

Tavish glanced once at Joseph before sitting down beside Katie. Something had happened before he arrived that had the usually calm Joseph Archer a bit on edge. An argument?

"Good day to you, Katie."

"Good day?" She gave him a scolding look. "I've not seen you since the céilí, and all you have to say to me is 'good day'?"

He took her hand. "Missed me, did you?"

"Perhaps."

She was not one to make things easy on him. He enjoyed that about her.

"Are you here to make up sweet to me?" she asked him. "Or have you come on business?"

Make up sweet to her? Katie would never have even joked about such a thing three months ago. "Both, Sweet Katie."

"What's your matter of business?"

"I should be offended you're more interested in my business than in getting sweet with me."

Katie bumped his shoulder with hers, smiling through her heightened color.

"My business." Tavish watched the children playing with Finbarr. Tavish sat close enough to Katie to touch shoulder to hip. Sitting with her that way was well worth losing time at his harvesting.

You're caught, and no denying it.

"I hadn't heard you found a place to live when the new housekeeper arrives."

Katie slumped against him, defeat heavy in her posture. He felt her shake her head even as she leaned it against his shoulder.

"I don't have anywhere to go," she whispered. "So much depends on me not failing, and I don't even have anywhere to live."

Anxiety crackled in every word. Poor Katie. He suspected she'd been holding back that panic for some time. The Irish had put a heavy burden on her.

He took her hand in his. "I think I know where you might find a room."

She went very still. "Do you, truly?"

Tavish rubbed his thumb along the back of her hand. She was tense yet. He hoped his idea would prove a good one.

"I haven't said anything to her yet," he said, "but would you consider staying with my granny?"

"I hadn't heard Mrs. Claire was looking for a boarder."

"She's not." He leaned against the railing at his back, looking more at her than at the commotion in the yard. The shift meant they were no longer touching, beyond her hand in his. He regretted that but wanted to put her mind at ease regarding her situation. If she could be calm and settled in town, he could move forward in earnest. "Her mind is sharp as ever. And despite her age and recent fall, she is in relatively good health. But I worry about her being alone during the winter." He worried about it a lot, in fact. "If she fell ill or was injured, no one would even know. She's not as able to care for herself as she once was."

She seemed uncertain. He didn't want her to feel forced into anything.

"You're very kind to my granny, but if living with her would drive you out of your mind—"

Katie shook her head immediately "I adore her. And I've wished so many times I could stop between deliveries and visit with her." Still, she looked hesitant. "Do you think she'd take me in?"

He could have rolled his eyes in exasperation with the woman. Did she have no idea how much everyone down the Irish Road adored her?

"Would she have you? You make yourself sound like a stray cat looking for a barn."

"I feel like one sometimes."

"You don't need to. And you'd truly be doing a favor for her. She'll have someone around to help her. She has an oven that is sitting cold and empty most of the time."

He saw a bit of hope enter Katie's eyes.

"I'll talk to Mrs. Claire, see if she's open to the idea of a boarder," Katie said.

Tavish didn't realize how worried he'd been about both of them until Katie took up his idea.

Katie looked up all of a sudden. Tavish did, as well. The children had grown quiet. The reason was immediately apparent. Jeremiah Johnson strode up the walk toward the house, dislike thick in his posture.

Joseph moved to the path, meeting Johnson there but a few paces from the steps. Tavish stood, intending to put a barrier between Johnson and Katie. There would be no repeat of Johnson's "filthy Irishwoman" insult.

"Good afternoon, Jeremiah." Joseph's greeting was not overflowing with enthusiasm, but he'd managed not to sound disgruntled. "What can I do for you?"

"I came regarding your order of yet another barrel of flour." Johnson's eyes swung in Katie's direction, hardening as his gaze settled there.

Tavish held his ground. Katie had risen, and in that moment shifted a bit behind him. She took hold of his arm, but didn't look at him. She kept a close eye on the new arrival. His Katie was no shrinking violet to crumble at a threat.

"Is there a problem with that order?" Joseph asked. "I assume you aren't out of flour."

Johnson shook his head. "But I think this is the last barrel I'll be able to sell you at the current price." No one could miss the warning in his tone.

Katie's grip on his arm tightened. Tavish knew the flour was for Katie and that Johnson was actually coming after her.

"You intend to cheat me?" Joseph Archer could sound every inch the steely man of business at times. He did in that moment.

Johnson wasn't intimidated. "The Irish pay a certain price, Joseph. They always have."

"I am not Irish."

Johnson's gaze slid contemptuously over them all. "I'd say you are the only one here who isn't."

Tavish looked over at Katie. Mr. Johnson clearly unnerved her. His brave Irish rose was closing up. He slipped an arm around her middle and pulled her up against his side.

"I know perfectly well, Joseph, that you are buying this flour for her." Johnson pointed his chin in Katie's direction. "She is trying to put me out of business. I won't stand for it."

"Miss Macauley is selling bread," Joseph said. "There is nothing in that to threaten you."

"The Irish aren't buying flour, Joseph. I cannot tell you the last time any of them bought sugar. She is undercutting me. I will not stand for it. I will not."

"I am only undercutting because *he* is overcharging," Katie whispered urgently.

"I know, darling, I know." Tavish was itching to jump into the fray. He had more than a few things to say to the man. But his more rational side kept him still. An argument from an Irishman would only make Johnson more angry. Joseph was more likely to be successful.

"Don't start this, Jeremiah," Joseph said. "We all know where this will go."

"I hope y'all do know." Again he eyed Katie and Tavish, even Biddy and her children. "We've danced this dance before. You Irish decide to throw your weight around. But in the end, you are always sorry for it."

"What does he mean by that?" Katie whispered.

He leaned in and lowered his voice. "In ten years of feuding, the Irish have never truly claimed a victory."

"Not even once?"

He shook his head.

A firmness entered Katie's expression. "We won't lose this time," she said. "He can rail against me all he wants, for years and years even, but he won't stop me."

Tavish held her tighter. *Years and years.* He liked the sound of that.

"Might I make a suggestion?" Joseph addressed the belligerent shopkeeper. "Flour will not put you out of business. You know it will not. But if you start this again, if you start punishing half this town with prices and restrictions, this will spiral. And it will not be only the Irish who suffer."

Johnson set his chin at a determined and angry angle. "Perhaps not. But they will be the ones who concede defeat. They always are."

Chapter Thirty-Seven

Katie's price for flour didn't increase. She asked Joseph how he'd managed to talk Mr. Johnson around, but he simply told her not to worry over it. She would have pressed the issue, if she weren't so ridiculously grateful for whatever he'd done. The man had earned the right to be left in peace. Without his intervention, she'd have been forced to give up her business.

She stepped out of the house late in the day nearly a week after Mr. Johnson's visit. She'd fully intended to call on Mrs. Claire sooner, but each time she set out, she turned back. Nothing about Mrs. Claire prevented the visit. 'Twas the Red Road. She had not once gone outside since Mr. Johnson's warning without finding at least one person standing out on the road, watching her. Gone were the occasional staring passersby. The Red Road seemed to have formed a permanent patrol.

She wasn't actually fearful for her safety, but she was uncomfortable beyond expressing. A man and woman stood just to the Red side of the fork in the road as Katie stepped out from behind the house. She didn't know their names, a sure sign they weren't Irish. Over the months she'd been in Hope Springs, Katie had met and developed a friendship with every family down the Irish Road. They'd embraced her like family.

The Red Road couple watched every step she took all the way to the bridge. She hadn't mentioned to Joseph the increase in people.

Her watchers always disappeared by the time he came in from the fields. They never came any closer than the road. Should Mrs. Claire be willing to take her in, Katie would be gone from the Archers' home just as soon as her replacement arrived. That, she'd been told by both Joseph and Tavish, would calm the Red Road considerably.

Even a full half-mile past the bridge, after the couple couldn't possibly still see her, Katie felt their eyes on her back. Every move she made was tracked. The Red Road wanted her safely tucked away among the Irish. The Irish had set their national pride and hopes for the future on her success. The tension was wearing on her.

She knocked at Mrs. Claire's door and was grateful she was able to open the door quickly. That boded well for Mrs. Claire's health.

"You seem to be walking better than you were," Katie said, seeing Mrs. Claire move about more spryly.

"Aye. I've not a foot in the grave yet, now."

Katie set the sweet rolls she'd brought near the cold stove. What had Mrs. Claire eaten that evening if not the tiniest bit of warmth remained in the stove? Though she'd not make the argument out loud, Katie could see Mrs. Claire needed her nearly as much as the Archers had when she'd first come. If only she didn't need to return to the Archers' so quickly that evening.

"I cannot stay long," Katie said, truly regretting the fact. "I need to set out my things for tomorrow's baking."

"I hope that means your business is doing well."

Katie nodded. "It is beginning to." How to approach her need for lodging without making Mrs. Claire feel like a charity case? Katie didn't think that of her but knew a person's pride often took a beating during times of need.

"'Tis something of a miracle," Mrs. Claire said. "It seems the only success the Irish have had here is the blacksmith. But without the Red Road being customers there, it'd fail. Even Tavish's berries depend on customers all over the territory. You're the only one who's made a success of her business exclusively among the Irish here in town. It's proof, I think, that we could thrive here."

"If not for the feuding, I'd say there's hardly another place on earth where we'd be more likely to blossom than here." Katie sat on the spindle-backed chair near the fireplace. "We have land and water and each other. I think we can make this work so long as we don't give up."

Mrs. Claire rocked back and forth, watching her. "And you don't mean to give up, do you?"

"Absolutely not." She made the declaration boldly, but she had her share of doubts. "Though I'll confess to you I worry over it something fierce. I have to make this bakery a roarin' success, or all me Irish neighbors'll simply decide they're in a sinkin' ship."

"Broadening the brogue, are you? That there's a sure sign you're upset."

She could smile a bit at that. "Joseph told me the same thing once. Apparently he knows I'm most upset when he can't understand a word I say."

"I've a feeling you're going to miss him when you move out of that house."

Katie nodded. "I'll miss them all." She would miss the girls dancing in her room while she played her fiddle.

Mrs. Claire gave her a searching look. "You'll miss them as a whole and not him in particular?"

An ache settled on Katie's heart. She would miss Joseph particularly. She would miss her conversations with him in the mornings as he drank his coffee and ate his midday meal. There would be no more quiet evenings spent gabbing about their days or talking through their troubles. She would miss that quite a lot, actually. But staying, she knew, would only make more trouble for everyone.

"What'll I do, Mrs. Claire, if things fall apart? Joseph's managed to keep my costs down, but I can't expect him to do that forever. Mr. Johnson is angry over losing business. He likely won't endure that long. A few raised prices or refusing to sell me what I need, and he'd stop me in my tracks."

Mrs. Claire didn't lose her air of calm serenity. Katie appreciated it in that moment. She needed someone she could talk to who wouldn't panic.

"For starters, Katie, you'd best call me Granny, as Mrs. Claire feels far too strange to my ear."

"Everyone calls you Mrs. Claire."

She shook her head. "But it feels wrong coming from you."

Katie pressed her lips together and pushed back an unexpected tear. She'd never known either of her own grandmothers. Katie didn't realize how large a void that had left in her life until that moment.

"You'd truly like me to call you Granny?"

Mrs. Claire nodded.

Warmth wrapped around Katie's heart. "I believe I can do that."

"As to your business"—Granny wasn't swayed in the slightest from the topic at hand—"there's no point greeting the devil 'til he's knocking at your door. That devil down at the mercantile might very well crush your bakery out of existence, but until that happens, I expect you not to give up."

"But if I fail, everyone'll give up."

"No, Katie." Granny stopped her rocking and leaned forward, capturing Katie's gaze with a steady, pointed one. "They will only give up if you do. We've tried and failed before. We're not afraid of failing. But if you'll keep fighting, so will they."

"I'm trying to keep going on," Katie said. "But there are so many what-ifs."

Granny sighed and leaned back in her rocker once more. "Aren't there always? I'd imagine among those unanswered questions is just what you'll do when Joseph brings to town his fancy new housekeeper."

"Indeed." Katie hadn't expected her to address so directly the very topic she'd meant to bring up subtly herself. Tavish had asked her to approach it carefully, to make certain his beloved granny didn't feel like they all felt sorry for her.

"Seems to me," Granny continued, "you need someone with extra room and an oven that's not being used all hours of the day. Someone down the Irish Road so you've some flexibility in your comings and goings and so our hot-tempered Red Road neighbors won't feel they're being invaded."

A twinkle of devilment shown in the woman's eye.

"Seems to me as well." Katie let her suspicions show.

"And seems to me further if that same someone were an old woman unable to climb the ladder to her own loft or see to much of a meal for herself, she'd be right happy to have you living with her and filling her house with the smell of fresh-baked bread."

Katie pointed a finger at her new granny. "I'm suspecting you've been plotting."

"'Twould be a further fine thing if that old helpless woman lived but a short walk across and up the road from a certain blue-eyed Irishman."

"Old and helpless, are you? Mischievous and unrepentant, more like."

"And is that a trait you look for in a potential landlady?" Granny was clearly enjoying herself.

Katie quickly got into the spirit of it. She rose from her seat and paced about, making quite a show of thinking through the situation. "I've lived under unrepentant landowners, though malicious seems a better word for them than mischievous."

"Aye. Aye." Granny nodded as she rocked.

"And you being old and helpless will make nipping off with your valuables a great deal easier." Katie spun to face her. "I do believe you've talked me into it."

"Just how long do I have before I need to hide the valuables—that is, how long before you'd be moving in?" Granny Claire acted flustered over her seeming slip, but the twinkle remained in her eyes. She would be a great deal of fun to share a house with.

"Just as soon as the Archers' new housekeeper has come. That might be a couple weeks yet. Likely longer. I'm not entirely certain."

"That'll do fine. Whenever you need a roof, you just bring yourself by."

A feeling of peace Katie hadn't known in three months settled over her. For once her future was not entirely mired in uncertainty. "And how much would you be wanting for rent?"

Granny waved a dismissive hand. "None of that. We're family now, you and I."

"But will you still think that a year or two from now when I'm living here for free and taking up space in your house?" Katie teased.

The dear woman shook her head. "Perhaps in five or ten years I'll start demanding a king's ransom from you. But not until then."

"Fair enough."

"And with you here, I suspect Tavish'll come visiting more often," Mrs. Claire added. "That'll be a treat. And I'll enjoy getting to know that handsome Joseph Archer a touch better as well."

"Joseph?"

"Oh, he'll be by, and don't you doubt it."

"So you're happy to keep me here in exchange for having handsome men hanging about the place?" Katie clicked her tongue. "Seems to me you're just using me. Hoping to find yourself a beau of your own, you are."

Granny laughed, her face wrinkling happily. "I'm hoping for something else as well, if you go to that of it."

"What is it you're wanting? I'd happily do anything for you."

"Promise you'll sit with me now and then and speak to me of Ireland." Such loneliness filled her eyes in that moment. Katie's heart ached to see it. "I haven't seen m' homeland in twenty-five years, but you were there only two years ago. I want to remember it, to go back there in my thoughts."

"Of course." Katie took her hand. "I miss Ireland myself."

"'Twill be a far finer winter having you here, Katie." Her thin hand squeezed Katie's. "I've spent the last four since my family died dreaming of Ireland all alone in this quiet house. I would sit here on my own and wish I could go back."

"We'll both of us enjoy talking of Ireland," Katie said, squeezing the dear woman's hand. "'Twill be something of a journey in itself. I'll tell you of the places I've lived, and you can tell me of the Ireland you knew."

Granny patted Katie's cheek as lovingly as she always did Tavish's. "'Tis glad I am that you'll be staying with me. A comfort and a friend you'll be."

The words remained with her as Katie walked back to the Archers'. Whether or not she stayed in a place or moved on had never been helpful nor important to anyone else. Being needed and wanted and useful felt good. More than good, in fact. Katie hadn't felt so peaceful since she was a tiny child.

That no one stood guard watching the Archer home as Katie walked back told her as nothing else could that Joseph had come in from the fields already.

She stepped inside the house and smiled broadly at the scene that met her eyes. Ivy sat on the table, loudly explaining something to Tavish, who was sitting on a chair listening with an overwhelmed look. Joseph sat exactly opposite him, talking to Emma about a book she held in her hands. Ivy and Joseph's voices competed to be heard over each other.

'Twas a lovely bit of chaos. Standing in the doorway watching it, Katie felt grateful she didn't have to leave it behind just yet. Mrs. Claire's home would be very quiet compared to the joyful laughter of the girls.

Tavish noticed her standing there in the next moment. His look of pleading made her laugh, pulling everyone's attention to her.

"Good evening, everyone. Are you having a party and didn't invite me?"

Tavish leaned back in his chair. "We have been playing with dolls, Katie. You missed all the fun."

"*You* have been playing with dolls?"

He nodded slowly and with emphasis. Apparently he'd been quite horribly tortured.

She pulled the kitchen door closed behind her and came fully inside. "I have played dolls with Ivy myself. She is the very best of playmates."

Ivy smiled broadly at the praise. She was not, however, the sister who generally needed to hear it. Katie went around to the side of the table where Emma sat with her father.

"Good evening to you, Emma." She gave the girl's shoulders a friendly squeeze.

"My new book has arrived." Emma held a leather-bound volume up for Katie to see. Lovely golden letters shone on the cover. "Isn't it beautiful?"

"Very." Katie brushed a finger along the book's surface. "What is the book called?"

Emma read each word slowly with the occasional stumble. "*Stories of Ireland and Her Four Provinces.*"

"Stories of *Ireland?*" Katie was full astonished. She looked to Joseph, wondering just what had inspired such a selection.

"Emma wished to learn more about where you come from," Joseph explained.

Katie gave Emma a hug. "What a sweet, sweet girl you are." She pulled back enough to smile at her and receive a smile in return.

"May I read them to you?"

"I would love for you to." Katie pressed a kiss to the top of Emma's head.

"No reading just now, Emma," Joseph said. "You and Ivy need to wash up for dinner."

"Yes, Papa." But Emma dragged her feet.

"You as well, Ivy." Joseph motioned his youngest daughter to the doorway.

The girls left, but not without protest and slow, lingering footsteps. Joseph followed them out. He helped them wash up every night.

Katie heard Tavish's footsteps as he approached the spot where she stood. She did not, however, expect him to wrap his arms about her, holding her tenderly.

"You're very affectionate this evening." She rested her arms on his.

"I sat here waiting for you to return and realized how much I've missed you."

She adored hearing that. Still, she opted to tease him rather than let him know as much. "Missed me, did you? Could it be you're feeling a bit jealous that I spent a good deal of time with your granny instead of with you?"

A wry smile spread slowly across his face. "I am not at all jealous of that."

"Not jealous 'of that'? Am I to assume you're jealous of something else, then?" she teased.

"I'll not admit to any more than I already have."

"But you've not admitted to anything."

Tavish bent down enough to whisper, "I think I have, Sweet Katie."

He took one of her hands in his and, in a flourish, spun her out of his embrace. Katie nearly giggled like a schoolgirl. Tavish grinned like the mischief maker she knew him to be.

"You've plenty of work to do tonight," he said. "Why don't you see to it, and I'll gather up Ivy's dolls?"

She accepted the offer, knowing she had far too much to do, especially considering how little sleep she'd had the past few nights trying to keep up with her work and her baking, as well as worrying over her prices and her neighbors. As she began her meal preparations, she talked with him.

"First you play with the dolls and then you willingly pick them up. I'm beginning to suspect you're a touch too good to be true, Tavish O'Connor."

He winked at her as he set the dolls in a pile on the work table. "Just keep reminding yourself of that."

Katie set to chopping vegetables. "Have you finished harvesting your berries?"

"Nearly. And then I'll be spending days on end with the women of my family canning preserves." He offered a dramatic shudder.

Katie set a hand on one hip, pointing her chopping knife in his direction as though she'd just had a tremendous insight. "Perhaps if you're particularly lucky, they'll play dolls with you as well."

He shook his head. "You shouldn't goad a man on that way, Katie."

She dumped the vegetables into a strainer and moved to the sink to rinse them. "Don't tell me you aren't equal to a little teasing?"

"Oh, I favor it to be sure." He walked slowly in her direction, gaze firmly set on her, his eyes capturing hers. "But, you see, m' father has a theory, he does, about just why a woman plagues a man that way."

He stopped directly in front of her where she stood at the sink facing him. Her heart began pounding, her lungs tight with tension.

"What is this theory of his?"

"That a woman who pricks at a man does so"—he set his hands on the sink's edge on each side of her—"because she's begging to be kissed, and to be kissed well and good."

Kissed? Katie could hardly breathe, let alone anything beyond. She'd been near dying for him to properly kiss her for weeks, but he'd never done more than place a kiss on her hand or, if she were particularly lucky, on her forehead or cheek. The man was driving her out of her mind.

"And are you a believer in this theory, as well?" The words only just came out whole.

He nodded and leaned in closer. She could feel each of his breaths against her lips. There was no contact between them, not so much as a brushing of hands.

Katie held herself perfectly still, both wishing for him to remain as close as he was and unnerved by his nearness.

"But you see, Katie, I've another theory as well." Each word brought his mouth achingly closer to hers. "A first kiss isn't something that ought to be begged for. 'Tis something that comes from a place deeper than that."

The slightest movement would press their lips together. Yet, Katie was frozen. She couldn't think, couldn't move, could barely breathe.

"And," Tavish whispered, "that first kiss shouldn't happen in another man's kitchen."

He lingered there but a moment before stepping back. Even with the added distance, Katie felt ready to burst. For him to come so close to kissing her only to pull away again was nothing short of torture.

Joseph returned in the next moment. She was happy to see him, as always, yet resented him being there at the same time. His gaze moved from her to Tavish before falling away all together.

"The girls will be down in a few more moments," he said. "I thought you might like to see this before they return."

He held out a letter to her.

"For me?"

Joseph nodded. "From a 'Mrs. Mary Macauley' in Belfast."

Katie was certain her heart stopped in that moment. "Mama." She hadn't heard from her mother in nearly a year, though she'd sent her new address to her parents before leaving Baltimore.

She took the letter and brushed her fingers along the tidy letters. Katie had learned to recognize the handwriting of her parents' priest the way one recognizes a loved one's voice.

Excitement warred with fear in her as it always did when a letter arrived from home. With each letter she received—there'd only been six in eighteen years—she would tell herself *this* letter would surely hold some words of tenderness. She would convince herself they'd written to say they loved her in spite of everything, or that she might come home even without the money to buy back the farm or place a proper headstone at

Eimear's grave. The letter she would receive would heal wounds so deep no one saw them but Katie herself.

She told herself with each letter that she'd find in it what she so desperately needed, but it was never the case. Mother only ever wrote of her brothers, briefly mentioned that Father worked hard as always, and little else. With each letter, Katie's heart broke all over again.

She turned to Tavish. "Would you read it to me?"

"Certainly." He took the envelope from her and broke the seal.

Katie swallowed against the thickness in her throat.

Tavish must have sensed her sudden, painful tension. He took one of her hands in his, squeezing it a moment before unfolding the letter.

"'My dear Katie,'" he read, "'I hope this letter reaches you in your new home. I'm pleased to hear you've found a position of such importance. To be a housekeeper is a fine thing.'"

Katie smiled to herself. 'Twas the closest either of her parents had come to saying they were proud of her.

Tavish kept reading. "'I've some bad news, Katie.'"

Bad news. Katie's breath caught in her lungs. *Bad news.*

"'Your father is ill. We've had the doctor in, and he fears 'tis a fatal ailment.'"

Pain stung Katie's throat. Panic surged through her. The word *fatal* repeated again and again in her mind.

"'He'll likely not live out the year, Katie. Your brothers mean to come and say their farewells. I don't know if you're able to come, but I wanted you to know so you can come if you'd like.'"

Father is dying. He's dying. Tears welled in her eyes as the thought repeated in her mind. She didn't have the money she needed yet. She couldn't give him his land. But he was dying. That meant she was too late. She couldn't give him what she owed him. She couldn't make amends.

She was too late.

"'I wish I had better things to tell you, Katie,'" Tavish continued. "'I wish so many things had gone differently in our lives.' And it is signed, 'Mother.'"

Tavish looked up at her with such compassion in his eyes. The emotion she barely held back rushed out. Tears fell unchecked. Her breath shuddered out.

"Katie—" He reached for her hand again, but she pulled back.

She rose so quickly her chair toppled to the ground. She shook her head, unable and unwilling to accept what she'd heard. With a sob, she spun and ran out the back door, straight for her clump of trees.

Her father was dying, and she might never have a chance to tell him she was sorry for all she'd done. In that moment, her very world was crashing down around her.

Chapter Thirty-Eight

Father is dying. Katie pressed her hand to her mouth, trying in vain to hold back her sobs. Her father. Her papa.

Katie couldn't stop the memories. No amount of pulling her thoughts kept them from going directly back to that time so long ago, before their eviction, before Eimear's death, before the loneliness of a cold floor to lie on under a table in Derry.

William and Danny and Brennan had all left for Manchester. Each departure had kept the family from ruin. Fewer mouths to feed meant their meager provisions stretched further, leaving more money to pay their rent. 'Twas how they'd managed to survive five years of The Hunger without a death and without losing their home. No one had been condemned to the workhouse. The boys' leaving was necessary, but in the end it wasn't enough.

Even at only eight years old she'd heard of the factories in the north of England. She'd heard of the enormous machines that filled wide, tall rooms. She'd known of the noise they made, of thick air that caught in the lungs, of workers growing ill and sickly.

She knew from Brennan, the last to leave, that the smallest of children in the factories were sent inside those machines when they stopped working. The children climbed inside with tools, assigned the task of unstopping the gears so the great monsters would run again. Those who were swift could slip out again before the great cogs and wheels crushed their tiny hands and arms and bodies.

Father sat Katie down at the start of winter the year she was eight years old to tell her he meant to send her to Manchester with her brothers. All she could think of was crawling into the belly of a dark, grinding machine, of being crushed, maimed, killed. She'd felt her lungs tighten at the thought of air so full of weaving waste that it seemed to be a fog indoors. She quaked at the picture that had long since formed in her mind of what the heartless, cold factories must have been like.

"Please don't send me there, Father," she'd pleaded. "Please don't send me."

"It isn't happy this makes me," he'd said. "And it's no pleasure I take from sending you away. But, Katie child, if you stay, there'll not be enough food for your sister and yourself both. There'll not be enough money for buying more nor paying our rents. You must be thinking on that, of what must be done to help everyone."

She'd begged for days on end. He told her clearly again and again that if she stayed with them in Ireland, there'd not be enough money or food for them all. The Famine had begun to wane but hadn't yet released its grip on the country. Her family had suffered much and continued to live daily in want and a breath away from disaster.

Katie halted her walk along the riverbank. She pushed air in and out of her lungs. Even breathing hurt. These were not easy memories. She looked over Joseph's fields and the abundance there. Three months in Wyoming had shown her how very hard the farmers worked for their crops. The rains were few; the soil was hard. Yet, the fields were healthy.

The sight kept her memories flowing as swift as the river she stood beside. The fields in Ireland those years ago had grown every bit as strong and lush as these, more so, even. There had been grains and crops in abundance, all of which had been harvested and gathered and shipped out of Ireland whilst the people starved to death by the millions.

Dark times, they'd been. Dark and desperate.

She could only just see the Archer home so far had she walked. Turning back seemed wise. 'Twouldn't do to wander so far afield she couldn't find her way home.

Now why was it that thought brought a lump of sadness to her throat? Cornagillagh was still home in her heart, but so was Hope Springs. It had become home, and the people there were like family.

"You disappoint me, Katie. You full disappoint me." Of all the things her father had ever said to her, those were the words she heard most often in her thoughts.

He'd spoken that reprimand as they dug about looking for any praties yet left in the ground, hoping to find some that were edible. Father had held up a potato obviously taken by the blight and reminded her again, in terms that left no room for argument, that they hadn't food enough for all four of them.

"You know Eimear is sickly. She was born in the midst of this Hunger, and she's never been strong. She'll not survive long if the food runs out, more especially without protection from the cold. Leaving home is a sacrifice for you, I know it. But you must think of her. She'll die if you stay. She'll die, Katie."

But Katie had been entirely certain she'd die herself if she went to the factories; she'd be crushed to death inside an enormous machine. If one of them had to die, Katie didn't want that someone to be her. So she'd shaken her head quite firmly and told him again. "I don't want to go, and I won't unless you make me. Not unless you tie me up and toss me on the boat screaming all the way. I'll not go."

Father's expression hardened. His shoulders grew tense beneath his ragged coat. "You disappoint me, Katie. You full disappoint me."

The passage of more than eighteen years hadn't dimmed the pain of that moment. Katie looked out at the silhouette of the distant mountains but saw in her mind that pitiful plot of land with its rotten potatoes. She saw her father's disheartened face.

She brushed at her wet cheeks with the palm of her hand. Her thoughts didn't stray far from those weeks of arguing with her father. That was the beginning of the darkest time of her life. She'd discovered a selfish part of herself she could only look back on with shame and regret. She'd worked hard to overcome that failing in the years since. Every wish and want she'd had from that time forward came up against rigorous evaluation. She hadn't so much as purchased thread for mending without asking herself if she did so out of selfishness or pride.

She'd lived her whole life attempting to clear her heart of her father's disappointment in her. How she wanted him to know she had become a better person, for him to tell her he was no longer disappointed in her.

She wanted that so badly it ached inside her. But he was dying. Her father was dying.

"Katie?"

Even in her distraction, she instantly knew the sound of Tavish's voice. Slowly she let her thoughts return to the present and focus once more. She'd reached the clump of trees where she often went to play her music and think. Tavish stood at the river's edge, watching her.

Katie swiped the tears from her eyes.

She fully intended to offer a simple hello. But what emerged was, "My father's dying, Tavish." Her voice broke with the quiet words.

"I know, darlin'." He stepped closer to her. "And I'm sorry."

"I was supposed to fix things with him. I was supposed to make things right. But I've run out of time."

Tavish stepped around her so they stood facing one another. "Your mother seems to think you'd have enough time to get there."

Katie shook her head. "But he won't want me there. Not yet."

"Katie." He cupped her face with his hand. "Of course he would want you there. You're his daughter."

"I have a debt I need to pay, a terribly heavy debt. He'd not want me back until I pay it."

"You owe him money?"

She turned to face the water, her heart tearing inside. "I need to buy back his land, Tavish. The land he lost in The Famine. I can't face him again until I can give him back his land."

"A lot of people lost land in The Hunger," Tavish said. "He'd not blame *you* for that."

"No. It was *my* fault. It was entirely my fault."

He only sounded more confused. "What was your fault? I don't understand."

She felt torn between wanting him to know and fearing what he'd think of her if he had the whole truth. Perhaps losing his regard was part of her penance.

"I've done some things I'm not proud of, things I've not told to another soul."

"You told me about your father's fiddle. Surely you can trust me with this, as well."

Katie wrapped her arms about herself. "This is different. You'll hate me when you hear what I've done. You'll walk away from me and never look back."

He set his hands on her shoulders from behind. "I never would, Katie."

She stepped away. In her tension and regret and guilt, his touch was nearly unbearable.

"Trust me this far. See if I can't bear some of this burden with you."

Katie looked back at him, uncertain. 'Twas almost as if the words came to her mind fully formed. She needed to tell him. If he despised her for her past, she'd know her guilt had not yet been washed away.

He held a hand out to her. "Trust me, Katie? Please?"

She'd told him of stealing her father's fiddle, and he'd not scolded nor condemned her. If she could trust anyone with the rest of her story, she could trust him.

She took his hand and allowed him to lead her to the canopy of trees. They sat side by side on the cool grass.

She took a moment to collect her thoughts and calm her nerves. "When first we met," she said at last, "I told you of my older brothers."

He nodded.

"I didn't tell you I had a sister."

"No, you didn't. You said you only had older brothers. You were very specific about that."

Katie dropped her gaze to her hands, her fingers fussing with each other. "I lied," she whispered. "I've been lyin' about her for years."

Tavish's silence didn't bode well for the much larger confession she had yet to make.

She pressed on, knowing the tale needed to be told regardless of the outcome. "Eimear was born during the earliest years of The Famine. She was always small and frail. My parents worried over her a great deal, spending what little money we had keeping her fed as much as they could. Each of my brothers left home for Manchester and jobs in the factories there in order to save the family the cost of feeding them, allowing more to be spent keeping Eimear alive."

"Aye," Tavish said quietly, "such things happened a lot during The Bad Times."

Katie nodded. "It wasn't enough. The praties were rotting in the ground again, and years of scarcity had driven high the price of what little food could be bought. The family either needed fewer mouths or more money, and we all knew we'd never manage the latter."

She clasped her hands tightly, pushing herself on. "There was nothing for it but to send me to Manchester as well, only I didn't want to go. I was afraid. Afraid of being killed in the factories, of growing ill as I heard so many did. I was frightened of being away from my family, away from Ireland. I couldn't imagine being happy anywhere but at home."

"I think that is understandable." Tavish spoke hesitantly, as if he could sense the history was growing worse.

"I refused to go," Katie said. "I argued over and over and over with my father. He'd have to force me to go, I said. He'd need to drag me there,

I said. He told me again and again, in words I understood plainly, that if I stayed, the food would run out and the money would run out. I'd seen us come close before with my brothers. And I'd watched other families we knew lose their homes. I knew people who'd died of hunger because their food ran out. I understood exactly what he meant."

For a moment her thoughts were filled with the memory of sunken eyes and swollen bellies, of tiny frames shrunken to nothing but bones. How well she'd known the fate of those left to starve.

"If I stayed, we'd be destitute. There'd be no chance of payin' rent; we'd lose our home and land. Without food, we'd suffer greatly. But Eimear wouldn't merely be miserable, she'd die. She was too frail to survive such suffering. I knew that. I knew it as surely as I knew the sun rose in the east every morning.

"A good-hearted child would have thought of her sister first, would have endured the worry and the work and the separation for the sake of her sister's life." She shook her head in firm disappointment with herself. "I knew just the arguments that would pierce my father's heart. I knew just what to say to burden him with such guilt he'd not send me away. Staying would cost us our home and put my sister's very life in danger, but I refused to go."

Katie rose swiftly to her feet. She couldn't keep still while recounting those days. "He finally relented. 'Twasn't long after that the food ran out. Father took what little money we had and bought more. But the rents came due, and he couldn't pay. He begged the land agent for time and received his answer in the darkest hours of night."

"When your house was burned down?" Tavish asked.

Katie nodded. "We lost our home and the land Father's family had worked for six generations. If I had gone to Manchester, we wouldn't have lost our home. He'd be there still. I need to give that back to him, but I don't have the money yet. I hardly have enough for . . . for Eimear's . . ."

She took a deep breath. "The history grows worse, Tavish," she warned.

"I haven't left yet, Katie."

She rubbed her arms. Though the night was warm, she felt chilled to her core.

"'Twas the beginning of winter, cold and bitter, and we had not so much as a roof over our heads, nor anything more than the clothes we'd slept in and the blankets we'd dragged out with us. We didn't even have shoes." They'd stolen clothes off clotheslines along the way, shoes off back porches. They'd gone from a family humbled by want, but honest and upright, to a family of thieves.

"I should have regretted then what I'd done to bring us so low. I should have felt repentant. As we walked the roads, my only thought was that at least I wasn't in the factories. My feet were burned in the fire, and every step I took was excruciating. I wept in agony but didn't regret saving myself from going to Manchester. I saw my parents stooped and aged with worry. I watched my sister grow thin and quiet, weak to the point Father had to carry her because she could no longer walk. And still I didn't regret it."

Katie rubbed a hand over her face, fighting the pain growing inside. She shook as though exposed to the bitter Irish winter once more, pushed back more tears at the memory of her poor sister's suffering.

A self-loathing she'd not allowed herself to feel in a decade or more surged inside. What a horrible child she'd been, an unfeeling and cold-hearted girl. She looked over the river, the sting of wind only adding to the tears forming in her eyes.

"We lost the only home my family had known for nearly two hundred years, just as Father had said we would. My sister was dying, just as Father said she would. I'd known what would happen, and still I'd done everything I could to keep from being sent away."

"You were very young, Katie."

She knew that argument wouldn't stand. "How old were you, Tavish, when The Famine taught you to know death?"

"I was seven." Something like resignation sounded in his voice. Katie didn't look back at him to see if his expression matched his tone. "A neighbor family lost two little ones."

"And, young as you were, you knew what death meant and that dying of hunger was a real thing, did you not?"

"I did," he said quietly.

"So did I." Katie rocked back and forth, from her toes to her heels, unable to hold still in the least. "We slept in abandoned barns and roofless skeletons of houses with hardly a bite to eat as the weeks dragged on. Day by day death crept into Eimear's eyes. I knew then I'd made a terrible mistake, but I realized it too late."

"What happened to her?" Tavish's voice was so quiet Katie hardly heard it over the sound of the river.

"'Twas nearly six weeks after we lost our home." Katie wrapped her arms tightly around her middle. "Father found us a barn for shelter, one hardly standing but better than huddling against a stone wall like we'd been doing. He laid Eimear down in the musty straw and told me to care for her while he and Mother walked to the nearest town, hoping to find a bit of bread or a day's work.

"'Look after your sister,' he said. 'She's in your charge and your care.' And I promised him I would. I was wrong to have put my worry over Manchester above Eimear's well-being. I vowed to my father I'd take care of her." For the first time since their house burned, Father had looked at her without disappointment.

"We lay there in that barn as still as could be. We were trespassing, after all. Eimear kept saying she was cold. 'I'm cold, Katie. I'm so cold.' She said it again and again. I was afraid we'd be found, so I shushed her, telling her to keep quiet."

She heard Tavish rise behind her, but his footsteps didn't trail off. Her gaze fell to the river bank directly in front of her.

"I covered her with as much straw as I could, our blankets were too worn to be of any use. She just kept saying how cold she was." Katie closed her eyes. 'Twas, perhaps, her clearest memory of Eimear. "'I don't want to be cold anymore,' she said, so quiet and so miserable. We'd all been freezing for six weeks. All on account of my selfishness."

Tavish didn't argue that point. He made no sound behind her. She only knew he hadn't left because she hadn't heard him go.

Katie lifted her eyes to the nearly dark horizon stretching out before her. She let out a slow breath. Best finish her story and let him go if he meant to.

"Hours passed before she stopped saying how cold she was. I lay there beside her, looking at the stars peeking through the missing pieces of the roof. I was relieved when she finally grew quiet. *Relieved.* Eventually I fell asleep. When I woke up, Eimear was still sleeping. I tried to nudge her awake."

For a moment Katie couldn't speak. Too much pain filled her. She trembled from deep within, tears falling from her eyes.

"She was so cold." Katie whispered. "So very, very cold."

A salty tear rolled over her lips. Katie brushed it aside, but another immediately took its place. Her lungs clenched. Only with great effort could she pull in the tiniest bit of air.

Tavish's hands settled gently on her shoulders. He didn't speak a word, simply stood behind her, silently listening.

"I sobbed with my hands over my mouth to stay quiet, afraid someone would hear and find us there. I wept alone all day. Mother and Father didn't return until nightfall." Her next breaths shook out of her. Her throat burned with emotion. "They knew before they even saw Eimear. My mother crumbled, dropped to her knees right there. Father— Father—"

One of Tavish's arms wrapped around her middle, holding her close to him. Katie wiped at her wet face. She struggled to regain control of her voice, to get even the smallest of breaths through.

"Father looked at me. He didn't speak to me again. Not ever."

She felt ill thinking back on those moments. The whole world fell apart that day.

"Father carried Eimear to the nearest town the next morning and asked the priest if she could be buried in the churchyard. We hadn't money for a casket or headstone or even a grave digger. Father dug the hole, and then we helped him fill it in."

More tears dripped off her face. Katie let them fall. With one hand Tavish gently caressed her arm, his other arm yet wrapped around her waist.

"All I could think was how cold she would be in the frozen ground without even a blanket. I could hear her voice in my mind. Over and over. 'I'm so cold, Katie. I'm so cold.'"

She pressed her hand over her mouth, stifling her gasping breaths. Without a word, Tavish stepped around her and pulled her into a proper embrace. She buried her face against his chest, clasping his shirt tightly. If she let go, Katie knew she'd simply collapse.

"If I'd gone to Manchester, she wouldn't have died. She would have been warm and safe and alive. It was all my fault, Tavish."

"You couldn't have known, love. Not truly." His arms tightened around her. "You were only a child yourself."

Katie shook her head against him. "I knew enough."

His fingers threaded into her hair, holding her ever closer to him. "Oh, Katie."

"My parents didn't speak to me again. Not the day we buried Eimear. Not all the way to Derry. They didn't say a word. Not one single word." Her tears had soaked his shirt front, and yet he didn't pull away.

"Have you been blaming yourself for this all your life?"

"I know what I did, Tavish. My parents knew it."

He rubbed her back as he held her. "Is that why your father left you in Derry?"

"I killed his daughter."

"You *are* his daughter."

Katie slid her arms around him, leaning against him for support. "The night after we buried Eimear, I lay beside them in an abandoned cottage, pretending to sleep. They were whispering to each other. Father said, 'I've lost everything, my land and all my children.'" She closed her eyes and concentrated on the warmth of Tavish holding her as he was. It did not stop the tears. "I was lying right there next to him and he said all his children were gone. *All* of them."

Tavish set his hands on either side of her face, raising her eyes to his. "I don't think he meant that you were not one of his children anymore."

"He did." She knew it.

"And that is why you mean to go back? To give him his land so he'll claim you as his own again?" Tavish shook his head. "Katie—"

"I mean to give him his land because it is the right thing to do. He was punished for a mistake *I* made. I can't expect any kind of forgiveness if I don't make that right. And my sister never had a proper headstone, nothing more than two sticks tied together in the shape of cross." She took a shuddering breath. "I mean to see to it she has a fine stone with her name on it. Years from now when people see it, they'll know her name. She'll not just disappear as if she never lived at all."

"My Sweet Katie." He brushed his fingers along the line of her jaw. Such a tender gesture.

"The only thing I can give him now is his fiddle. But that won't be enough."

"Your mother said she wanted you to come home. Sounds to me as though just yourself would be plenty enough."

That set the tears falling again. "She didn't, though. She told me time was short, in case it mattered to me. She didn't ask me back." She sniffled against the continuing tears. "And Father didn't say anything at all. He never sends word to me. Never asks Mother to send his greetings or his love to me. Even dying he didn't ask me back."

Tavish pulled her more fully into his arms. "So what do you mean to do, darlin'?"

"I don't know. I hate the idea of not seeing him again, of not even trying to make things right with him."

His hand rubbed her back in wide circles. "But?"

She leaned more heavily against him. "What if I go and spend what I have to buy his land back, even find a job to eventually get Eimear a headstone? What if I do all that, and he still hates me? What if it's not enough? I will have given up everything I have here for nothing."

His hand stilled. "Given it up? But you'd come back, love. Surely you'd come back."

She wiped at a tear. "I'd have nothing left. Every penny would be gone."

"Begorra, Katie." She felt him take a tense breath. "I knew you'd come here planning to leave, but I thought that had changed in the past months. I thought you'd come to think of this as home. I never imagined you'd even think of leaving us for good."

She pulled back a little, enough to look up into his face.

His brow pulled in tight. "You would truly leave for good? How could you do that? How could you even think it?"

He wasn't yelling, hadn't even raised his voice. But Katie heard disappointment in his tone. *You full disappoint me.* 'Twas her father's words she heard in her head but in Tavish's voice. She'd done it again. She'd failed in the eyes of someone she loved.

"I'm sorry," she whispered. "I'm sorry."

Katie pulled away and moved swiftly back toward the house, only just keeping herself from running. Why couldn't life continue on a sure and certain path? And why must that path be filled with such deep and constant pain?

Chapter Thirty-Nine

Joseph opted to give Katie space. He remembered very well the feelings of loss and pain when he'd heard of his father's passing. Katie had walked around the house in the two days since her mother's letter arrived, with tears constantly brimming in her eyes. The cheerful, determined Katie had disappeared.

He knew there was little he could do to ease her pain, but he wanted to help in any way he could.

He hung back after lunch when he would usually have returned to the fields. Katie had her basket filled with loaves and ready for delivery.

"I'd like to help you make your deliveries, Katie, if you don't mind."

Her smile was heartbreakingly shaky. "I would appreciate that. Biddy was supposed to help but couldn't spare the time. Are you sure *you* can spare it? I know you've a crop to tend."

"Finbarr is capable of seeing to things for an hour or two." He took up her basket and walked with her out the door. The buggy was hitched up and waiting.

"I can see you were pretty confident I'd agree to your offer of help."

"Because I know you're smart." He set her basket in the backseat of the buggy.

At his offered hand up into the buggy, she shook her head but not in refusal. "Do you know no one ever handed me up or down before I came here?" She let him hand her up. "I was always just a servant. And servants don't matter."

He stepped up and grabbed the reins. "Well, you have certainly mattered here."

"*Have.* I think you've heard I may be leaving."

He had. "You apparently told Biddy, and she told Ian. Ian told me."

Her shoulders drooped. "Likely all of the Irish Road has heard by now." Her brow creased. Her mouth turned down. "Do you think they'll be disappointed in me if I choose to go?"

He set the buggy in motion. "They'll be sad to see you leave, Katie, but I don't think they'll be 'disappointed' in you."

She looked away from him. Something in the set of her shoulders told him she was fighting her own emotions. *Poor Katie.* News of her father was a blow. But to add to that the weight of half a town's dependence on her would crush anyone.

They pulled around the house and rolled toward the road.

"I think you must have scared off my wardens," Katie said in a small voice. "The Red Road's watchers are usually here this time of day."

"I know."

That brought her eyes to him again. "You knew it all along? I'd not mentioned they'd become constant."

"They may have been keeping an eye on you, but I was keeping an eye on them." Had one of them so much as set a single foot off that road, they would have had him to deal with, no matter what it did to his neutral stance. Both roads knew his home and land were off limits to their feud.

"Well, I'm glad you sent them off."

"I didn't, actually," he said.

Her gaze returned to the fork in the road. "Then where do you suppose they went?"

"I believe word has reached the Red Road that there is a high likelihood you are leaving. They don't feel the need to intimidate you any longer."

Katie hung her head a little, her gaze on her wringing hands. "The Red Road feels they've won?"

He couldn't think how to answer that without inflicting more pain. The Red Road absolutely felt victorious. Katie was the first real threat to their control over the Irish's economic standing. Even Seamus Kelly, despite having the only smithy in town and the Red Road's need for it, didn't have a business that benefited only the Irish, that depended only on their patronage, that took income away from the mercantile. She was the first to dare to live off the Irish Road. Were she to leave, no matter the reason, the Red Road would claim the victory.

They didn't say much through Katie's deliveries. He could see her mind was heavy and didn't know what he could possibly say to help ease her mind. At every stop, the Irish held Katie back, talking at great length, and she came back looking more burdened than she'd been before.

Mrs. Claire didn't keep Katie as long as the others. Still, Katie looked even more upset after that quick delivery.

"How does Mrs. Claire feel about you contemplating leaving Hope Springs rather than moving in with her?" he asked as he set the horses in motion again.

"She only told me I had to choose the right path for me." She spoke in little more than a whisper. "Everyone else is so . . . disappointed."

"Your departure would be a blow, but they have survived worse." He could see that was not a helpful answer.

"Am I to assume, then, you also don't think I should go?"

"Have many people lectured you about leaving?" While he could understand everyone's wish for her to stay, he had seen her pain every day since the letter came. He knew what she was living with.

"Not lectured so much as pleaded." She sighed, slumping down on the buggy bench. "I've been happy here, and I don't truly want to give that up. But if I don't go, I'll never see my father again. And, yet, the Irish are convinced their whole world will fall apart if I leave."

He pulled the buggy to a stop at Ian and Biddy's place. Katie's hinted-at question was best left unanswered. She carried enough guilt as it was.

The delivery was quickly made, no doubt due to whatever obligation had kept Biddy from making deliveries with Katie. Joseph thought he'd avoided her question, but she took it up just as soon as she returned to the buggy.

"What would my going back to Ireland to do them all, Joseph? *Would* everything fall apart?"

He wanted her to feel free to make whatever choice she needed to, but he refused to lie to her. "Whenever the Red Road comes out victorious in these battles, they make things that much worse for their Irish neighbors."

"Like higher prices at the mercantile?"

He nodded. "Or not allowing them to buy things they need most. Or letting animals out of barns. Or keeping the Irish from going into town for church or, after harvest, keeping the Irish children away from the schoolhouse."

She stayed quiet as the buggy rolled down the road. Lines of worry creased her face. "I thought those were things they did *during* a battle, not afterward."

"They often choose a means of revenge in order to remind the Irish 'where they belong,' as Reverend Ford summed up so nicely your first Sunday here."

Katie rubbed at her forehead. "They'll be mistreated because of me. No wonder they're so disappointed. But if I don't go back, my mother'll be disappointed."

There was that word again. Katie obviously worried about letting people down. But did she ever think of what was best for her?

"I think, Katie, regardless of which path you choose, there will be disappointments. You simply have to choose the regrets you can best endure."

Katie's expression only grew more burdened. "I don't know that there is anything truly simple about that choice."

"Believe me, I am painfully aware of that." Regrets had been part of his life for years.

"Do you have a great many regrets, then, Joseph?"

He flicked the reins. Did he have regrets? Here was a woman he'd come to care about more than he'd thought possible. He'd kept his affections a secret, waiting for the day she didn't live under his roof. He hadn't planned on that day being the one on which she left the town and the country all together.

"More regrets all the time," he answered quietly.

In time the basket was empty, and the buggy was turned back toward home. The afternoon had clearly been hard on Katie. Joseph didn't want to add to that, but he needed to talk to her.

"I have to make a confession."

She looked equal parts intrigued and wary.

"When Tavish didn't return to the house after going looking for you the night the letter came, I went out looking myself. I wanted to be certain you were all right."

He could see she was alarmed.

"I know I should have left once I realized you were fine, especially after realizing you were having a private conversation, but I stayed and listened." He shouldn't have. He'd told himself as much, even as he'd stood out of sight but within hearing.

Katie kept her eyes trained on the passing fields. She was probably upset, offended. He couldn't blame her.

"I have wondered so much about you since you first came," he admitted, not looking at her as he drove back toward home. "You always seemed to be holding back, keeping part of yourself locked away. I couldn't understand why you so adamantly pushed the girls away or why such obvious pain lurked in your eyes. All of that made more sense after hearing what you said."

She folded her arms across her chest, her gaze straight ahead. "You had no right to listen in on my confessions, Joseph Archer."

"I know, and I'm sorry."

Katie's mouth pulled in a taut line. "And I suppose you rather despise me now, knowing the kind of person I am."

He'd heard that soul-crushing guilt in her voice out by the river. She did not see herself clearly enough. "Oh, I knew before the kind of person you are. Knowing more about your past only helped explain what brought you to the place where you are now."

He slowed the buggy but didn't stop. He wanted a chance to talk to her, but they were quickly approaching the bridge leading off the Irish Road.

"I have heard many of our Irish neighbors talk about going back to Ireland but only ever in the vaguest of terms, the way one dreams of something far-fetched. You are the only one who spoke of it as a settled thing, as an inevitable destination. As near as I could tell, every decision you'd made in life pointed to that end. For the life of me, I couldn't understand what would give a person that much motivation."

"Guilt," Katie whispered.

"More regret than guilt, I would say." She was plagued by heartache over mistakes she made before she was even truly old enough to understand such things.

"What if I go back and do all these things and my father still won't forgive me? What if, even on his deathbed, he won't love me again?"

Joseph could not even imagine turning his back on his daughters at any point in his life, let alone in his last moments. Yet, there was a history of neglect between Katie and her father. She said he stopped talking to her after her sister's death. He had never written to her in all the years they'd been apart.

"His pardon is his to give, Katie. You cannot control that."

She turned a little on the bench, facing him. "I do worry about that. I might go all the way there, and he'll not see me. Or he will, but he won't forgive me."

"You can't really know without trying."

She let out a tense breath. Her emotions seemed close to the surface. "You think I should go, then?"

Joseph kept his eyes on the road as he guided his horse. If he looked at her, she would see the truth of his feelings in his eyes. "I only want you to be happy, Katie. Whether that means staying here or returning to Ireland, I want you to do what you need to do. I don't want you to spend the rest of your life with so much weight on your heart."

"You are the first person I've spoken to about this who has said anything other than that I shouldn't go." Her smile was fleeting and half-formed. "Perhaps you're simply hoping to be rid of me so you won't have to pay my salary any longer."

"If you do stay, you'll be at Mrs. Claire's as it is and not on my payroll any longer." She had no idea how grateful he would be to have her down the road. "I will miss not having you in the house. Knowing you aren't even in the country would be far worse."

Her smile turned more genuine. "I would miss you too, Joseph. Knowing you has restored my faith in people likely more than you realize."

He kept his eyes focused ahead. "That feeling is mutual," he said quietly. "And, for the record, I don't want you to go. I truly don't. I'm only acknowledging that leaving may be what you need to do."

A stiff breeze blew across the road, rustling Joseph's jacket and Katie's skirts. The chill it brought reached deep into him. He would let her go if she needed to leave. He would even help her in any way he could. But a weight settled in his chest at the thought of losing her.

"'Tis a dilemma I have, Joseph Archer. If I go, the Irish'll see it as a defeat, and they'll be punished for it. If I don't go, I won't get to see my father before he dies."

Joseph nodded. She had a hard choice ahead of her.

"You look like you understand that well."

"Sometimes the dilemma is between what is best for someone else and what is easiest for oneself. Not unlike that song you told me about, the one in which the man is in love with a lady but doesn't tell anyone, not even her, because their circumstances would keep them apart regardless. It would be best for her if he keeps silent, but doing so is torturous for him."

"Aye. Choosing between hard things it is."

He turned the buggy down the path toward the barn. "How does the song end?" he asked. "Does the man's patience ever pay off? Do they find a way to be together?"

"No, they don't."

He had expected as much. "Life is hard sometimes, Katie."

She nodded. "Aye. It is that."

They pulled up in front of the barn. Joseph hopped down, wrapping the horse's reins around the hitching post as he made his way to Katie's side of the buggy. He moved quickly enough to reach her side before she'd climbed down herself.

He reached up and gently lowered her to ground.

"I thank you for helping me with my deliveries," she said. "And for helping me sort out my difficulties."

He knew his smile was a little sad. "You're welcome." He made for the barn, needing a moment to himself to let her go for good.

"And, Joseph?"

"Yes?" He spoke without looking at her.

"Thank you for giving me my job back all those months ago."

He glanced back. "That was one of the better decisions I have made in my life," he said. "And one of the reasons we'll miss you regardless of how far away you go."

Chapter Forty

Katie hardly recognized her own reflection in the Archers' front windows. As she cleaned the glass, her gaze continually drifted back to the dark circles clearly visible beneath her eyes, to the weary downturn of her lips, to the sag in her posture. Life had, once again, dealt her a hard blow.

In the background of her own reflection she could see a small gathering of people off a pace down the road leading to town. She glanced back over her shoulder, heart hammering a bit at the possibility of the small group proving to be Reds with unfriendly intentions.

She recognized Mr. and Mrs. O'Donaghue quite quickly and felt immediate relief. A moment more and she knew the others, as well. Irish, every last one of them.

Their arms gestured sharp and broad as their voices rose. Katie couldn't make out their words, but she could see the tension in their faces. She set her wash rags aside and stepped from the porch.

Two wagons sat still in the road beside each other, the drivers standing about on the road. Thomas Dempsey rode his horse over the bridge in the next moment. Katie could see in his face the moment he noticed the discussion ahead.

"What's this?" he asked when they met up at the fork in the road.

Katie held her hands up in a show of uncertainty. "Something's worked them all up."

She walked closer but quickly fell behind Thomas's horse. By the time she reached the small crowd—the O'Donaghues, Callaghans, and Kirkpatricks, she realized—he'd already dismounted.

"Twice the price," Mr. O'Donaghue was saying. "We can't pay twice the price no matter how much the children need shoes."

Mrs. O'Donaghue wrung her hands. A deep furrow creased her brow. "Winter's comin' soon enough. The two littlest have worn holes clear through their shoes. The oldest can't hardly squeeze into his."

Winter with no shoes. Katie could feel the terrible pain of bitter cold. She could clearly see the icy countryside, the pitiful wrappings around her bloodied feet.

"The mercantile raised the price of the children's shoes." She didn't need to pose it as a question. She knew it was true.

Mr. Callaghan nodded. "And he just now hinted at a higher Irish price for wool as well."

The distress in Mrs. O'Donaghue's expression grew with each word. "How are we to make coats without wool?"

No coats. No shoes. Katie's heart ached at the thought. They'd not all survive the winter under such conditions.

"That is a terribly mean-spirited thing for any person to do," Katie said. "He must know the little ones'll suffer most of all."

"They're punishing us, Katie." Thomas shook his head, his mouth turned down. "We stood up to them, had one of our own living past the bridge, boasted an independent Irish business. They're punishing us for trying, and they're further punishing us for failing."

He shoved his hands into the pockets of his trousers, eyes glancing up the road toward town.

"Failing?"

"You're leaving, aren't you?" he pointed out. "In their eyes, that's us failing again."

Guilt gnawed at her in that instance. She was leaning more heavily toward leaving Hope Springs. She'd very nearly decided, though she still harbored some doubts.

"I likely am, but not because the Reds drove me off. They're not the reason I'd be leaving."

"It won't matter." Thomas moved slowly in the direction of two men just arrived from over the bridge. "They'll claim the victory and all the spoils that go with it."

This is my fault. Once again she was choosing what *she* wanted at the expense of someone else's welfare. How many of the Irish children would suffer that winter while their Red Road neighbors gloated?

Katie looked in the faces of her friends and saw worry and frustration. 'Twas the defeat she saw there that broke her heart. They'd resigned themselves to losing again.

Seamus Kelly came riding up in the next moment. Katie groaned at seeing him. Though she liked Seamus well enough, his temper never did bode well in difficult moments.

"I heard about Johnson's latest bit of robbery," he called out to the others, dismounting as he reached the group. "Couldn't starve us out before, so he means to freeze us out."

Mr. O'Donaghue pulled himself up proudly. "We've starved and frozen before. We can endure it again."

Mrs. Connelly was not so easily persuaded. "But can we endure the cries of our children? 'Tis a different matter entirely when you yourself aren't the only one suffering."

Katie ached for them all, for the dismal future laid out before them. "Surely there's something that can be done," she said.

Seamus's glance held a note of empathy. "Don't fret yourself, Katie. You'll likely be long on your way back to Ireland before we have to face this latest setback."

Though he spoke with no malice, Katie felt the comment as a slice to her soul. By leaving, she would be abandoning them to the coming disaster.

"Don't you pay him no nevermind," Mrs. O'Donaghue said. "Your father is dying. None of us blames you in the least for wanting to be with him. Though we do all hope you'll decide to stay."

"Are you entirely certain only the Irish are being charged so much for shoes and woolens? Perhaps the price has gone up for everyone." Her conscience sincerely hoped that was the case.

Mr. O'Donaghue shook his head. "Johnson said we'd be paying 'the Irish price.'"

Seamus Kelly's expression immediately hardened. "What do you say we exact an 'Irish price' of our own?" He jerked his chin in the direction of the fork in the road, pulling everyone's gaze that way.

Bob Archibald and two of his neighbors had only just reached the point where the Red Road met the Irish Road directly in front of the Archer home. All three men eyed the gathered Irish with disdain and distrust.

"Get out of the road," Mr. Archibald spat at them. "You can't stand around blocking the path."

They were, indeed, cutting off the roadway. Mr. Archibald might have driven around, but such a thing would have proven tricky. And, Katie suspected, he'd see doing such a thing as a sign of weakness, of giving in to the Irish. So his wagon came to a stop, his horses nearly nose to nose with those of the Scotts.

Seamus pushed his way to the front of the group, his neck turning a deep shade of red, his fists clenched hard at his sides. "We've as much right to this roadway as any of you do. You want to get past? You can just drive round."

"And suppose I mean to drive straight through?" Mr. Archibald growled.

"Your little wagon plowing through two of ours, plus a few horses? Even your wee little brain must know you'd come out the loser in that."

"Are you calling me stupid, Paddy?" Mr. Archibald managed to make 'Paddy' sound like the worst of profanities. He tossed the reins to the man up next to him on the wagon bench and jumped down to the ground.

Katie didn't have to wait to know what would come next. There'd be a fistfight in a lick of a cat's ear. Already the men were waving their wives away from the road, out of the coming fray. For her part, Katie moved around the wagons, closer to the men glaring each other down. 'Twas no longer just Seamus and Mr. Archibald. The other two Red Road men were fair itching for a fight, and the Irish seemed more than happy to oblige them.

"Don't do this, Seamus," Katie called out. "A brawl can only make things worse."

But she was ignored entirely. Seamus and Mr. Archibald circled one another, fists at the ready, anger etched into every line of their faces.

"I'd think on this long and hard if I were you, Archibald." Seamus spoke slowly, confidently. "You know perfectly well I'm a better fighter than you are."

"Is that so, Irishman? I believe you'll have to show me."

Seamus's fist flew on the instant. Mr. Archibald ducked out of the way, receiving no more than a glancing blow.

"Stop!" Katie shouted. "Stop this!"

A person could shout at the waves to stop crashing into the shore for all the good it would do. The men were at each other with a fervor. A fistfight in the street would hardly solve their difficulties.

Katie looked to the other men, hoping cooler heads existed some-where in the group. Other than Thomas, who shouted more strongly worded expressions of frustration at them, stubborn chins, fiery eyes, and fists at the ready were the order of the day. Soon dust was flying, the men forgoing brawling partners and all going at each other at once.

"Quit being idiots," Katie shouted at them all, knowing her words would do no good.

The fighting went on all around her. She made to duck around them, figuring taking refuge with the ladies was her best option in the moment, even if it felt terribly cowardly.

A sudden jolt of pain in her right shoulder was her only warning before she landed on her backside against the unforgiving ground. Her lungs seemed to stiffen, unable or unwilling to take in air. Tears stung at her eyes. She grabbed at her shoulder, pulsing with pain.

Around her the men continued throwing punches, pummeling each other in their pent-up rage. Thomas Dempsey braved the fray to offer her a hand up. She'd only just regained her feet when someone in the scuffle landed Thomas a telling blow to the back. He swayed a bit before steadying himself.

Thomas turned red at the ears. He spun about.

"You'd hit a man while he assisted a woman from the ground?" he snapped. "What kind of uncivilized savages—"

With that, he, too was full into the fray.

Katie took a quick step backward, still holding her shoulder. It hurt like the devil, but it didn't feel dislocated. Either she'd been struck by one of the combatant's fists or caught a thrown-back elbow.

A loud crack rent the air. The horses nickered and fidgeted. The men stopped their brawling, though they kept their fists at the ready.

"Go on home, all of you." Joseph Archer stood on the road, horse-whip in hand, eyes flashing with anger as he looked over the group. "Breaking each other's noses and blacking each other's eyes isn't going to solve anything."

There was a slight shuffling of feet but little else.

"Go on." Katie'd never heard Joseph's voice snap the way it did in that moment.

Whilst the Irish took the reins of their skittish animals, Bob Archibald did the same with his. "It's not like you to involve yourself in this," he grumbled to Joseph.

Joseph took a single step closer, pointing the end of his whip in Mr.

Archibald's direction. "Any time I see a woman felled by a man's fist, you can be certain I will involve myself."

"I didn't mean to hit her," Mr. Archibald muttered. "She got in the middle of it, is all."

"You are obviously headed into town." Joseph's tone left no room for further arguments. "I suggest you continue on your way. Perhaps you could purchase some liniment at the mercantile for your black eye."

"I'd've gone there directly, except these Paddies were blocking the road." Mr. Archibald's mouth turned down, twisting as though he'd smelled something foul.

The O'Donaghues and Scotts and the others had already begun to make their way toward the fork, having yielded the road to the Reds. Katie's heart ached at the terrible irony of that. Once again they had been the ones to give ground.

Joseph motioned Mr. Archibald on down the road. In a moment's time, no one remained on that spot except Katie and a very quiet Joseph Archer.

"They were ready to tear each other to pieces right here in the road," she whispered. "I couldn't talk any sense into them."

"This feud has quickly passed the point of sense. There'll be no reasoning with anyone now."

Katie could have cried right there. Not only from the agony in her shoulder but even more from the frustration of seeing people she cared about come to the point of brawling with their neighbors in broad daylight. They were afraid and broken and angry, and far too much of that could be laid at her feet.

Joseph sighed, the sound filled with bone-deep weariness. "Come on up to the house. We need to look at that shoulder."

Katie shook her head. "'Tis nothing so bad as that." The weight sitting heavy on her heart bothered her more than the pain in her shoulder.

"You took almost the full brunt of a man's swing, Katie." He set a hand on her back and gently nudged her toward the house. "You will be fortunate to walk away with nothing more than an enormous bruise and a terribly stiff shoulder."

She walked at his side, thoughts heavy and difficult. "This is going to be horrible, isn't it?"

"A bruise at the very least—"

"No. I mean the feud. The fighting." She looked up into his face. "People are going to be hurt, aren't they?"

He nodded, slowly and reluctantly. "At the very least."

She rubbed at her aching shoulder. "If I stayed—" Even posing the possibility in terms of *if* set her stomach to spinning. Could she really give up the chance to see her father one last time? "If I stayed, would it help? Would they stop fighting?"

"No." He spoke so matter-of-factly, she couldn't doubt him in the least. "Nothing will likely stop it now."

They stepped through the front door. Joseph shut the door behind them. She stopped in the entryway, too burdened to move further.

"It wouldn't do any good, then? Is it already too late?" How terribly familiar that was. She'd been too late to help Eimear as well.

"Tell me directly, Joseph. No sweetening your words or skirting about the question. If I stayed, would it help in the least?"

He hesitated only a moment. "You would give the Irish an extra helping of confidence, a feeling of having an extra bit of strength on their side. But, Katie"—he looked her direct in the eye—"this feud will one day escalate into the war we all see coming, regardless of what you choose to do."

Chapter Forty-One

The céilí bore little resemblance to the cheerful, festive affair of even one week before. Tavish knew precisely what had caused the change. Everyone in town knew of the brawl out on the road. And everyone was holding his breath to see which side would seek revenge first and how. There'd be no stopping the feud now. The future loomed before them all dark as a thundercloud.

Katie arrived among them but a few minutes into the weekly party. The heaviness Tavish had seen in her countenance the first day they met had returned tenfold. He didn't realize until that moment how much of her worry and sadness had melted away in the months he'd known her.

"Poor Katie," Ian said, standing beside him. "Carrying the weight of the world on her shoulders, she is. Biddy says our Katie feels responsible for our latest troubles."

Add to that guilt the weight of her own regrets and any person would crumble under that crushing burden. But not his Katie. There she stood, facing them all with a brave smile and teary eyes.

"You'll be excusing me, brother. I've a woman to go make up to."

Ian gave him an encouraging slap on the shoulder. Tavish weaved his way through the somber crowd.

"I'm praying you aren't going to leave us, Katie," Rose McCann said in the very moment Tavish arrived at Katie's side. "I know we've not much to offer you, but we need you so badly. We need you."

Katie stood there, slumped by the weight but still able to meet her inquisitor's eye. "'Tis my *father*. I'd like to see him again before he dies, but coming back takes more money than I have."

"But, Katie, the Reds'll tear us to bits if you go. They'll have no reason to play nice. You've seen yourself what they'll do"

Katie held her hands up in a gesture of helplessness. "I know, and I don't want that to happen. I swear to you, I don't."

"You'll be excusing me," Tavish interrupted. He offered Rose an apologetic smile. "I'm wishing for a moment with Miss Katie."

If Tavish had doubted his feelings for Katie were well known, the look of empathetic understanding on Rose's face would have told him as much.

Alone with her at last, Tavish offered his arm. She didn't accept it immediately.

"Do you mean to lecture me? Because I warn you, I haven't—" Her voice broke, but she rallied. "I haven't the strength for it."

He took her hand, though she hadn't truly offered it. "No lectures. No scolding. I give you my word."

Her nod was small and weary.

"First of all," he said, "I mean to ask after your shoulder. I know you took a blow during the scuffle yesterday, but you'd already gone to bed for the evening when I stopped at Archers' to inquire after you."

"I've a colorful bruise, I have. And Joseph had to wash all the dishes today as my arm was too stiff."

He'd have to thank Joseph for that when next he saw him. "But otherwise you're well? You don't suspect it's broken or any such thing?"

Katie shook her head.

"Will you walk about with me?" he asked.

She set her other hand on his arm, moving to walk at his side. "How far are we going?"

That, there, was the question sitting heaviest on his mind. He opted to answer in literal terms rather than burden her with his feelings. "Just up to the back of the house."

Katie rested her head against his shoulder. He hoped that meant she didn't entirely hold against him his lack of support the night she'd received her letter. He had been so blindsided by her declaration that going meant staying in Ireland that he hadn't been as understanding as he should have been.

He led her to a bench not far from the back door. He took the spot directly beside her. "Have you decided to go, then?

"If I don't go, I'll never see my father again."

He took her hand once more, squeezing it. "I know, Sweet Katie."

"But if I go, my loved ones here will be made to suffer. I've seen that already."

"I know that as well. And I'd be lying if I said I wasn't broken up at the thought of you leaving."

He could hear emotion shaking each breath she took. He wanted to beg her with every ounce of strength he had not to go, but he kept himself quiet. She didn't need him adding to the pressure she felt.

"If you choose Ireland, how long would it be, do you think, before you go?"

She slipped her arm through his, her other hand held in his own. 'Twas almost as if she was embracing his arm. "As soon as can be. Joseph's new housekeeper should arrive in the next couple weeks, but he said if I needed to leave sooner, he would understand."

A couple weeks was the most he would have? It was almost too painful to contemplate. "I don't know what I'd do without you. I don't know that I can live without you here."

He stood and paced away a bit. Hurting Katie was the last thing he wanted to do, but he was dying inside. "What if I lent you the money for your return?" He'd likely have to take out a second note on his land to give her that, but he would if it meant she would come back. "If you had that, you could go back to see your da and still return to Hope Springs."

But she shook her head. "It's more than just the money. My mother would have the land after my father died." She seemed to struggle on the word a bit. "I'd have to stay and help her. She'd be all alone."

"Does your mother want the land back? I remember you saying how much it meant to your da, but you never once included your ma in that."

She blinked a few times, contemplation heavy on her face. "She is family, Tavish. A person should be willing to give anything for family."

Like go work in a dangerous factory at eight years old. He knew that was a big reason for her insistence on going. She had, in her mind, chosen a selfish route over one that would have helped her family. Returning to Ireland and giving up the life she had in Hope Springs was some kind of proof in her mind. He suspected she couldn't forgive herself without hearing from her father that he forgave her. Tavish worried deeply that she wouldn't ever hear that from him, even if she reached him before he died.

"You're giving up your entire life, Katie. You speak of family, but I think you've forgotten that you have loved ones *here*. Biddy sees you as a sister. Granny has outright adopted you. Those little Archer girls love you clear to pieces. Every Irish family in this town would do anything for you. They've bought bread and they've braved the wrath of the mercantile and the troubles from the Red Road's fear of you without flinching because they care about you." Saints, he didn't want to pain her, but she needed to see things clearly. "Family is who you choose to care for, Katie, and who choose to care for you."

She wrapped her arms around herself as she sat there taking the blow of words. He very much feared she was going to choose Ireland for the wrong reasons. He couldn't let that happen.

"But my father cares for me." She spoke in a small voice. "Deep down in some part of himself, I know he cares for me."

Tavish hesitated for only a breath before speaking the admittedly harsh response that had immediately sprung to his mind. "He hasn't sent so much as a word in nearly twenty years. Your mother only a half-dozen letters in that time." She'd told him as much herself.

"Only because I haven't made amends yet. I've not made my restitution. You can't blame them for—"

He hunched down in front of her and took her hand in his again, careful not to overtax her shoulder, and looked up into her face. "If they have not forgiven you after all these years for a decision you made as a child, a wee tiny child, and a decision that never should have been yours to make in the first place, then grand gestures and acts of atonement aren't likely to change that."

She shook her head again and again. "I've counted on this all my life. I need it. Eimear's forgiveness is out of my reach. But my father's is not. I need to hear him say he forgives me."

He lightly brushed her cheek with his hand. "I believe, darlin', 'tis not your father's forgiveness you've needed all these years, but your own."

Her gaze fell away from his face, dropping to their clasped hands. "I can't forgive myself if he still hates me for what I did, if he still thinks I'm no better than the selfish little girl I was then. I can't. I never could."

"There are more ways to prove that to your own self than buying a plot of land and a slab of stone."

She pulled free of his grasp and rose from the bench. Her quick, tense steps took her into the shadows behind the house. Tavish followed cautiously. He suspected he had offended her. But what else could he have said that would have driven the point home? He did not want to lose her over a fool's errand.

"I'm sorry to speak to you so sharply, Katie. I wouldn't say the difficult things if I cared for you any less than I do. But you've wanted this so long, depended on your father someday telling you that you're a good person. The only thing that could prove the kind of person you are is nothing more nor less than the way you live your life."

She didn't say anything, didn't look back at him.

"You can show him the person you've become by writing and telling him of the life you've lived, of the good you're doing here. I'll write to him, myself. Every Irish family in Hope Springs would write and tell him of their admiration for you, of how much they all care for you." Tavish would pay the postage himself if need be.

Though she didn't say as much, indeed, didn't so much as glance at him, he thought he saw the tiniest thread of contemplation in her expression. How he hoped she would at least consider it.

"I suppose I mostly just want you to know that, though your blood family is back in the old country, you have full half a town here that cares deeply what happens to you. And you've proven to them time and again that you're in no way the selfish person you paint yourself."

"What about his fiddle? How can I give that back to him if I don't go back?"

He rubbed at the back of his neck, brow furrowed deeply. "That I can't tell you, Katie."

She shook her head. "I don't know. What if . . . What if it isn't enough?"

Katie finally looked at him. The worry and pain and uncertainty in her eyes cut him to the quick. He couldn't bear to see it there. "Do you need to go back, Katie? Is going back what you need to find peace?"

She hesitated. After a moment her shoulders drooped anew. "I don't know anymore."

He leaned closer, his mouth a breath from hers. "I hope you know I love you, Sweet Katie. I will love you no matter what you choose."

Tears rushed to her eyes immediately. She opened her mouth, but no words emerged. Her lips quivered a moment before she simply pressed them closed again.

He brushed his lips against hers, the touch no more substantial than a breeze. Her hands rested gently against his chest. He lightly kissed her again. Many times he'd held back, kept himself from pulling her into his arms and truly kissing her. Their first real kiss, and it was a sad and brokenhearted one.

Tavish pulled back by a hair's breadth. For a moment he didn't move or speak. He simply stood there, silently holding her to him.

He pressed a brief kiss to her forehead, then one more, and turned away. He didn't know what else to say. He very much feared she was leaving, and though he understood why, he was still dying inside.

Chapter Forty-Two

Life, for Katie, had always been a matter of passing through. She'd never anticipated facing the same decision she had faced as an eight-year-old girl. Once again she had to choose between leaving a place that was home to her for the sake of her father, or remaining in the one place she truly felt loved.

She sat on the edge of her bed, her mother's letter in her hand.

"Your father hasn't sent even a word to you in nearly twenty years." Tavish's words had pierced her. They were painful but true. She would be leaving behind people who embraced her and loved her, who she knew would rally around her if ever she needed them to, for the thin hope that this man who'd not acknowledged her in nearly two decades would finally decide to do so.

And, yet, he *was* her father. She loved him whether or not he returned that affection. She loved him, and he was dying.

He'd never written to her. But she had never sent word directly to him, either. She asked mother to give him her greetings, but nothing beyond. Tavish's suggestion from the night before rushed back to her. She could write to her father. She could write her apologies, tell him of the life she was living and the person she'd become, and hope her words arrived in Ireland before her father left the world for good. It wasn't a final decision *not* to go. She couldn't quite commit herself to that. Not quite.

If Joseph was still willing to send her words as a telegram, the letter could reach Belfast in a fortnight. That was time enough. She could apologize. She could reach out to her father. It was not the full atonement she'd always meant to make, but it was a beginning.

Katie slipped her mother's letter into the old biscuit tin where she kept her savings. Was she truly brave enough to risk writing to him? Surely she was. If she was willing to give up the life she had in Hope Springs to see him again, she could certainly summon the courage to send a letter.

She set her mind to it, committed herself to the task. An almost immediate, unexpected sense of peace settled over her in that moment. For days on end she'd agonized over the obligation she felt to return to Ireland. Even eighteen years of working toward that goal hadn't been enough to make her feel truly at ease with the decision. But writing a letter, beginning that way, felt right.

The family had returned from services more than an hour earlier, though Katie had not come out of her room to greet them. The time had come to stop hiding and begin taking control of things.

She went looking for Joseph, determined to ask if he was yet willing to send a telegram on her behalf. The calmness she felt didn't disappear, didn't lessen. The choice to stay or go had twisted about inside her every minute of every day since her mother's letter arrived. Yet, she found an uncharacteristic peace of mind in this new path.

Joseph wasn't in the kitchen nor the dining room nor the parlor. Where in heaven's name was the man?

In the next moment she heard voices, low men's voices, from just beyond the parlor windows. On the front porch?

Katie opened the front door but didn't step out immediately. She didn't want to interrupt Joseph's conversation with his visitor.

"Are you sure about this?" Joseph was asking.

"I've never been more certain of anything in my life." 'Twas Tavish, of all people.

Katie peeked out enough to confirm it really was him. He and Joseph shook hands. But what were they shaking on?

"I'll need a fortnight or so to make all the arrangements," Joseph said.

Tavish nodded. "Let me know." He stepped off the porch and made his way up the path.

Katie stepped out but didn't stop him. Their parting at the céilí hadn't been the happiest. Watching him walk away tore into her.

"Tavish came by, did he?" Katie couldn't pull her eyes away from Tavish's retreating form. He'd not even stopped in to say hello to her. 'Twas all she could do not to run after him and ask him not to go.

"He did," Joseph said. "Tavish had some business to see to."

"Business?" Her heart dropped further. Tavish hadn't come with her in mind at all.

"He came to sell me his land," Joseph said.

Her head snapped round, as she stared at him, wide-eyed. "He *what?*" Though she understood his words, her mind refused to accept them. "He's selling his land? All of it?"

Joseph nodded solemnly.

In her mind Katie could hear her father's voice, the words he'd spoken quietly around the hearth at home when talk of impossible land payments arose. "A man belongs to the land, not the other way around. If he loses that, he might as well lose his very soul."

His very soul.

"Why would Tavish do that, Joseph? I don't understand."

Joseph clearly thought she should have pieced the puzzle together already. "Tavish wishes to follow a certain town baker woman to Ireland, but he doesn't have the money to make the journey. The only thing he has of any value is his land."

Oh, saints above. "He's not giving up his land on my account, is he?"

The thought set her nearly into a panic. "Good heavens, Joseph. He can't do that. He can't."

Joseph's expression was tight. "On the contrary, he is quite determined to."

Merciful heavens. Something very like fear gripped her. Tavish couldn't do this. He couldn't give up his land for her, and for something she wasn't entirely sure she wanted anymore.

Her heart raced and pounded, her mind spinning.

Joseph watched her closely but didn't speak.

"I don't know what to do." Her heart ached. "I don't know what to do."

Joseph stepped closer. She'd come to realize in the weeks she'd known him that Joseph Archer was a man of compassion. She saw that in him again. "What does your mind tell you, Katie?"

"That if I don't go back to Ireland, I'll never see my father again, that it doesn't make sense to delay my travels even a day with his time so nearly at an end." Grief settled on her shoulders, a mourning for a loss she knew was coming but was powerless to prevent.

Joseph's gaze didn't waver, though his expression softened. "And what does your *heart* tell you?"

"My heart?"

He nodded. "In my greatest moments of indecision, when I think I have no idea what I truly want, I have found my heart knows the answer."

What does my heart *say?* Katie pushed away the arguments her mind made in both directions, and focused solely on what she felt. *What does my heart say?*

A flood of memories and faces and moments rushed over her like a warm wave. The beloved almost-green farms, so different from Ireland but so dear to her. The stubbornly optimistic families of the Irish Road. Biddy's precious friendship. Sweet Ivy. Darling little Emma. Joseph, a man of wealth and influence who respected and valued her—that would certainly never happen in Ireland.

And Tavish. Kind, loving Tavish, who'd lost one sweetheart to death and, his heart being tender as it was, still couldn't bring himself to speak of her. A man capable of loving that deeply was well worth keeping. Tavish, who'd heard all of Katie's history and loved her still. Who brought smiles to her face when all she felt capable of was crying. Who was willing to give up his home and his family for her.

That was what she wanted. All of it. That was the reason for her doubts. Her mind insisted she keep to her lifelong plans, but her heart knew what it wanted and needed.

Her eyes focused once more to find Joseph still standing there, watching her. He gave her a look of understanding. "I think you need to at least go talk to him."

She nodded but couldn't find her voice.

"If you hurry, you might catch him before he gets too far."

Catch him. That was exactly what she intended to do.

Katie took hold of her skirts and rushed down the porch steps.

"Tavish?" But he was too far ahead already to hear her.

Faster she ran toward the bridge to the Irish Road, ignoring the pain each jarring step sent through her sore shoulder. He hadn't yet crossed all the way over the bridge.

"Tavish?" she called out.

He turned back, stopping when he saw her.

She stopped at the end of the bridge. He stood near the other end, looking at her.

"Why are you selling your land?"

Frustration entered his face. "Joseph wasn't supposed to say anything to you."

The river rushed by beneath their feet. Wind rustled the bushes and trees growing along the river bank. Katie stood there in the quiet, her mind spinning, no idea how to say what she felt.

"You would give that up for me?" She swallowed against the thickness in her throat.

"I'd do anything for you, Katie Macauley." He didn't step closer, nor did he move away. "If going to Ireland will make you happy, then I want you to go. But I won't live here without you. I won't spend the rest of my life wondering what might have happened if I'd gone with you."

She saw heavy regret in Tavish's eyes. Though she knew he would walk away from his house and his land and never blame her for it, he would regret the loss. He would.

She took a single step in his direction. "I have been thinking about Ireland, Tavish."

He shook his head. "This is precisely why I told Joseph not to say anything to you. I won't have you guilting yourself into a hasty decision."

"No. Not guilt. That you'd do this for me means more than I can tell you." Tears fell slowly from her eyes as overwhelming emotion nearly enveloped her. "You would give up your land for me, Tavish. My own father fully meant to give *me* up for his land."

She didn't bother to wipe away the tears. The determined and stubborn set of his posture eased, his gaze firmly on her.

"I love you, Tavish. I know I haven't said it before, but I mean it. I've felt it for some time now." Not since she lost her parents had she said those words to anyone. Part of her wondered if she even truly understood what they meant. "You said you'd always wonder what might have happened between us."

He moved slowly, uncertainly, in her direction.

"I'd rather find out than look back and wonder," she said. "And neither do I want to find myself years from now sitting in a damp flat in Belfast, thinking back on Hope Springs and regretting that I gave it up, not realizing I had a home here. A home where I needn't spend the rest of my life all alone."

It wasn't at all like Tavish to remain silent for so long. Had she said something wrong? Was he unconvinced? She didn't want him to think he'd forced her into changing her mind or that she'd made this decision out of guilt or a feeling of obligation.

"I'm needed here," she rushed to explain. "I haven't been needed anywhere since I was tiny. If I stay, the Red Road won't feel like they've won. I might even save the Irish some troubles in the future. And the sweet Archer girls, I cannot just abandon them. My job at the Archer home is the best I've had yet. And to sell my own bread, to have a business of my own, that'd never happen in Ireland. Not ever. Granny—"

He'd reached her side and brushed his hand along her cheek, cutting off her words mid-sentence.

"You're choosing to stay?" He whispered the question.

She nodded.

"Are you certain, Katie? I'll not have you burdened by this like you've been the last years."

She leaned into his touch. "We choose the regrets we can live with. I would always regret losing the home and family I have here. Always. I finally realized why I've struggled to make this decision, why there have been so many doubts. *This* is what I want. It's what I need."

"Are you certain?" he asked. "Absolutely certain."

"This feels right in a way going back hasn't in days," she said. "Weeks, really." Warmth began slowly spreading through her.

His thumb rubbed at her cheek, his hand slipping around the back of her neck. "If you ever change your mind, Katie, if going back ever becomes necessary to you again, promise you'll tell me. Promise you won't hold back out of a feeling of obligation or guilt or any such thing."

Bless the man. "I'll tell you. I swear to it."

His other hand slipped around the other side of her neck, so he held her head in his hands, looking directly into her eyes. "I love you, Katie Macauley."

Her heart seemed to swell, almost to bursting.

"Will you let me court you properly now that you don't mean to skip out?"

That was something she not only happily agreed to, but looked forward to wholeheartedly. "I believe I can accommodate you in that."

His grin spread wide as the River Foyle. She laughed at his whoop of delight. No person had ever seemed *that* happy to have her around.

In a movement so swift she hardly noted it, his arms wrapped about her middle and he swung her about, lifting her feet off the ground.

Tavish set her on her feet once more. He turned in the direction of the Archer house. With one hand cupped beside his mouth, the other arm tucked closely around her, he called out. "She's decided to stay!"

Katie looked over to see just who Tavish was speaking to. There stood Joseph, halfway out his door.

"Our Katie has decided to stay!" Tavish shouted loudly enough that even the Red Road must have heard him.

Joseph certainly did. He smiled back at them. Even from that distance, Katie fancied she saw honest relief in his eyes. Who could have imagined she would ever have found a place where she was wanted as much as she was in Hope Springs?

"Come on, then, Sweet Katie." Tavish tugged her by the hand, pulling her across the bridge.

"Just where are we going?"

"I've an enormous family, love, and they'll all be dancing jigs of joy to hear you won't be leaving us."

Jigs of joy. Good heavens, what a lovely thought. She joined her free hand with the one he held, clasping his warm, strong fingers. He meant to court her. To court her properly. Tears mingled with her contented smile, but they were tears of relief and happiness this time.

He looked back at her and, on the instant, halted his steps. They'd not even traveled as far as his granny's house. "What's the matter?" he asked.

She smiled ever broader. "Not anything. I am simply very happy."

"As am I, my Sweet Katie." He put his arms around her, his hands resting at the middle of her back. "Very, very happy."

Katie put a single hand to his cheek, relishing the feel of his face beneath her fingers. She could grow used to such a thing. Tavish held her close, filling her with warmth and flutterings.

She smiled from deep inside, happier than she remembered being in a long time. Something in his sparkling eyes brought heat to her cheeks.

"I've thought about kissing you for weeks and weeks, Katie Macauley."

Her heart made a valiant attempt to jump straight out of her ribs. Her gaze dropped of its own accord to his upturned lips. "I wish you'd just done it, Tavish, rather than merely thinking on it."

The mischievous grin he wore grew. "Take a moment, then, to prepare yourself sweetheart, because I'm done thinking."

He leaned close, his lips as near to touching hers as possible without actually doing so. He kept very still. She could feel his breath against her mouth. She brushed her thumb along his cheek, closing her eyes as she memorized that moment.

His fingers splayed across her back, holding her to him. He lightly brushed his lips once over hers, then again. Her pulse strummed through every inch of her.

At last he kissed her quite thoroughly, and she melted into him. Her arms wrapped about his neck as naturally as anything.

Tavish trailed kisses from her mouth to her temple before resting his cheek against hers. "Courting you, my Sweet Katie, is going to be a pleasure, indeed."

She turned her head a bit, just enough to look into his face. His gaze met hers. The smile he gave her turned her knees weak all over again. She kissed his cheek, then leaned her forehead against his jaw.

For the first time since her childhood, perhaps in all her life, she felt truly and deeply hopeful. She'd spent the past eighteen years so entirely alone. Home had ever been a distant goal, something she only dreamed of finding again.

But it was there in a town torn by its own history. It was there among people who had embraced her as family. And it was there in the arms of a man who had willingly given up everything for the chance to have her in his life.

Her troubles were far from over, life far from settled. Hope Springs hadn't found the way of peace. She yet had a father to mourn and a past that in many ways still haunted her, perhaps always would.

But in that moment, Katie knew she had, indeed, found home.

Sequel to

LONGING FOR *Home*

COMING SPRING 2014

Chapter One

However long the day, night must eventually fall. Katie Macauley knew that truth well. For every bit of joy she'd known, life had served her an ever-increasing portion of pain and grieving. Her Irish heart was just stubborn enough to keep going despite it all and just foolish enough to believe someday the balance would tip in her favor.

Finding a home amongst her displaced countrymen in a tiny town far from nowhere in the dry and unforgiving vastness of the American West seemed a fine argument in favor of optimism. Logic told her the odds of that happening were far too slim to be anything but a gift of fate. And yet the town of Hope Springs wasn't without its problems, a great many problems, in fact.

"Michael, bring the butter crock, lad. We're eating without your father if he's not here in another five minutes." Biddy, Katie's dearest friend in all the world, gave her a look of utter exasperation. "I can't imagine what's kept that man in town so long. He and his brother had best return with a broken axle or a three-legged horse to explain their lateness."

Katie set out the last of the dinner plates. She'd been invited to have her evening meal with Biddy and her family, an offer she appreciated more than any of them realized. Though she worked for a family who treated her with kindness and had the heart of a wonderful man—Biddy's husband's brother, in fact—she often felt alone.

"Put the spoon in the colcannon, Mary," Biddy told her little girl. "Then fetch the soda bread, if you will."

Colcannon and soda bread. 'Twas a bit of the Emerald Isle thousands of miles from Ireland.

Biddy crossed to the narrow front window. "What is keeping that man?"

Katie joined her there, looking out at the dimming light of dusk. "Ian realizes he's late and knows you're likely cross as a bag of cats. I'll warrant he's staying away out of fear of you."

Biddy gave a firm nod. "And well he should, the troublesome man. My supper's a full thirty minutes late from waiting for him. He'll need to butter me up sweet if he means to be forgiven for this night's troubles."

Katie smiled. She knew her friend too well to believe she was truly angry. Indeed, Katie could see Biddy was more concerned than anything else. She and her Ian had the happiest marriage Katie had ever seen, though her experience of such things was admittedly limited.

"Never fear, Biddy. Tavish'll round him up and bring him home to make his apologies."

"And not a moment too soon, it seems." Biddy looked back toward the rough-hewn table, where little Mary was carefully setting down the plate of soda bread. "Thank you, love. Now you and Michael go wash your hands."

"With soap?" Mary clearly hoped the answer was no.

"Aye. Soap and plenty of it." Biddy eyed both her children. "On with the two of you, then." She shook her head at their retreating backs. "I swear to you, Katie, they'd eat out in the muddy fields if I'd let them."

"And return to the house so filthy you could toss them against a wall and they'd stick," Katie added.

Biddy smiled, as Katie hoped she would. But just as quickly as the lightness appeared, it faded. Biddy turned back to the window. "Where is that man? It's not his way to be late."

Katie set a reassuring hand on Biddy's harm. "He and Tavish likely ran into Seamus or Eoin or Matthew and are busy telling wildly exaggerated tales of the glories of their pasts."

Biddy gave a single, quick laugh. "Men. I swear they've tongues that could clip a hedge, so sharpened are they on their own teeth."

"Indeed."

Biddy set one hand on her hip and rubbed at her forehead with the other. Her gaze lingered at the window.

"I am certain all's well." Katie spoke with all the conviction she could muster, but Biddy's worries were beginning to settle heavy on her as well. Tavish had left over an hour earlier and could easily have gone to town and back in that time.

As if making a finely timed entrance, the turning of wagon wheels and the pounding of hooves sounded from the yard.

"At last," Biddy breathed and made her way to the door. She pulled it open. "The two of you had best—" Biddy's eyes opened in shock, her words ending abruptly.

Katie moved swiftly to the doorway. Tavish was climbing over the back of the wagon bench to the bed. His mouth was drawn in a tense line, his eyes snapping with something very much like anger and also a great deal of fear.

"What's happened?" Katie called out.

"Come help me," he answered. "Quick, Katie."

Biddy stepped out with her.

"Just Katie." Tavish's voice was insistent, sharp. "Just Katie."

Alone she moved quickly over the short distance to the waiting wagon. Tavish had made his way to the back and offered a hand to help her up.

"What's happened?" she asked again, her voice low.

Ian was nowhere to be seen. The wagon was empty except for a few crates and a messy pile of blankets.

"Why've you returned without Ian?"

"I haven't." He spoke too solemnly for Katie's peace of mind.

Tavish took hold of the nearest corner of the blanket and tossed it back.

Heavens above. 'Twas Ian beneath the blanket. Ian, bloodied and bruised and unmoving. Katie's very breath rushed from her. *Saints preserve us.*

"Keep calm, Sweet Katie. Biddy'll need you to be strong."

Katie struggled to find air enough to speak. "Is he dead?" she whispered.

"He was still breathing when I found him. But he's in a bad way."

He was, indeed. The man's face was swollen, discolored. She'd never seen anyone lie so utterly still. "Had he an accident with the wagon, or was he thrown from a horse or something?"

Tavish shook his head. The man generally wore smiles and mirthful twinkles in his deep blue eyes. Katie was not at all accustomed to seeing him somber.

"I'd wager my entire farm he was set upon by a mob."

Katie's heart fell clear to her feet. "A mob? Good heavens. Who'd do such a thing?"

And yet, she knew the answer. Hope Springs was ten years deep in a feud. Half the town was Irish. The other half hated the Irish with a passion. So, the Irish had opted to return the sentiment and hate their neighbors with equal fervor.

She set her hand lightly at Ian's heart. His chest rose and fell faintly, as though his breath was hardly there. "I'm afeared for him, Tavish."

"And it's right you should be. He needs doctoring."

Katie glanced quickly at the doorway. Little Mary and Michael had joined their mother. The three of them looked on with fearful expressions.

Merciful heavens. Someone had beaten the father of these children to within an inch of his life. Beyond, perhaps.

"This is more of the feud, then, is it?"

"Aye." Tavish sounded neither surprised nor horrified. Clearly this sort of thing had happened before.

"How bad is it likely to become?"

He set his hand lightly on her arm, his eyes heavy with worry. "How bad? Oh, Sweet Katie, this is only the beginning."

Acknowledgments

With gratitude to the following:

The Ryan family of Tramore, Ireland, for welcoming us into their home and proving that Irish people are every bit as kind and witty and good as I have always believed them to be.

Ranee S. Clark and Krista Lynne Jensen, who answered countless questions about Wyoming, saved me from frequent embarrassment, and helped add an aura of authenticity to this work I could never have achieved without their insights.

Pam van Hylckama Vlieg, who has seen me through innumerable hiccups, detours, and temporary roadblocks on this crazy journey. An author couldn't possibly hope for a better cheerleader, advisor, and all-around go-to gal.

Annette Lyon, Heather Moore, J. Scott Savage, LuAnn Staheli, Michele Holmes, and Robison Wells, the world's greatest critique group, for countless hours of encouragement and support and for teaching me so much about being a good writer and a good friend.

To my family, for putting up with late hours and frozen-waffle dinners, and for listening to me talk endlessly about the characters and stories in my head. Their support and willingness to embrace this madness has made it all possible.

Discussion Questions about LONGING FOR *Home*

1. Katie firmly believes her refusal to go to England to work in the factories led to her sister's death and her family's losing their land. In what ways is she correct? In what ways is she wrong? How might her life and that of her family have turned out differently if she had gone to England as her father wanted her to?

2. Katie began working as a servant at the age of eight and spent the eighteen years that followed very much alone. She didn't have family or anyone else to truly care for her and help her make sense of the terrible tragedies she had passed through. How might her perspective on her losses have been different if she hadn't been left alone to sort through all that had happened?

3. Katie wonders, when watching Emma's aching need for her father's affection, if any father realizes how important his opinion of his daughter truly is. How can a daughter's relationship with her father influence the woman she becomes and the choices she makes? What other people play a crucial role in shaping the lives and beliefs of children? How can we be better influences in the lives of the children we interact with?

4. In recounting her reasons for keeping her father's fiddle, Katie confesses she hoped he would come back for it so she could see him again. What reasons, whether noble or ignoble, might her father have had for

never returning? What reasons might he have had for remaining so silent over the years, not even sending so much as a greeting?

5. Katie says, "No one was a child after The Famine. We were nothing but cobbled-together pieces of the children we once were." Why, and in what ways, can traumatic experiences be more devastating to the children who pass through them than to the adults? Conversely, why and in what ways do children often prove to be more resilient than adults?

6. When Katie was a child, starving and homeless, she was told that bad things wouldn't be happening to her if she were a good person. Why do some people believe that bad things happen only to bad people despite enormous evidence to the contrary? What might convince someone to say such a thing to a person in the midst of struggles? How do such unfeeling and unkind declarations add to a person's suffering?

7. Tavish and Joseph each view the other as having the advantage in courting Katie. In what ways might each of them be correct about the other? In what ways might each be incorrect? Is Joseph right not to let his feelings for Katie show, or ought he to tell her what is in his heart? Why do you think Tavish doesn't talk about his late fiancée? What might that tell us about his internal conflicts?

8. Tavish and Joseph are both vying for Katie's heart, though she doesn't fully realize it. What does each have to offer that she needs? Who do you think is the better match for Katie? Why?

9. Katie has spent her life in pursuit of her father's forgiveness as well as that of her dead sister. Yet Tavish tells her that the person whose forgiveness she needs most is her own. Why is the act of forgiving ourselves often the hardest of all? How might the restitution Katie has always planned to make help her find the forgiveness she seeks? Would making those sacrifices be enough for her to find peace?

10. In her mind, Katie has always been on the road back to her home in Ireland in search of forgiveness and the family and home she lost there. What else has she been looking for over the years, perhaps without even

realizing it? In what ways has she actually found in Hope Springs what she has been seeking?

11. In the end, Katie chooses to remain in Hope Springs but reaches out to her father in a letter. Why was this the best choice for her? What difficulties or regrets might this decision cause for her later on? Do you think her father will respond? In what way?

12. Music has always been a balm for Katie. It is a reminder of home and happier times, as well as a soothing and calming influence. What things in your life give you comfort in times of sorrow or struggle?

Let's Talk History

Land in Ireland in the nineteenth century was owned and worked under a centuries-old tenant system. The families who worked and lived on the land didn't own it. Though many had lived in the same home on the same plot for generations, they could be evicted with little or no notice. The crops produced on all but the tiniest pieces of that land belonged to the landlord. As a result, the poor in Ireland depended almost entirely on the potatoes they could grow in the small plot allowed them for their personal use.

When potato blight spread throughout Europe in the 1840s, only in Ireland did the loss of this single crop lead to widespread starvation. The suffering of the Irish, more or less ignored by the government, combined with the abundance of healthy crops shipped out of Ireland to foreign markets, a death toll estimated at over one million, and a desperate exodus of more than a million Irish in the few short years of The Famine made this time in Irish history a rallying cry, one recalled decades later in the uprising of the twentieth century that would eventually lead to Irish independence.

1. How might feelings of resentment toward the indifference of their government, the perception that the Irish, as a people, were not heard by their own government, and the seemingly unreachable goal of freedom

have influenced the decision of the Irish fleeing the famine to settle in the United States rather than in other destinations?

2. How might the tenant system in Ireland have influenced the desire of Irish immigrants in the United States to seek out land in the American West?

When the starving and desperate throngs of poor Irish immigrants arrived in the United States, they found themselves in a country unprepared for such an enormous and sudden influx of people. Their sheer numbers (by 1850, more than half the people of Boston's North End were Irish-born), extreme poverty, lack of resources, and constant new arrivals led to widespread resentment, discrimination, and even hatred.

For the newly arrived Irish, jobs were scarce, housing conditions were often unsanitary and inhumane, and communicable disease claimed lives at alarming rates. The immigrants worked the most menial jobs when they could find them, earning wages that could not possibly lift them from their desperate poverty. The story of the Irish in America during this time was all too often lacking in hope.

3. America had long been seen as the land of opportunity, where a person could overcome hardship and poverty to live a life of comfort. What must it have been like for the Irish immigrants, having just escaped starvation in their homeland, to find waiting for them across the Atlantic harsh conditions and fewer opportunities than they expected?

4. Irish uprisings during the many centuries of British rule were plentiful, though unsuccessful. The Irish viewed their American counterparts as sympathetic comrades who had shared their feeling of being oppressed by a government in which they were not truly represented. No doubt Irish immigrants who arrived during the nineteenth century, having suffered under what they clearly felt was the cold indifference of their government, expected to find empathy and a welcome acceptance among those who had overthrown the very rule they themselves were suffering under. Instead, they felt generally unwanted, unwelcome, and often despised.

What kind of responses and feelings must this reception have engendered in the Irish?

5. The United States was a relatively young country at the time of the mass exodus from Ireland. How might the sudden and then constant arrival of so many people in such desperate need have alarmed citizens of the United States?

6. The Irish came in such large numbers that they quickly changed the cultural and ethnic makeup of many Eastern cities. Furthermore, their poverty and their desire to recreate the closeness they had once known in their homeland led them to keep to themselves, creating tight-knit and exclusionary communities. How might this characteristic have further fueled the flames of resentment and prejudice?

7. Desperation, discouragement, and lack of employment and basic necessities led to a great deal of resentment within the Irish slums of cities such as Boston and New York. How might these situations have added to the perception of the Irish as lazy, drunken troublemakers?

8. The American Civil War began fifteen years after the earliest flood of Irish immigrants arrived on American shores. How might the tensions that led to this war have contributed to the challenges the immigrants encountered? How might the presence of Irish immigrants among both Confederate and Union troops have added to the resentment many in the country felt toward them?

The post–Civil War railroad boom in the American West led to a sudden opportunity for employment among the poor and desperate Irish. The work was dangerous, backbreaking, and poorly paid, and many were unwilling to undertake it. The Irish, like immigrants from various Asian countries who settled along the American West Coast, answered the call. This led to a westward movement by many Irish immigrants.

Land was plentiful and inexpensive. The completion of the railroads made supplies easier and cheaper to obtain. Towns began popping up throughout the American West, many with sizable Irish populations.

9. Having lost land in Ireland, land they never held title to and could

not have called their own, the promise of land ownership must have been an almost irresistible opportunity to many Irish immigrants. How might the passage of time since their years as farmers in Ireland combined with the drastically different farming conditions of the West have made the adjustment difficult?

10. Many non-Irish Americans also made the move west and, in many instances, brought with them the resentment they felt toward this group of people. What kind of difficulties might that have caused? How might the problems have been avoided?

11. How do the experiences of Irish immigrants during this time parallel those of other immigrant groups throughout history, both in the United States and throughout the world?

12. What can we learn from this era in history about prejudice, poverty, desperation, compassion, and so forth? What could have been done differently—both by the Irish immigrants themselves and by American citizens and their local, state, and federal governments—to have improved the situation?

13. Anti-Irish sentiment is all but unheard of today in the United States. What influence would the following have had on extinguishing the flames of hatred, prejudice, and resentment exhibited toward this particular group?

- The passage of time
- Assimilation into mainstream America by the Irish as accents disappeared among the second generation who adopted more "American" ways of speaking and behaving
- An Irish voice in government, something Americans initially feared
- A growing acceptance of Catholicism, though it was still an issue as recently as the 1960 election of President John F. Kennedy
- Other problems that captured the nation's attention
- A significant slowing of Irish immigration
- The sheer number of Irish immigrants

About the Author

SARAH M. EDEN is the author of several well-received historical romances, including Whitney Award finalists *Seeking Persephone* (2008) and *Courting Miss Lancaster* (2010). Combining her obsession with history and an affinity for tender love stories, Sarah loves crafting witty characters and heartfelt romances. She happily spends hours perusing the reference shelves of her local library and dreams of one day traveling to all the places she reads about. Sarah is represented by Pam van Hylckama Vlieg at Foreword Literary Agency.

Visit Sarah at www.sarahmeden.com